THE TERRORISTS

Maj Sjöwall and Per Wahlöö

Translated from the Swedish by Joan Tate

VINTAGE BOOKS
A Division of Random House
New York

FIRST VINTAGE BOOKS EDITION, January 1978

Library of Congress Cataloging in Publication Data

Sjöwall, Maj, 1935–
The terrorists.

Translation of Terroristerna.
I. Wahlöö, Per, 1926–1975, joint author.
II. Title.
[PZ4.S61953Te5] [PT9876.29.J63] 839.7'3'74 77-3192
ISBN 0-394-72452-6

Manufactured in the United States of America
89

THE TERRORISTS

1.

The National Commissioner of Police smiled.

He usually reserved his smile, boyish and charming, for the press and television and only seldom bestowed it on such members of the inner circle as Superintendent Stig Malm, of the National Police Administration, Eric Möller, chief of Security Police, and Martin Beck, chief of the National Homicide Squad.

Only one of the three men smiled back. Stig Malm had beautiful white teeth and liked smiling to show them off. Over the years he had quite unconsciously acquired a whole register of smiles. The one he was using now could only be described as ingratiating and fawning.

The chief of the Security Police suppressed a yawn and Martin Beck blew his nose.

It was only half-past seven in the morning, the National Commissioner's favorite time for calling sudden meetings, which in no way meant that he was in the habit of arriving at the station at that time. He often did not appear until late in the morning and even then he was usually inaccessible even to his closest colleagues. "My office is my castle" might well have been inscribed on the door, and indeed it was an impenetrable fortress, guarded by a well-groomed secretary, quite rightly called "The Dragon."

This morning he was showing his breezy and benign

side. He had even had a Thermos of coffee and real china cups brought in, instead of the usual plastic mugs.

Stig Malm got up and poured out the coffee.

Martin Beck knew that before he sat down again he would first pinch the crease in his trousers and then carefully run his hand across his well-cut wavy hair.

Stig Malm was his immediate superior and Martin Beck had no respect for him whatsoever. His self-satisfied coquettishness and insinuating officiousness toward senior potentates were characteristics that Martin Beck had ceased to be annoyed by and nowadays found simply foolish. What did irritate him, on the other hand, and often constituted an obstacle to his work, was the man's rigidity and lack of self-criticism, a lack just as total and destructive as his ignorance of everything to do with practical police work. That he had risen to such a high position was due to ambition, political opportunism and a certain amount of administrative ability.

The chief of the Security police put four lumps of sugar into his coffee, stirred it with a spoon and slurped as he drank.

Malm drank his without sugar, careful as he was of his trim figure.

Martin Beck was not feeling well and did not want coffee this early in the morning.

The National Commissioner took both sugar and cream and crooked his little finger as he raised his cup. He emptied it in one gulp and pushed it away from him, simultaneously pulling toward him a green file that had been lying on the corner of the polished conference table.

"There," he said, smiling again. "Coffee first and then on with the day's work."

Martin Beck looked gloomily at his untouched cup of coffee and longed for a glass of cold milk.

2

"How are you feeling, Martin?" said the Commissioner, with feigned sympathy in his voice. "You don't look well. You're not planning to be ill again, are you? You know we can't afford to be without you."

Martin was not planning to be ill. He already was ill. He had been drinking wine with his twenty-two-year-old daughter and her boy friend until half-past three in the morning and knew that he looked awful as a result. But he had no desire to discuss his self-inflicted indisposition with his superior, and moreover he didn't think that the "again" was really fair. He had been away from his work with the flu and a high temperature for three days at the beginning of March and it was now the seventh of May.

"No," he said. "I'm fine. A bit of a cold, that's all."

"You really don't look good," said Stig Malm. There was not even feigned sympathy in his voice, only reproach. "You really don't."

He looked piercingly at Martin Beck, who feeling his irritation rising said, "Thanks for your concern, but I'm fine. I assume we're not here to discuss my appearance or the state of my health."

"Quite right," said the Commissioner. "Let's get down to business."

He opened the green file. Judging by the contents—three or four sheets of paper at the most—there was some hope that today's meeting would not drag on for too long.

On top lay a typed letter with the mark of a large green rubber stamp beneath the scrawled signature and a letterhead that Martin Beck could not make out from where he was sitting.

"As you will remember, we have discussed our to some extent imperfect experience when it comes to the security measures to be taken during state visits and in similar delicate situations—occasions when one can expect demonstrations of a particularly aggressive nature and well- and less-well-planned attempts at assassination," the Commissioner began, falling automatically into the pompous style that usually characterized his public appearances.

Stig Malm mumbled in agreement, Martin Beck said nothing, but Eric Möller objected.

"Well, we're not that inexperienced, are we? Khrushchev's visit went off fine, except maybe for that red-painted pig someone let loose in front of Logård steps. So did Kosygin's, organizationally as well as security-wise. And the Environmental Conference, to take a maybe slightly different example."

"Yes, of course, but this time we're faced with a more difficult problem. What I'm referring to is the visit by this senator from the United States at the end of November. It could turn out to be a hot potato, if I may use that expression. We've never been confronted with the problem of VIPs from the States before, but now we are. The date's been set and I've already received certain instructions. Our preparations must be made well ahead of time and be extremely thorough. We have to be prepared for anything."

The National Commissioner was no longer smiling. "We'll probably have to be prepared for something more violent than egg-throwing this time," he added grimly. "You should bear that in mind, Eric."

"We can take preventive measures," said Möller.

The Commissioner shrugged. "To some extent, yes," he said. "But we can't eliminate and look up and intern everyone who might make trouble. You know that as well as I do. I've got my orders to go by and you'll be getting yours."

And I've got mine, thought Martin Beck gloomily. He was still trying to read the letterhead on the letter in the green file. He thought he could discern the word "police" or possibly "policia." His eyes ached and his tongue felt as rough and dry as sandpaper. Reluctantly he sipped at the bitter coffee.

"But all that will come later," said the Commissioner. "What I want to discuss today is this letter." He tapped the paper in the open file with his forefinger. "It is in every way relevant to the problem at hand," he said. He gave the letter to Stig Malm, to pass around the table before he continued.

"It is, as you see, an invitation, in response to our request to be allowed to send an observer during an impending state visit. As the visiting president is not particularly popular in the host country, they will be taking all possible measures to protect him. As in many other Latin American countries, they have had to deal with a number of assassination attempts—of both native and foreign politicians. Consequently, they have considerable experience, and I would think that their police force and security services are the best qualified in that area. I'm convinced that we could learn much by studying their methods and procedures."

Martin Beck glanced through the letter, which was written in English in very formal and courteous terms. The president's visit was to take place on the fifth of June, hardly a month away, and the representative of the Swedish police was welcome to arrive two weeks earlier, so that he could study the most important phases of the preparatory work. The signature was elegant and totally illegible, but elucidated in typescript. The name was Spanish, long, and appeared in some way to be noble and distinguished.

When the letter had been returned to the green file, the Commissioner said, "The problem is, who shall we send?"

Stig Malm thoughtfully raised his eyes to the ceiling, but said nothing.

Martin Beck feared that he himself might be suggested. Five years earlier, before he had broken out of his unhappy marriage, he would have been delighted to undertake an assignment that would take him away from home for a while. But now, the last thing he wanted to do was to go abroad, and he hastened to say, "This is more of a Security Services job, isn't it?"

"I can't go," said Möller. "In the first place, I can't be absent from the department—we've got some reorganizational problems in Section A that will take some time to clear up. In the second place, we're already experts on these matters and it would be more useful if someone went who was unfamiliar with security questions. Someone from the Criminal Investigation Bureau, or maybe someone from the Regular Police. Whoever goes will pass on what he learns to the rest of us when he gets back, so everyone will benefit anyway."

The Commissioner nodded. "Yes, there's something in what you say, Eric," he said. "And, as you point out, we can't spare you at the moment. Nor you, Martin."

Martin Beck inwardly sighed with relief.

"In addition, I cannot speak Spanish," said the chief of Security Police.

"Who the hell can?" said Malm, smiling. He was aware of the fact that the Commissioner did not master the Castilian language, either.

"I know someone who can," said Martin Beck.

Malm raised his eyebrows. "Who? Someone in Criminal Investigation?"

"Yes, Gunvald Larsson."

Malm raised his eyebrows yet another millimeter, then smiled incredulously and said, "But we can't send him, can we now?"

"Why not?" said Martin Beck. "I think he'd be a good man to send."

He noticed that he sounded slightly angry. He did not usually speak up for Gunvald Larsson, but Malm's tone of voice had annoyed him and he was so used to disagreeing with Malm that he opposed him almost automatically.

"He's a bungler and totally unrepresentative of the force," said Malm.

"Does he really speak Spanish?" asked the Commissioner doubtfully. "Where did he learn it?"

"He was in a lot of Spanish-speaking countries when he was a sailor," said Martin Beck. "The city we're talking about is a large port, so he's almost certainly been there before. He speaks English, French and German, too, all fluently. And a little Russian. Look in his file and you'll see."

"He's a bungler all the same," insisted Stig Malm.

The Commissioner looked thoughtful. "I'll look at his qualifications," he said. "I thought of him myself, as a matter of fact. It's true he has a tendency to behave somewhat boorishly, and he's much too undisciplined. But he's undeniably one of our best inspectors, even if he does find it difficult to obey orders and stick to regulations."

He turned to the chief of the Security Police. "What do you say, Eric? Do you think he'd be suitable?"

"Well, I don't like him much, but generally speaking I've no objections."

Malm looked unhappy. "I think it would be extremely inappropriate to send him," he said. "He would disgrace the Swedish force. He behaves like a boor and uses language more suited to a longshoreman than a former ship's officer."

"Perhaps not when he's speaking Spanish," said Martin Beck. "Anyway, even if he does express himself a little crudely sometimes, at least he chooses his moments."

That was not strictly true. Martin Beck had recently heard Gunvald Larsson call Malm "that magnificent asshole" in the man's presence, but fortunately Malm had not realized that the epithet was intended for him.

The Commissioner did not seem to take much notice of Malm's objections. "It's perhaps not a bad idea," he said thoughtfully. "I don't think his tendency to uncivilized behavior will be much of a problem in this case. He can behave well if he wants to. He has a better background than most. He comes from a wealthy and cultured family, he's had the best possible education and an upbringing that has taught him how to behave correctly in all possible circumstances. That shows, even if he does his best to conceal it."

"You can say that again," mumbled Malm.

Martin Beck sensed that Stig Malm would very much have liked the assignment and that he was annoyed at not even being asked. He also thought it would be good to be rid of Gunvald Larsson for a while, as he was not much liked by his colleagues and had an unusual capacity for causing rows and complications.

The Commissioner did not seem wholly unconvinced even by his own reasoning, and Martin Beck said encouragingly, "I think we should send Gunvald. He has all the qualifications needed for the job."

"I've noticed that he's careful of his appearance," said the Commissioner. "His way of dressing shows good taste and a feeling for quality. That undoubtedly makes an impression."

"Exactly," said Martin Beck. "It's an important detail." He was conscious of the fact that his own clothing could hardly be called tasteful. His trousers were unpressed and baggy, the collar of his polo sweater was wide and limp from many washings, his tweed jacket was worn and missing a button.

"The Violence Division is well-staffed and ought to be able to manage without Larsson for a few weeks," said the Commissioner. "Or does anyone have any other suggestion?"

They all shook their heads. Even Malm appeared to have perceived the advantage of having Gunvald Larsson at a safe distance for a while, and Eric Möller yawned again, apparently pleased that the meeting was drawing to a close.

The National Commissioner rose to his feet and closed the file. "Good," he said. "Then we are agreed. I shall personally inform Larsson of our decision."

Gunvald Larsson received the information without much enthusiasm, nor was he especially flattered by the assignment. His self-esteem was pronounced and imperturbable, but he was not entirely unaware that some of his colleagues would heave a sigh of relief when he left, and regret only that he was not leaving for good. He was aware that his friends on the force could be easily counted. As far as he knew, there was only one. He also knew that he was regarded as insubordinate and troublesome, and that his job often hung by a thread.

This fact did not disturb him in the slightest. Any other policeman of his rank and salary grade would at least have felt some anxiety over the constant threat of being suspended or actually dismissed, but Gunvald Larsson had never spent a sleepless night over the prospect. Unmarried and childless, he had no dependents, and he had long since broken off all communication with his family, whose snobbish upper-class existence he despised. He did not worry much about his future. During his years as a policeman, he had often weighed the possibility of returning to his old profession. Now he was nearly fifty and he realized that he would probably never again go to sea.

As the day of his departure approached, Gunvald Larsson discovered that he was genuinely pleased about the assignment, which, while regarded as important, could hardly be expected to be especially difficult. It involved at least two weeks' change in his daily routine, and he began to look forward to the journey as if to a holiday.

On the evening before his departure, Gunvald Larsson was standing in his bedroom in Bollmora, clad in nothing but underpants, looking at his reflection in the long mirror on the inside of his wardrobe door. He was delighted with the pattern on the underpants, yellow moose against a blue background, and he owned five more pairs. Half a dozen of the same kind, though green with red moose, were already packed in the large pigskin case that lay open on his bed.

Gunvald Larsson was six feet tall, a powerful and muscular man with large hands and feet. He had just showered and routinely stepped onto the bathroom scales, which registered two hundred and twenty-four pounds. During the last four years, or perhaps it was five, he had put on about twenty pounds, and he looked with displeasure at the roll of fat above the elastic of his underpants.

He pulled in his stomach and it occurred to him that he ought to visit the station gym more often. Or begin swimming when the pool was completed.

Except for the spare tire, though, he was really quite pleased with his appearance.

He was forty-nine years old, but his hair was thick and abundant and his hairline had not crept back and made his forehead higher. It was low, with two marked lines across it. His hair was cut short and so fair that the gray in it didn't show. Now that it was wet and newly combed, it lay smooth and shiny across his broad skull, but when it had dried it would rise and look bristly and untidy. His eyebrows were bushy and of the same fair color as his hair, and his nose was large and well formed, with wide nostrils. His pale china-blue eyes looked small in that rugged face and were a trifle too close together, which sometimes, when they were empty of expression, made him look deceptively stupid. When he was angry—and that was often—a furious crease appeared between his eyes, and his light-blue eyes could strike terror into the most hardened criminals, as well as into the hearts of subordinates.

The only person who had never been on the receiving end of Gunvald Larsson's fury was Einar Rönn, a colleague in the Stockholm Violence Division and his only friend. Rönn was a placid and taciturn northerner with a perpetually running red nose, which dominated his face to such a degree that one hardly noticed the other details of his appearance. He carried about within him an inextinguishable longing for his home district around Arjeplog in Lapland.

As Gunvald Larsson and Rönn served in the same department, they saw each other nearly every day, but they also spent a good deal of their spare time together. When it was possible, they took their leaves at the same time and went to Arjeplog, where they mostly devoted themselves to fishing. None of their colleagues was able to understand this friendship between two such different personalities, and many wondered how Rönn, with stoic calm and few words, could turn a raging Gunvald Larsson into a meek and mild lamb.

Now Gunvald Larsson inspected the row of suits in his well-filled closet. He was well acquainted with the climate of the country he was to visit, and he remembered several suffocatingly hot spring weeks in that port many years before. If he was to endure the heat he would have to be lightly clothed, and he had only two suits that were sufficiently cool. For safety's sake, he tried them on and discovered to his dismay that he couldn't get the first on and that the trousers of the second would only just fasten if he made an effort and inhaled deeply. They were also tight across the thighs. At least he could button the jacket without difficulty, but it was tight across the shoulders and either it would limit his freedom of movement or the seams would split.

He hung the useless suit back in the wardrobe and laid the other one across the lid of his case. It would have to do. He had had it made for him four years earlier, from thin Egyptian cotton, nougat-colored with narrow white stripes.

He completed his packing with three pairs of khaki trousers, a shantung jacket and the suit that was too tight. In the pocket on the inside of the lid, he put one of his favorite novels. Then he closed the lid, fastened the brass buckles on the wide straps, locked the case and took it into the hall.

He cared about his own EMW too much to let it stand in the airport parking lot, so Einar Rönn was to pick him up in his car the next morning and drive him to Stockholm's Arlanda Airport. Like most Swedish airports, Arlanda was a dismal and misplaced establishment and succeeded excellently in giving expectant visitors an even more distorted view of Sweden than the country deserved.

Gunvald Larsson threw the blue-and-yellow moose underpants into the hamper in the bathroom, put on his pajamas and went to bed. He did not suffer from travel fever and fell asleep almost immediately.

2.

The security expert did not reach even to the middle of Gunvald Larsson's upper arm, but he was very neat and elegant in his light-blue suit with its flared and beautifully pressed trousers. With the suit, he wore a pink shirt, shiny torpedo-toed black shoes and a lilac-colored tie. His hair was almost black, his skin light brown and his eyes olive-colored. The only discordant note was the pistol holster bulging under his left armpit. The security expert's name was Francisco Bajamonde Cassavetes y Larrinaga; he came from an extremely distinguished family.

Francisco Bajamonde Cassavetes y Larrinaga spread the security plan out on the balustrade, but Gunvald Larsson was looking instead at his own suit; it had taken the police tailor seven days to make it, and the result was excellent, as this was a country where the level of the art of tailoring was still high. Their only difference of opinion had been over the space for a shoulder holster, which the tailor had taken for granted. But Gunvald Larsson never used a shoulder holster. He carried his pistol in a clip in his belt. Here abroad, of course, he was not armed, but he would be using the suit in Stockholm. There had been a brief dispute and naturally he had had his way. What else? With deep satisfaction he glanced down at his well-tailored legs, sighed contentedly and looked around at his surroundings.

They were standing on the eighth floor of the hotel, a spot chosen with great care. The motorcade would pass below the balcony and stop at the provincial palace a block away. Gunvald Larsson glanced politely at the plan, but without much enthusiasm, as by now he knew it all by heart. He knew that the harbor had been closed to all traffic that morning and the civilian airport had been closed since the presidential plane had landed.

Straight ahead lay the harbor and the azure-blue sea. Several large passenger liners and cargo boats were anchored at its outer edges. The only ships moving were a warship, a frigate and a few police boats in the inner harbor. Below them lay the paseo, edged with palm and acacias. Across the street was a rank of taxis, and beyond that a row of colorful horse-drawn cabs. All these had been thoroughly checked.

Every person in the area, apart from the military police and gendarmes forming an arm's-length barrier along each side of the paseo, had passed through metal detectors of the kind with which most larger airports were now equipped.

The gendarmes' uniforms were green, while the military police wore blue-gray. The gendarmes wore boots, the military police high shoes.

Gunvald Larsson suppressed a sigh. He had done a dummy run along this stretch at the rehearsal that morning. Everything had been in its place except the President himself.

The motorcade was made up as follows. First, a motorcycle party of fifteen specially trained security police. After that, an equal number of motorcycle police from the regular force, followed by two cars loaded with security men. Then came the presidential car, a black Cadillac with bulletproof blue glass. (During the dummy run, Gunvald Larsson had sat in the back seat as a stand-in, unquestionably an honor.) Next came an open car full of security men, on the American pattern. And finally, more motorcycle police, followed by the radio reporters' bus and cars full of other authorized journalists. In addition, civilian security men were spread along the road from the airport.

All the street lamps were decorated with pictures of the President. The route was fairly long, indeed very long, and Gunvald Larsson had had time to become quite bored with that bull-necked head, puffy face and black enamel steel-framed glasses.

That was the ground protection. The airspace was dominated by army helicopters at three levels, with three choppers in each group. In addition, a division of Starfighters was sweeping back and forth, guarding the upper airspace.

The entire operation was organized with such perfection that unpleasant surprises ought to be fairly unthinkable.

The heat at this time of the afternoon was, to put it mildly, oppressive. Gunvald Larsson was sweating, but not excessively. He could not imagine that anything could go wrong. Preparations had been singularly detailed and thorough, and planning had been going on for several months. A special group had been assigned to look for faults in the planning, and a number of corrections had been made. Add to this the fact that every attempted assassination in this country—and there had been quite a few—had failed. The National Commissioner had probably been right when he said that they were the world's greatest experts in their field.

At a quarter to three in the afternoon, Francisco Bajamonde Cassavetes y Larrinaga glanced at his watch and said, "Twenty-one minutes to go, I presume."

There had been no need for a Spanish-speaking delegate. The security man spoke the Queen's English as used in the most sophisticated clubs of Belgravia.

Gunvald Larsson looked at his own chronograph and nodded. At that moment, to be more precise, it was exactly thirteen minutes and thirty-five seconds to three on Wednesday the fifth of June, nineteen hundred and seventy-four.

Outside the harbor entrance, the frigate was turning to sound the welcoming salute, which was its only real assignment. High above the paseo the eight fighter planes drew white zigzag lines in the bright blue sky.

Gunvald Larsson looked around. Down the paseo was a huge brick bullring with curved arcades plastered in red and white. In the other direction they were just turning on the multicolored sprays of a tall fountain; there had been a severe drought all year and the fountains—this was not the only one—were only set going on especially grand occasions.

Now they could hear the drone of helicopters and the sirens on the motorcycles. Gunvald Larsson checked the time. The motorcade seemed to be ahead of schedule. Then his china-blue gaze swept the harbor and noted that all the police boats were now in action. The harbor installations themselves were much the same as when he had been at sea, only the ships completely different. Supertankers, container ships, huge ferries on which cars were more important than passengers—they were all unfamiliar to him from his own years at sea.

Gunvald Larsson was not alone in his observation that the order of events was ahead of the prescribed schedule. Cassavetes y Larrinaga spoke swiftly but calmly into his radio, smiled at his fair-haired guest and looked out over the sparkling fountains, where the first scooter group of specially trained security police was already appearing between the lines of green-uniformed gendarmes.

Gunvald Larsson shifted his gaze. Immediately below them a cigar-smoking security man was strolling along the middle of the street keeping an eye on the sharp-shooters posted on the surrounding roofs. Behind the line of gendarmes was the row of taxicabs with blue lines along their sides, and in front of them an open yellow-and-black horse-drawn carriage. The man on the box was also dressed in yellow and black, and the horse had yellow-and-black plumes in the band round its forehead.

Behind all this were the palms and acacias and a few lines of curious people. A few of them carried the only sign approved by the authorities, a picture of that bull-necked head, puffy face and black enamel steel-framed glasses. The President was not a particularly popular visitor.

The motorcade was moving very quickly. The first of the Security Service cars was already below the balcony. The security expert smiled at Gunvald Larsson, nodded assuringly and began to fold up his papers.

At that moment, the ground opened, almost directly beneath the bulletproof Cadillac.

The pressure waves flung both men backward, but if Gunvald Larsson was nothing else, he was strong. He grabbed the balustrade with both hands and looked upward.

The roadway had opened like a volcano from which smoking pillars of fire were rising to a height of a hundred and fifty feet. Atop the flaming pillars were diverse objects. The most prominent were the rear section of the bulletproof Cadillac, an overturned black cab with a blue line along its side, half a horse with black and yellow plumes in the band round its forehead, a leg in a black boot and green uniform material, and an arm with a long cigar between the fingers.

Gunvald Larsson ducked as a mass of flammable and nonflammable objects began to rain down on him. He was just thinking about his new suit when something struck him in the chest with great force and hurled him backward onto the marble tiles of the balcony.

The roar of the explosion finally faded away, and there were sounds of cries, desperate calls for help, someone weeping and another person screaming hysterical curses, before all human sounds were drowned by the sirens of ambulances and the wail of a fire engine.

Gunvald Larsson got to his feet, found himself not seriously hurt and looked about to see what it was that had knocked him down. The object lay at his feet. It had a bull neck and a puffy face, and strangely enough, the black enamel steel-framed glasses were still on.

The security expert scrambled to his feet, clearly unhurt, even if some of his elegance had been dissipated. He stared incredulously at the head and crossed himself.

Gunvald Larsson looked down at his suit. It was ruined. "Goddammit," he said.

Then he looked at the head lying at his feet. "Maybe I ought to take it home," he said to himself. "As a souvenir."

Francisco Bajamonde Cassavetes y Larrinaga looked questioningly at his guest. "Catastrophe," he said.

"Yes, you could say that," said Gunvald Larsson.

Francisco Bajamonde Cassavetes y Larrinaga looked so unhappy that Gunvald Larsson felt duty-bound to add, "But no one could really blame you. And anyhow, he had an unusually ugly head."

3.

The same day that Gunvald Larsson had his strange experience on the balcony with the lovely view, an eighteen-year-old girl named Rebecka Lind was being tried in Stockholm city court on a charge of armed robbery of a bank.

The public prosecutor in her case was Bulldozer Olsson, who for some years had been the judiciary's expert in armed robberies, which were spreading over the country like a plague. He was, as a result, an extremely harried man with so little time to spend at home that it had taken him three weeks, for instance, to discover that his wife had left him for good and been replaced by a laconic message on his pillow. This had not made all that much difference, as with his usual swiftness of action he had found himself another within three days. His new life partner was one of his secretaries who admired him unreservedly and devotedly, and certainly his suits appeared to be slightly less rumpled from that day on.

On this day he arrived breathlessly, two minutes before the trial was to begin. He was a corpulent but light-footed little man with a joyous countenance and lively movements. He always wore bright pink shirts, and his ties were in such indescribably bad taste that they had driven Gunvald Larsson almost insane when he had worked in Bulldozer's special group.

He looked round the bare and ill-heated anteroom of the court and discovered a group of five people, among them his own witnesses, and a person whose presence surprised him enormously. It was, in fact, the chief of the Homicide Squad.

"What on earth are you doing here," he said to Martin Beck.

"I've been called as a witness."

"By whom?"

"The defense."

"The defense? What does that mean?"

"Braxén, counsel for the defense," said Martin Beck. "He drew this case, apparently."

"Crasher," said Bulldozer, clearly upset. "I've already had three meetings and two arrests today, and now I'll have to sit and listen to Crasher for the rest of the afternoon, I suppose. Do you know anything about this case?"

"Not much, but Braxén's argument convinced me I ought to come. And I don't have anything special at the moment."

"You people in Homicide don't know what real work is," said Bulldozer Olsson. "I've got thirty-nine cases on the books and just as many on ice. You should work with me for a while, then you'd find out."

Bulldozer Olsson won all his cases, with very few exceptions indeed. This, to put it delicately, was not especially flattering to the judiciary.

"But you'll have an amusing afternoon," said Olsson. "Crasher'll give you a good show, for sure."

Their discussion was interrupted by the case being called, and those involved, with one important exception, filed into the courtroom, a singularly dismal sector of the principal city courthouse. The windows were large and majestic, which in no way excused but possibly explained why they clearly had not been cleaned for a very long time.

The judge, assistant judge and seven jurymen on a platform behind a long connecting pulpit were staring with dignity out into the courtroom.

The accused was brought in through a small side door, a girl with shoulder-length fair hair, a sulky mouth and distant brown eyes. She was wearing a long, pale-green embroidered dress of some light, thin material and had black clogs on her feet.

The court was seated.

The judge turned to the girl, who was sitting to the left of the bench, and said, "The accused in the case is Rebecka Lind. Are you Rebecka Lind?"

"Yes."

"May I ask you to speak a little louder?"

"Yes."

"You were born on the third of January, nineteen hundred and fifty-six?"

"Yes."

"I must ask the accused to speak louder." He said this as if it had to be said ritualistically, which was true, as the acoustics in the courtroom were singularly poor.

"Counsel for the Defense Hedobald Braxén appears to have been delayed," he went on. "In the meantime, we can summon the witnesses. Counsel for the prosecution has called two witnesses—Kerstin Franzén, bank cashier, and Kenneth Kvastmo, police assistant. The defense has called the following: Martin Beck, chief inspector, Homicide Squad; Karl Kristiansson, police assistant; Rumford Bondesson, bank director; and Hedy-Marie Wirén, home economics teacher. Counsel for the defense has also called Walter Petrus, business executive, to testify, but he has declared himself unable to attend and has also declared that he has nothing whatsoever to do with the case."

One of the jurymen sniggered.

"The witnesses may now leave the court."

The two policemen—as always on these occasions wearing uniform trousers and black shoes plus dreary blazers—Martin Beck, the bank director, the home economics teacher and the bank cashier all trooped out into the foyer. Only the accused, her guard and one spectator remained in the courtroom.

Bulldozer studied his papers busily for about two minutes, then looked curiously at the spectator, a woman Bulldozer reckoned to be about thirty-five. She was sitting on one of the benches with a stenographer's notebook open in front of her. She was of below average height and had dead-straight blond hair, not especially long. Her clothes consisted of faded jeans, a shirt of indefinite color and strap sandals. She had broad, sunburnt feet with straight toes, flat breasts with large nipples that could be seen quite clearly through her shirt. The most remarkable thing about her was her small, angular face with its strong nose and piercing blue gaze, which she directed in turn on those present. Her gaze rested especially long on the accused and Bulldozer Olsson; in the latter case so piercingly that the public prosecutor rose and fetched himself a glass of water and moved into a position behind her. She at once turned and caught his eye.

Sexually she was not his type, if he even had a type, but he was intensely curious about who she could be. Viewed from behind, he could see that she was compactly built, without being in the least plump.

If he had asked Martin Beck, who was standing around in a corner of the foyer, he might have learned something. For instance, that she was not thirty-five but thirty-nine, that she had a considerable background in sociology, and that at present she was working for the social welfare services. Martin Beck knew a great deal about her in fact, but had very little information he wished to proffer, as most of it was of a personal nature. Possibly he would have said, if anyone had asked him, that her name was Rhea Nielsen.

Twenty-two minutes after the prescribed time, the doors were thrown open and Crasher appeared. He was carrying a lighted cigar in one hand and his papers in the other. He studied the documents phlegmatically and the judge had to clear his throat meaningfully three times before he absently handed the cigar to the court official to remove from the courtroom.

"Mr. Braxén has now arrived," said the judge acidly. "May we ask whether there is any further objection to starting the case?"

Bulldozer shook his head and said, "No, certainly not. Not as far as I'm concerned."

Braxén rose and walked to the middle of the floor. He was considerably older than anyone else in the room, a man of authority with an impressive stomach. He was also remarkably badly and unfashionably dressed, and a none too squeamish cat could have made a good meal from the food stains on his waistcoat. After a long silence, during which he fixed Bulldozer with a peculiar look, he said, "Apart from the fact that this little girl should never have been brought to court, I have no judicial objections. Speaking purely technically."

"Would the counsel for the prosecution now introduce the case," said the judge.

Bulldozer leaped up from his chair and with his head down he began plodding round the table on which his papers lay.

"I maintain that Rebecka Lind on Wednesday the twenty-second of May this year committed armed robbery of the PK Bank's branch in Midsommarkransen, and thereafter was guilty of assaulting an official in that she resisted the policemen who came to take her into custody."

"And what does the accused say?"

"The accused pleads not guilty," said Braxén. "And so it is my duty to deny all of this . . . drivel."

He turned to Bulldozer again and said in melancholy tones: "What does it feel like to persecute innocent people? Rebecka is as innocent as the carrots in the ground."

Everyone appeared to ponder this novel image. Finally the judge said, "It is for the Court to decide that, is it not?"

"Unfortunately," said Crasher.

"What is meant by that remark?" said the judge, with a certain sharpness. "Would Mr. Olsson please now state his case?"

Bulldozer looked at the spectator, who, however, returned his gaze so directly and demandingly that after a brief glance at Braxén, he let his gaze wander over the judge, the assistant judge and the jury, after which he fixed it on the accused. Rebecka Lind's own gaze seemed to be fixed in space, far from crazy bureaucrats and all other possible good and evil.

Bulldozer clasped his hands behind his back and began walking back and forth. "Well, Rebecka," he said in a friendly way, "what has happened to you is unfortunately something that happens to many young people today. Together we will try to help you . . . I suppose I may use your first name?"

The girl did not seem to have heard the question, if it was one.

"Technically speaking, this is an open-and-shut case, about which there can be little discussion. As was evident at the arraignment—"

Braxén had appeared to be sunk in his thoughts, but now he suddenly jerked a large cigar out of his inside pocket, pointed it at Bulldozer's chest and cried, "I object! Neither I nor any other lawyer was present at the arraignment. Was this girl Camilla Lund even informed of her right to counsel?"

"Rebecka Lind," said the assistant judge.

"Yes, yes," said Crasher impatiently. "That makes her arrest illegal."

"Not at all," said Bulldozer. "Rebecka was asked and she said it didn't matter. It didn't, either. As I will shortly show, the case was crystal clear."

"The very arraignment was illegal," said Crasher conclusively. "I would like my objection to be entered in the record."

"So, Rebecka," continued Bulldozer, with that winning smile that was one of his main assets. "Let us now, clearly and truthfully, try to clarify the actual course of events, what happened to you on the twenty-second of May and why it happened. You robbed a bank, certainly out of desperation and thoughtlessness, and then assaulted a policeman."

"I object to counsel's choice of words," said Crasher. "I object to counsel for the prosecution's attitude toward both myself and this girl."

Bulldozer for once appeared put out. But he soon collected himself and, in as good form as ever, gesticulating and smiling, pursued his case to its conclusion, despite the fact that Braxén interrupted him no fewer than forty-two times, often with totally incomprehensible objections.

Briefly, the case was as follows: Shortly before two

o'clock on the twenty-second of May, Rebecka Lind had walked into the PK Bank's branch in Midsommarkransen and gone up to one of the tellers. She had been carrying a large shoulder bag, which she placed on the counter. She then demanded money. The teller noticed that she was armed with a large knife and set off the police alarm with her foot as she began to fill the bag with bundles of notes, amounting to a sum of five thousand Swedish kronor. Before Rebecka Lind had time to leave the bank with her booty, the first of the radio patrol cars arrived. Two policemen with guns drawn went into the bank and disarmed the robber, at which a certain tumult arose, during which the notes were scattered over the floor. The police arrested the robber, and the prisoner offered violent resistance, inflicting on the policemen damage to their uniforms. They drove her to the station on Kungsholm. The robber, who turned out to be eighteen-year-old Rebecka Lind, was taken first to the Criminal Division duty office and was then transferred to the special department concerned with bank robberies. She was immediately charged with suspected armed robbery of a bank and assault of a policeman, and the following day was formally arraigned at a singularly brief transaction before the Stockholm assize court.

Bulldozer admitted that certain judicial formalities had not been observed in connection with the arraignment, but pointed out that, technically speaking, these were of no importance. Rebecka Lind had herself been quite uninterested in her defense, and she had also immediately confessed that she had gone to the bank to get money.

Everyone began to glance at the clock, but Bulldozer Olsson did not approve of adjournments and promptly called his first witness, Kirstin Franzén, the bank cashier. Her testimony was short and confirmed in all respects what had already been said.

Bulldozer asked: "When did you realize that this was a holdup?"

"As soon as she threw her bag on the counter and demanded money. And then I saw the knife. It looked awfully dangerous. A kind of dagger."

"Why did you hand over the money?"

"We've had instructions not to offer resistance in situations like this, but to do what the robber says."

This was true. The banks did not wish to run the risk of paying out life insurance and expensive damages to employees who were injured.

A clap of thunder seemed to shake the venerable courtroom. In fact it was Hedobald Braxén belching. This did not happen all that seldom and was one of the many reasons for his nickname.

"Has the defense any questions?"

Crasher shook his head. He was busy writing something down on a piece of paper.

Bulldozer called his next witness.

Kenneth Kvastmo stepped up and laboriously repeated the oath. His testimony began with the usual litany: occupation police assistant, born in Arvika in nineteen hundred and forty-two; first served in patrol cars in Solna and later in Stockholm.

Bulldozer said, foolishly, "Tell us in your own words."

"What?"

"What happened, of course."

"Yes," said Kvastmo. "She was standing there, the murderess. Well, she didn't manage to murder nobody, of course. Karl didn't do nothing, as usual, of course, so I threw myself on her like a panther."

The image was unfortunate. Kvastmo was a large,

shapeless man with a fat bottom, a bull neck and fleshy features.

"I got hold of her right hand just as she was trying to pull out the knife, and then I told her she was under arrest and then I just arrested her. I had to carry her out to the car and in the back seat she resisted arrest violently and then it turns out she was assaulting an officer of the law because one of my shoulder flaps almost come off and my wife was furious when she had to sew it on because there was something on TV she was going to watch and also a button had almost came off my uniform and she didn't have no blue thread, Anna-Greta, my wife, I mean. And when we was done in the bank, then Karl drove us to the station. There wasn't nothing else after that except she called me a pig, but that's not really insulting a policeman. A pig don't cause no disrespect or contempt of the force, I mean neither to the individual officer which in this case was me, or to the force as a whole does it? She's the one, over there, that said it." He pointed to Rebecka Lind.

While the policeman was revealing his narrative abilities, Bulldozer was watching the woman spectator, who had been busily taking notes and was now sitting with her elbows on her thighs, her chin in her hands, as she attentively watched both Braxén and Rebecka in turn. Her face looked troubled, or rather expressed profound unease. She bent down and scratched an ankle with one hand as she chewed a nail on the other hand. Now she was looking at Braxén again and her half-closed blue eyes expressed a mixture of resignation and hesitant hope.

Hedobald Braxén appeared to be only just physically present, and there was no indication whatsoever that he had heard a word of the evidence.

"No questions," he said.

Bulldozer Olsson was satisfied. The case was open-and-shut, exactly as he had said from the start. The only fault was that it had taken so long. Now when the judge suggested an hour's adjournment, he nodded his approval enthusiastically and rushed toward the door with short, bouncing steps.

Martin Beck and Rhea Nielsen used the break to go to the Amarante. After open sandwiches and beer, they finished off with coffee and brandy. Martin Beck had had several boring hours. He had gone up to the station for a spell with Rönn and Strömgren, but that had not been particularly rewarding. He had never liked Strömgren and his relationship with Rönn was complicated. The simple truth was that he no longer had any friends left at the station on Kungsholmsgatan; both there and at the National Police Administration there were a number of people who admired him, others who detested him and a third group, the largest, who quite simply envied him. Out at Västberga, too, he had no friends since Lennart Kollberg had left. Benny Skacke had applied for the job and got it, on Martin Beck's recommendation. Their relationship was fairly good, but from that to genuine warmth was a long step. Sometimes he just sat and stared into space, wishing Kollberg were back; to be perfectly honest—and he found that easy nowadays—he mourned for him the way you mourn for a child or a lost love.

He sat chatting for a while in Rönn's room, but not only was Rönn indifferent company, he also had a lot to do.

"Wonder how things are with Gunvald," said Rönn. "I wouldn't mind trading places with him. Bullfights and palm trees and expense-account dinners, boy oh boy!"

Rönn specialized in giving Martin Beck a guilty conscience. Why couldn't he have been offered that trip, he who certainly needed more encouragement than anyone else?

It was impossible to tell Rönn the truth—that he had actually been discriminated against simply because they considered it impossible to send out a runny-nosed northerner, a man with a notably unrepresentative appearance who could only with the greatest goodwill be said to speak passable English.

But Rönn was a good detective. He had been nothing much to start with, but now he was undoubtedly one of the section's greatest assets.

As usual, Martin Beck tried but failed to find something encouraging to say, and shortly he left.

Now he was sitting with Rhea, and that in truth was quite a different matter. The only trouble was that she seemed sad.

"This trial," she said. "Christ, it's depressing! And the people who decide things! The prosecutor is just a buffoon. And the way he stared at me, as if he'd never seen a girl before."

"Bulldozer," said Martin Beck. "He's seen lots of girls and anyhow he's not your type."

"And the defense lawyer doesn't even know his client's name! That girl hasn't a hope in heaven."

"It's not over yet. Bulldozer wins almost all his cases, but if he does lose one occasionally, it's always to Braxén. Do you remember that Swärd business?"

"Do I remember!" said Rhea. She laughed hoarsely. "When you came and stayed at my place the first time. The locked room and all that. Two years ago almost. How could I not remember?"

She looked happy, and nothing could have made him happier. They had had good times since then, full of talk, jealousy, friendly quarrels and, not least, good spells of sex, trust and companionship. Although he was over fifty and thought he had experienced most things, he had still opened up with her. Hopefully, she shared his feelings about the relationship, but on that point he was more uncertain. She was physically stronger and the more free-thinking of the two of them, presumably also more intelligent, anyhow quicker-thinking. She had plenty of bad points, among others that she was often cross and irritable, but he loved them. Perhaps that expression was stupid or far too romantic, but he could find no better one.

He looked at her and became aware that he had stopped being jealous. Her large nipples were thrusting out beneath the material, her shirt was carelessly buttoned, she had taken off her sandals and was rubbing her naked feet against each other under the table. Now and again she bent down and scratched her ankles. But she was herself and not his; perhaps that was the best thing about her.

Her face became troubled at this moment, the irregular features set in an expression of anxiety and distaste. "I don't understand much about the law," she said, with little truth, "but this case appears lost. Can't you say something to change it when you testify?"

"Hardly. I don't even know what he wants out of me."

"The other defense witnesses seem useless. A bank director and a home economics teacher and a policeman. Were any of them even there?"

"Yes, Kristiansson. He was driving the patrol car."

"Is he as dumb as the other cop?"

"Yes."

"And I don't suppose the case can be won on the closing argument, the defense's, I mean?"

Martin Beck smiled. He should have known she would get this seriously involved.

"No, it doesn't seem likely. But are you sure the defense ought to win and that Rebecka isn't guilty?"

"The investigation is a load of rubbish. The whole case ought to be turned back over to the police—nothing's been properly investigated. I hate the police on that score alone. They hand over cases to the prosecutor's office that aren't even half completed. And then the prosecutor struts around like a turkey cock on a garbage heap and the people who are supposed to judge are only sitting there because they're politically useless and no good for anything else."

In many ways she was right. The jurymen were scraped from the bottom of the political party barrels, they were often friends of the prosecutor, or let themselves be dominated by strong-willed judges who fundamentally despised them.

"It may sound odd, I know," said Martin Beck, "but I think you underestimate Braxén."

On the short walk back to the courthouse, Rhea suddenly took his hand. That seldom happened and always meant that she was worried or in a state of great emotional tension. Her hand was like everything else about her, strong and reliable.

Bulldozer came into the foyer at the same time as they did, one minute before the court was to reconvene. "That bank robbery on Vasagatan is all cleared up," he said breathlessly. "But we've got two new ones instead, and one of them . . ."

His gaze fell on Kvastmo and he set off without even finishing the sentence. "You can go home," he told Kvastmo. "Or back on duty. I would take it as a personal favor."

This was Bulldozer's way of bawling someone out.

"What?" said Kvastmo.

"You can go back on duty," said Bulldozer. "Every man is needed at his post."

"My evidence took care of that gangster dame, didn't it?" said Kvastmo.

"Yes," said Bulldozer. "It was brilliant."

Kvastmo left to carry on his struggle against the gangster community in other arenas.

The court reconvened and the case continued.

Braxén called his first witness, Rumford Bondesson, bank director. After the formalities, Braxén suddenly pointed at the witness with his unlit cigar and said inquisitorially, "Have you ever met Rebecka Lind?"

"Yes."

"When?"

About a month ago. The young lady came to the head office of the bank. She was dressed in the same clothes as now, but she was carrying an infant in some kind of harness on her chest."

"And you received her?"

"Yes. I had a few moments to spare, as it happened, and I am also interested in modern young people."

"Especially the female kind?"

"Yes. I don't mind admitting it."

"How old are you, Mr. Bondesson?"

"Fifty-nine."

"What did Rebecka Lind want?"

"To borrow money. Clearly she had no idea whatsoever about the simplest financial matters. Someone had told her that banks lend money, so she went to the nearest big bank and asked to speak to the manager."

"And what did you reply?"

"That banks were commercial enterprises which didn't lend money without interest and security. She replied that she had a goat and three cats."

"Why did she want to borrow money?"

"To go to America. Just where in America she didn't know, and neither did she know what she was going to do when she got there. But she had an address, she said."

"What else did she say?"

"She asked if there was a bank that was not so commercial, that was owned by the people and to which ordinary people could go when they needed money. I replied, mostly in fun, that the Credit Bank, or the PK Bank as it is called nowadays, was at least officially owned by the state, and so by the people. She appeared to be satisfied with that answer."

Crasher went up to the witness, jabbed the cigar against his chest and asked, "Was anything else said?"

Mr. Bondesson did not reply, and finally the judge said, "You're under oath, Mr. Bondesson. But you do not have to answer questions which reveal criminal activities on your part."

"Yes," said Bondesson, with obvious reluctance. "Young girls are interested in me and I in them. I offered to solve her short-term problems."

He looked around and caught an annihilating look from Rhea Nielsen and the glint of a bald head from Bulldozer Olsson, who was deep in his papers.

"And what did Rebecka Lind say to that?"

"I don't remember. Nothing came of it."

Crasher had returned to his table. He rummaged around in his papers and said, "At the police interrogation, Rebecka said that she had made the following remarks: 'I loathe dirty old men' and 'I think you're disgusting.' " Crasher repeated in a loud voice: "Dirty old men." With a gesture of his cigar, he implied that as far as he was concerned the interrogation was over.

"I do not understand at all what this has to do with the case," said Bulldozer without even looking up.

The witness stepped down with an injured air.

Then it was Martin Beck's turn. The formalities were as usual, but Bulldozer was now more attentive and followed the defense's questions with obvious interest.

"Yesterday," said Crasher when the preliminaries were over, "I received word that a certain Filip Trofast Mauritzon had been refused the right to appeal to the High Court. As you may remember, Chief Inspector Beck, Mauritzon was convicted over eighteen months ago of murder in connection with armed robbery of a bank. The prosecutor in the case was my perhaps not-all-that-learned friend, Sten Robert Olsson, who at that time went under the title of Royal Prosecutor. I myself had the thankless and for my profession often morally burdensome task of defending Mauritzon, who undoubtedly was what we call in everyday speech a 'criminal.' I would now like to ask one single question: Do you, Chief Inspector Beck, consider that Mauritzon was guilty of the bank robbery and the murder connected with it, and that the investigation presented by present counsel for the prosecution, Mr. Olsson, was satisfactory from a police viewpoint?"

"No," said Martin Beck.

Although Bulldozer's cheeks had suddenly taken on a pink tone which matched his shirt and enhanced even further his monstrous tie with its golden mermaids and hula-hula dancers, he smiled happily and said, "I, too, would like to ask a question. Did you, Chief Inspector Beck, take any part in the investigation of the murder at the bank?"

"No," said Martin Beck.

Bulldozer slapped his hands together in front of his face and nodded in a self-satisfied way.

Martin Beck stepped down and went to sit beside Rhea. He rumpled her blond hair, which won him a cross look. "I thought there'd be more than that," she said.

"I didn't," said Martin Beck.

Watching them, Bulldozer Olsson's eyes were almost insane with curiosity. Crasher, however, appeared quite unaware of the situation. With his limping walk he had moved over to the window behind Bulldozer. In the dust on the pane he wrote the word IDIOT.

Then he said, "As my next witness I call Police Assistant Karl Kristiansson."

Kristiansson was shown in. He was an uncertain man who had lately come to the conclusion that the police force constituted a class system of its own, in which superiors behave as they did, not to exploit anyone, but quite simply to make the lives of their subordinates hell.

After a long wait, Crasher turned around and began to walk back and forth across the room. Bulldozer did the same, but at quite a different pace, so that they looked like two somewhat peculiar sentries on duty. Finally, with a colossal sigh, Crasher began the interrogation.

"According to my information, you've been a policeman for fifteen years."

"Yes."

"Your superior officers consider you lazy, unintelligent, but honest and generally as suitable—or unsuitable—as your other colleagues on the Stockholm Police Force."

"Objection! Objection!" cried Bulldozer. "Counsel is insulting the witness."

"Am I?" said Crasher. "If I were to say that the counsel for the prosecution, like a zeppelin, is one of the country's, yes even the world's most interesting and eloquent gasbags, there'd be nothing insulting about that, would there? Now I'm not saying that about the counsel for the prosecution, and as far as the witness is concerned, I am merely pointing out that he is an experienced policeman, as capable and intelligent as the other policemen who adorn our city. I'm just trying to bring out his excellent qualifications and good judgment."

Rhea Nielsen laughed out loud. Martin Beck placed his right hand over her left one. She laughed even more loudly. The judge pointed out that spectators were expected to keep quiet, then turned to look irritably at the two lawyers. Bulldozer gazed so intently at Rhea that he almost missed the beginning of the interrogation.

Crasher, on the other hand, showed no reaction. He asked, "Were you first into the bank?"

"No."

"Did you seize this girl, Rebecka Olsson?"

"No."

"Rebecka Lind, I mean," said Crasher, after a few sniggers.

"No."

"What did you do?"

"I grabbed the other one."

"Were there two girls present at the robbery?"

"Yes."

"Why?"

Kristiansson pondered a moment. "So she wouldn't fall."

"How old was this other girl?"

"About four months."

"And so it was Kvastmo who seized Rebecka Lind?"

"Yes."

"Do you think you might say that he employed violence or excessive force in doing so?"

"I don't understand what counsel for the defense is trying to get at," said Bulldozer banteringly.

"I mean that Kvastmo, whom we all saw earlier today . . ." Crasher rummaged for a long time among his papers. "Here it is," he said. "Kvastmo weighs over two hundred pounds. He is, among other things, a specialist in karate and wrestling. He is regarded by his superiors as a keen and zealous man. Inspector Norman Hanson, who submitted the evidence, says however that Kvastmo is all too often overzealous on duty and that many of those taken into custody complain that Kvastmo used violence against them. The evidence also says that Kenneth Kvastmo has received various reprimands and that his ability to express himself leaves much to be desired."

Crasher put down the document and said, "Would the witness now answer the question as to whether Kvastmo used violence."

"Yes," said Kristiansson. "You could say that." Experience had taught him not to lie where duty was concerned, at least not too much or too often. Also, he disliked Kvastmo.

"And you took custody of the child?"

"Yes, I had to. She was carrying it in a sort of harness, and when Kvastmo was taking the knife away from her, she almost dropped the child."

"Did Rebecka offer any resistance?"

"No. When I took the kid, she just said, 'Careful you don't drop her!' "

"That all seems clear enough," said Crasher. "I will return to the possible continued use of force later. Instead, I should now like to ask you about another matter—"

"Yes," said Kristiansson.

"Since no one from the special department concerned

with protecting the banks' money visited the scene of the crime," said Crasher and stopped short with an imperious look at the prosecutor.

"We work day and night," said Bulldozer, "and this was considered an insignificant case, one of many."

"Which means that the initial interrogations were conducted by whatever police happened to be present," said Crasher. "Who spoke to the teller?"

"Me," said Kristiansson.

"And what did she say?"

"She said the girl came up to the counter with the kid in a harness and put her shoulder bag on the marble slab. The teller saw the knife right away, so she started stuffing notes in the bag."

"Did Rebecka take out the knife?"

"No, she had it in her belt. Around in the back."

"Then how could the teller have seen it?"

"I don't know. Yes, of course, she saw it afterward when Rebecka turned around, and then she screamed, 'A knife, a knife, she's got a knife!' "

"Was it a sheath knife or a stiletto?"

"No, it looked like a small kitchen knife. Like the kind you have at home."

"What did Rebecka say to the teller?"

"Nothing. Anyhow, not right away. Then they said she laughed and said, 'I didn't know it was so easy to borrow money.' And then she said, 'I suppose I have to leave a receipt or something.' "

"The money appears to have been scattered all over the floor," said Crasher. "How did that come about?"

"Well, Kvastmo was standing there holding onto the girl while we waited for reinforcements. And then the teller started counting the money to see if any was missing. And then Kenneth started shouting, 'Stop, that's illegal.' "

"And then?"

"Then he yelled, 'Karl, don't let anyone touch the loot.' I was carrying the kid so I only got hold of one of the handles and dumped it on the floor by accident. It was mostly small bills, so they flew all over the place. Well, then along came another patrol car. We gave the child to them, and then took the prisoner to the station on Kungsholm. I drove and Kenneth sat in the back seat with the girl."

"Was there trouble in the back seat?"

"Yes, a little. At first she cried and wanted to know what we'd done with her kid. Then she cried even louder and then Kvastmo was trying to put handcuffs on her."

"Did you say anything?"

"Yes, I said I was sure she didn't need them. Kvastmo was twice as big as her and anyway she wasn't offering any resistance."

"Did you say anything else in the car?"

Kristiansson sat in silence for several minutes. Crasher waited silently.

Kristiansson gazed at his uniform-clad legs, looked guiltily around and said, "I said, 'Don't hit her, Kenneth.' "

The rest was simple. Crasher rose and went over to Kristiansson. "Does Kenneth Kvastmo usually hit the people he arrests?"

"It has happened."

"Did you see Kvastmo's shoulder flap and the almost torn-off button?"

"Yes. He mentioned it. Said his wife didn't keep his things in order."

"When did this happen?"

"The day before."

"The prosecution's witness," said Crasher gently.

Bulldozer caught Kristiansson's eye and held it. How

many cases had been wrecked by dumb policemen? And how many had been saved?

"No questions," said Bulldozer lightly. Then, as if in passing, "The prosecution withdraws the charge of assaulting a police officer."

What happened next was that Braxén requested a recess, during which he lit his first cigar and then made the long trek to the washroom. He came back after a while and stood talking to Rhea Nielsen.

"What sort of women do you run around with?" Bulldozer Olsson asked Martin Beck. "First she laughs at me while the court's in session and now she stands there chatting with Crasher. Everyone knows Crasher's breath can knock an orangutan unconscious at fifty yards."

"Good women," answered Martin Beck. "Or rather, one good woman."

"Oh, so you've married again? Me, too. It gives life a little more zip."

Rhea came over to them. "Rhea," said Martin Beck, "this is the senior public prosecutor, Mr. Olsson."

"So I gather."

"Everyone calls him Bulldozer," said Martin Beck. He turned to Olsson. "I think your case is going badly."

"Yes, one half has collapsed," said Bulldozer. "But the rest of it'll stick. Bet me a bottle of whisky?"

At that moment the case was called again and Bulldozer Olsson rushed into the courtroom.

The defense called its next witness, Hedy-Marie Wirén, a suntanned woman of about fifty.

Crasher sorted his papers, finally finding the right one, and said, "Rebecka did not do well in school. She left at sixteen with grades far too low to enable her to go on to high school. But did she do equally poorly in all subjects?"

"She was good at my subject," said the witness. "One

of the best pupils I've ever had. Rebecka had a lot of ideas of her own, especially when it came to vegetables and natural foods. She was aware that our present diet is objectionable, that most of the food sold in supermarkets is in one way or another poisoned. Rebecka realized at a very early age the importance of a healthy way of life. She raised her own vegetables and was always prepared to gather what nature had to offer. That was why she always carried a gardening knife in her belt. I have talked a great deal to Rebecka."

"About biodynamic turnips?" Crasher yawned.

"Among other things. But what I would like to say is that Rebecka is a sound child. Her academic education is perhaps limited, but that was a conscious decision on her part. She does not wish to burden her mind with a mass of inessentials. The only thing that really interests her is how the natural environment can be saved from total destruction. She is not interested in politics other than that she finds society as such incomprehensible and its leaders either criminal or insane."

"No more questions," said Crasher. At this stage he appeared bored, interested in nothing but going home.

"I'm interested in that knife," said Bulldozer, suddenly jumping up from his place. He went over to the table in front of the judge and picked up the knife.

"It's an ordinary gardening knife," said Hedy-Marie Wirén. "The same kind she's always had. As anyone can see, the handle is worn and the tool well used."

"Nonetheless, it can be said to be a dangerous weapon," said Bulldozer.

"I don't agree at all. I wouldn't even attempt to kill a sparrow with that knife. Rebecka also has a totally negative attitude toward violence. She doesn't understand why it occurs and she herself would never dream of giving anyone so much as a slap."

"Nevertheless, I maintain that this is a dangerous weapon," said Bulldozer, waving the gardening knife about.

He did not, however, seem altogether convinced, and although he was smiling at the witness, he was forced to summon up all his benignity to accept her next comment with his famous good humor.

"That means that you are either malevolent or else simply stupid," said the witness. "Do you smoke? Or drink?"

"No more questions," said Bulldozer.

"The interrogation is now over," said the judge. "Does anyone wish to ask any questions before the character appraisals and the closing arguments?"

Braxén, limping and smacking his lips, approached the bench.

"Character appraisals are seldom more than routine essays, written to allow the writer to earn his fifty kronor, or whatever it is. So I would like—and I hope other responsible people will join me—to ask Rebecka Lind herself some questions."

He turned to the accused for the first time. "What is the name of the King of Sweden?"

Even Bulldozer looked surprised.

"I don't know," said Rebecka Lind. "Do I have to know that?"

"No," said Crasher. "You don't. Do you know the name of the Prime Minister?"

"No. Who is that?"

"He is the head of the government and the leading politician of the country."

"Then he's a bad man," said Rebecka Lind. "I know that Sweden has built an atomic power station in Barse-båck in Skåne, and it's only twenty-five kilometers from the center of Copenhagen. They say the government is to blame for the destruction of the environment."

"Rebecka," said Bulldozer Olsson in a friendly way, "how do you know about things like atomic power when you don't even know the name of the Prime Minister?"

"My friends talk about that sort of thing, but they aren't interested in politics."

Crasher let everyone think that over. Then he said, "Before you went to see this bank director, whose name I have unfortunately forgotten, presumably forever, had you ever been inside a bank before?"

"No, never."

"Why not?"

"What for? Banks are for the rich. I and my friends never go into such places."

"And nevertheless you did go there," said Crasher. "Why?"

"Because I needed money. One of my friends said that you could borrow money from a bank. Then when that horrible bank manager said that there were banks owned by the people, I thought maybe I could get some money there."

"So when you went to the PK Bank, you really thought you could borrow some money from them?"

"Yes, but I was surprised it was so easy. I never even had time to say how much I needed."

Bulldozer, who had now realized what line the defense was taking, hurried to intervene. "Rebecka," he said, a smile covering his face, "there are some things I simply don't understand. How is it possible, with all today's mass media, that a person can avoid learning the simplest facts about society?"

"Your society isn't mine," said Rebecka Lind.

"You're wrong, Rebecka," said Bulldozer. "We live together in this country and we have mutual responsibility for what is good or bad. But I would like to know how a person can avoid hearing what is said on the radio and television and entirely miss what is written in the newspapers."

"I have neither radio nor TV and the only things I read in the papers are the horoscopes."

"But you went to school for nine years, didn't you?"

"They just tried to teach us a lot of nonsense. I didn't listen."

"But money," said Bulldozer, "money is something everyone's interested in."

"Not me."

"Where did you get the money to live on?"

"Welfare. But I needed very little. Until now."

The judge then read out the character appraisal which was not quite so lacking in interest as Braxén had predicted.

Rebecka Lind was born on January 3, 1956, and grew up in a lower middle class home. Her father was an office manager in a small building firm. Their home circumstances had been good, but Rebecka had very early on rebelled against her parents, and this antagonism had culminated when she was sixteen years old. She had been remarkably uninterested in school and had left after the ninth grade. Her teachers considered her fund of knowledge to be frighteningly inadequate. Although she did not lack intelligence, her attitudes were strange and divorced from reality. She had not been able to find work and showed no interest in doing so. When she was sixteen years old, life at home had become difficult and she moved out. Questioned by the investigator, the father said that this had been best for them all, as the parents had other children who were less of a disappointment to them.

At first she lived in a country cottage, which she had

on more or less permanent loan from an acquaintance and which she kept after she managed to acquire a little cold-water apartment in the southern part of Stockholm. At the beginning of 1973 she met an American deserter named Jim Cosgrave and moved in with him. Rebecka soon became pregnant, which was her own wish, and in January 1974 she gave birth to a daughter, Camilla. Cosgrave had wanted to work but could find no job because he was long-haired and a foreigner. The only work he had during his years in Sweden was as a dish-washer for two weeks one summer on one of the ferries to Finland. Moreover, he longed to return to the United States. He had job experience and considered that he would have little difficulty in arranging things for him-self and his family once he got home.

At the beginning of February, Cosgrave made contact with the United States Embassy and declared himself prepared to return voluntarily, provided he was given certain guarantees. They were anxious to get him home and promised him that his punishment would be mere formality.

Cosgrave flew back to the States on February 12. Rebecka had reckoned on being able to follow in March, when her boy friend's parents had promised to help with money, but the months had gone by and no word had come from Cosgrave. She went to the social welfare office and was told that because Cosgrave was a foreign citizen, they could do nothing. That was when Rebecka decided to go to the United States on her own, to find out what had happened. To get money, she turned to a bank, with known results.

The character appraisal was mainly positive. It pointed out that Rebecka had been an excellent mother and that she had never sunk to vice or shown criminal tendencies. She was incorruptibly truthful, but had an unrealistic attitude toward the world and often showed signs of exaggerated gullibility. Cosgrave was also appraised briefly. According to his acquaintances, he was a purposeful young man who had not attempted to evade his responsibilities and who had implicitly believed in a future for himself and his family in the United States.

Bulldozer Olsson now rose to give his summation.

Rhea observed him through half-closed eyes. Apart from his hopeless clothes, he was a man who radiated enormous self-confidence and an intense interest in what he was doing. He had seen through Crasher's line of defense, but he was not going to let his actions be influenced by it. Instead, he expressed himself simply and briefly and stuck to his previous line of argument. He puffed out his chest—in fact mostly stomach—looked down at his unpolished brown shoes and began in a silky voice.

"I wish to limit my summation to a repetition of proven facts. Rebecka Lind went into the PK Bank, armed with a knife and equipped with a capacious shoulder bag in which she intended to put her booty. Long experience with bank robberies of the simpler variety—in fact there have been hundreds during this last year—convinces me that Rebecka was behaving according to a pattern although her lack of experience caused her to be immediately apprehended. I personally feel sorry for the accused, who while so young has allowed herself to be beguiled into committing such a serious crime. All the same, my regard for the law obliges me to demand unconditional imprisonment. The evidence that has been produced in this court is incontestable. No amount of argument can undo it."

Bulldozer fingered his tie, then concluded: "I therefore submit my case for the approval of the court."

"Is counsel for the defense prepared for his summation?" asked the judge.

Crasher was apparently not in the least prepared. He shuffled his papers together unsorted, regarded his unlit cigar for a moment, then put it into his pocket. He looked round the courtroom, staring curiously at each person in turn, as if he had never seen any of them before. Then he rose and limped back and forth in front of the judge.

Finally he said, "As I have already pointed out, this young lady who has been placed on the accused's bench, or perhaps I should say chair, is innocent, and a speech in her defense is largely unnecessary. Nevertheless, I shall say a few words."

Everyone wondered nervously what Crasher might mean by "a few words."

Crasher unbuttoned his jacket, belched with relief, thrust out his stomach and said, "As counsel for the prosecution has pointed out, a great many bank robberies occur in this country. The wide publicity they are given, as well as the often spectacular attempts of the police to stop them, have not only made the public prosecutor a famous man but have also caused a general hysteria."

Crasher paused and stood for a moment with his eyes on the floor, presumably trying to concentrate, then resumed.

"Rebecka Lind has not had much help or joy from society. Neither school, nor her own parents, nor the older generation in general have on the whole offered her support or encouragement. That she has not bothered to involve herself in the present system of rule cannot be blamed on her. When, in contrast to many other young people, she tries to get work, she is told that there is none. I am tempted here to go into the reasons why there is no work for the younger generation, but I shall abstain.

"At any rate, when she finally finds herself in a difficult situation, she turns to a bank. She has not the slightest idea of how a bank works, and is led to the mistaken conclusion that the PK Bank is less capitalistic, or that it is actually owned by the people.

"When the bank teller catches sight of Rebecka, she at once thinks the girl has come to rob the bank, partly because she cannot understand what such a person would be doing in a bank, and partly because she is inflamed by the innumerable directives that have been heaped onto bank employees recently. She at once sounds the alarm and begins to put money into the bag the girl has placed on the counter. What happens then? Well, instead of one of the public prosecutor's famous detectives, who have no time to bother with such futile little cases, along come two uniformed policemen in a patrol car. While one of them, according to his own words, leaps on the girl like a panther, the other manages to scatter the money all over the floor. Beyond this contribution, he also questions the teller. From this interrogation it appears that Rebecka did not threaten the bank staff at all and that she did not demand money. The whole matter can then be called a misunderstanding. The girl behaved naively, but, as you know, that is no crime."

Crasher limped over to his table, studied his papers, and with his back to the judge and jurymen said, "I ask that Rebecka Lind be released and that the charge against her be declared void. No other plea is possible, because anyone with any sense must see that she is not guilty and that there can be no question of any other verdict."

* * *

The court's deliberations were quite brief. The result was announced in less than half an hour.

Rebecka Lind was declared free and immediately released. On the other hand, the charges were not declared void, which meant that the prosecution could appeal the verdict. Five of the jurymen had voted for release and two against. The judge had recommended conviction.

As they left the courtroom, Bulldozer Olsson came up to Martin Beck and Rhea and said, "You see? If you'd been a bit quicker, you'd have won that bottle of whisky."

"Are you going to appeal?"

"No. Do you think I've nothing better to do than sit in the High Court for a whole day arguing the toss with Crasher? In a case like this?" He rushed away.

Crasher also came up to them, limping worse than ever. "Thanks for coming," he said. "Not many people would have done that."

"I thought I understood your train of thought," said Martin Beck.

"That's what's wrong," said Braxén. "Lots of people understand one's train of thought, but hardly anyone will come and support it."

Crasher looked thoughtfully at Rhea as he snipped off the top of his cigar.

"I had an interesting and profitable conversation with Miss . . . Mrs. . . . this lady during the recess."

"Nielsen's her name," said Martin Beck. "Rhea Nielsen."

"Thank you," said Crasher with a certain warmth. "Sometimes I wonder if I don't lose a lot of cases just because of this name business. Anyhow, Mrs. Nilsson should have gone in for law. She analyzed the whole case in ten minutes and summarized it in a way that would have taken the public prosecutor several months, if he were bright enough to manage it at all."

"Mmm," said Martin Beck. "If Bulldozer wanted to appeal, he would be unlikely to lose in a higher court."

"Well," said Crasher, "you have to reckon with your opponent's psyche. If Bulldozer loses in the first instance, he doesn't appeal."

"Why not?" said Rhea.

"He would lose his image as a man who is so busy that he really has no time for anything. And if all prosecutors were as successful as Bulldozer usually is, then half the population of the country would be in prison."

Rhea grimaced.

"Thanks again," said Crasher and limped away.

Martin Beck watched him go with some thoughtfulness, then turned to Rhea. "Where do you want to go?"

"Home."

"Your place or mine?"

"Yours. It's beginning to be a long time ago."

To be precise, long ago was four days.

4.

Martin Beck lived in Köpmangatan in the Old City, as close to the middle of Stockholm as one could get. The building was well maintained—it even had an elevator—and all but a few incorrigible snobs with villas and grand gardens and swimming pools in Saltjöbaden or Djursholm would have called it an ideal apartment. He had been in luck when he found the place, and the most extraordinary thing was that he didn't get it through cheating or bribery and corruption—in other words, the way police generally acquired privileges. This stroke of luck had in turn given him the strength to break up an unhappy marriage of eighteen years.

Then his luck ran out again. He was shot in the chest by a madman on a roof and a year later, when he was finally out of the hospital, he had truly been out in the cold, bored with work and horrified at the thought of spending the rest of his working life in a swivel chair in a carpeted office with originals by established painters on the walls.

But now that risk had been minimized. The upper echelons of the police force appeared convinced that even if he wasn't actually crazy, he was certainly impossible to work with. So Martin Beck had become head of the National Homicide Squad and would remain so until that antediluvian but singularly efficient organization was abolished.

Ironically, that very efficiency had engendered some criticism of the Squad. Some said that the Squad's extraordinary rate of success was due to the fact that it had too good a staff for its relatively few cases.

In addition, there were also people in high places who disliked Martin Beck personally. One of these had even let it be known that, by various unjust means, Martin Beck had persuaded Lennart Kollberg, who had been one of the best policemen in the country, to resign from the force to become a part-time revolver sorter at the Army Museum, compelling his poor wife to take on the burden of being the family breadwinner.

Martin Beck seldom became really angry, but when he heard this gibe, he came close to going up to the person in question and slugging him on the jaw. The fact was that everyone had gained from Kollberg's resignation. Kollberg himself not only escaped from a distasteful job but also managed to see his family more often, and his wife and children very much preferred seeing more of him. Another beneficiary was Benny Skacke, who took Kollberg's place and thus could hope to collect more credits toward his great purpose in life, that of becoming chief of police. And last but by no means least to benefit were certain members of the National Police Administration who, even if they were forced to admit that Kollberg was a good policeman, never could get over the fact that he was "troublesome" and "caused complications." When you came down to it, there was only one person who missed Kollberg, and that was Martin Beck.

When he had come out of hospital more than two years earlier, he also had problems of a more personal nature. He had felt lonely and isolated in a way he had never felt before. The case he had been given as occupational therapy had been unique in that it seemed to come straight from the world of detective stories. It concerned a locked room, and the investigation had been mystifying and the solution unsatisfactory. He had often had the feeling that it was he himself who was seated in the locked room, instead of a rather uninteresting corpse.

He had found the murderer, although Bulldozer Olsson at the subsequent trial had chosen to have the accused charged with murder in connection with a bank robbery, of which the man in question was entirely innocent—the case that Braxén had referred to earlier in the day. Martin Beck had found things a bit difficult with Bulldozer since then, as the whole affair had been so deliberately manipulated, but their relations weren't all that bad. Martin Beck was not resentful and he liked talking to Bulldozer, even if it did amuse him to put a spoke in the public prosecutor's wheel as he had done earlier that day.

But luck had come his way again—in the shape of Rhea Nielsen. When he met her, it took him only ten minutes to realize he was extremely interested, and she had made little effort to hide her interest in him. Perhaps most meaningful to him, at least at first, was that he had made contact with not only a human being who had at once understood what he meant, but also one whose own intentions and unspoken questions had been quite clear, without misunderstandings or complications.

So it had begun. They had met often, but only at her place. She owned an apartment house in Tulegatan and ran it, more and more dejectedly during the last year, as a kind of collective household.

Several weeks had gone by before she had come to the Köpmangatan apartment. She had cooked dinner that evening, because good food was one of her interests. The evening had also revealed that she had certain other interests, and that their interests on that point were more or less mutual.

It had been a good evening. For Martin Beck, perhaps the most successful ever.

They had had breakfast together in the morning, Martin Beck preparing it as he watched her dress. He had seen her naked several times before, but he had a strong feeling that it would be many years before he had looked his fill. Rhea Nielsen was strong and well built. It could be said that she was rather stocky, but also that she had an unusually functional and harmonious body—just as it could be said that her features were as irregular as they were strong and individual. What he liked most of all were five widely disparate things:

her uncompromising blue eyes, her flat round breasts, her large light-brown nipples, the fair patch of hair at her loins, and her feet.

Rhea had laughed hoarsely. "Go on looking," she said. "Sometimes it's damned good to be looked at." She pulled on her pants.

Soon afterward they were breakfasting on tea and toast and marmalade. She looked thoughtful, and Martin Beck knew why. He was troubled himself.

A few minutes later, she left, saying, "Thanks for one hell of a nice night."

"Thanks yourself."

"I'll call you," said Rhea. "If you think too long's gone by, then call me." She looked thoughtful and troubled again, then thrust her feet into her red clogs and said abruptly, "So long then. And thanks again."

Martin Beck was free that day. After Rhea had gone, he took a shower, put on his robe and lay down on the bed. He still felt troubled. He got up and looked at himself in the mirror. It had to be admitted that he did not look forty-nine, but it also had to be admitted that he was. As far as he could see, his features hadn't altered markedly for a number of years. He was trim and tall, a man with slightly yellow skin and a broad jaw. His hair showed no signs of going gray. No receding at the temples, either.

Or was that all an illusion? Just because he wanted it to be that way?

He went back to the bed, lay down on his back and clasped his hands behind his head.

He had had the best hours of his life. At the same time, he had created a problem that appeared insoluble. It was damned good sleeping with Rhea. But what was she really like? He was not sure he wanted to put it into words, but maybe he should. What was it someone had said once in the house on Tulegatan? Half girl and half ruffian?

Stupid, but it fitted somehow.

What had it been like last night?

The best in his life. Sexually. But he hadn't had a great deal of experience in that field.

What was she like? He would have to answer. Before he got to the central question.

She had thought it was fun. She had laughed sometimes. And sometimes he had thought she was crying.

So far so good, but then his thoughts took a different turn.

It won't work.

There's too much against it.

I'm thirteen years older. We're both divorced.

We have children, and even if mine are grown up, Rolf nineteen and Ingrid soon twenty-three, hers are still pretty young.

When I'm sixty and ready to retire she'll be only forty-seven.

It won't work.

Martin Beck did not call her up. The days went by, and over a week had passed since that night, when his own telephone shrilled at half-past seven in the morning.

"Hi," said Rhea.

"Hi. Thanks for last week."

"Same to you. Are you busy?"

"Not at all."

"God, the police *must* be busy," said Rhea. "When *do* you work, by the way."

"My department is having a quiet time at the present. But go into town and you'll find a different story."

"Thanks, I know what the streets are like."

She paused briefly, coughed hoarsely, then said, "Is it talking time?"

"I guess so."

"Okay. I'll put in an appearance whenever you say. It'd be best at your place."

"Maybe we might go out and eat afterward," said Martin Beck.

"Yes," she said hesitantly, "we might. Can you eat out in clogs these days?"

"Sure."

"I'll be there at seven then."

It was an important conversation for them both, despite the brevity. Their thoughts seemed always to run along roughly the same tracks, and there was no reason to suppose they had not done so this time. More than likely they had come to similar conclusions in a matter that was of undeniable significance.

Rhea came at exactly seven o'clock. She kicked off her red clogs and stood on tiptoe to kiss him.

"Why didn't you call me?" she asked.

Martin Beck did not answer.

"Because you'd finished thinking," she said. "And weren't pleased with the result?"

"Roughly."

"Roughly?"

"Exactly," he said.

"So we can't move in together or marry or have any more children or any other dumb thing. Then everything would become too complicated and muddled and a good relationship would have considerable chances of going to hell. Chewed to pieces and worn through."

"Yes," he said. "You're probably right. However much I'd like to deny it."

She gazed straight at him with her strange, peering, clear blue eyes and said, "Do you want to deny it very much?"

"Yes, but I won't."

For a moment she seemed to lose control. She walked over to the window, struck aside the curtain and said something in such a muffled voice that he could not catch the words. A few seconds later she said, still without turning her head, "I said I love you. I love you now, and I'll probably go on loving you for quite a long time."

Martin Beck felt bewildered. Then he went over and put his arms around her. Soon afterward she raised her face from his chest and said, "What I mean is, I'm staking a claim and will go on doing so as long as both of us do. Does that make sense?"

"Yes," said Martin Beck. "Shall we go and eat now?"

Though they seldom went out to eat, they had gone to an expensive restaurant where the headwaiter had looked at Rhea's clogs with distaste. Afterward they had walked home and lain in the same bed, which neither of them had planned on.

Since then almost two years had gone by and Rhea Nielsen had been to Köpmangatan innumerable times. Naturally she had to some extent left her mark on the apartment, especially in the kitchen, which was wholly unrecognizable. She had also stuck a poster of Mao Tse-tung above the bed. Martin Beck never expressed opinions on political matters and said nothing this time, either. But Rhea had said, "If anyone wanted to do an 'At Home With . . .' article, you'd probably have to take it down. If you were too cowardly to leave it up."

Martin Beck had not answered, but the thought of the tremendous dismay the poster would cause in certain circles decided him at once to leave it there.

When they went into Martin Beck's apartment on the fifth of June, 1974, Rhea began at once to take off her sandals.

"These damned straps rub," she said. "But they'll be all right in a week or two." She flung the sandals aside. "What a relief," she said. "You did a good job today. How many policemen would have agreed to testify and answer those questions?"

Martin Beck continued to say nothing.

"Not one," said Rhea. "And what you said turned the whole case. I could tell right away." She studied her feet and said, "Pretty sandals, but they rub like hell. It's nice to get them off."

"Take everything else off if you like it," said Martin Beck. He had known this woman long enough to know exactly how the situation might develop. Either she would immediately fling off all her clothes, or she would start talking about something completely different.

Rhea glanced at him. Sometimes her eyes looked luminous, he thought. She opened her mouth to say something and at once closed it again. Instead she flung off her shirt and jeans, and before Martin Beck had time to unbutton his jacket, her clothes were lying on the floor and she herself lay naked on the bed.

"God, how slowly you undress," she said, with a snort. Her mood had suddenly changed. This showed too in that she lay flat on her back almost throughout, her legs wide apart and straight up, the way she thought was the most fun, which was not to say that she always or even usually thought it was the best way.

They came simultaneously and that had to be that for the day.

Rhea rummaged in the wardrobe and extracted a long lilac-colored knit sweater, which was clearly her favorite piece of clothing and which she had found as difficult to leave behind at Tulegatan as her personal integrity. Before she had even put it on, she began to talk about food.

"A hot sandwich or maybe three, or five, how does that sound? I've bought all sorts of goodies, ham and paté, the best Jarlsberg cheese you've ever tasted."

"I believe you," said Martin Beck. He was standing over by the window, listening to the wolf howls of police cars, which could be heard very clearly, although in fact he lived in a very secluded spot.

"It'll be ready in five minutes," said Rhea.

It was the same every time they slept together. She at once became extremely hungry. Sometimes it was so urgent that she rushed stark-naked out to the kitchen to start cooking. Her preference for hot food didn't make things easier.

Martin Beck had no such problems—on the contrary. True, his stomach trouble seemed to have left him as soon as he left his wife. Whether the trouble had been due to her erratic cooking or whether it had had psychosomatic origins was not easy to say. But he could still easily satisfy his caloric needs—especially when on duty or when Rhea was not within reach—with a couple of cheese sandwiches and a glass or two of milk.

But Rhea's hot open sandwiches were very difficult to resist. Martin Beck ate three of them and drank two bottles of Hof. Rhea devoured seven, drank half a bottle of red wine and was still hungry enough fifteen minutes later to go foraging in the refrigerator for more.

"Are you staying over?" Martin Beck asked.

"Yes, please," she said. "It seems to be that sort of day."

"What sort of day?"

"The sort of day that suits us, of course."

"Oh, that sort of day."

"We could celebrate Swedish Flag Day, for instance. And the King's name day. We'll have to think up something original when we wake up."

"Oh, I expect that can be arranged."

Rhea curled up in the armchair. Most people would probably have thought she looked comical in her strange position and that mysterious long sweater. But Martin Beck did not think so. After a while it looked as if she had fallen asleep, but at that moment she said, "Now I remember what it was I was going to say just as you raped me."

"Yes? What was it?"

"That girl, Rebecka Lind, what'll happen to her?"

"Nothing. They released her."

"Sometimes you really do say stupid things. I know they released her. The question is what might happen to her psychologically. Can she look after herself?"

"Oh, I think so. She isn't as apathetic and passive as a lot of her contemporaries. And as far as the trial—"

"Yes, the trial. What did she learn from it? Presumably that it's possible to be arrested and maybe sent to prison without ever having done anything." Rhea frowned. "I'm worried about that girl. It's difficult to manage on your own in a society you don't understand at all, when the system is alien to you."

"From what I could gather that American boy is okay and really does want to take care of her."

"Maybe he just can't," said Rhea, shaking her head.

Martin Beck looked silently at her for a while, then said, "I'd like to disagree with you, but the fact is I was worried myself when I saw that girl. Another fact is that unfortunately we can't do much to help her. Of course we could help her privately, with money, but I don't think she'd accept that kind of help and anyway I don't have any money to give away."

Rhea scratched the back of her neck for a while. "You're right," she said. "I think she's the type who wouldn't accept charity. She'll never even go willingly to the social welfare office. Perhaps she'll try to get herself a job, but she'll never find one." She yawned. "I haven't the energy to think anymore," she said. "But one thing seems clear. Rebecka Lind will never become a noted citizen in the land."

She was wrong there, and soon afterward fell asleep.

Martin Beck went out to the kitchen, did the dishes and put things away. He was still there when Rhea woke up and he heard her switch on the TV. She had decided not to have a set of her own, presumably for the sake of the children, but she occasionally liked to watch his. He heard her call something, put down what he was doing and went into the room.

"There's a special news bulletin," she said.

He had missed the actual beginning, but there was no doubt about the subject matter. The newscaster's voice sounded dignified and serious.

". . . the assassination occurred before the arrival at the palace. An explosive charge of very great force was detonated beneath the street just as the motorcade was passing. The President and the others in the bulletproof car were killed immediately and their bodies badly mutilated. The car itself was thrown over a nearby building. A number of other people were killed by the explosion, among them several security men and civilians in the area. The chief of the City Police announced that sixteen people had definitely been killed, but the final number may be considerably higher. He also emphasized that security measures for the state visit had been the most comprehensive ever undertaken in the history of the country. In a broadcast from France immediately after the assassination, it was said that an international terrorist group called ULAG had accepted responsibility for the act."

The newsman lifted his telephone receiver and listened for a few seconds, then said, "We now have a film transmitted by satellite and made by an American television company covering this state visit that has come to such a tragic end."

The broadcast was of poor quality, but nevertheless so revolting that it should never have been shown.

At first there were a few pictures of the arrival of the President's plane and the noble gentleman himself, rather foolishly waving at the reception committee. Then he unenthusiastically inspected the honor guard and greeted his hosts with a smile plastered on his face. There followed a few pictures of the motorcade. The security measures seemed singularly reassuring.

Then came the climax of the broadcast. The television company appeared to have had a cameraman very strategically, or perhaps fortunately, placed. If the man had been fifty yards nearer, he would probably no longer be alive. If on the other hand he had been fifty yards farther away, he would probably not have had any pictures to show. Everything happened very quickly; first an enormous pillar of smoke, cars, animals and people all thrown high into the air, bodies torn apart, swallowed up in a cloud of smoke that looked almost like the mushroom cloud from an atomic bomb. Then the cameraman panned around the surroundings, which were very beautiful; a fountain playing, a wide palm-lined street. And then came the terrible paroxysms beside a heap of metal that might once have been a car, and something which a short time before had probably been a living human being.

Throughout the film the reporter kept up a ceaseless commentary in that eager, exalted tone that only American news reporters seem to achieve. It was as if he had —with enormous pleasure—just witnessed the end of the world.

"Oh, God," said Rhea, burying her face in the chair cushion. "What a goddamn awful world we live in."

But for Martin Beck it was going to be slightly more difficult.

The Swedish newsman reappeared and said, "We have just learned that the Swedish police had a special observer at the site of the assassination, Inspector Gunvald Larsson, from the Violence Division in Stockholm."

The screen was filled with a still picture of Gunvald Larsson looking mentally deficient, his name, as usual, misspelled.

"Unfortunately there is no news at the moment of what has happened to Inspector Larsson. The next newscast will be the regularly scheduled news on the radio."

"Goddammit," said Martin Beck. "Goddammit to hell."

"What's the matter?" asked Rhea.

"Gunvald. He's always right there when the shit hits the fan."

"I thought you didn't like him."

"But I do. Even if I don't say so very often."

"You should say what you think," said Rhea. "Come on, let's go to bed."

Twenty minutes later he had fallen asleep with his cheek against her shoulder.

Her shoulder soon grew numb, and then her arm. She didn't move, but just lay awake in the dark, liking him.

5.

The last commuter train of the night from Stockholm's Central Station stopped at Rotebro and dropped a single passenger.

The man, wearing a dark blue denim suit and black sneakers, walked briskly along the platform and down the steps, but as he left the bright lights of the station behind him, he slowed down. He continued unhurriedly through the older villa section of the suburb, past the fences, low walls and well-cut hedges that surrounded the gardens. The air was chilly, but still and full of scents.

It was the darkest part of the night, but it was only two weeks to the summer solstice and the June sky arched deep blue above his head.

The houses on either side of the road lay dark and silent, the only sound that of the man's rubber shoes against the sidewalk.

During the train journey, he had been uneasy and nervous, but now he was feeling calm and relaxed, his thoughts wandering their own ways. A poem by Elmer Diktonius came to his mind, its cadence matching his steps.

Walk carefully along the road
But never count your steps,
For fear will kill them.

From time to time he had tried to compose poetry himself, with indifferent results, but he liked reading poetry and had learned by heart many poems written by his favorite poets.

As he walked he kept his hand firmly clenched around the solid iron bar, over a foot long, that he was carrying thrust up the right sleeve of his denim jacket.

When the man had crossed Holmbodavägen and was approaching the area of row-houses, his movements grew more cautious and his stance more alert. Up to now he had met no one and he was hoping his luck would hold for the short stretch remaining before he reached his goal. He felt more exposed here, the gardens were behind the houses, and the vegetation in the narrow strip between the fronts of houses and the sidewalk consisted of flowerbeds, bushes and hedges that were too low to offer any protection.

The houses along one side of the road were painted yellow, those opposite red. This appeared to be the only difference; their exteriors were otherwise identical, two-story houses of wood, with mansard roofs. Between the houses were garages or toolsheds, squeezed in as if to link the houses together as well as to separate them.

The man was on his way to the farthest row of houses, beyond which the buildings ceased and fields and meadows took over. He slipped swiftly and silently up to the garage next to one of the houses by the corner of the road, as his eyes swept the terraces and the road. There was no one to be seen.

The garage had no doors, and there was no car inside, only a woman's bicycle leaning against the wall just inside the entrance, and opposite that a garbage bin. Farthest in, by the far wall, were two large rectangular wooden crates standing on end. He had been worried that someone might have moved them away. The hiding place had been decided on beforehand and he would have found it difficult to find another one as good.

The space between the packing cases and the wall

was narrow, but wide enough for him to squeeze into. He wriggled in behind the crates, which were solidly constructed of rough pine and about the same size as coffins. When he had assured himself that he was completely hidden he drew the iron bar out of his sleeve. He lay facedown on the damp, cold cement floor, his face buried in the crook of his arm. In his right hand was the iron bar, still warm from the heat of his body. Now he had only to wait as the summer night outside gradually grew lighter.

He was awakened by the twittering of birds. Getting to his knees, he looked at his watch. Almost half-past four. The sun was just rising; he had four more hours to wait.

Just before six, sounds began to come from inside the house. They were faint and indefinite and the man behind the wooden crate felt like pressing his ear to the wall, but dared not as he would then be visible from the road. Through a narrow slit between the two crates he could see a bit of the road and the house opposite. A car passed, and shortly after he heard an engine start up nearby and then saw another car go by.

A half-past six he heard steps approaching on the other side of the wall; it sounded like someone in clogs. The thumping faded away and came back several times, and finally he heard a deep female voice saying quite clearly, "Bye, then. I'm going. Will you call me this evening?"

He could not make out the reply, but heard the front door open and close. He stood quite still with his eye to the crack.

The woman in clogs came into the garage. He could not see her, but heard a small click as she unlocked the bicycle and then the crunch of her steps on the gravel path leading out to the road. The only thing he saw as she cycled past was that her trousers were white and her hair long and dark.

He scanned the house across the road. The blinds were down in the only window that was within his field of vision. He clamped the iron bar under his jacket with his left arm and moved three steps away from the protection of the crates, put one ear against the wall and listened, his eye on the road outside. At first he could hear nothing, but he soon caught the sound of steps vanishing up some stairs.

The road was empty. Far away he heard a dog bark and the distant grumble of a diesel engine, but in the immediate neighborhood everything was quiet and still. He pulled on his gloves, which had been rolled up inside his jacket pockets, slipped quickly along the garage wall, stepped around the corner and pressed down the handle of the front porch door.

As he had expected, it was unlocked.

He held the door ajar, heard footsteps up on the next floor, established with a swift glance that the road was still empty, and slipped inside.

The tiles of the porch were a step lower than the parquet flooring of the hall, and he stood there looking to the right, through the hall and into the large living room. He was already familiar with the layout of the house. There were three doors to the right, the middle one open—that was the kitchen. The bathroom lay behind the door to the left in the hall. Then the stairs to the upper floor. Beyond them was the part of the living room hidden from him facing the garden at the back of the house.

To his left hung a row of outdoor clothes, and on the tile floor beneath them were rubber boots and some sandals and shoes. Straight ahead of him, immediately opposite the door from the porch, was yet another door. He opened it, went in and shut it soundlessly behind him.

He found himself in a kind of combined storage and utility room. The boiler for the central heating was there. Washing machine, dryer and pump stood along one wall beyond the heating unit. Along the other wall were two large cupboards and a workbench. He glanced into the cupboards. In one hung a ski suit, a sheepskin coat and other clothing seldom used, or put away for the summer. The other held a few rolls of wallpaper and a large can of white paint.

The sounds from above had ceased. The man held the iron bar in his right hand as he opened the door crack and listened.

Suddenly steps could be heard coming down the stairs and he hurried to close the door, but remained standing there with his ear to the door. The steps could not be heard so clearly down here, probably because the person out there was either barefooted or in his stocking feet.

There was a clatter in the kitchen, as if a saucepan had fallen to the floor.

Silence.

Then steps approached and the man tightened his grip on the iron bar. But he relaxed it again when he heard the bathroom door open and then the rush of water in the toilet. He opened the door a crack again and peered out. Over the sound of rushing water, he heard the peculiar sounds that arise when someone tries to sing while cleaning his teeth. This was followed by gargling, throat clearing and spitting. Then the song started up again, clearer now and with shrill power. He recognized the song despite the fact that the rendering of it was horribly out of tune and that he had not heard it sung for at least twenty-five years. "The Girl in Marseille" he thought it was called.

". . . but then one dark night, in the Mediterranean moonlight, I lay dead in an alley, down by the old harbor . . ." came from the bathroom as someone turned on the shower.

He stepped out and on tiptoe crept up to the half-open bathroom door. The noise of the shower did not drown the song, which was now mixed with snorts and puffings and blowings.

The man stood with the iron bar in his hand and looked into the bathroom. He looked at the reddening shiny back with two rolls of fat hanging between the round cushions over the shoulder blades and the place where the waist should have been. He looked at the sagging buttocks, trembling over dimpled thighs, and the bulging veins at the back of the knees and knobby calves. He looked at the fat neck and the skull, which shone pink between thin strands of black hair. And as he looked and took the few steps toward the man standing in the bath, he was filled with loathing and disgust. He raised his weapon, and with the force of all his hatred, split the man's skull with one blow.

The fat man's feet slid backward on the slippery enamel and he fell facedown, his head thumping against the edge of the bath before his body came to rest with a smacking sound under the shower.

The killer leaned over to turn off the faucets and saw how blood and brain tissue had mixed with the water and were swirling down the drain, which was half blocked by the dead man's big toe. Revolted, he grabbed a towel and wiped the weapon, threw the towel over the corpse's head and thrust the iron bar up the wet sleeve of his jacket. Then he closed the bathroom door and went into the living room, opening the glass doors into the garden, where the lawn bordered on the broad fields surrounding the area.

He had to walk a long stretch across open fields to reach the edge of the woods on the other side. A beaten path ran diagonally across the field and he began to follow it. Farther on, the ground was cultivated and green with sprouting seed. He did not turn around, but out of the corner of his left eye he sensed the long rows of houses with their angled roofs and shining windows in the pointed gables. Every window was an eye staring coldly at him.

As he approached the first group of trees on a small rocky slope surrounded by thick bushes, he turned off the path. Before he pushed his way through the prickly blackthorn bushes to vanish among the trees, he let the iron bar slide out of his sleeve and vanish into the tangled undergrowth.

Martin Beck was sitting alone at home, leafing through an issue of *Longitude* as he listened to one of Rhea's records. Rhea and he did not really have the same tastes in music, but they both liked Nannie Porres and often played her records.

It was a quarter to eight in the evening and he had considered going to bed early. Rhea was at a meeting of the parent-teacher association of her children's school, and anyway they had already celebrated Swedish Flag Day in a satisfactory manner that morning.

The telephone rang in the middle of "I Thought About You," and as he knew it could hardly be Rhea, he was in no hurry to answer it. It turned out to be Chief Inspector Pärsson in Märsta district, known to some people as Märsta-Pärsta. Martin Beck considered the nickname infantile and always thought of him as Pärsson in Märsta.

"I called the duty officer first," Pärsson said, "and he thought it'd be okay to call you at home. We've got a case out here in Rotebro which is clearly murder. The man's had his skull bashed in with a powerful blow to the back of his head."

"Where and when was he found?"

"In a row house on Tennisvägen. The woman who lives in the house and appears to be his mistress came home at about five and found him dead in the bath. He was alive when she left the house at half-past six in the morning, she says."

"How long have you been there?"

"She called us at five thirty-five," said Pärsson. "We got here almost exactly two hours ago."

He paused for a moment and then went on. "I imagine it's a case we could manage on our own, but I thought I'd better inform you as soon as possible. It's difficult at this stage to decide just how complicated the investigation will be. The weapon hasn't been found."

"So you want us to come in on it?" said Martin Beck.

"If I hadn't known that you weren't actually working on a case at the moment, I wouldn't have bothered you at this stage. But I wanted your advice, and I'm told you usually like to come on a case when it's reasonably fresh."

Pärsson sounded slightly uncertain. He admired all notabilities, and Martin Beck could be considered one of those, but most of all he respected his professional skill.

"Of course," said Martin Beck. "You're quite right. I'm glad you called me up so soon."

It was true. Often the police in country areas waited

too long before calling in National Homicide, either because they overestimated their own resources and skills or misjudged the scope of the investigation, or because they themselves wanted to rap the experts in Stockholm over the knuckles and have the honor of solving a murder. When they finally had to admit their limitations and Martin Beck and his men went to the place, they were often faced with a situation in which all the clues had been destroyed, all reports were illegible, witnesses had lost their memories, and the culprit had already established residence in Tahiti or had died of old age.

"When can you come?" said Pärsson, noticeably relieved.

"I'll get started right away. I'll just call Koll . . . Skacke, and see if he can drive me out."

Martin Beck thought of calling Kollberg in situations like this out of habit. He supposed it was because his subconscious would not accept the fact that they were no longer working together. During the first few months after Kollberg resigned, he had actually called him several times in emergencies.

Benny Skacke was at home and as usual sounded eager and enthusiastic. He lived in southern Stockholm with his Monica and their one-year-old daughter. He promised to be at Köpmangatan within seven minutes, and Martin Beck went down to the street to wait for him. Exactly seven minutes later Skacke arrived in his black Saab.

On the way out to Rotebro he said, "You heard about Gunvald, didn't you? That he got hit in the stomach by the President's head?"

Martin Beck had heard and said, "He was lucky to get away with just that."

Benny Skacke drove for a while in silence, then said,

"I was thinking about Gunvald's clothes. He's always so careful about them and always gets them ruined. He must have gotten absolutely covered with blood."

"Must have," said Martin Beck. "But he got out of it alive, so he's still ahead of the game."

"*Ahead* is right!" said Skacke with a snort of laughter.

Benny Skacke was thirty-five and during the last six years had often worked with Martin Beck. He reckoned he had gained all his basic knowledge of criminal work by observing and studying the work of Lennart Kollberg and Martin Beck. He had also noted the special rapport that existed between the two men and had been amazed how easily they read each other's thoughts. He realized that such rapport would never arise between himself and Martin Beck, and he was aware that in Martin Beck's eyes he was a poor substitute for Kollberg. This insight often made him unsure of himself in Martin Beck's company.

On his side, Martin Beck understood very well how Skacke felt and did his best to encourage him and show that he appreciated his efforts. He had watched Skacke mature during the years he had known him and he knew Skacke worked hard, not only to do well in his career but also to become a really good policeman. He regularly spent his free time building up his physique and practicing on the firing range, and he studied constantly —law, sociology and psychology—and he also kept himself well-informed on what was happening within the force, both technically and organizationally.

Skacke was also a good driver and had a better knowledge of Stockholm and all its new suburbs than any taxi driver. He had no difficulty finding the address in Rotebro and stopped at the end of the row of parked cars on Tennisvägen.

A few representatives of the press had already arrived, but at least for the moment they were being held in check by a couple of policemen in civilian clothes who were standing by their cars and talking to them. The photographers immediately recognized Martin Beck and ran up clicking their cameras. The driveway leading to the house and garage was barred, but the policeman on duty let Martin Beck and Skacke through with a polite gesture toward his cap.

Inside, the house was seething with activity. The men from the crime lab were hard at work, a man squatting in the hall dusting a table lamp on a low chest by the telephone for fingerprints, and the flare of a flashbulb revealing a photographer in another room.

Chief Inspector Pärsson came up to Martin Beck and Skacke. "That was quick," he said. "Do you want to look in the bathroom first?"

The man in the bath was not a pretty sight, and neither Martin nor Skacke stayed in there any longer than necessary.

"The doctor just left," said Pärsson. "He says the man's been dead at least eight and at most fifteen hours. The blow killed him at once, and he thinks the weapon may have been an iron lever or a crowbar, or something like that."

"Who is he?" asked Martin Beck, nodding toward the bathroom.

Pärsson sighed. "Unfortunately someone the evening papers will eat up. Walter Petrus, the film director."

"Oh, Christ," said Martin Beck.

"Or Valter Petrus Pettersson, film director, as it says in his papers. His clothes, wallet and briefcase were lying in the bedroom."

The men who had come to collect the body were standing impatiently waiting to get past, and Martin

Beck, Pärsson and Skacke went into the living room to get out of the way.

"Where's the woman who lives here?" asked Martin Beck. "And who is she? Don't tell me she's a film star."

"No, thank God," said Pärsson. "She's upstairs. We've got a man talking to her at the moment. Her name's Maud Lundin. She's forty-two and works in a beauty salon in Sveavägen."

"How does she seem?" asked Skacke. "Is she in shock?"

"Well," said Pärsson, "she seemed more shaken. I think she's fairly calm now. She can't sleep here tonight, but she says she's got a friend in town who'll put her up until we've finished here."

"Have you had time to question the neighbors?" asked Martin Beck.

"We've only spoken to the people who live in the houses on either side, and to the neighbor across the road. None of them saw or heard anything unusual, they say. But we'll have to go to the other houses along the road tomorrow. Maybe we'll have to talk to everyone in Rotebro. This is the sort of place where people know each other—their kids go to the same school, they shop at the same shops, and the ones who haven't got cars use the same buses and trains."

"But this Walter Petrus, does he live here, too?" asked Benny Skacke.

"No," said Pärsson. "He comes a few times a week and spends the night with Mrs. Lundin. He lives with his wife and three children in a house in Djursholm."

"Has the family been informed?" asked Martin Beck.

"Yes," said Pärsson. "We were lucky—there was a receipt from a private doctor in the briefcase. We called him and he seems to be their doctor and knows the family well. He offered to tell the family and look after them."

"Good," said Martin Beck. "We'll have to question them tomorrow, too. It's getting a little late now, so all we can do is try to finish up here."

Pärsson looked at his watch. "Half-past nine," he said. "Not that late. But you're right. We can maybe leave his family in peace for a while."

Pärsson was a tall, thin man with snow-white hair and a freckled complexion, which always made him look slightly sunburnt. He gave an aristocratic impression, with his narrow hooked nose, thin lips and small, elegant, deliberate movements.

"I'd like to talk to Maud Lundin for a while," said Martin Beck. "You said you have a man upstairs with her. Would it be all right if I went up?"

"Yes, sure," said Pärsson. "That'll be fine. You're the boss anyhow, so do as you please."

They could hear voices and noises outside and Pärsson went into the kitchen to look out the window. "Those damned reporters," he said. "They're like vultures. I'd better go out and talk to them." He walked toward the front door with dignified posture and serious face.

"You could look around a little," said Martin Beck to Skacke.

Skacke nodded, went over to the bookcase and began to study the titles.

Martin Beck went up the stairs, which led into a large square room with wall-to-wall white carpeting. The furniture consisted of eight bulging armchairs in light-colored leather in a circle around a huge circular glass-topped table. There was a very complex and evidently very expensive stereo setup against one wall and white-painted loudspeakers on shelves in each corner. The ceiling was angled and the view through the large window facing out over the back of the house was rural and peaceful, with the shifting green of the forest beyond the wide field.

There was only one door in the room, and that was closed. Martin Beck could hear the murmur of voices through it. He knocked and went in.

Two women were sitting on a double bed with a white coverlet of some furlike material. They fell silent and looked up at him as he stood in the doorway.

One of the women was heavily built and considerably taller than the other. She had powerful features, dark eyes, and her hair was parted in the center and hung straight and glossy down her back. The other woman was slim and slightly angular, with lively brown eyes and very short dark hair.

"Martin," she said. "Hi! I didn't know you were here."

Martin Beck was surprised too, and hesitated before answering. "Hi, Åsa," he said. "I didn't know you were here, either. Pärsson said he had a man up here."

"Oh," said Åsa Torell, "he calls everyone his men, even if they're women."

She turned back to the other woman. "Maud, this is Chief Inspector Beck. He's the head of the National Homicide Squad."

The woman nodded at Martin Beck, who nodded back. He had not really collected himself after the sudden meeting with Åsa. Five years earlier he had almost been in love with her.

He had met her eight years ago, when her fiancé and his youngest colleague, Åke Stenström, had been shot dead, together with eight other people in a bus. Åsa had mourned Åke for a long time and had eventually decided to join the police. She was an assistant to Pärsson in Märsta now.

One summer night in Malmö, five years earlier, Martin Beck and Åsa had slept together. It had been a good night, and had never been repeated. He was glad now. Åsa was a sweet girl and their relationship was good and friendly whenever they met on duty, but after Rhea it was impossible for him to have sexual feelings for any other woman. Åsa was still unmarried, apparently wholly absorbed in her job, and she had become a very skillful policewoman.

"Go down to Pärsson, will you," said Martin Beck. "He's sure to need you down there."

Åsa nodded cheerfully and went.

As Martin Beck knew how adept Åsa was, especially at establishing a relationship with the person she was questioning, he thought he would keep his conversation with Maud Lundin brief.

"I imagine you're upset and tired after what's happened," he said. "I won't trouble you for long, but I'd very much like to know what your relationship to Mr. Petrus was. How long have you known each other?"

Maud Lundin tucked her hair behind her ears and looked at him steadily. "For three years," she said. "We met at a party and he asked me out to dinner once or twice after that. That was in the spring. In the summer he was going to start filming, and he gave me a job in makeup. We went on meeting."

"But you aren't working for him now?" asked Martin Beck. "How long did you work for him?"

"Only on that one film. Then it was a while before he got started on a new production, and I got a good job in a beauty salon."

"What sort of film did you work on?"

"It was a film made for export only. It hasn't been shown in Sweden."

"What was it called?"

"Love in the Midnight Sun."

"How often did you and Mr. Petrus meet?"

"About once a week. Sometimes twice. He usually came here, but sometimes we went out to eat and dance."

"Did his wife know about your relationship?"

"Yes. But she didn't mind as long as he didn't divorce her."

"Did he plan to?"

"Sometimes. Earlier. But I think he thought things were all right the way they were."

"And what about you? Did you think things were all right?"

"I probably wouldn't have said no if he'd asked me to marry him, but on the whole I thought things were all right. He was kind and generous."

"Have you any idea who could have killed him?"

Maud Lundin shook her head. "Not the slightest," she said. "It seems crazy. I can't really believe it's happened."

She was silent for a while and he looked at her. She seemed strangely unmoved.

"Is he still down there?" she asked finally.

"No, not any more."

"Can I stay the night here, then?"

"No, we haven't completed the investigation yet."

She looked at him darkly and shrugged her shoulders. "It doesn't matter," she said. "I can sleep in town."

"How did he seem when you left him this morning?" asked Martin Beck.

"Like always. There was nothing special. I usually

leave before him—he doesn't like rushing in the mornings. Sometimes we went to town together. He always took a cab when he was here, but I usually ride my bike to the station and take the train."

"Why did he take a cab? He had a car, didn't he?"

"He didn't like driving. He's got a Bentley, but mostly other people drove him."

"What other people?"

"His wife, or someone from the office. Sometimes the man who does his gardening."

"How many employees are there in his office?"

"Only three. A man who looks after the accounts, a secretary, and someone who sees to the contracts and sales and so on. He hires extra people when he's producing a film, according to what's needed."

"What sort of films did he produce?"

"Well, I don't quite know how to describe them. To be honest, they were pornographic films. But very artistic ones. He made an ambitious film once, with good actors and all that. It was based on a famous novel, and I think it got a prize at a festival, too. But he didn't make much money on it."

"But now he was earning a lot of money on his films?"

"Yes, a lot. He bought this house for me. And you should see his house in Djursholm. A real villa, with a huge garden and swimming pool and everything."

Martin Beck began to understand what kind of person Walter Petrus had been, but he was not really sure about the woman beside him.

"Did you love him?" he asked.

Maud Lundin gave him an amused look. "Frankly, no, I didn't. But he was kind to me. Spoiled me and didn't interfere with what I did when we weren't together."

She sat silent for a moment, then said, "He wasn't exactly handsome. Nor a particularly good lover. He had difficulty with his potency, if you know what I mean. I was married for eight years to a man who really was a man. He was killed in a car crash five years ago."

"So you had other men, apart from Petrus."

"Yes, now and then. When I met someone I liked."

"And he wasn't ever jealous?"

"No, but he wanted me to tell him what it was like with the others. In detail. He liked that. I made most of it up to keep him happy."

Martin Beck looked at Maud Lundin. She was sitting very erect and met his gaze calmly.

"Could you say that you were really only with him for his money?" he said.

"Yes, you could say that. But I don't regard myself as a whore, even if maybe you do. My need for money is great. I like things that money can buy. And it isn't easy for a woman of forty with no particular education to get money any other way than through a man. If I'm a whore, then so are most married women."

Martin Beck got up. "Thank you for talking to me, and for being so honest."

"You needn't thank me for that. I'm always honest. May I go to my friend now? I'm tired."

"Of course. Just tell Inspector Pärsson where we can get in touch with you first, all right?"

Maud Lundin got up and picked up a small white leather bag that had been lying at the end of the bed. Martin Beck watched her leave the room. She held herself very erect and seemed calm and collected. Her long, powerful body was well built and strong, and she must have been a whole head taller than the fat little film director.

He thought about what she had said about money and

what you could get with it. Walter Petrus had gotten a pretty good woman with his.

6.

The definitive medical report fixed Walter Petrus's death as having occurred between six and nine in the morning. There was no reason to doubt Maud Lundin's statement that he had been alive when she left home at half-past six. Neither Åsa Torell nor Martin Beck thought she had anything to do with the murder.

The fact that the front door had been unlocked had made it easy for someone to get into the house and surprise Petrus as he stood in the shower, but how the killer got there without being seen was more of a puzzle. Either he had come by car, which seemed the most likely, or by train, but it was strange that no one living nearby had noticed him. In an area where everyone knew one another, or at least knew their nearest neighbors and their cars, the chances of being seen ought to have been greatest during just that period between half-past six and nine in the morning. That was everyone's most active time—the men were on their way to work, the children were walking to school and the housewives were at home starting their cleaning or gardening.

Nevertheless, though the knocking on nearby doors went on for several days, until practically every inhabitant in that part of Rotebro had been questioned, it was established that no one had noticed anyone or anything that could be linked with the murder. Pärsson and his "men," in fact mostly Åsa Torell, had begun working on the theory that the killer lived in the neighborhood, but they had not yet come across anyone who either knew Petrus or could have had a motive for killing him.

Martin Beck and Benny Skacke devoted their time to trying to clarify Walter Petrus's private life, professional activities and financial circumstances. The last of these was particularly difficult to shed any light on. Petrus appeared to have been involved in tax evasion on a major scale. His films were sold abroad, and he could be presumed to have fat accounts in Swiss banks. There was no doubt that he had juggled his accounts and tax declarations, or that he had used skilled legal advisers. Martin Beck knew nothing about the intricacies of such financial finagling and he was only too happy to let the experts in that field try to clarify the picture.

Petrus Films, Inc., had its office on Nybrogatan. The office, which had once been a residential apartment, had been lovingly renovated and consisted of six rooms and a kitchen. The three employees had an office each, and their modern office furniture looked strangely out of place surrounded by tiled stoves, oak panels and plasterwork ceilings. Walter Petrus himself had presided from behind an enormous desk of jacaranda wood in a large, beautiful corner room with high windows. There was also a screening room with seats for ten people, and another room which appeared to be used as an archive and storeroom.

Martin Beck and Skacke spent a couple of mornings in the screening room trying to assess the results of Walter Petrus's cinematic activities. They watched one film from beginning to end, plus extracts from seven others, each one more appalling than the last. Skacke wriggled with embarrassment at first, but after a while started yawning. The films were all technically very bad, and for Maud Lundin to have called them "artistic" was not just an exaggeration but a downright lie. In this particular case she had not been honest, thought Martin Beck, unless she entirely lacked judgment.

The actors, if such a term could be used to describe the collection of obvious amateurs appearing on the screen, were for the most part naked. When any of them did wear clothes, it was only in order to remove them as quickly as possible.

Three teenage girls kept reappearing in all the films—sometimes separately and sometimes all together. One of them seemed painfully embarrassed and glanced uncertainly into the lens every now and then as she wiggled her tongue and rolled her eyes and twisted her body like an eel to the obvious instructions of someone behind the camera. The young men were all blond—with the exception of one who was black—and well-built. The props were minimal, most of the action taking place on the same old couch, which occasionally changed covers.

Only one of the films appeared to involve any kind of plot, and that was the one Maud Lundin had referred to—*Love in the Midnight Sun.* It had obviously been filmed in the islands outside Stockholm and began with the main character, a girl of fifteen or so, paddling out to an island in a canoe to celebrate midsummer in a traditional Swedish way. She had with her a picnic basket containing a bottle of aquavit, glasses, plates and some silver, a white linen tablecloth, a head of lettuce and a loaf of bread.

After carrying the basket and a fishing rod ashore, she immediately took her clothes off, slowly and with strange writhing movements, her mouth open and her eyes downcast. Then she sat down at the water's edge with her legs apart and began masturbating with the handle of the fishing rod. After tossing her head and letting out a few groans, she adroitly cast the line and immediately landed an enormous dead salmon. Delighted with her catch, she jumped around the rocks for a while, stretching her legs, wriggling her hips and thrusting out her breasts. She quickly built a gigantic bonfire of driftwood which happened to be lying about in a convenient heap on the shore, and placed the fish on a spit over the fire. Then she laid the tablecloth and poured aquavit into what looked like a champagne glass.

Just as she was swallowing the drink, a naked blond youth appeared out of the sea. She invited him to join her in her meal, and between drinks—which they took from the same glass—they ate the salmon, which by now was smoked and thinly sliced. Night had fallen, although the sun was still high in the sky, and the young couple carried out a kind of ritual dance around the smoking bonfire. Then they wandered hand in hand toward the island's green meadows, found a convenient haystack and indulged in fifteen minutes of intercourse in twenty different positions. In the final scene, the two young people wandered out into the glittering sun-drenched sea.

The end.

The sales manager of Petrus Films, Inc., suggested that they might like to look at some additional films of the same type, such as *Lust and Love in Sweden* or *Three Nights with Swedish Eva,* but Martin Beck and Skacke had had enough and politely refused the invitation. They were told that *Love in the Midnight Sun* was the firm's biggest hit and had been sold to eight countries. The girl who starred in it was now in one of these countries, he could not remember which, Italy perhaps, to further her career. Mr. Petrus had arranged an engagement for one of the other girls with a German company, the sales manager told them, so the girls had probably been richly rewarded over and above the thousand kronor that was the usual fee for the star part in a film.

Martin Beck left Skacke to continue rummaging in Petrus Films, Inc.'s dirty laundry and decided that it was time to go and visit the bereaved family. He had called the house in Djursholm on Friday, but had only been allowed to speak to the family doctor, who had said briefly and authoritatively that Mrs. Petrus was not in a state to receive visitors, least of all policemen. The doctor gave him to understand that it was most callous and unfeeling of him not to leave the poor widow in peace at least over the weekend.

Now the weekend was over, it was Monday the tenth of July, and when Martin Beck came out onto Nybrogatan, the sun was shining. The summer was just beginning, holiday time had come, and the sidewalks were crowded with people in varying states of frenzy. He walked down the street toward Östermalm Square and when he got to the Seventh Precinct's new station, he went inside and up the stairs to borrow a telephone.

A woman answered at the Petrus house. She asked him to wait, returned after a long while and said that Mrs. Petrus was prepared to receive him on condition that his visit be kept short.

He promised not to stay long, then he called a cab.

The house in Djursholm was surrounded by a large parklike garden and the driveway to the house was lined with tall poplars. The high wrought-iron gates were open and the cabdriver asked if he was to drive in, but Martin Beck told him to stop outside the gates and he paid and got out.

As Martin Beck walked up the drive, he studied the villa and its surroundings. The hedge along the road was thick and high and carefully and artistically trimmed. Once inside the hedge, the drive divided and continued to the right toward a large garage. The enormous garden looked very well kept, the lawns had sharp edges where narrow gravel paths twisted among shrubs and flower beds, and to judge from the height of the poplars and the age of the fruit trees the whole thing must have been laid out many years before.

In that setting there was every reason to expect an ancient house of the type that was common in such wealthy areas, but the house Martin Beck was approaching along the newly raked gravel path was a modern two-story architectonic creation with a flat roof and gigantic windows.

A middle-aged woman in a black dress and white apron opened the door before he even had a chance to put his finger to the bell. She walked ahead of him in silence through a large hall, past a broad staircase, through two more rooms, and then stopped in a wide archway opening into a sunny room, the end wall of which was entirely glass.

The floor of light plastic-treated pine was sunken and Martin Beck did not see the step, so he stumbled into the room where Walter Petrus's widow was waiting for him, lying in a deck chair in the corner by the glass wall. On the terrace outside were several similar chairs lined up as if on the sun deck of an ocean liner.

"Oopsie!" she said, as she waved away the black-clad woman as one waves away a fly.

As the woman turned to go, Mrs. Petrus changed her mind and said, "No, wait a minute." She looked at Martin Beck. "Would you like something to drink, Inspector? Coffee, tea, beer or perhaps a drink? I'll have a sherry myself."

"Thank you," said Martin Beck. "A beer would taste good."

"One beer and a large glass of sherry," she said in commanding tones. "And, Mrs. Pettersson, perhaps you'd bring some of those Dutch cheese biscuits."

Martin Beck considered the odd fact that Walter Petrus Pettersson's widow had the same name as her maid, or whatever this fortunately rare occupational group was called nowadays. They must also have been about the same age.

He had already dug out some facts about Mrs. Petrus and knew, among other things, her last name had also been Pettersson before she married; that her Christian names were Kristina Elvira, though nowadays she called herself Chris; that she was fifty-seven years old; and that she had been married to Petrus for twenty-eight years. In her youth she had worked in an office and just before her marriage she had been a secretary in the firm that Petrus had been running at the time. Walter Petrus, film director, was a relatively new phenomenon; for many years he had been called Valter Pettersson and had dealt in inadequately renovated used cars, a lucrative but not particularly honest activity which harsher laws and stricter control of the trade had forced him to abandon.

Martin Beck was still standing in the middle of the room, looking at the woman in the deck chair. Sunburnt beneath her makeup, she had bleached hair and was wearing a black shantung blouse over well-tailored black linen slacks. She was very thin and her face looked harrowed and worn under the modern curly hairstyle.

He went up to her and she graciously held out a small wrinkled hand as he offered his condolences and apologized for having to intrude, phrases he seemed to have used hundreds of times in similar situations.

He did not really know what to do with himself—the deck chair stood by itself there in the corner. But finally she got up and went over to two enormous leather sofas placed in the middle of the room on either side of a long marble-topped table. She sat down in the corner of one sofa and Martin Beck sat down on the one opposite.

Outside the glass wall, which was equipped with sliding doors, there was a paved terrace and below that a swimming pool. Beyond the pool a large lawn sloped down toward a row of tall birches about fifty yards from the house. The lawn was thick and smooth and there were no trees, shrubs or flower beds here. Through the gauzy green of the birches he caught a glimpse of the blue surface of Great Värta.

"Yes, it's a lovely view, isn't it?" said Chris Petrus, following Martin Beck's gaze. "It's a pity we don't have the lakeshore lot as well. Then I'd have the birches cut down to see the water better."

"Birches are pretty too," said Martin Beck.

Mrs. Pettersson came in and placed a tray on the table, handed Martin Beck a beer and put a large glass of sherry and the bowl of cheese biscuits in front of Mrs. Petrus. Then she picked up the tray and left the room without a word.

Mrs. Petrus raised her glass and nodded to Martin Beck before drinking. Then she put down the glass and said, "We've always liked it so much here. When we bought the property six years ago, there was a dreadful old place here, but we had it demolished and built this house instead. One of Walter's acquaintances who is an architect designed it for us."

Martin Beck was sure the old place had been pleasanter to live in. What he had seen of the house so far seemed bare and inhospitable, and the ultramodern and certainly extremely costly décor seemed designed more for show than for comfort and warmth.

"Isn't it cold in the winter with such large windows?" said Martin Beck conversationally.

"Oh, no, we've got infraheat in the ceiling and heating coils in the floor. On the terrace, too. And we're not here very much in the winter. We go to warmer climes —Greece or Algarve or Africa."

Martin Beck had a feeling that the woman in front of him had not yet realized that a change had occurred in her life. Or perhaps the change had not been so great. She had lost her husband, but not his money. Perhaps she had even wished for his death. Practically everything can be bought for money, even murder.

"What was the relationship between you and your husband like?" he asked.

She looked at him in astonishment, as if she had thought all along that he'd come to talk about the house and the view and trips abroad.

"It was very good," she said. "We'd been married for twenty-eight years and we have three children. That alone is enough to keep a marriage together."

"But it doesn't necessarily mean the marriage was happy," said Martin Beck. "Was it?"

"You get used to each other over the years, you overlook each other's faults and you adapt," she said. "Do you believe yourself that there is such a thing as a really happy marriage? Ours was free of friction at least, and neither one of us ever considered divorce."

"Did you know very much about your husband's business?"

"Not a thing. The film company didn't interest me in the slightest and I never interfered in my husband's business affairs."

"What did you think of the films your husband's company produced?"

"I've never seen them. Of course, I know what kind of films they are, but I'm not prejudiced and refuse to express opinions. Wally worked hard and did his best to give me and the children a decent life. Our eldest son is twenty-six. He's a naval officer and lives here when he's in Stockholm, but he's usually at sea or in Karlskrona. Pierre is twenty-two and has an artistic bent. He also wants to work in films, but times are bad and right now he's traveling around making contacts and gathering impressions. He has his room upstairs and lives at home when he's not abroad. I cabled his last address in Spain but haven't heard from him yet, so I don't even know if he has learned that his father is dead."

She took a cigarette from a silver box on the table and lit it with a table lighter, also silver and of monstrous proportions.

"Then there's Titti. She's only nineteen, but she's already doing very well as a photographer's model. She lives here at home part of the time, and part of the time in her little den in the Old City. She isn't home at the moment, or else you could meet her. She's awfully pretty."

"I'm sure she is," said Martin Beck politely, thinking that if she was she must not take after her father.

"Even if you weren't interested in your husband's affairs, you must have met some of his business friends," he went on.

Chris Petrus ran her fingers through her hair and said, "Yes, I did. We often had dinner parties here for all kinds of film people. And then there were all the parties and receptions Wally had to go to, though lately I hardly ever went with him."

"Why not?"

Mrs. Petrus looked out the window. "I didn't want to," she said. "There were always so many people I didn't know, and lots of young people with whom I had nothing in common. And Wally didn't think it was necessary for me to go. I have my own friends whom I prefer to be with."

In other words Walter Petrus had not wanted his fifty-seven-year-old wife with him at parties where he could meet teen-age girls. He had been sixty-two, fat and ugly and impotent, and his reputation as a film producer had gradually grown shabbier and shabbier, although in some circles he still lived off a prizewinning production, generally known as ambitious and artistic. But the attraction of the film world for many young girls was so great that they were prepared for any sacrifice or degradation to enter it.

"I suppose you've had time to think about who might have killed your husband, Mrs. Petrus?" said Martin Beck.

"I can only imagine it was someone who was utterly insane. It's terrible that he hasn't been caught yet."

"There was no one close to him who could have had any reason to—"

She interrupted him, for the first time apparently upset. "No one except an absolute maniac could have had any reason to do such a thing, and we have no lunatics among our friends. Whatever people thought of my husband, there was no one who hated him that much."

"I didn't mean to criticize your husband or your friends," said Martin Beck. "I just wondered whether he might have been threatened or whether someone might possibly have felt he'd been badly treated—"

She interrupted him again. "Wally didn't treat people badly. He was kind and did his best for all his employees. It was a tough and difficult world he worked in, and now and again you have to be ruthless to keep your head above water; he said that himself sometimes. But it's simply absurd to think he could have treated anyone that badly."

She emptied her sherry glass, lit another cigarette, and Martin Beck waited for her to calm down.

He looked out through the glass wall. A man in blue work clothes was walking across the lawn.

"Someone's coming," said Martin Beck.

Mrs. Petrus glanced at the man. "That's Hellström, our gardener," she said.

The man in blue overalls turned right by the swimming pool and vanished from their sight.

"Does anyone else work for you besides Mrs. Pettersson and the gardener?"

"No. Mrs. Pettersson looks after the housekeeping, and twice a week we have extra cleaning help. When we have dinner parties we hire staff, of course. And Hellström isn't just our gardener; he looks after several gardens in the neighborhood. He doesn't live here, either. He lives in a small house on the grounds next door."

"Does he take care of the car, too?"

She nodded. "Wally hated driving, so Hellström had to be the chauffeur, too. Sometimes I'd be going into town at the same time as Wally, but I prefer to drive my own car, and Wally preferred the Bentley."

"Didn't your husband ever drive himself?"

She fingered her glass and looked toward the doorway. Then she got up and said, "I'm just going to call Mrs. Pettersson. The only thing wrong with this house is that there's no bell to the kitchen."

She went out and he heard her calling to Mrs. Pettersson to bring the sherry decanter. Then she came back and sat down on the sofa.

Martin Beck waited with his next question until Mrs. Pettersson had put the decanter on the table and gone. He took a sip of beer, which had begun to get warm and flat, and said, "Did you know that your husband had relationships with other women, Mrs. Petrus?"

She replied immediately, looking straight at him. "Naturally I knew about his relationship with the woman he was with when he was killed. She had been his mistress for a year or two. I don't think he had any other relationships, one or two brief ones perhaps, but he was no longer a youngster. As I told you before, I'm not prejudiced and I let Wally live his life the way he wanted."

"Have you ever met Maud Lundin?"

"No. And I don't want to. Wally had a certain taste for cheap women, and I presume Mrs. Lundin is the type."

"Have you yourself had relationships with other men?" asked Martin Beck.

She looked at him for a moment, then said, "I don't think that has anything to do with it."

"But it has, or else I wouldn't have asked."

"If you think that I've got a lover who killed Wally out of jealousy, then I can tell you you're wrong. I have in fact had a lover for several years, but he and Wally were good friends and my husband accepted our relationship as long as it was conducted discreetly. I'm not going to give you his name."

"Maybe that won't be necessary," said Martin Beck.

Chris Petrus ran the back of her hand across her forehead and closed her eyes. The gesture looked theatrical. He noticed that she had false eyelashes.

"Now I really must ask you to leave me in peace," she said. "I really don't enjoy sitting here discussing Wally's and my private life with a perfect stranger."

"I'm sorry, but it's my job to try to find out whoever killed your husband. So I have to ask indiscreet questions in order to get some idea of what could have caused his death."

"You promised on the phone to keep it short," she said plaintively.

"I won't bother you with any more questions now," said Martin Beck. "But I may have to come back. Or send one of my colleagues. In that case, I'll call you first."

"Yes, yes," said Mrs. Petrus impatiently.

He got up and again she graciously extended her hand.

As he went out through the archway, this time without stumbling over the step, he heard the gurgling of the decanter as she poured herself another sherry.

Mrs. Pettersson must have been in the upper part of the house. He could hear her steps and the hum of the vacuum cleaner. Nor was there any sign of the gardener, and the garage doors were closed. As he went out through the gates, he saw that the gateposts were equipped with photocells, presumably connected to some signaling system up in the house. That explained why Mrs. Pettersson had let him in without his having to ring the bell.

As he passed the house next door, he saw Hellström, the gardener, through the ironwork of the gate. He stopped and considered going in to speak to him, but the man, who had been bending over doing something on the lawn, straightened up and walked quickly away. With a swishing sound, a sprinkler began to throw a fine cascade of water over the rich green grass.

Martin Beck continued along the road in the direction of the station. He was thinking now about Rhea and how he would describe the Petrus family to her when they met. He knew exactly what she would say.

7.

The day after the midsummer holiday, a young man walked into the police station in Märsta and handed the duty officer a long, narrow, heavy object wrapped in newspaper.

Nineteen days had gone by since the murder in Rotebro and the investigation had produced very few results. The technical examination had brought out nothing remarkable or interesting, not even a fingerprint which did not belong to Walter Petrus himself, or to Maud Lundin and her friends, or to other people who had legitimate reasons for being in the house. The only thing that might possibly have been linked to the killer was a blurred footprint outside the glass doors leading to the garden.

Innumerable questions had been asked of neighbors, members of the family, employees, friends and acquaintances; and the more extensive the material grew, the clearer the picture of Walter Petrus became. Behind a jovial and generous facade was a hard, unscrupulous man who was utterly ruthless when it came to pursuing his own ends. His unprincipled behavior, especially in business, had earned him a great many antagonists, but the people closest to him, who might have been thought to have had sufficiently strong motives for killing him, all had alibis for the time of the crime. Apart from his wife and children, there was no one who would gain financially from his death.

The duty officer handed the parcel to Chief Inspector Pärsson who opened it, glanced at the contents and called the young man in.

"What is this, and why did you bring it to us?" he said, pointing to the iron bar which had been rolled up in the newspaper.

"I found it in Rotebro," said the man. "I thought maybe it might have something to do with the murder of that man Petrus. I read about it in the papers and it said the weapon hadn't been found. A friend of mine lives across the street from the house where it happened, and I slept over at his place last night. We talked about the murder, of course, among other things, and when I found that thing this morning I thought it might be the murder weapon. Anyhow, I figured I ought to take it to the police." He looked eagerly at Pärsson and went on hesitantly: "For safety's sake. You never know."

Pärsson nodded. A few days earlier a woman had sent a wrench through the mail along with a letter accusing her neighbor of the murder. She had found the wrench in the neighbor's garage and since there was obviously blood on the tool and the neighbor had previously committed a murder, all the police had to do was come and take him away, she wrote. Pärsson had investigated the matter and it turned out that the woman was neurotic and paranoid, and that she was quite convinced her neighbor had killed her cat, which had been missing for three months. It also turned out that the blood on the wrench was red paint.

The young man looked uncertainly at him and Pärsson said in a friendly voice, "Thank you for coming. Do you think you could show us the place where you found it, if necessary?"

"Oh, yes. I put a stick in the ground, just in case."

"Good," said Pärsson. "Very sensible. Leave your name and telephone number out there, will you, and we'll let you know if we need your help."

An hour later the parcel was on Martin Beck's desk at the South police station. He examined the iron bar and then the enlarged close-ups of the fracture of the victim's skull. Then he lifted the receiver and called the State Crime Lab in Solna. He asked to speak to Oskar Hjelm, the boss.

Hjelm sounded irritable, but then he usually did. "What is it this time?" he said.

"An iron bar," said Martin Beck. "As far as I can see, it might very well be the one Walter Petrus was killed with. I know you've got a lot to do, but I'd appreciate it if you'd take care of it as quickly as you can. All right?"

"As quickly as I can," said Hjelm. "We've got work out here to last us to Christmas and all of it has to be done as quickly as we can. But send it out. Anything special you want done, apart from the usual?"

"No, just the usual. See if it fits the wound, and whatever else you can get out of it. It's been lying outdoors for a while so it'll probably be difficult to find anything on it, but do your best."

Hjelm sounded offended when he answered. "We always do our best."

"I know," said Martin Beck quickly. "I'll send it out right away."

"I'll call you when it's done," said Hjelm.

Four hours later, just as Martin Beck was cleaning up his desk to go home, Hjelm called.

"Hjelm here," he said. "Yes, it fits exactly. There are only minute traces of blood and brain tissue, but I managed to confirm the blood type. It's the right one."

"Nice going, Hjelm. Anything else?"

"A little cotton fiber. Of two kinds, in fact. Some white, probably from the towel used to wipe the blood off. And some navy blue, maybe from his clothes."

"Great job, Oskar," said Martin Beck.

"The iron bar itself is four hundred and twenty-four millimeters long, thirty-three in diameter, octagonal, wrought iron, and judging by the corrosion it's been outdoors for quite a long time. Several years, maybe always. It's hand-wrought and has been soldered at both ends."

"Soldered to what? Do you have any idea what it was used for?"

"It appears to be fairly old, maybe sixty or seventy years. Might have been in some kind of railing."

"And you're sure it's the weapon used on Petrus?"

"Definitely," said Hjelm. "Unfortunately the surface was so rough it was impossible to get any fingerprints."

"We'll have to do without them," said Martin Beck. He thanked the other man and, with a grunt, Hjelm put down the receiver.

Martin Beck called Pärsson in Märsta and told him what Hjelm had said.

"Then that's one step forward," said Pärsson. "We'd better send out some men to comb the area. Not that I think it'll be much use after such a long time, but still . . ."

"Do you know exactly where the iron bar was lying?" asked Martin Beck.

"The young man who found it marked the place. I'll call him now. Do you want to come and see?"

"Okay. Just tell me when you're going and I'll come."

Martin Beck went back to shuffling papers and files about, gradually succeeding in achieving some kind of order on his desk. Then he leaned back in his chair and opened a file that Åsa Torell had handed in earlier that morning. The file contained the report of her interviews with two girls who had known Walter Petrus. Åsa was obviously acquainted with one of them from her earlier work with the Vice Squad.

The girls' stories agreed, on the whole. Their descriptions of Petrus were not flattering, and neither one of them seemed to mourn or regret his demise. As far as one of his characteristics was concerned, they were very much in agreement—he had been extremely miserly. He had, for instance, never ever bought them a dinner, or a cocktail, or given them so much as a pack of cigarettes or a candy bar. On one occasion he did take one of them to the movies, but she pointed out that he had free tickets for the show.

At fairly regular intervals he used to call them up and summon them to his office, always in the evenings after the staff had gone home, and they agreed that his sexual efforts were lamentable. He was almost always impotent, and those so-called moments of passion in his office, usually unsuccessful, did not make him any more generous. Once or twice they had been given their cab fares home after their long, tiresome and fruitless efforts to give him sexual satisfaction, but mostly he simply sent them away, whining and discontented.

One of the reasons why the girls had had anything to do with him at all was his generosity with alcohol and hash. He kept a well-stocked bar and he always had a supply of Cannabis or marijuana. The other reason the girls stuck around was his persistent promises of important parts in future films, constant prospects of trips, to the Cannes Festival perhaps, and a life of luxury and fame.

One of the girls had stopped seeing him six months earlier, but the other had been with him as recently as a few days before his death. She admitted that at first she had been stupid enough to believe his promises, but had gradually realized that he was using her. After their last meeting she had been so disgusted with him that she had decided to say a few well-chosen words and slam down the receiver the next time he called. Now she needn't worry about it any more.

Her epitaph for Walter Petrus certainly showed no signs of any warm feelings. Åsa had taken her at her word and written it down: "You can quote me. Say I've a good mind to do a go-go dance on his grave, if any-one's gone to the trouble of digging a grave for that asshole." Åsa had also clipped a note to the report. Martin Beck unfastened it and read:

> MARTIN,
> This girl is a junkie—not known to the narcotics squad—but shows all the signs of abuse of harder stuff than hash. Denies that WP supplied her with anything else, but wouldn't it be worth looking into?

Martin Beck put the paper into his desk drawer, closed the file and went and stood by the window with his hands in his pockets. He thought about Åsa's suggestion that Walter Petrus might have been involved in the steadily increasing drug traffic. It was an aspect of the case that might open new roads for investigation, but might also complicate matters. There had been nothing in his office or his home to indicate that Petrus was involved with drugs, but then they hadn't been looking for anything, either. Now he would have to bring in the Narcotics Squad and see what they could find out.

The telephone rang. It was Pärsson in Märsta, informing him that he'd got hold of the youth who could show them the place where the iron bar was found, and that they would be driving out there in a little while.

Martin Beck promised to come and went to find Skacke, but Skacke had gone home or was out on some errand. He lifted the receiver to call a cab, but then changed his mind and called a garage instead. It would cost almost a hundred crowns to go to Rotebro and back by cab and this month's bundle of cab receipts was already alarmingly thick. Although he drove a car only very reluctantly, and only when absolutely necessary, he had no choice this time. He took the elevator down to the garage where a black Volkswagen was waiting for him.

Pärsson was at the agreed meeting place in Rotebro, and together with the young man, they walked across the field to the blackthorn bushes where the iron bar had been found. The weather had taken a turn for the worse, the air was cold and damp, the evening sky low and gray with heavy rain-filled clouds. Martin Beck looked over toward the houses on the other side of the field.

"Funny he came this way, where he could be seen so easily."

"Maybe he had a car over on the Enköping road," Pärsson suggested. "I think we can start with that and examine the ground from here to the road tomorrow."

"It looks like rain," said Martin Beck, "and almost three weeks have gone by. It doesn't seem likely you'll find anything."

His feet were cold and he longed to be home with Rhea. The blackthorn bushes had not produced any answer to the question of who had murdered Walter Petrus, and it was getting dark.

"Let's go," he said, starting to walk back toward the cars.

He drove straight to Tulegatan, and while Rhea fried meat rissoles out in the kitchen, he lay in the bath and thought about how he would organize the next day's work.

The Narcotics Squad would have to be informed and brought into the picture.

A thorough search would have to be made of the house in Djursholm, of the film company's office and of Maud Lundin's house.

Benny Skacke would have to spend the day finding out if Petrus had some secret address, an apartment or premises rented under a false name.

The girl Åsa had talked to would have to be pressed a bit harder. That would be up to Narcotics.

He himself thought about going out to the house again to speak to Mrs. Pettersson and Hellström the gardener, but that could wait. Tomorrow he would have to stay in his office. Åsa could talk to the help in Djursholm. He wondered what Åsa was up to. She had not been seen all day.

"Food's ready," called Rhea. "Do you want wine or beer?"

"Beer, thanks," he called back.

He climbed out of the bath and stopped thinking about the next day.

8.

The National Commissioner of Police smiled at Gunvald Larsson, but there was no trace of boyish charm in the smile. It showed only two rows of sharp teeth and a barely concealed dislike of his visitor. Stig Malm was in position, which meant just behind his boss's shoulder, trying to look as if none of this had anything to do with him.

Malm had reached his present post by means of what might be called clever careerist maneuvering, or, in rather more direct language, ass-licking. He knew how dangerous it was to offend some higher-ups, but he was also aware of the fact that it could be disastrous to sit too heavily on some subordinates. The day might come when they in their turn were given the chance to sit on him. So for the time being he was observing the situation with an open mind.

The Commissioner raised his hands an inch or two and let them fall flat on the table again. "Well, Larsson," he said, "there's no need to tell you how genuinely pleased we are that you escaped from that terrible business without serious injury."

Gunvald Larsson glanced at Malm, who did not look the least bit pleased. But when Malm saw that he was being observed, he tried to repair the damage with a wide smile. "Yes, indeed, Gunvald," he said. "You certainly gave us an anxious morning."

The chief turned and looked icily at his second-in-command, and Malm realized he'd gone too far. He at once suppressed the smile, looked down and thought despondently: Whatever you do, it's wrong.

He did in fact have good reason for a certain misanthropy. If he or the Commissioner made some slight error that evening papers could splatter all over their front pages, it was Malm who got blamed. And when some subordinate erred, it was Malm again who got shot down. If he had shown a little more spunk, this might not have been the case, but Stig Malm never carried his reasoning that far.

The Commissioner, who for some reason thought long pauses increased his authority, now said: "What seems slightly peculiar is that you stayed there for eleven days after the assassination, although you had a flight booked for the following day. You should have left on June sixth, and yet you weren't back until the eighteenth. How do you explain that?"

Gunvald Larsson had prepared an answer to that question. "I had a new suit made," he said.

"Does it take eleven days to have a suit made?" asked the Commissioner in astonishment.

"Yes, if you want the job done properly. It can be done more quickly of course, but there's bound to be some sloppy work here and there."

"Mmm," said the Commissioner irritably. "As you know, we have our auditors, and things like suits may be difficult to fit into the budget. Why couldn't you buy a new suit here?"

"I don't buy my suits," said Gunvald Larsson, "I have them made. And there's hardly a tailor in Europe who could have done the job the way I wanted it. So, since I was there and had to wait for my suit, I took the opportunity to try to find out what had happened."

"Doesn't sound very constructive," said the chief. "The police on the spot did a very thorough investigation. They sent us all the information while you were still out there, in fact, so they might just as well have given you the papers."

"Personally, I'm convinced that the Security Service made several mistakes," said Gunvald Larsson, "and that the conclusions the police came to are incorrect, particularly with regard to several important details. I've got a copy of the report in my office. They gave it to me before I left."

There was a brief silence in the room. Then Malm risked opening his mouth. "This may be important for the visit in November."

"Wrong, Stig," said the chief. "This isn't just important, it's extremely important. We must call a meeting at once."

"Exactly," said Malm. He was good at meetings. They were part of life itself. Without them, nothing would ever get done. Society would quite simply collapse. "Who should we ask?" Malm was already standing by the telephone.

The Commissioner was deep in thought. Gunvald Larsson was pulling at his large fingers one by one, cracking the knuckles.

"Gunvald will have to be there, of course, to introduce it," prompted Malm.

"After this, he should be there as an expert," said the Commissioner. "But I was thinking about something else. The special team hasn't been selected yet. True, we've quite a bit of time, but it's a big and demanding assignment. I think it's high time we gathered together a small team of key men."

"Chief of Security."

"Yes, of course, obviously. And the chief of the Regular Police and the Stockholm City chief."

Gunvald Larsson yawned. When he thought about the City Police chief, with his silk ties and the countless armed numskulls under his so-called command, he was always overcome with weariness. As well as a certain amount of fear. Deep down inside.

The Commissioner went on: "We'll need experts of all kinds. We'll have to borrow equipment and men from the army and the air force. Perhaps from the navy, too. Naturally, the final responsibility for what happens will rest on one single person—me. But there's one other thing. If we are to make preparations now to bring together all this expertise, gradually adding more and more, like Psychological Defense for example, then we ought to have a chief of operations right from the start. An experienced policeman and a decent administrator. A man who can coordinate all of the forces involved. A man who possesses all these qualifications plus criminological acumen, and who is also a good psychologist. Who is that man?"

The Commissioner looked at Gunvald Larsson, who nodded without saying anything, as if the answer were self-evident.

Stig Malm unconsciously straightened up. The answer was indeed self-evident, he thought. Who else apart from himself had the qualifications for this difficult task? The fact that he had once served as chief of operations in a case that had ended in disaster could be ascribed to bad luck and coincidence.

"Beck," said Gunvald Larsson.

"Exactly," said the Commissioner. "Martin Beck. He's our man." Especially if something goes wrong, he thought. Aloud he said, "The final responsibility is mine anyhow."

That sounded all right. Still, he wondered if it would be more effective to say, for instance, "The ultimate responsibility nevertheless rests on my shoulders."

"Why don't you start calling them?" The Commissioner was looking questioningly at Malm.

"Beck's on a case," said Malm, pulling himself together. "He is in fact subordinate to me, in my division."

"Oh, so the Homicide Squad is working on a case?" said the Commissioner. "Well, I'm sure he'll find the time. Anyhow, the Homicide Squad may soon work itself right out of existence."

"I'm on eleven cases myself," said Gunvald Larsson.

"But you're not in my division," said Stig Malm.

"No, thank the good Lord in heaven. Or some such."

* * *

They all arrived at the prescribed time, except Möller. Stig Malm and Gunvald Larsson greeted each other and the Commissioner, not especially warmly, but then it was not the first time they had met on this rather dreary July day. Martin Beck was there, wearing a denim jacket and baggy trousers, and the Stockholm City Police chief was sporting the usual white silk tie.

But Möller was missing.

They were already seated down around the conference table when the National Commissioner noticed the fact and remarked cleverly, "Where's Möller? We simply can't start without him. You know what a fuss there is whenever Security's involved."

Eric Möller was head of the State Security Police, better known as Säpo, but it was questionable whether even he himself really knew what he was in charge of. The actual Security Police was nothing special. It employed about eight hundred people who supposedly spent their time on two things: first, exposing and catching foreign spies; and second, counteracting organizations and groups considered dangerous to the security of the state. Over the years, however, its role had become more and more confusing, since everyone knew that Säpo's only task was to register, persecute and in general make life a misery for people with left-wing views.

When Säpo finally reached the point where they were keeping dossiers on members of the ruling Social Democratic party, the supposedly socialist government began to find it more and more difficult to control its embarrassment.

Eric Möller arrived at the conference room thirty-three minutes late. His face was perspiring and he was puffing and blowing.

Even if Möller were a spy or a counterspy or whatever, it would have been extraordinarily difficult for him to appear in disguise. Though roughly the same age as the others, he was much more overweight and had a wreath of foxy-red hair around a bald head and large ears that stuck out at a striking angle. None of the others knew him very well, as he kept to himself, perhaps because of his profession.

The only person present who genuinely loathed Möller was Gunvald Larsson, who said: "How're things with your Croatian terrorist friends? Do you still have tea parties in the garden on Saturday afternoons?"

The chief of the Security Police, however, was too out of breath to reply.

The National Commissioner then opened the meeting, gave an account of the somewhat unpopular senator's coming visit on Thursday the twenty-first of November and said that Gunvald Larsson had brought back some interesting and useful material from his study trip. He spoke of the difficulty of the task and its enormous importance for the prestige of the police. Then he went on to the various special missions each of those present could expect to be assigned.

Pity I didn't bring that head back with me and put it in a jar of Formalin, thought Gunvald Larsson. Now that would really be interesting and useful material.

The news of his very first assignment as chief of operations reached Martin Beck in the middle of a yawn. He suppressed it as best he could and said, "Just a minute, please. Are you talking about me?"

"Precisely, Martin," said the Commissioner heartily. "What is this if not a preventive murder investigation? You'll be given all the resources you need, you can choose whom you like and use your staff as you think best."

Martin Beck at first thought of shaking his head, and

then he thought, good God, the fact is he can order me to do it. Then he noticed that Gunvald Larsson was nudging him in the side and turned to him.

Gunvald Larsson murmured, "Tell him you'll organize the whole protective apparatus, preliminary investigation, long-range security and everything."

"How?"

"With staff from the Homicide Squad and the Violence Division. But only if someone else takes charge of short-range security, to see to it that no one pops up and bashes the senator's head in with a brick or something."

"Gentlemen, would you stop mumbling and speak up, please," said the Commissioner.

Glancing swiftly at Martin Beck, Gunvald Larsson said, "Beck and I figure that with personnel mainly from Homicide and Violence, we can undertake to coordinate all long-range activity—preventive measures and everything. But we'd rather not have to deal with the close-range protection. That assignment seems made for Möller and his gang."

The Commissioner cleared his throat and said, "What do you think, Eric?"

"Fine," said Möller. "We'll take that on."

He was still having difficulty with his breathing.

"That particular job is really embarrassingly simple," said Gunvald Larsson. "I could do it with the twenty dumbest cops in the city. And Möller, after all, has several hundred numskulls out there in the bushes in disguise. I heard one of them photographed the Prime Minister as he was giving his May Day speech and reported that he appeared to be a dangerous communist."

"Cut it out, Larsson," said the Commissioner. "That's enough. So you'll take the job, Beck?"

Martin Beck sighed, but nodded his agreement. He saw the assignment ahead of him with all of its wretched complications—endless meetings, officious politicians and military people meddling in everything. Still, he could not in fact refuse to carry out a direct order, and Gunvald Larsson seemed to have some sort of idea of how the whole thing could be handled. He had already succeeded in getting rid of the Security Police, and that was a very good thing.

"Before I go on, I'd like to know one thing," said the Commissioner. "Something our friend Möller should be able to answer."

"Oh, yes," said the security man stoically, opening his briefcase.

"Well, this organization called UGH or whatever it's called, what do we know about it?"

"It isn't called UGH," said Malm, stroking his hair.

"But it ought to be," said Gunvald Larsson.

The Commissioner burst out laughing. Everyone except Gunvald Larsson looked at him in surprise.

"It's called ULAG," said Malm.

"That's it," said the Commissioner. "What do we know about it?"

Möller took a single piece of paper out of his file and said laconically, "Practically nothing. That is, we know it has carried out several assassinations. The first time was in March last year, when the president of Costa Rica was shot as he stepped out of a plane in Tegucigalpa. An assassination attempt was unexpected and the security measures do not appear to have been very satisfactory. If ULAG itself had not taken the responsibility, the assumption would have been that the assassin was some individual psychopath."

"Shot?" asked Martin Beck.

"Yes, apparently by a long-range sniper who lay hidden in a van. The police did not succeed in tracing him."

"And the next time?"

"In Malawi, where two African prime ministers were meeting to discuss a border dispute. The whole building suddenly exploded and more than forty people were killed. That was in September. The security measures were extremely comprehensive."

Möller wiped the sweat from his forehead. Gunvald Larsson reflected with satisfaction that his own physical condition was not all that bad by comparison.

"Then the organization carried out two assassinations in January. First, a North Vietnamese minister, a general and three members of his staff were all killed when their car was attacked by mortar fire. They were on their way to a conference with some senior South Vietnamese, and the convoy had a military escort.

"Only a week later, the organization struck again in one of the northern states of India. When the president of the state visited a railway station, at least five men threw hand grenades at both the train and the station building. Then the terrorists fired several salvos with machine pistols. It was their bloodiest attack to date. Several hundred schoolchildren had gathered to cheer the president and about fifty of them were killed. All the police and security men on the spot were also killed or severely injured and the president himself was blown to bits. This was also the only time anyone saw the criminals. They were masked and wearing some kind of commando uniform. They drove away in several different cars and could not be traced.

"Then there was one more case in Japan in March, where a well-known and controversial politician visited a school. In this case, too, the building was blown up and the politician killed along with a good many other people."

"Is that all you know about ULAG?" asked Martin Beck.

"Yes."

"Did you prepare that summary yourself?"

"No."

"When did you get it?"

"About two weeks ago."

"May I ask who supplied you with it?" said Gunvald Larsson.

"Yes, you may, but I don't have to give you an answer."

They all knew, anyhow. Möller said with a resigned expression, "The CIA. It's no secret that we exchange information with the USA."

"So the Security Police knew nothing about ULAG before that?" said Martin Beck.

"No," said Möller. "No more than what was in the newspapers. It doesn't seem to be a communist group."

"Nor Arab," said Gunvald Larsson.

"Now let's hear what Larsson has to say," said the Commissioner. "What more do you know about this ULAG, or whatever it's called?"

"I know just as much about ULAG as Möller has down on that piece of paper, plus a little more. I was in on most of the investigation after the assassination on the fifth of June, and I'll merely point out that there are countries whose security men do more than subscribe to mimeographed material from the CIA."

"Don't be so long-winded, Gunvald," said Martin Beck.

"If we look at these assassinations, certain conclusions can easily be drawn," Larsson said. "For instance, they have all been directed at prominent politicians, but those politicians have nothing else in common. Costa Rica's president was more or less a social democrat and the two Africans were nationalists. The Vietnamese, in contrast to what Möller said, were not North Vietnamese but connected to the PRG—that is, the provisional government in South Vietnam—and were communists. The state president in India was a liberal socialist, and the Japanese an ultraconservative. The president whose demise I witnessed was a fascist and ran a dictatorship of many years' standing. However you twist and turn it, there is no clear political pattern. Neither I nor anyone else I know of is in a position to offer even a possible explanation."

"Perhaps they do the jobs to order," said Martin Beck.

"I've thought of that, but it doesn't seem likely. It just doesn't fit somehow. Another thing that strikes me is that all the assassinations were so well planned and carried out. They have used a whole series of different methods and all of them have functioned perfectly. These people know their job and are extremely dangerous. They are evidently well trained and educated, and they seem to have considerable resources at their command. They must also have some kind of base."

"Where?" asked Martin Beck.

"I don't know. I could make a guess, but I'd rather not. But regardless of what their ultimate aims may be, I find it hard to imagine anything more unpleasant than a terrorist group that always succeeds in its assassination attempts."

"Tell us what happened out there," said the Commissioner.

"It took me a while to figure it out," said Gunvald Larsson. "The explosion was extremely powerful. Twenty-six people were killed in addition to the president and the governor—most of them police and security men, but also the drivers of several taxis and horse-drawn cabs parked nearby. There was even one person walking along another street who was killed when what was left of the car landed on his head. What made the explosion so powerful was that the bomb had been placed in one of the city's gas mains, so it must have been detonated by radio by someone who was quite some distance away."

"And what do you think the police did wrong?" asked Martin Beck.

"There was nothing much wrong with the actual security plan," said Gunvald Larsson. "It was roughly the same one the United States Secret Service worked out after the assassination of President Kennedy. But since this guest was obviously unpopular, they shouldn't have published the route of the motorcade beforehand."

"But then people don't get a chance to cheer and wave flags," said the Stockholm City chief.

"And it's hell to keep changing the route," said Möller. "I remember what a brouhaha there was when Khrushchev was here."

"I seem to remember when he left he said he'd never seen so many policemen's backs before anywhere in the world," said Martin Beck.

"That was his own fault," said Möller. "He didn't even have enough sense to be scared."

"Another mistake they made was in starting their preventive measures too late," Gunvald Larsson went on. "They set up controls at the ports and airports only two days before the state visit. But people like these boys in ULAG come weeks ahead."

"That's sheer guesswork," said Möller.

"Not so. The police over there produced quite a lot of interesting information. And the information from that assassination in India wasn't as meager as you made out. A policeman who was badly injured and later died said that the terrorists weren't really masked, they were just wearing some kind of helmets, like the ones construction workers wear. He also said he was sure that, of the three he saw, two were Japanese and the third was European, a tall man about thirty. When this man jumped into the car, his helmet fell off and the wounded policeman saw that he had blond hair and sideburns. Naturally the Indian police were checking everyone who left the country, especially foreigners, and among them was a man who fit that description. He had a Rhodesian passport and they took his name. But the policeman in the hospital didn't give his description until the next day, and by that time the man was long gone. The authorities in Rhodesia said the name wasn't known to them."

"But at least it's something," said Martin Beck.

"The security police down where I was had had no previous contact with the Indian police. But they did keep track of everyone leaving the country at the time, and it turned out later that one of them was a person with the same name and the same passport. The passport is almost a hundred percent certain to be false, as well as the name."

"What name did he use?" asked Martin Beck.

"Reinhardt Heydrich," said Gunvald Larsson.

The chief cleared his throat. "This ULAG seems very unpleasant."

"How are we going to defend anyone against people who use radio-controlled bombs?" said Möller gloomily.

"We'll manage, I expect," said Gunvald Larsson. "As long as you take care of the close-range protection."

"That's not so easy if we all go flying into the air all of a sudden," said the security chief. "How do we protect him then?"

"Don't worry about bombs. We'll take care of that."

"I was just thinking about one thing," said Martin Beck. "If long-range protection was really functioning down there, then whoever set off the bomb couldn't have been close enough to see what was happening."

"I'm sure he wasn't," said Gunvald Larsson.

"Could he have had an accomplice nearby?"

"I don't think so."

"Then how did he know when to set the thing off?"

"What I think is that he just listened to the regular radio broadcast or watched it on television. Radio and TV were both sending the whole state visit live. They usually do in most countries when anything special is going on. We know that ULAG always strikes at very well-known political figures. And always when the intended victim is doing something unusual or spectacular, like making an official state visit for example. This'll be just the kind of occasion when they might try something."

"What do we do about prevention?" asked Möller. "Shall I lock up all the crackpots?"

"No," said Gunvald Larsson. "Anyone who wants to can go out and demonstrate, of course."

"You don't know what you're saying," said the Stockholm chief. "We'd have to bring in every policeman in the country. McNamara was supposed to go to Copenhagen a few years ago, and he simply had to cancel when he heard about the demonstrations they were expecting. And when Reagan was in Denmark to lunch on the royal yacht two years ago, it was hardly mentioned in the newspapers. He was there on a private visit and didn't want any publicity. He said so himself. Imagine: Reagan . . ."

"If I were free this particular day, I might well go out and demonstrate against this bastard myself," said Gunvald Larsson. He's a lot worse than Reagan."

They all looked distrustfully and gravely at Gunvald Larsson, all except Martin Beck, who appeared to be sunk in his own thoughts. They were thinking: Is this really the right man for the job?

Then the Commissioner decided it had probably been a joke.

"This has been very productive," he said. "I think we're heading in the right direction. Thank you, all of you."

Martin Beck had finished thinking. He turned to Eric Möller.

"I've been offered this assignment and I've accepted it. That means you'll have to follow my directives. Directive number one is that there's to be no preventive detention of people whose political opinions are different from your own, unless there are really compelling reasons and unless we others, myself in particular, approve. You've been given an important assignment, the close-range protection, and I want you to stick to that. You're to try to remember that people have the right to demonstrate, and I forbid you to use provocation and unnecessary force. Any demonstrations are to be handled properly and you're to work together with the chiefs for Stockholm and the Regular Police. All plans must be submitted to me."

"But what about all the subversive elements in this country? Am I just supposed to ignore them?"

"As far as I can see, the subversive elements are a product of your imagination and your wishful thinking. Your primary job is the close-range protection of the senator. Demonstrations are inevitable, but they are not to be broken up by force. If the Regular Police get sensible directives, there won't be any complications. I want to be informed of all your plans. Of course you're free to deploy your eight hundred spies however you like provided it's legal. Is that clear?"

"It is," said Möller. "But I presume you know I can go over your head if I feel I have to."

Martin Beck did not answer.

The Stockholm chief went over to the wall mirror and began adjusting his white silk tie.

"Gentlemen," said the Commissioner, "the conference is over. The fieldwork can begin. I've complete confidence in you all."

A little later that day, Martin Beck was visited by Eric Möller, an event that had never occurred before.

Martin Beck himself was still at Kungsholmsgatan, although he ought to have been either at his office in Västberga, or in Rotebro, or Djursholm. He was anxious to crack the Petrus case before this new assignment began to take up too much of his time, and he still had nowhere near the same faith in Benny Skacke as he'd had in Lennart Kollberg. Lennart Kollberg had been an excellent criminal investigator, systematic and inventive. In fact, Martin Beck had sometimes had the feeling that in many respects Kollberg was a better policeman than he himself.

There was nothing wrong with Skacke's ambition and energy, but he had never shown any blinding acumen, and he would certainly never be brilliant. He might well develop, considering his relative youth—he was just thirty-five and was already showing signs of admirable persistence and a total fearlessness—but Martin Beck would probably have to wait a long time before he could hand over difficult cases to Skacke with complete confidence. On the other hand, Benny Skacke and Åsa Torell were not a bad team at all, and would certainly make some headway as long as they weren't hampered too much by Märsta-Pärsta's directives.

Nevertheless, he would soon have to transfer Skacke temporarily to this new assignment and thus further weaken the Homicide Squad. He himself was capable of dealing with two complicated jobs at once, but he very much doubted Benny Skacke's capacity to do the same.

As far as he was concerned, his double assignment had already started. They had already discussed where their headquarters was to be—Command Headquarters, as Stig Malm had martially expressed it—and just now he was discussing the composition of the escort with Gunvald Larsson, simultaneously thinking about the villa in Djursholm.

In the midst of this discussion there was a knock on the door and in came Möller, paunchier and more fox-like than ever. He glanced blankly at Gunvald Larsson, then turned to Martin Beck.

"I presume you've already contemplated what the escort will look like?"

"Have you got secret microphones in here, too?" said Gunvald Larsson.

Möller totally ignored him. Eric Möller was unflappable. If he hadn't been, he would probably never have become the head of Säpo.

"I've got an idea," he said.

"Really?" said Gunvald Larsson.

"The senator will, I presume, be traveling in the bulletproof limousine?" said Möller, still addressing himself only to Martin Beck.

"Yes."

"In that case, my idea is that we let someone else go in the limousine, while the senator goes in a less ostentatious car, a police car, for instance, farther back."

"Who would that other person be?" asked Gunvald Larsson.

Möller shrugged. "Oh, anyone."

"Typical," said Gunvald Larsson. "Are you really so goddamned cynical—"

Martin Beck saw that Gunvald Larsson was beginning to get seriously angry and hurriedly interrupted.

"It's not a new idea. It's been used many times, sometimes successfully, sometimes not. In this case it's clearly out of the question. The senator himself wants to ride in the bulletproof car, and anyway the television broadcast will show him getting in."

"There's lots of tricks," said Möller.

"We know that," said Martin Beck. "But we're not interested in your tricks."

"Oh, I see," said the chief of Säpo. "Goodbye, then."

And he left.

Gunvald Larsson's complexion slowly returned to normal. "Tricks," he said.

"There's no point in getting annoyed with Möller," said Martin Beck. "It doesn't affect him. It's like pouring water on lard. Now I really have to get out to Västberga."

9.

The days went by and grew into weeks, and as usual the much-longed-for summer seemed to be passing much too swiftly.

But now it was still July, the peak of summer, with its cold and rain and very occasional sunny days.

Martin Beck had little time to notice the weather. He was fully occupied and some days hardly ever left his office. He often stayed long into the evenings when the police station was silent and virtually uninhabited. Not that this was always necessary; he often stayed simply because he didn't want to go home, or because he wanted to think about problems he hadn't had time for during a hectic day of constant telephone calls and visitors.

Rhea had taken her children for a three-week holiday in Denmark, where their father lived.

Martin Beck missed her, but she would be back in a week, and meanwhile he filled his life with work and calm solitary evenings at home in the Old City.

The death of Walter Petrus occupied a large part of his time and thoughts. Over and over again, he studied the voluminous collection of material that had been gathered from various quarters, with an irritating sense of constantly reaching a dead end. Now, after a month and a half, the case was being handled mainly by Benny Skacke and Åsa Torell. He could rely on their judgment and thoroughness and he left them to work largely on their own.

The Narcotics Division had made a report after long and careful inquiries. They found, first, that Walter Petrus had not handled drugs on a large scale and there was nothing to indicate that he was a dealer. Presumably the quantity he had possessed had never been very great.

Second, they found that Petrus personally had not been a drug user on any great scale, though he occasionally smoked hash or took stimulants. In a locked drawer at his home they found packages bearing the names of various foreign drug manufacturers which he had probably brought back with him from his trips abroad, but there was no sign of any extensive smuggling.

He was a known customer on the Stockholm narcotics market and seemed to have gone to three different suppliers for his somewhat modest purchases. He had paid the going price and returned at fairly long intervals without any of the signs of desperation common to addicts.

They had also interrogated several girls with experiences similar to those of the two girls Åsa had questioned. They had all been offered drugs, but only during visits to his office. He had definitely refused to give them any to take away with them.

Two of the girls questioned by the Narcotics Division had been in one of his films; not the great international production with Charles Bronson in the main part as Petrus had promised, but in a pornographic film with a lesbian theme. They admitted that during the filming they had been so under the influence of drugs that they had hardly known what they were doing.

"What a bastard!" Åsa had cried when she read the report.

Åsa and Skacke had been out to Djursholm and spoken to Chris Petrus again, and to the two children who were home. The younger son was still abroad and had not been heard from, although the family had cabled his last known address and had also put an advertisement into the personal column of the *International Herald Tribune.*

"Don't worry, Mother, he'll show up when his money runs out," the elder son had said acidly.

Åsa had also had a talk with Mrs. Pettersson, who by and large gave one-syllable replies to all her questions.

She was a faithful servant of the old school, and in the few words she actually uttered she spoke highly of the family.

"I felt like giving her a lecture on women's liberation," said Åsa later on to Martin Beck.

Benny Skacke had spoken to Walter Petrus's gardener and chauffeur, Sture Hellström. He was as taciturn as the maid when it came to opinions on the Petrus family, but he was happy to talk about gardening.

Skacke also spent quite a lot of time out at Rotebro, which was really Åsa's territory. No one really knew what he was doing out there, and one day when they were having coffee in Martin Beck's office, Åsa said teasingly, "You haven't gone and fallen in love with Maud Lundin, have you, Benny? Watch out for her. I think she's a dangerous woman."

"I think she's pretty mercenary," said Skacke. "But I've talked quite a bit to a guy out there—the sculptor who lives across the street. He makes things out of scrap iron, really nice things."

Åsa also disappeared for long periods of the day without saying where she was going. Finally Martin Beck asked her what she was up to.

"I go to the movies. Watch dirty films. I take them in small doses, one or two a day, but I'm determined to see all of Petrus's movies. It'll probably make me frigid, on top of everything else."

"What do you want to see them for?" asked Martin Beck. "What do you think you can find? One was enough for me—that *Love in the Glow of the Midnight Sun,* or whatever it was called."

Åsa laughed. "That was nothing compared to some of the others. Some of them are considerably better from a technical point of view—color and wide screen and all that. I think he sold them to Japan. But it's no fun to sit and watch them. Especially for a woman. You get simply furious."

"I can understand that," said Martin Beck sincerely. "But you didn't answer my question about why you think you have to see them."

Åsa ruffled her untidy hair. "Well, you see, I look at the people in the films, and then I try to find out what sort of people they are, where they live and what they do. I've interviewed a couple of boys who were in several of the films. One's a professional, works at a sex club and regards it as a job. He was fairly well paid. The other one works in a men's clothes shop and did it for fun. He got practically nothing. I've got a long list of people I'm going to check up on."

Martin Beck nodded thoughtfully, giving her a doubtful look.

"Not that I know anything'll come of it," said Åsa, "but if you have no objections, I'm going on."

"Do, if you can take it," said Martin Beck.

"There's only one more I haven't seen," said Åsa. "*Confessions of a Night Nurse,* I think it's called. Horrors."

The week went by and on the last day of July, Rhea returned.

That evening they celebrated with smoked eel, Danish cheeses and Elephant beer and aquavit she had brought back with her from Copenhagen. Rhea talked almost without stopping until she fell asleep in his arms.

Martin Beck lay for a while feeling happy that she was back, but the Elephant beer took its toll and soon he was asleep too.

Things began to happen the next day. It was the first of August, the name day was Per, and it was pouring rain.

Martin Beck awoke bright and alert, but ended up late for work anyway. Three weeks was a long time, and Rhea's eagerness to tell him about her visit to the Danish island, combined with the food, beer and aquavit, had caused them to fall asleep before they could give expression to how much they'd missed each other. They made up for it in the morning, and as the children were still in Denmark they were undisturbed and took their time, until Rhea finally pushed him out of bed and commanded him to think about his responsibilities and his duty as chief to set a good example.

Benny Skacke had been waiting for him impatiently for two hours. Before Martin Beck had time to sit down, he was in the office, shuffling his feet.

"Morning, Benny," said Martin Beck. "How're things with you?"

"Fine, I think."

"Do you still suspect that scrap-iron artist?"

"No, that was only at first. He lived so close-by and his workshop was full of iron bars and pipes and things, I thought he seemed like a good bet. He knew Maud Lundin quite well and he would only have had to run across the road with one of his iron bars or lead pipes and kill the old man, after he'd seen Maud Lundin go off to work. It looked obvious."

"But he had an alibi, didn't he?"

"Yes, a girl was with him all night and went into town with him in the morning. Anyway, he's a nice guy and had nothing to do with Petrus. His girl seems straight, too. She says she sleeps badly, so was reading after he'd fallen asleep, and she says he slept like a log until ten in the morning."

Martin Beck looked at Skacke's eager face with amusement. "So what have you found now?"

"Well, I've been out there quite a bit, walking and

looking around and sitting talking to that sculptor. Yesterday I was out there and we were having a beer together, and I sat there looking at those big crates standing in Maud Lundin's garage. They're his crates—he uses them for packing his sculptures when he sends them to exhibitions. He hasn't got room for them in his garage, so Maud Lundin let him put them in hers. They've been there since March and no one has touched them since. It occurred to me that whoever killed Petrus could have gone to the house that night, when there wasn't any risk of being seen, and waited behind those crates until the old man was alone."

"But then he walked right across the field where everyone could see him," said Martin Beck.

"Yes, I know. But if he did hide behind the crates, it must have been because Walter Petrus used to leave the house shortly after Maud Lundin, so he had to make use of that brief period when the old man was alone in the house. And from his hiding place behind the crates, he could hear when she left."

Martin Beck rubbed his nose. "Sounds plausible," he said. "Have you checked whether it's actually possible to hide in there? Aren't they right up against the wall?"

Benny Skacke shook his head. "No. There's a space just large enough. Kollberg might not be able to squeeze in there with his stomach, maybe, but a person of normal build could."

He fell silent. Negative statements about Kollberg didn't go over too well with Martin Beck, but he didn't seem offended, so Skacke went on.

"I looked behind the crates. There's quite a lot of sand, dust and loose earth on the floor. Couldn't we do some lab work? Spray for footprints and sieve the soil and see if we can find anything?"

"Not a bad idea," said Martin Beck. "I'll get somebody on it right away."

When Skacke had gone, Martin Beck phoned to request an immediate technical examination of Maud Lundin's garage.

As he put the receiver down, Åsa Torell came into his office without knocking. She was as breathless and eager as Skacke had been.

"Take a seat and calm down," said Martin Beck. "Have you been to another blue movie? What were the night nurse's confessions like, anyhow?"

"Awful. And her patients were really something. Surprisingly healthy, I must say."

Martin Beck laughed.

"I hope that's the last skin flick I ever have to watch," said Åsa. "But now listen."

Martin put his elbows on the desk and adopted a listening attitude with his chin in his hands.

"You know that list I told you about?" said Åsa. "The one I made of all the people who were in Petrus's films?"

Martin Beck nodded and Åsa went on.

"In some of the worst films—I think you saw some of them yourself—black-and-white shorts of people screwing on an old sofa and that kind of thing—there was a girl called Kiki Hell. I tried to get hold of her, but it turned out she was no longer in Sweden. But I got hold of a friend of hers and learned quite a lot. Kiki Hell's real name is Kristina Hellström and a few years ago she lived in Djursholm on the same street as Walter Petrus. What do you say to that?"

Martin Beck sat up straight and struck his forehead. "Hellström," he said. "The gardener."

"Exactly," said Åsa. "Kiki Hellström is the daughter of Walter Petrus's gardener. I haven't managed to find out much about her yet. It seems she left Sweden a few years ago and no one knows where she is now."

"It does sound as if you've got something there, Åsa. Do you have your car here?"

Åsa nodded. "It's in the parking lot. Shall we go out to Djursholm?"

"Right away," said Martin Beck. "We can talk on the way."

In the car Åsa said, "Do you think it's him?"

"Well, he's got plenty of reason to dislike Walter Petrus," said Martin Beck. "If what I suspect is true. Petrus used the gardener's daughter in his films and when her dad found out, he can't have been all that pleased. How old is she?"

"She's nineteen now. But the films are four years old, so she was only fifteen when they were made."

After a spell of silence, Åsa said, "Suppose it was the other way around?"

"What do you mean?"

"That her dad encouraged her to be in the films to get money out of Petrus."

"You mean he sold his own daughter? Åsa, watching all that filth has given you a dirty mind."

They parked the car at the edge of the road and walked through the gate to the house next door to the Petruses'. There were no photocells in the gateposts there. A wide gravel path led to the left along the hedge up to a garage and a yellow stucco bungalow. Between the bungalow and the garage was a smaller building which seemed to be some kind of workshop or toolshed.

"That must be where he lives," said Åsa, and they began to walk toward the yellow house. The garden seemed enormous, and the house itself, which they had seen from the gateway, was here quite hidden by tall trees.

Hellström must have heard their footsteps on the gravel through the open door of the toolshed. He came to the doorway and watched them guardedly as they approached.

He looked about forty-five, tall and powerfully built, and was standing quite still, his feet apart, his back slightly bowed.

His eyes were blue and half-closed, his features heavy and serious. His dark untidy hair was streaked with gray and his short sideburns were almost white. He was holding a plane in one hand and some curls of light wood clung to the dirty blue of his coverall.

"Are we interrupting your work, Mr. Hellström?" said Åsa.

The man shrugged his shoulders and glanced behind him. "No," he said. "I was just planing some moldings. They can wait."

"We'd like to talk to you," said Martin Beck. "We're from the police."

"A policeman's already been here," said Hellström. "I don't think I've got anything else to say."

Åsa got out her identification, but Hellström turned around without looking at it, went over and put the plane down on a workbench inside the door.

"There's very little to say about Mr. Petrus," he said. "I hardly knew him, just worked for him."

"You have a daughter, haven't you?" said Martin Beck.

"Yes, but she doesn't live here anymore. Has anything happened to her?" He was standing half-turned away from them, fiddling with the tools on the bench.

"Not that we know of. We'd just like to talk with you about her," said Martin Beck. "Is there anywhere we can go to talk in peace and quiet?"

"We can go to my place," said Hellström. "I'll just get this thing off."

Åsa and Martin Beck waited while the man took off his coverall and hung it up on a nail. Under the coverall he was wearing blue jeans and a black shirt with the sleeves rolled up. He had a wide leather belt round his hips, with a large brass buckle in the shape of a horseshoe.

It had stopped raining, but heavy drops were splashing through the branches of a large chestnut tree by the house.

The outside door was not locked. Hellström opened it and waited on the steps while Åsa and Martin Beck stepped into the hall. Then he went ahead of them into the living room.

The room was not large and they could see into the bedroom through a half-open door. Apart from the little kitchen, which they had seen from the hall, the house had no more rooms. A sofa and two unmatched armchairs filled almost the whole of the living room. An old-fashioned television set stood in the corner, and along one wall was a home-made bookcase, half-filled with books.

While Åsa went over and sat on the sofa and Hellström vanished into the kitchen, Martin Beck looked at the titles of the books. There were a number of classics, among them Dostoyevsky, Balzac and Strindberg, as well as a surprising amount of poetry—several anthologies and poetry-club editions, but also hardback editions of authors like Nils Ferlin, Elmer Diktonius and Edith Södergran.

Hellström turned on the taps in the kitchen and a few moments later appeared in the doorway, wiping his hands on a dirty kitchen towel. "Shall I make some tea?" he said. "It's all I have to offer. I don't drink coffee myself, so there isn't any here."

"Don't put yourself to any trouble," said Åsa.

"I was going to have some myself," said Hellström.

"In that case, tea would be nice," said Åsa.

Hellström returned to the kitchen and Martin Beck sat down in one of the armchairs. An open book lay on the table. He turned it over and looked at the jacket. *Sermon to the Dogs* by Ralf Parland. Walter Petrus's gardener obviously had rather good and advanced tastes in literature.

Hellström brought mugs, a sugar bowl and a carton of milk out to the table, went back to the kitchen and returned with the teapot. He sat down in the other armchair and took a flattened pack of cigarettes and a book of matches out of his jeans pocket. When he had lit a cigarette, he poured out the tea and looked at Martin Beck. "You want to talk about my daughter, you said."

"Yes," said Martin Beck. "Where is she?"

"The last time I heard from her, she was in Copenhagen."

"What does she do there?" asked Åsa. "Does she work?"

"I don't really know," said Hellström, looking at the cigarette between his sunburnt fingers.

"When was it that you heard from her?" Martin Beck asked.

Hellström did not answer at once. "I didn't really hear from her at all," he said finally. "But I was down to visit her a while back. In the spring."

"And what was she doing then?" asked Åsa. "Has she met a man there?"

Hellström smiled bitterly. "You could say that. Not just one, either."

"Do you mean she's . . ."

"She's a whore? Yes," he interrupted, almost spitting out the words. "She walks the streets, in other words. That's what she lives on. I got the social services down there to help me find her, and she was pretty down. She didn't want anything to do with me. I tried to get her to come home with me, but she wouldn't."

He paused and fingered his cigarette.

"She'll be twenty soon, so no one can stop her from living her own life," he said.

"You brought her up on your own, didn't you?"

Martin Beck sat in silence, letting Åsa handle the conversation.

"Yes, my wife died when Kiki was only a month old. We didn't live here then. We lived in town."

Åsa nodded and he went on.

"Mona took her own life and the doctor said it was because of some sort of depression after the baby was born. I didn't understand anything. Of course, I saw she was depressed and down, but I thought that was because of money worries and the future and all that, what with having a child."

"What sort of work did you do then?"

"I was a church caretaker. I was twenty-three, but I didn't have any kind of education. My father was a garbage man, and my mother did cleaning jobs now and then. There was nothing for me to do but start work as soon as I finished school. I was an errand boy and worked in a warehouse and that sort of thing. Things were tight at home and I had several younger brothers and sisters, so we needed the money."

"How did you come to be a gardener?"

"I worked in a truck farm in Svartsjöland. The old boy who owned it was all right and took me on as an apprentice. He paid for me to learn to drive and get my license, too. He had a truck and I drove vegetables and fruit to Klara market."

Hellström took a last draw on his cigarette and then stubbed it out in the ashtray.

"How did you manage to take care of the child and work at the same time?" asked Åsa, while Martin Beck drank his tea and listened.

"I had to," said Hellström. "When she was little, I took her with me everywhere. Later, when she went to school, she had to manage alone in the afternoons. It wasn't the best way to bring up a child, but I had no choice."

He sipped his tea and added bitterly, "You can see the result."

"When did you come here to Djursholm?" Åsa asked.

"I got this job ten years ago. A free house if I looked after the garden here. And then I got gardening jobs at several other places, so we managed pretty well. I thought this neighborhood would be good for Kiki—a good school and fine friends. But I guess it wasn't all that easy for her. All her school friends had rich parents who lived in big houses and she was ashamed of the way we lived. She never brought anyone home here."

"The Petrus family has a daughter about the same age. Did the girls get along? They were neighbors, after all."

Hellström shrugged. "They were in the same class, but they never played outside school. Petrus's daughter looked down on Kiki. The whole family did, in fact."

"You were chauffeur to Petrus, too."

"It wasn't really my job, but I often drove him places. When the Petrus family moved here, they hired me as gardener and they never mentioned chauffeuring. But I got some extra pay for taking care of the cars."

"Where did you drive Mr. Petrus?"

"To his office, and other places when he had other things to do in town. And sometimes when he and his wife went to a party."

"Did you ever drive him to Rotebro?"

"A few times. Three or four, maybe."

"What did you think of Mr. Petrus?"

"I didn't think anything about him. He was just one of the people I worked for."

Åsa thought for a while and then said, "You worked for him for six years, didn't you?"

Hellström nodded.

"Yes, just about. Since they built the house here."

"Then you must have talked to him quite a bit, in the car for instance."

Hellström shook his head. "We almost never talked in the car. And when we did, it was mostly about what had to be done in the garden and that kind of thing."

"Did you know what kind of films Mr. Petrus made?"

"I've never seen any of them. I hardly ever go to the movies."

"Did you know your daughter was in one of his films?"

Hellström shook his head again. "No," he said curtly.

Åsa looked at him, but he did not meet her eyes. After a while he said, "As an extra?"

"She was in a pornographic film," said Åsa.

Hellström glanced swiftly at her. "I didn't know that."

Åsa looked at him for a moment and said, "You must have been very fond of your daughter. Perhaps more than most fathers. And she of you. You only had each other."

Hellström nodded. "Yes, we only had each other. When she was little she was the only thing I lived for."

He straightened up and lit another cigarette. "But

she's grown up now and does as she pleases. I'm not going to try to interfere with her life anymore."

"What were you doing that morning when Mr. Petrus was murdered?"

"I was here, I suppose."

"You know which day I'm talking about—Thursday the sixth of June?"

"I'm usually here and usually start work pretty early. So that day was probably like any other."

"Can anyone vouch for that? Any of your employers, for instance?"

"I don't know. It's a fairly independent job. As long as I do what has to be done, no one bothers about when I do it. I usually start work about eight." He paused, then added, "I didn't kill him. I didn't have any reason to."

"Maybe you didn't," said Martin Beck, speaking up for the first time, "but it'd be nice if someone could confirm that you were here on the morning of June sixth."

"I don't know if anyone can. I live alone, and if I'm not out in the garden, then I'm usually in the workshop. There's always something that needs fixing."

"We may have to talk to the people you work for, and anyone else who might have seen you," said Martin. "Just to be sure."

Hellström shugged. "It was so long ago," he said. "I can't remember what I was doing on that particular morning."

"No, maybe not," said Martin Beck.

"What happened in Copenhagen when you saw your daughter?" asked Åsa.

"Nothing special," Hellström replied. "She was living in a little apartment where she met her customers.

She told me that straight out. She went on about some movie she was supposed to be in, and said that this other thing was just temporary, but she didn't have anything against being a whore, since it paid well, but she was going to stop soon, she said, as soon as she got this movie job. She promised to write, but I haven't heard from her yet. That was all. She got rid of me after an hour, said she didn't want to come back home with me, and there wasn't any point in me going to see her again. And I'm not going to either. As far as I'm concerned, she's lost for good. I just have to accept it."

"How long is it since she left home?"

"Oh, she left as soon as she finished school. Lived with some friends in town. She came here sometimes to see me. Not very often. Then she disappeared completely, and after a while I found out she was in Copenhagen."

"Did you know about her relationship with Mr. Petrus?"

"Relationship? No, there was no relationship between them. Maybe she got some kind of job in a movie, but otherwise she was just the gardener's daughter to him. Like the rest of the family. I can see why she didn't want to stay in a snobbish place like this, where everyone looks down on you if you don't have any money."

"Do you know if there's anyone at home up at the house?" Martin Beck asked. "Maybe I could go up and see if anyone saw you here that morning."

"I don't know if they're at home," said Hellström. "But you can go up and see. Not that I think they keep track of what I'm up to."

Martin Beck winked at Åsa and got up. Åsa took the cue, poured out another cup of tea for herself and Hellström and leaned back in the sofa.

* * *

The lady of the house was at home, and to Martin Beck's question replied that no, indeed, she did not keep track of what the gardener did, as long as he did the work expected of him. She reminded him that the gardener didn't work just for them but for other households as well, and came and went as he liked.

Martin Beck thanked her and took his leave, walking back through the garden down to Hellström's house. He knew that Åsa was good at getting people to talk and had thought she would manage better with Hellström on her own.

He stopped and looked into the garage. It was empty except for a couple of spare tires, a rolled-up hose and a large gasoline can. The door to the workshop was ajar, so he pushed it open and walked in.

The lathe Hellström had been working on was screwed down to the bench. Along one wall were garden tools of various kinds, and above the bench hung tools on hooks and pegs. Just inside the door was a power-mower, and leaning against the wall beyond it was a row of newly painted greenhouse frames.

Martin Beck was standing by the bench, running his forefinger along the newly planed surface of the pine moldings when he suddenly saw something half-hidden in a corner behind a heap of black plastic sacks. He went over and pulled the object out. It was a square wrought-iron grating with four octagonal bars soldered into a strong frame. A wide space in the middle and two rough surfaces indicated that there should have been a fifth.

Martin Beck picked up the grating and went back to Hellström's house.

Åsa was sitting with her mug of tea in her hand, talking to Hellström, when Martin Beck came in. When she saw what he had in his hand, she fell silent.

"I found this in your workshop," said Martin Beck.

"It's from the old house they tore down when Petrus built his new one," said Hellström. "It was in one of the cellar windows. I thought I'd find a use for it, and it's been here ever since."

"You did find a use for it, didn't you?" said Martin Beck.

Hellström did not reply. He turned to the table and carefully stubbed out his cigarette.

"One of the bars is missing," said Martin Beck.

"It always has been," said Hellström.

"I don't think so," said Martin Beck. "I think you'd better come with us so we can try and clear this up."

Hellström sat still for a moment. Then he got up, went out into the hall and put on his jacket. He walked ahead of them through the gate and waited calmly by the car while Martin Beck put the grating into the trunk.

He sat beside Martin Beck in the back, while Åsa drove.

None of them said a word the whole way to the police station.

10.

Almost three hours went by before Sture Hellström confessed to murdering Walter Petrus.

It didn't take long to establish, however, that the iron bar used as the murder weapon was the missing piece from the grating Martin Beck had found in Hellström's workshop. Faced with this evidence, Hellström repeated that the bar had been missing at the time that he had taken the grating, six years before, and that anyone could have taken it.

The technical examination of the sand behind the crates in Maud Lundin's garage produced clear prints of a buckle of the kind on Hellström's belt, probably made as he lay waiting. It also produced a few footprints, as incomplete and blurred as those found in the garden but undoubtedly from the soles of a pair of sneakers found in Sture Hellström's wardrobe. They also found a few strands of hair and some fibers from some dark-blue cotton fabric.

While Martin Beck patiently exhibited and explained the evidence that more and more clearly bound Sture Hellström to the crime, the latter patiently continued to deny it. He didn't say much, just shook his head and lit one cigarette after another.

Martin Beck had had tea and cigarettes brought in, but Hellström didn't want anything to eat.

It had begun to rain again and the monotonous patter on the windowpane and the gray light in the smoke-filled office created a strange atmosphere of timelessness and isolation in the room. Martin Beck looked at the man in front of him. He had tried to talk to Hellström about his childhood and youth, about his struggle for his own and his child's existence, about his books, about his feelings for his daughter, and about his work. At first the man had answered with stubborn defiance, but then he had gradually become more and more taciturn, and now he was sitting with his shoulders hunched, his melancholy eyes directed toward the floor.

Martin Beck sat in silence, too, and waited.

At last Sture Hellström straightened up and looked at Martin Beck. "I haven't really anything left to live for," he said. "He destroyed my daughter and I hated him as much as it's possible for me to hate anyone."

He sat in silence for a while, looking down at his hands. There was dirt under the rims of his cracked stubby nails. Then he raised his eyes and looked out at the pouring rain.

"I still hate him, even though he's dead," he said.

Now that he had decided to talk, all Martin Beck had to do was insert a question here and there.

He told how it was on his journey back from Copenhagen that he decided to kill Petrus. His daughter had told him how Petrus had treated her, and her story had come as a shock to him.

As early as when she was still in school, Petrus had enticed Kiki up to his office. For a long time she didn't dare go but he told her about her rare charm and unique radiance and promised her that if he could put her in a film, she'd be an instant star.

The very first time she visited him, he offered her hash. She went on seeing him, and he soon switched over to giving her amphetamines and heroin. After a while, she became totally dependent on him and finally agreed to be in his films if only he'd supply her with drugs.

When she left school and moved away from home, she was already an addict and could no longer manage on what Petrus gave her. She moved in with some other addicts, and turned to prostitution to pay for her habit. Finally she went to Copenhagen with a whole gang of young people, and there she had stayed.

When her father came to see her, she admitted that she was hopelessly addicted and said she wasn't even going to try to do anything about it. Her habit had grown and she had to work hard to pay for it.

He did what he could to persuade her to go home with him and go into a clinic, but she said she didn't want to live much longer and was going to go on until it killed her, which she figured wouldn't take long.

At first Sture Hellström had blamed himself, but when he thought about the talented and lovely girl his daughter had been before Walter Petrus got his hands on her, he began to see that the fault had been entirely Petrus's.

Hellström knew that Petrus visited Maud Lundin regularly, and he decided to kill him there. He began to follow Petrus to Rotebro and soon realized that he was often alone in the house for a while in the mornings.

On the night of June sixth, when he knew Petrus was going to Maud Lundin's, he took the train to Rotebro, waited in the garage until morning and then went into the house and killed Petrus before the man knew what had hit him.

That was the only thing he regretted. With the weapon he had available, he had been forced to take Petrus by surprise. If only he had had a gun to threaten him with, then he would have told him first that he was going to kill him, and why.

Hellström had left the house by the back door, walked across the field, through some woods and an old overgrown garden, then out onto the Enköping road. Then he had walked back to the station, taken the train to Central Station, a bus to the East Station and returned home on the Djursholm train.

That was all.

"I never thought I'd be able to kill a human being," said Sture Hellström. "But when I saw my daughter as deep in shit as a person can get, and then had to watch that swine walking around the place all fat and smug there was nothing else I could do. I was almost happy once I'd made up my mind."

"But it didn't help your daughter," said Martin Beck.

"No. Nothing can help her. Or me, for that matter."

Sture Hellström sat in silence for a while, then said, "Maybe we were doomed from the start, both Kiki and me. But all the same I think I did right. Anyhow, he can't do anyone else any harm now."

Martin Beck sat looking at Sture Helström, who looked tired, but quite calm. Neither of them said anything. Finally Martin Beck switched off the tape recorder that had been revolving for the last hour, and then got up.

"Let's go, then," he said.

Sture Hellström got up at once and walked ahead of Martin Beck toward the door.

11.

In the middle of August, Rebecka Lind was evicted from her apartment in south Stockholm.

The building was old and run down, and now it was going to be demolished, to be replaced by a new apartment house from which the landlord could extract at least three times the rent after installing all kinds of substandard but modern conveniences, and unnecessary decorative touches of poor quality but luxurious appearance.

After her month's notice had expired she took her little daughter and their few possessions and moved in with some friends who shared a large apartment in a similar substandard building in the same area, also due for demolition.

Rebecka furnished the maid's room with her mattress, four large red-enameled beer kegs that served as shelves, a large basket for sheets, towels, clothes, and Camilla's bed, which Jim had made before he left. Under Camilla's bed she shoved the small suitcase she had brought with her from home, but which she had never really unpacked. Inside it were drawings she had done at school, photographs, letters and some small articles she had inherited from her mother's aunt, wrapped up in an old embroidered cloth.

Rebecka was content to have a roof over her head. She enjoyed being with her friends and liked her little room, which faced out onto a large yard where two tall trees spread their broad branches. She was still waiting to hear from Jim. When one of her friends advised her to forget him, she calmly replied that she knew him too well to believe that he would abandon her without a word of explanation.

Inwardly, however, she began to feel certain that something must have happened to him, and her anxiety increased day by day. Before her ill-fated attempt to borrow money for the journey to America, she had written to Jim's parents at the address he had given her. She had had no reply. It had been a great effort to get the letter together; the English she'd learned at school had improved considerably during her year with Jim, but she still had great difficulty with spelling.

One evening, when Camilla was asleep, she sat down crosslegged on her mattress and using one of the beer kegs as a table she wrote another letter to Jim's parents.

Dear Mister and Missis Cosgrave, she wrote slowly, carefully making the letters as clear as possible.

Sins Jim left me and oure dauhter Camilla in januari I have not herd from him. It is now 5 months that have gon. Do you now were he is? I am worryd about him and it wold be very nice if you cold write me a letter and say if you now waht has happend to him. I now that he wold write to me if he cold, becouse he is a very god and honest boy and he loves me and oure little dauhter. She is nou 6 month and a very fine and beutiful girl. Pleas, Mister and Missis Congrave, write to me and tell wat has happend to Jim. With many thanks and god greetings. Rebecka Lind.

Then all she could do was go on waiting. With autumn coming soon, the person who had first right to her room would be back and she would be forced to move again. She did not know where, but hoped to find someplace with friends.

Just before Rebecka was about to move, the reply to her letter to Jim's parents arrived.

Jim's mother wrote that they had recently moved to another state, far away from where they had lived before. Jim's punishment had not been the mere formality he had promised; he had been sentenced to four years' imprisonment for desertion. They could not visit him because the prison was too far away, but they could write to him. They presumed that the prison authorities censored his mail and that was why Rebecka had not heard from him. Rebecka could try to write, but his mother could not be certain the letters would reach him. They could do nothing to help either him, her, or the child, as Jim's father was very ill and was undergoing expensive medical treatment.

Rebecka read the letter carefully several times, but the only words that really penetrated her mind were "four years' imprisonment."

Camilla had fallen asleep on the mattress on the floor.

She lay down next to her, curled up with the child held close to her and wept.

Rebecka did not sleep that night and it was not until it began to grow light that she fell asleep. When she was awakened by Camilla a short while later, she at once knew to whom she should turn for help.

12.

Hedobald Braxén's office was as shabby as the man himself, though centrally located on David Bagaresgatan. He had no secretary and no waiting room, only one single room with filthy windows and a kitchenette where he occasionally made coffee—when there was any coffee, and if the supply of plastic cups had not run out.

In the room, which was very small, there were two cats and a cage containing a rather tatty and bald old canary. The greater part of the floor space was taken up by a big desk, extremely old and so large that it was amazing that some brilliant moving men had ever succeeded in getting it through the door. Crasher himself, in jest no doubt, used to say that it had been built inside the room when the building was constructed seventy years before.

That Rebecka Lind's case had been allotted to Crasher had been a stroke of luck for her, at least so far.

"Well," he said to her, stroking the cat from its nose right out to the tip of its tail, "we won the case. They did not appeal. All the better. There are blockheads in the High Court who simply regard the laws in the light of their own peculiar literal interpretations. It would have been very difficult to convince them of the truth—sometimes I doubt the word is even included in their vocabulary."

He noticed that the girl was looking distressed.

"So, Roberta . . ."

"Rebecka," said the girl.

"Exactly, yes, Rebecka," he said. "So, Rebecka, what's on your mind? Has something happened?"

"Yes, and you're the only person who has ever helped me."

Crasher relit his cigar, which had gone out. Then he put another cat on his knee and scratched it behind the ears until it began to purr.

He did not interrupt her once during her presentation of the case.

Finally she said helplessly, "What shall I do?"

"You can go to Social Welfare or the childcare office. Since you're unmarried, you've probably got a social worker already."

"No," she said immediately. "Certainly, definitely *not*. Those people already chase me like I was an animal. And when they had Camilla while I was locked up, they didn't take care of her."

"They didn't?"

"No, they gave her the wrong kind of food. It took me three weeks to get her stomach functioning normally again."

Then she repeated, "What shall I do?"

Braxén lifted the cat aside, an unusually ugly specimen, mottled yellow-ocher, black and white, and said, "A long lifetime's struggle against various authorities, and especially those who have more power than others, has taught me that one can seldom get anyone to listen, and even more seldom convince them that you're right."

"Who rules this shitty country?" she said.

"Officially, Parliament, but in practice the cabinet and the committees and the capitalists and a number of people who have been chosen because they either have money or can control politically important groups, the trade-union bosses. The head bossman so to speak, is—"

"The King?"

"No, the King has no say in the matter. I mean the head of the government."

"The head of the government?"

"Haven't you ever heard of him?"

"No."

"The head of the government, or the Premier or the Prime Minister or the Minister of State or whatever you like to call him. He is the leader of the country's politics."

Crasher rummaged around on his desk. "Here," he said. "Here's a picture of him in the paper."

"How awful. And who is that in the cowboy hat?"

"An American senator who is shortly coming on an official visit. He was governor of the very state your boy friend comes from, as a matter of fact."

"My husband," she said.

"Well, one never knows what word to use nowadays," said Crasher, with a belch.

"Can a person go and talk to that man who's head of the government? He does speak Swedish, doesn't he?"

"Yes, but it would still be difficult. He doesn't receive just anyone, except just before an election. But one can draw up a writ, which means sending a letter."

"I couldn't do that," she said resignedly.

"But I could," said Crasher.

From the bowels of his remarkable desk, Hedobald

Braxén unfolded a flap on which an ancient Underwood was mounted. He pushed two pieces of typing paper with a carbon paper between them into the machine, then started typing easily and nimbly.

"Won't it be very expensive?" said Rebecka uncertainly.

"As I see it, it's like this," said Crasher. "If someone who is really guilty of something criminal or who injures society can receive free legal aid, then a person who is totally innocent should certainly not have to pay expensive lawyer's fees."

He glanced through the letter, gave the original to Rebecka and put the copy away in a file.

"What shall I do now?" she asked.

"Sign it," said Braxén. "My address here is at the top of the paper."

She signed it, her hand trembling a little, while Braxén addressed the envelope. Then he sealed the envelope, affixed a stamp showing a picture of their powerless king and gave her the letter.

"If you turn right when you go out of the building and then turn right again, you'll find a mailbox."

"Thank you," she said.

"Goodbye, Ro . . . Rebecka. Where can I get hold of you?"

"Nowhere at the moment."

"Then come back here. In a week's time at the earliest. We cannot expect a reply before then."

When she had closed the door behind her, Braxén folded the flap with the typewriter on it back again and lifted the mottled cat back onto his lap.

13.

The tall, blond man had a British passport, made out in the name of a businessman called Andrew Black. He arrived in Sweden on the fifteenth of October and used the best possible entry, from Copenhagen via hydrofoil to Malmö, where the passport police, if they are even on duty, spend most of their time yawning and drinking coffee.

In Malmö he bought a rail ticket to Stockholm, slept soundly as the cold Swedish rain hammered against the compartment window, arrived in Stockholm in the morning and took a taxi to the six-room apartment in south Stockholm which a dummy operation of ULAG's had long since rented as a visitor's apartment for its business contacts. The first unpleasantness he experienced in Sweden was the lengthy wait for a cab outside the railway station. Apart from that, he had met with no problems; nowhere had he had to show more than the front of his passport, he had not given his name to anyone, nor had anyone opened his bags. These had false bottoms and their contents were highly interesting. And yet a normal customs official, not used to anything more than rummaging about for liquor or tobacco, would certainly not have noticed anything unusual.

At lunchtime he went out and ate at something called a "bar," noting that the food was revoltingly bad and astonishingly expensive. Then he bought some Swedish newspapers and took them back home. After a while he found that he was able to understand the text surprisingly well.

His real name was Reinhard Heydt and he was a South African, brought up in a family speaking four languages—Dutch, Afrikaans, English and Danish. Later on he had learned to speak French and German fluently and could get by in half a dozen other languages. He had been to school in England, but his practical education had been paramilitary. At first he had fought in the Congo, and later he had been on the losing side in Biafra. He had also been involved in the coup in Guinea, and after being in the Portuguese intelligence services for a few years, he had joined an irregular special unit fighting the Frelimo guerrillas in Mozambique. From there he had beeen recruited into ULAG.

Heydt had been trained as a terrorist in camps in Rhodesia and Angola. The training had been extremely hard and the slightest sign of physical or mental weakness had meant an immediate transfer to administrative assignments. Treachery or cowardice was punished by death.

ULAG had been formed and organized by private interests with financial support from the governments of at least three countries. Its ultimate purpose was to form a highly efficient terrorist group, which could then be brought in to support the increasingly wavering white regimes in southern Africa. External contact lines were few, but they did exist. There was, for example, a solemn club in London where a job could be ordered from ULAG. Up to now only one of that kind had been carried out, the one that Gunvald Larsson had happened to witness. What otherwise made the organization's activities so frightening and inexplicable was that they had been carried out as exercises.

The terrorist groups quite simply had to prove that they were competent, but in the process they were able to achieve another goal—the creation of distrust and general political unease. In this they had succeeded, for the coup in Malawi had led to a tremendous quarrel between the three countries involved, with promising military and political complications. The assassination in India had also brought about great political unrest; and in Peking and Moscow, intelligence services still found it difficult to believe that neither the CIA nor the Thieu regime had been behind the mortar attack in Vietnam.

The people who had created ULAG were perfectly aware of the problems that automatically follow the use of terror as a political weapon. It either develops into a situation such as the one in Ulster, where the activists are badly trained and armed (no one is especially impressed when an unsophisticated Irish laborer blows himself to kingdom come because he fails to understand the construction of a bomb or how to handle it), or as in the numerous Palestinian actions, it leads to the death of the terrorists because their opponents are so well equipped and so utterly uncompromising.

Consequently, what they were trying to create was a group that never failed and that, even if not large, was truly in a position to create terror.

At present ULAG contained no more than a hundred men, consisting of ten activist groups of four men each, ten in reserve and another twenty in training. The rest were in the administration, which was kept to an absolute minimum for reasons of security. In the beginning, ULAG's central core had consisted of men who had seen action in Biafra and Angola, but even that group was multinational, and since then the organization had been reinforced with people from many countries, including some Japanese of an ultranationalistic variety who felt that they were serving their country in this way.

Reinhard Heydt had been at the top of his training class and could justifiably regard himself as one of the ten most dangerous men in the world, a thought that tickled him enormously. He was otherwise an educated man of attractive appearance who very much enjoyed his profession.

Three days after Heydt, the two Japanese in the group came to Stockholm. They had come via Finland and arrived on one of the big pleasure ferries from Mariehamn. One of the passport police on duty indifferently stamped their false passports as he listened with weary distaste to one of them asking for the nearest pornographic movie of beautiful Swedish girls.

That question about beautiful Swedish girls also caused the customs official to scribble a hasty chalk mark on their luggage.

"We should have some goddamn brochure in Japanese and English with addresses of whores and sex clubs in it. We could just hand them out to Japs and other idiots," said the customs man to his colleague.

"That's racist," shouted a youth in line. "Don't you realize that? It's against the law to discriminate between people because of race and color!"

As they were arguing about this, the second Japanese also got his luggage through without a search. He was a large man whose hands were as hard as boards.

The two Japanese had been involved in the Indian affair, but not in Latin America. Reinhard Heydt knew they were enormously competent—cold and ruthless and utterly reliable. They were boring to live with, though. They seldom said anything, just sat playing an incomprehensible game with a lot of small blocks. Their faces were so expressionless that it was impossible to make out who was winning or losing, or even whether the game had ended or was to be continued the next day.

In contrast to these two, Heydt had never been to Stockholm before, so during those first days he moved around town quite a bit to form an impression of the place as a whole. He rented a car, using the papers that identified him as the British citizen Andrew Black.

A week later he received a large crate from the freight terminal; it had been sent care of general delivery. As it had obviously come through customs without being examined, he had no need to bother with the two crates that followed a short while later. These would be returned to the sender after a certain period of time.

A little later he visited an office in Kungsholm, identified himself as a representative of a Dutch contractor and bought the complete plans of the city subway, sewage, electric and gas supply systems. This contact had been established beforehand; the man had been contacted well in advance by letter and had replied submitting an estimate.

On the thirty-first of October, Reinhard Heydt had already been in Sweden for seventeen days. The two Japanese went on playing their strange game, with breaks to go out into the kitchen and cook strange food. They appeared to buy the ingredients in ordinary stores in town.

All the material was ready at hand, and there were three more weeks to go before the senator's visit. Reinhard Heydt drove out to the international airport at Arlanda, looked at it without interest and then drove back into town. The route along which the famous American would be transported appeared to be fairly obvious.

After Heydt had passed the Royal Palace, he swung up and parked on Slottsbacken. Then he took out his Stockholm map and, as any other tourist might have done, went down to Logårds steps, stopped and looked around for a long time.

This was a good place, that was clear, whatever method he chose. He had more or less decided to use a bomb, but there was the risk that the King might be killed at the same time. No one had mentioned a king, and in some way Heydt could not reconcile himself to the idea. There was something special about a king. He looked at the palace again and thought it a massive and ugly heap of stones. As he had already crossed the road, he decided to leave the car where he had parked it and take a short walk through the Old City. This was the only part of Stockholm he liked.

Reinhard Heydt walked on until he came to Stortorget. He inspected Brunkeberg Pump and then walked eastward along Köpmangatan, when suddenly a woman came out of an alley right in front of him and fell into step ahead of him.

Scandinavian women were supposed to be tall and blonde, he thought. His Danish mother had been. But this one was noticeably short, with quite broad shoulders. She had straight fair hair and was wearing red rubber boots, jeans and a black duffle coat, her hands thrust deeply into the pockets. She was walking with her head down, with determined steps, at exactly the same speed as he.

As he continued walking a few yards behind her along Bollhusgatan, she suddenly turned her head, as if she had felt she was being followed, and looked at him, her eyes screwed up and as blue as his own. She regarded him searchingly, looked at the map he was still holding folded in his hand, then took a step to one side so that he could pass.

When he was back in the car he saw her again, striding down toward Skeppsbron. Once she appeared to glance over in his direction, a swift and observant look. For some reason he again thought of his Danish mother, who was still alive and lived near Pietermaritzburg. When they finished this job, he would have to go and see her.

That same day he called up the group's radio specialist, a Frenchman who had long been in readiness in Copenhagen. Heydt told him that he was to come to Stockholm on the fourteenth of November at the latest and that the method used would be essentially the same as the last time.

On Monday of the following week, Reinhard Heydt was so bored with his silent, constantly game-playing Japanese colleagues that he decided to try and find a woman. This in itself was a break in routine; he had never before had anything to do with women while preparing for action. Now searching about for one, he found that the great numbers of prostitutes in Stockholm depressed him, especially the number of girls in their early teens who seemed willing to do almost anything to get drugs.

After observing this dismal traffic for a while, he visited one of the better hotels in town and went into the bar.

Heydt never drank, but occasionally enjoyed a glass of tomato juice and tabasco. As he sipped his drink, he thought about what he wanted: preferably a fairly tall, ash-blonde woman who was twenty-five years old. He himself was thirty, but twenty-five was a kind of *ideé fixe* of his. What he definitely could not contemplate was any kind of professional lady or one of those who worked for an establishment. He no longer believed in beautiful Swedish girls; they seemed to be a myth, just another of the many lies the regime had spread as propaganda.

As he was drinking his second glass of spiked tomato juice, a woman came in and sat down at the other end of the bar. She seemed to be drinking orange juice with a red cherry in it and a neatly sliced piece of lemon on the edge of the glass.

They looked at each other a couple of times, disclosing their mutual interest, and Heydt decided to ask the bartender if he might buy her the next drink. The answer was yes. Shortly after that the stool next to her became vacant. He looked questioningly at it, and again she nodded.

After he had moved over, he entertained her for half an hour or so in Scandinavian. He told her he was a Danish engineer named Reinhard Jörgensen—it was always simplest to stick to the truth as closely as possible, and his mother's maiden name had been Jörgensen. She said her name was Ruth Salomonsson. He at once asked her how old she was, and she replied that she was twenty-five. She was almost perfect; her hair was not blond but ash-colored and her eyes were blue. She was tall, slim and well built.

It took him about fifteen minutes to discover that she was in the bar on exactly the same errand as he was. Then it was just a matter of going out and asking the hall porter to call them a cab.

As was common with women in bars, Ruth Salomonsson had a woman friend with her. The friend was talking to a man at a table in the bar, and as they waited for the cab to come, Heydt chatted politely with her.

He had made a good choice and had a very pleasant evening. It was not until some hours later that he filled a gap by asking a question. He had told her a little about his own affairs and travels. Now he inquired, "What do you do for a living?"

She lit a cigarette from his, blew out a cloud of smoke and said, "I'm with the police."

"Police?" he said. "You work for the police?"

"Yes. It's called police assistant."

"Is it interesting work?"

"It's not always particularly exciting," she said. "I work at what's called the Investigation Bureau."

He said nothing, feeling surprise more than anything else, but in some way she now became slightly more interesting in his eyes.

"I purposely didn't mention it before," she added. "Some people react in such a peculiar way if you tell them you're a policewoman."

"That's silly," said Heydt, pulling her toward him.

He did not get back to his Japanese until about seven the next morning. They looked at him reproachfully, then went back to bed.

14.

Gunvald Larsson was looking at his new suit.

Would it be a bad omen if he wore it on the great day? Would he be showered with the obnoxious senator's intestines or something similar? Not impossible—and in defiance he decided there and then to wear the suit the following Thursday.

Today he put on his ordinary clothes—fur-lined jacket, brown trousers and heavy Danish walking shoes with crepe soles—looked in the mirror and shook his head. Then he went off to work.

Gunvald Larsson did not like getting older. He

would soon be fifty, and wondered more and more often what the point of his life was. It had been fun squandering most of his inheritance, memorable both for himself as well as others. He had quite liked being in the navy and even more in the merchant navy, but why on earth had he become a policeman, voluntarily putting himself in a position in society where he was often forced to act against his own convictions?

The answer was simple. It had been the only job he could get with his odd education, and at the time he had also hoped to be of some use. But had he succeeded?

And why had he not married? There had been plenty of opportunities but now it was virtually too late.

Anyhow, what a time to be asking that sort of question.

He parked the car when he arrived and then took the elevator up to the Violence Division, where the special group had its headquarters. The rooms were decrepit, the walls were peeling, and the building itself appeared to be in the process of collapsing from the pressure of the ostentatious new police headquarters growing up just outside the windows.

Gunvald Larsson looked at the wall clock. Three minutes past eight. It was the fourteenth of November, exactly a week until the great day.

The headquarters had four rooms at its disposal. Martin Beck was usually there, and Gunvald Larsson and Einar Rönn were nearly always there, as were Benny Skacke and Fredrik Melander, who was otherwise a chief inspector in the Larceny Division but had many years' experience in both National Homicide and Violence.

Melander was a strange man and an invaluable asset. His memory functioned like a computer, only better, and by letting all information pass through him they were able to guard against diverse faults, duplicated orders and much else. Personally, he was a tall, even-tempered man, slightly older than the others, who mostly sat studying his papers and fiddling with his pipe, and if he was not to be found at his desk, then he would be in the men's room, a fact half of Stockholm's police were aware of and considered hugely amusing.

Gunvald Larsson nodded at Rönn before going on in to Martin Beck, who was sitting on his desk, dangling his legs and talking on the telephone as he leafed through a thick bundle of reports.

"Goodbye," he said, putting down the receiver.

Gunvald Larsson looked at him inquiringly.

"Air force," said Martin Beck.

"Ugh," said Gunvald Larsson.

"Yes, that's what I was trying to tell them, only a little more politely. They wanted to know if we need more than one division of fighter planes."

"And what did you say?"

"I happened to say that we didn't need any airplanes at all."

"You said that?"

"Yes. The general got a bit steamed up. 'Airplane' is evidently a dirty word."

"It's like calling the deck of a boat the floor."

"Oh, that bad, is it?" said Martin Beck. "I'll have to apologize to him if he calls again."

He glanced at the date indicator on his watch and said, "Your friends from ULAG don't seem to have put in an appearance."

Control of the borders and incoming traffic from abroad had been tremendously thorough during the last week or two.

"Mmm."

"Was that a statement?" asked Martin Beck.

Gunvald Larsson strode up and down the room a couple of times. Finally he said, "I think we should go on the assumption that they're here."

"But there must be several of them. Do you really mean they've managed to get in without our catching even one of them?"

"It seems peculiar," said Gunvald Larsson, "but . . ." He fell silent.

"Of course they may have come in before the border checks began," said Martin Beck.

"Yes," said Gunvald Larsson, "that's a possibility."

As if to steer the course of the conversation in another direction, Martin Beck asked, "Did you see any interesting films yesterday?"

Gunvald Larsson had been detailed to study a number of films the Security Service had acquired of state visits.

"Yes," said Gunvald Larsson. "I noticed that Nixon traveled in an open car through Belgrade with Tito. Same thing in Dublin—Nixon and de Valera paraded in an ancient Rolls-Royce with an open top. As far as I could see on the film, there was only one security man. On the other hand, about half the country was barricaded off when Kissinger was in Rome."

"Did they show the great classic, too? The Pope in Jerusalem?"

"Yes, but unfortunately I'd seen that before."

The Pope's visit to Jerusalem had been handled by the Jordanian security service, who had messed things up to a degree that probably lacked any precedent in the history of the world. Not even Stig Malm could have achieved anything like it.

The telephone rang.

"Yes. Beck."

"Hi," said the chief of the Regular Police. "Have you seen the papers I sent up?"

"Yes, I was just looking at them."

"As you see, there's going to be a bit of a shortage of Regular Police in the rest of the country on those two days."

"I can see that."

"I just wanted you to be aware of it."

"That's not my business. Ask the National Commissioner if *he* realizes it."

"Okay, I'll call Malm."

Rönn came in with his reading glasses on the red tip of his nose and a paper in his hand.

"This CS list that I found on my desk . . ."

"That should be in my 'in' tray," said Gunvald Larsson. "Put it there. Who the hell moved it, anyhow?"

"Not me," said Rönn.

"What list is that?" asked Martin Beck.

"People who should be on station duty," said Gunvald Larsson. "The ones who are best at sitting in the duty room playing tic-tac-toe, if you know what I mean."

Martin Beck took the list from Rönn and looked at it. It was headed by a number of not unexpected names: Bo Zachrisson, Kenneth Kvastmo, Karl Kristiansson, Victor Paulsson, Aldor Gustafsson, Richard Ullholm and so on. "I understand perfectly," said Martin Beck. "Station duty seems like a sound idea for them. But what does CS stand for?"

"Clod Squad," said Gunvald Larsson. "I didn't want to express myself too directly."

They went into the larger room, where Rönn and Melander had their desks and where they had tacked up a large copy of the city plan and drawn in the motorcade's preliminary route. Like most command offices this one was fairly messy. The telephone rang incessantly and now and again people came in and left internal messages in brown perforated envelopes.

Melander was in the process of talking into the telephone without taking his pipe out of his mouth. When he saw them he said, "Yes, he's just come in," and silently handed the receiver to Martin Beck.

"Yes. Beck."

"Glad I got hold of you," said Stig Malm.

"Uh-huh."

"Congratulations on the fantastically elegant solution of the Petrus murder, by the way."

A bit late in the day, and rather overstated.

"Thanks," said Martin Beck. "Was that what you called for?"

"No," said Malm. "Unfortunately not."

"What's it about then?"

"The chief of the air force has just called the National Commissioner."

Swift action, thought Martin Beck. Aloud, he said, "Yes?"

"The general seems to have been . . ."

"Annoyed?"

"Well, let's say that he seemed disappointed in the police's will to cooperate in this affair."

"I see."

Malm cleared his throat in embarrassment.

"Have you got a cold?"

What a goddamn awful superior, thought Martin Beck. Then it struck him that at present it was in fact the other way around; he could regard himself as Malm's superior. So he said, "I've got quite a lot to do. What is it you wanted?"

"Well, we consider that our relations with the defense forces are both sensitive and important. So it would be desirable if conversations with the defense forces could be carried out in a spirit of cooperation. Of course, as you know, it's not me talking."

Martin Beck laughed. "Who the hell is it then? Some kind of answering device?"

"Martin," said Malm pleadingly, "you know the position I find myself in. It's not easy—"

"Okay," said Martin Beck. "Anything else?"

"Not for the moment."

"So long, then."

"So long."

The telephone rang again. Melander answered it. This time it was Möller, who wished to speak about his struggle against what he called "subversive forces." In simpler language: communists. They let Melander handle the conversation. He was superb at that kind of job, replying briefly and patiently to everything, never swerving from the point and never raising his voice. When the conversation was over, the person who had called had had no hearing at all, and yet he had been received kindly and had nothing to complain about.

The others were studying the motorcade route.

The schedule for the Senator's visit was very simple. His special plane, presumably checked ten times daily by selected mechanics, was to land at Stockholm Arlanda at 1:00 P.M. A representative of the government was to meet him at the plane and they were to walk to the VIP room. The government had gracefully declined the offer of a military honor guard; instead, the government representative and the guest were to step into the bulletproof car for transport to the Parliament Building in Sergel Square. Later that same day the Senator, or rather four naval officers from an American warship which just happened to be in Oslo harbor, would be laying a wreath in memory of the former king.

There had been a good deal of fuss about this mark of respect to the dead monarch. It had all begun when the Senator was asked whether he had any special requests. He had replied that he would like to pay homage to the recently deceased King, as the latter had been regarded as the greatest Swede of his day, not only by the Senator personally but also by a large number of people in the United States.

No one had been especially pleased with this request. Several ministers had been slightly shocked by the outburst of uninhibited royalism that had occurred at the death of the old King and the proclamation of the new one. They considered that this was already more than enough, and through diplomatic channels the Senator had been asked just what was meant by "recently" (more than a year had passed since the death of King Gustaf VI Adolf) and it was strongly hinted that the government was not interested in contributing to the veneration of dead kings. But the Senator had remained inflexible. He was hell-bent on laying a wreath and that was what he was going to do.

The United States Embassy ordered a wreath so large that two florist firms had to be brought in to do the job. The Senator had himself decided on the size of the wreath and the kinds of flowers to be used. The four naval officers arrived in Stockholm on the twelfth of November and were fortunately of athletic build, not one of them less than six foot in his stocking feet. This showed some foresight, because it was possible that men of smaller size would not have been able even to shift the mountain of flowers.

After the ceremony, at which the Prime Minister, after a great many ifs and buts, had promised to be present, the motorcade was to go to the Parliament Building. During the afternoon the guest was to meet a number of ministers for informal political discussions.

In the evening the government was to host a banquet at Stallmästaregården, where the leaders of the opposition party and their wives would also have the opportunity to speak to the man who had once almost become President of the United States. The Senator's political caliber was such that the leader of the Swedish Left—that is, the chairman of the Communist party—had in fact declined the invitation to dine in such company.

After the banquet the Senator was to spend the night in the guest apartment at the embassy.

Friday's agenda was brief. The King was to be host at a luncheon at the palace. The royal secretary had not yet announced exactly how this was to be organized, but the preliminary arrangements called for the King to go out and meet his guest at Logården, after which they would enter the palace buildings.

After lunch the Senator, together with one or two members of the government, was to proceed directly to Arlanda airport, say goodbye and fly back home. End of schedule.

There was nothing especially complicated or remarkable about any of this. The whole thing was to be published in the newspapers, including the actual route. Radio and television were to broadcast live the eminent guest's arrival, as well as the motorcade into the city, the wreath-laying and the meeting with the King. In fact, it was ridiculous that so many policemen of all ranks should have to be involved in protecting one single person.

Melander ended his telephone call and got up and joined the others in front of the map.

"Mmm," he said. "Now, like the rest of you, I've read all the material available on this sabotage group."

"And where would you place an explosive charge?" asked Martin Beck.

Melander lit his pipe and said with stoic countenance, "Where would the rest of you put this hypothetical bomb?"

Five forefingers were raised to the city map and placed on the same spot.

"Oh, dear, oh, dear," said Rönn.

They all felt slightly silly. Finally Gunvald Larsson said, "If five people like us come to exactly the same conclusion, then it must be wrong as hell."

Martin Beck took a few steps to the side, propped his elbow against a filing cabinet over the wall and said, "Frederik, Benny, Einar and Gunvald. Within ten minutes I want your reasons, in writing. And I want you to write them independently. I'll do one myself, too. Very brief."

He went into his office. The telephone rang. He let it go on ringing, put a piece of paper into his typewriter and typed with his two forefingers:

> If ULAG attempts an assassination, then everything indicates they will use a remote-controlled bomb. With the type of security service we are in the process of forming, the bomb-in-gas-main method appears to be the one most difficult to protect against. This is also their best method of achieving an adequate explosive effect. My independent view that the most likely site is the logical entry to Stockholm from the airport is based on the fact that the motorcade cannot be directed onto an alternate route without great difficulty, es-

pecially as far as disposition of police is concerned. At this particular place, there are plenty of underground tunnels and passages; first the internal communication system of the subway line presently under construction; secondly a complicated division of the drainage system. This area can also be reached by way of a number of street wells and other entrances by anyone familiar with the underground communication network of the city. We should also reckon with the fact that alternative explosive charges may be placed, and try to localize the logical positions of these.

BECK

Skacke came in with his statement before Martin Beck had finished. Melander and Gunvald Larsson followed. Rönn came last. His statement had taken him almost twenty minutes. He was no writer.

All of them had similar points of view, but Rönn's study was the one most worth reading. He wrote:

The underground bomber, even if he uses radio detonation has to be able to put the bomb in a gas main where there is one. There are several (five) just where I pointed and if he has to put the bomb somewhere there, then he either has to dig himself a tunnel like a mole or else use the underground passages that are already there. Just where I pointed, there are a lot of already dug passages and then if the bomb itself is as small as Gunvald says, it is impossible to proceed with measures if we do not want at this moment to call out a huge lot of underground policemen and thus create an underground police commando, but they have no experience and would probably be useless.

EINAR RONN. *Deputy Inspector.*

But we do not know if there are any bomb assassination terrorists down in the ground, but if there are, neither surface nor underground police can deal with them, but they might also swim through the sewers and then we will also need a sewer commando of frogmen.

The author wriggled as Martin Beck, without a smile, read the epistle aloud. Then Martin Beck put the document down on the top of the heap.

Rönn thought clearly, but wrote somewhat strangely. Perhaps that was why he had still not been promoted to inspector. Sometimes his reports were circulated by malicious people, causing a great deal of mocking laughter. It was true that police reports were often pure gibberish, but Rönn was an experienced detective and should have been able to do better, people said.

Martin Beck went over to the cooler and drank a glass of water. Then he propped up his elbow again in the usual old way, scratched his head and said, "Benny, will you tell the switchboard we're not taking any calls or receiving any visitors. Whoever they are."

Skacke complied, but said, "What if it's the Commissioner or Malm?"

"We'll kick Malm out," said Gunvald Larsson. "As for the Commissioner, he can play solitaire. There's a pack of cards in my desk drawer. It's Einar's actually, and he inherited it from Åke Stenström."

"Okay," said Martin Beck. "First of all, Gunvald has something to tell us."

"It's about ULAG's bomb technique," said Gunvald Larsson. "Immediately after the assassination on the fifth of June, the police bomb squad, together with experts from the army, started searching for other explosive charges in the city gas mains. Eventually they found two undetonated charges. But they were so small and well hidden and cleverly placed that they didn't find one of them for three months and the other one was only found last week. Both of them were on the planned motorcade route for the next day, and the bomb squad more or less had to dig its way forward yard by yard. The bombs were a much improved version of the explosive charges the plastic-bombers used in their day in Algeria. The radio-control arrangements were technically enormously sophisticated."

He fell silent.

Martin Beck said, "That's that. Now we're going to talk about something else, and it is a detail that must definitely remain between us. Only the five of us here may know anything about it. There will be one exception, but we'll come to that later."

The talk went on for almost two hours. All of them had points of view.

Martin Beck felt extremely satisfied afterward. Apart from the personal views some of them had of each other, this was a good group. True, he'd had to explain himself rather often, which as usual caused him to miss Kollberg.

Skacke checked to see who had telephoned. It was a considerable list: the National Commissioner; the Stockholm chief; the Commander of the Armed Forces; the Army Chief of Staff; the King's Adjutant; the head of Swedish Radio; Malm; the Minister of Justice; the chairman of the Conservative party; the chief of the Regular Police; ten different newspapers; the United States ambassador; the chief of the Märsta Police; the Prime Minister's secretary; the head of the Security Guard at the Parliament Building; Lennart Kollberg; Åsa Torell; the public prosecutor; Rhea Nielsen and eleven unknown citizens.

Martin Beck looked worriedly at the list and sighed deeply. Of course there would be trouble in one way or another, perhaps in many ways.

He ran his forefinger down the long list of names, pulled the telephone toward him and dialed Rhea's number.

"Hi!" she said happily. "Am I disturbing you?"

"You never disturb me."

"Are you coming home tonight?"

"Yes, but probably late."

"How late?"

"Ten, eleven, around there."

"What have you eaten today?" she said inquisitorially.

Martin Beck didn't reply.

"Nothing, eh? Remember what we said about telling the truth."

"You're right. As usual."

"Come back to my place then. If you have a chance, call me half an hour beforehand. I don't want you to drop dead of starvation before that slob even lands."

"Okay. Be good."

"And you."

They divided up the rest of the calls, a number of which were rapidly dealt with, while others were long and involved. Gunvald Larsson took Malm.

"What do you want?" he asked Malm brusquely when he got him on the line.

"Beck seems to be trying to blame us because a lot of policemen are being called in from rural areas. The chief of the Regular Police telephoned about the matter an hour or two ago."

"So what?"

"Here at National Headquarters we just wish to point out that you have no reason to get mixed up in a whole lot of peripheral crimes which haven't yet been committed."

"Have we done that?"

"The Commissioner thinks the question of responsibility is important. If crimes are committed elsewhere, that's not our fault. It has nothing to do with National Headquarters."

"Extraordinary," said Gunvald Larsson. "If I were at National HQ I'd see to it that preventive measures were taken. What do you people do up there? What do you think your job is?"

"It isn't our responsibility, it's the government's."

"Okay, then, I'll call the Minister."

"What?"

"You heard perfectly well what I said. Goodbye."

Gunvald Larsson had never before spoken to a member of the government. For that matter, he had never wanted to, but now he dialed the Department of Justice with a certain gusto. He was put straight through and got the Minister of Justice on the line.

"Good afternoon," he said. "My name's Larsson and I'm from the police. I'm involved in security for the Senator's visit."

"Good afternoon. I've heard about you."

"There has arisen what strikes me as an unpleasant and meaningless discussion about whose fault it is that there won't be any policemen in, say, Enköping and Norrtälje next Thursday and Friday."

"And?"

"I'd appreciate an answer to the question, so I can stop arguing about it with all kinds of idiots."

"I see. Naturally, the government as a whole takes full responsibility. I can't see any point in trying to pin the blame on some individual—whoever it was, for example, who insisted on making the invitation in the first place. I shall personally point out to the National Police Headquarters that they must do everything in their power to strengthen crime prevention in districts where there is a severe shortage of manpower."

"Excellent," said Gunvald Larsson. "That's what I wanted to hear. Goodbye."

"Just a moment," said the Minister of Justice. "I myself telephoned to find out what the situation is on the security front."

"We consider it good," said Gunvald Larsson. "We're working according to a definite but flexible plan."

"Excellent."

He really seemed quite sensible, thought Gunvald Larsson, but then the Minister of Justice had the reputation of being a shining exception among the career politicians who were busily steering Sweden down the long and evidently unavoidable slope.

The day continued with numerous conversations, most of which were largely meaningless. File clerks ran in and out in a constant stream.

At about ten in the evening, Gunvald Larsson was handed a file, whose contents caused him to sit still for almost half an hour, his head propped in his hands.

Both Skacke and Martin Beck were still there, but about to go home, and Gunvald Larsson did not want to spoil their evening, so at first he thought he would say nothing about what was in the file until the next day. Then he changed his mind and without comment handed it to Martin Beck, who equally impassively placed it in his briefcase.

Martin Beck did not reach the house in Tulegatan until twenty past eleven that night.

He opened the street door with his own key, then

went up two flights and rang the bell, using their agreed signal.

Rhea had keys to his apartment, but he did not have any to hers. Martin Beck couldn't see that he needed any, as he'd have no reason to be there if she wasn't home. And when she was home, the door was usually unlocked.

Thirty seconds or so later she came running to open the door in her bare feet. She was looking unusually lovely, wearing nothing but a soft, fluffy blue-gray jersey that came halfway down her thighs.

"Damn," she said. "You didn't give me enough time. I've made something that has to be in the oven for half an hour."

When he was inside, she said, "God, you look tired. Shall we take a sauna? It'll relax you."

The year before, Rhea had had a sauna built in the basement for her tenants. When she wanted to use it privately, she simply stuck a note on the basement door.

Martin Beck changed into an old bathrobe he kept in the bedroom wardrobe, while she went on ahead and got the sauna going. It was a good sauna—dry and very hot.

Most people sat silently and enjoyed the heat, but Rhea was not that kind of person.

"How're things going with your peculiar job?" she asked.

"Pretty well, I think, but . . ."

"But what?"

"It's hard to know for certain. I've never done anything like it before."

"Imagine inviting that s.o.b.," said Rhea. "What is it, a week now? Until he comes?"

"Not even that. Next Thursday."

"Will it be on the radio or TV?"

"Both."

"I'll go down to Köpmangatan and watch."

"Aren't you going to demonstrate?"

"Maybe," she said moodily. "I ought to. Maybe I'm getting a bit old for demonstrating. It was different a few years ago."

"Have you ever heard of something called ULAG?"

"I've read something about it in the papers. What they stand for seems vague. Do you think they might do something here?"

"There's the possibility."

"They sound dangerous."

"Very."

"Have you had enough now?"

The thermometer showed almost a hundred degrees Celsius. She threw a few scoops of water onto the stones and an almost unbearable yet oddly pleasant heat sank from the ceiling.

They went and showered, then toweled each other down.

When they got back up to the apartment, a very promising aroma was coming from the kitchen.

"It smells done," she said. "Can you manage setting the table?"

That was about all he could manage—except eating, of course.

The food was very good and he ate more than he had for a long time. Then he sat in silence for a while, his wineglass in his hand.

She looked at him. "You look absolutely done in. Go to bed."

Martin Beck really was done in. The day of uninterrupted telephoning and conferring had exhausted him. But for some reason he did not want to go to bed at once. He felt too comfortable in this kitchen, with its plaits of garlic bulbs and bunches of wormwood, thyme and rowanberries. After a while he said, "Rhea?"

"Yes?"

"Do you think it was wrong of me to take on this job?"

She thought for a long time before answering, then said, "That would require quite an involved analysis. But I more than understand that friend of yours who resigned."

"Kollberg."

"He's a nice man. I like his wife, too. And I think he did the right thing. He saw that the police as an organization devoted itself to terrorizing mainly two categories of people, socialists and people who couldn't make it in our class society. He acted according to his conscience and convictions."

"I think he was wrong. If all good policemen got out, because they take on other people's guilt, then only the dumb ones, the dregs, would be left. We've talked about this before, anyhow."

"You and I have talked about practically everything before. Have you ever thought about that?"

He nodded.

"But you asked a concrete question, and now I'll answer it. Yes, darling, I think you were wrong. What would have happened if you'd refused?"

"I'd have been given a direct order."

"And if you'd refused a direct order?"

Martin Beck shrugged his shoulders. He was very tired, but the conversation interested him. "I might possibly have been suspended. But to be honest, that's unlikely. Someone else would simply have been given the job."

"Who?"

"Stig Malm, probably, my so-called chief and immediate superior."

"And he'd have made a worse job of it than you? Yes, most likely, but I think you should have refused all the same. That's what I feel, I mean. Feelings are difficult to analyze. I guess what I feel is this: Our government, which maintains it represents the people, invites a notorious reactionary to come on a visit—a man who might even have been President of the United States a few years ago. Had he been, we would probably have had a global war by now. And on top of all that, he is to be received as an honored guest. Our ministers, with the Prime Minister in the lead, will sit politely chatting with him about the recession and the price of oil and assure him that good old neutral Sweden is still the same bulwark against communism it has always been. He'll be invited to a damned great banquet and be allowed to meet the so-called opposition, which has the same capitalist interests as the government, only slightly more honestly expressed. Then he'll have lunch with our half-witted puppet king. And all the time he has to be protected so goddamn carefully that presumably he won't be allowed to see a single demonstrator or even hear that there is any opposition, if Säpo or the CIA don't tell him. The only thing he'll notice is that the head of the Communist party isn't at the banquet."

"You're wrong there. All demonstrators are to be allowed within sight."

"If the government doesn't get scared and talk you out of it, yes. What can you do if the Prime Minister suddenly calls you up and says all the demonstrators are to be transported to Råsunda stadium and kept there?"

"Then I'll resign."

She looked at him for a long time, her chin resting on her drawn-up knees and her hands clasped around her ankles. Her hair was tangled after the sauna and shower and her irregular features were thoughtful.

He thought she looked beautiful.

Finally she said, "You're great, Martin. But you've got a hell of a job. What sort of people are they you get for murder and other horrors? Like the last one—some poor working slob who tried to hit back at the capitalist bastard who had destroyed his life. What'll he get?"

"Twelve years, probably."

"Twelve years," she said. "Well, I suppose it was worth it to him." She did not look happy.

Then she changed the subject, abruptly, as she often did.

"The kids are upstairs with Sara, so you can sleep without them jumping on your stomach. On the other hand, I may step on you when I go to bed."

It often happened that she went to bed after he had fallen asleep.

She changed tack again. "I hope you're aware that this highly honored guest has tens of thousands of lives on his conscience. He was one of the most active forces behind the strategic bombing in North Vietnam. And he was right in there even during the Korean War. He supported MacArthur when he wanted to drop atomic bombs on China."

Martin Beck nodded. "I know." Then he yawned.

"Go to bed now," she said firmly. "I'll bring you breakfast in the morning. What time shall I wake you?"

"Seven."

"Okay."

Martin Beck went to bed and fell asleep more or less instantaneously.

Rhea cleaned up in the kitchen, then went into the bedroom and kissed him on the forehead. He did not react at all. It was warm in the apartment and she took off her jersey, curled up in her favorite armchair and read for a while. She had difficulty sleeping and was often awake long into the small hours. At one time she had tried to cure her insomnia with red wine, but nowadays she made a virtue out of necessity and read a great number of boring papers and suchlike at nights.

Tonight she read a paper on character appraisal that she herself had written a few years earlier. When she finished it, she looked around and caught sight of Martin Beck's briefcase. Rhea Nielsen was inquisitive, mostly in a very straightforward way, so she opened it without much thought and began to study the papers, thoroughly and with interest, finally opening the file Gunvald Larsson had handed to Martin Beck just before he left. She examined the contents for a long time, with intense attention and not without a certain surprise.

At long last she put everything back into the briefcase and went to bed. She stepped on Martin Beck, but he was sleeping so soundly he didn't wake up.

Then she lay down close to him with her face turned toward his.

15.

The Army Museum in Stockholm was on Riddargatan in Östermalm, in the old barracks behind a spacious yard containing neatly kept and grouped old artillery pieces. It filled the whole block between Sibyllegatan and Artillerigatan. The nearest building was not very military: Hedvig Eleonora Church, which despite its fine dome was not one of the city's historic buildings, nor much to cheer about.

Nowadays there was not much to cheer about in the Army Museum either, especially since it had been revealed that part of the Security Service had been tucked away in the building, with the museum as an innocent front.

The heart of the museum was a great hall filled with ancient cannons and various old muskets, but it was not an interest in history that had brought the chief of the Homicide Squad on a visit.

A fat man was sitting at a desk in a small office studying a chess problem. It was an unusually difficult one, mate in five moves, and now and again he made a note in a shorthand notebook, which he then almost immediately crossed out again. There was a possibility that this was not what he was supposed to be doing, as on the table lay a dismembered pistol and beside his chair a wooden crate full of firearms, some of them with cardboard labels that carried no information at all.

The man with the chess problem was Lennart Kollberg, Martin Beck's closest colleague during many difficult years. He had said farewell to the police force about a year before, and his resignation had caused considerable uproar and some acid comment. The fact that one of the country's best policemen—a man with a solid position of command—had resigned because he could no longer stand being a policeman had not looked so good. Stig Malm had chased through the corridors like a dog with its tongue hanging out trying to carry out the Commissioner's order that the matter not be made public.

Naturally, it got out all the same, although the newspapers, by and large, found it no more remarkable that an old policeman should resign than that a sports journalist, satiated with travel, bribes and drink, should say to hell with it all and decide to spend his time with his children watching football on TV. For Martin Beck personally, it had been a misfortune, but he'd get over it. They seldom met privately, but even so a number of tankards had been raised in either Kollberg's apartment in Skårmarbrink or Martin Beck's in Köpmangatan.

"Hi," said Kollberg now, pleased to see Martin Beck but showing no overwhelming enthusiasm.

Martin Beck said nothing but thumped his old friend on the back.

"This is quite interesting," said Kollberg, nodding at the crate. "A heap of old pistols and revolvers, mostly from various police districts. A lot of people handed in funny old popguns when Parliament made those new laws on the possession of firearms. But the ones who voluntarily brought in their arsenals were, of course, those who'd never even considered trying to shoot with them. No one here has the time or the desire to go through the whole lot and catalogue them properly," said Kollberg. "But someone thought I'd do for the job, even if half the top brass in the police keep calling me a communist."

That someone had been right. Few people could rival Kollberg when it came to being systematic.

He pointed at the dismantled pistol. "Look at that, for instance. An automatic Russian Nagant, eleven millimeters and as old as the hills. I managed to get it apart, but now don't know how the hell I'm going to get it together again. And here . . ." He rummaged in the crate and picked out a gigantic old Colt revolver. "Have you ever seen the likes of this Peacemaker? Well looked-after, too. Åsa Torell kept one like that under her pillow after Stenström was killed. And she kept the safety catch off, for good measure."

"I've seen quite a lot of Åsa this summer," said Martin Beck. "She's with the Märsta force."

"With Märsta-Pärsta?" said Kollberg with a laugh.

"She and Benny did a good job on that murder in Rotebro."

"What murder in Rotebro?"

"Don't you read the newspapers?"

"Yes, but not that kind of thing. Benny? Every time I hear that slob's name, I'm reminded that he actually saved my life once. Of course, if he hadn't been such an idiot just beforehand, he wouldn't have *had* to."

"Benny's okay," said Martin Beck. "And Åsa's become a good policewoman."

"Well, well, the ways of the Lord are indeed strange."

Although Kollberg had left the church some years earlier, he not infrequently came out with religious quotations.

"You know," he went on, "I always thought you and Åsa would get together. It would have been a good solution, and she would have made you a good wife. And you were in love with her, too, though you would never admit it. On top of everything else, she was damned good-looking."

Martin Beck smiled and shook his head.

"What happened that time in Malmö, anyhow?" Kollberg asked. "You know the time I fixed you up with adjoining hotel rooms?"

"You'll probably never know," said Martin Beck. "How's Gun, for that matter?"

"Great. She loves working and gets more and more beautiful every day. And I really like looking after the kids sometimes. I've even learned to cook. Even better than before," he added modestly.

Suddenly his eye lit on something lying near the dismantled pistol, and his hand shot out. "Got it!" he said. "This pin. Have you ever seen such a helluva pin before? I knew I'd find it, of course. This pin is the key to the whole construction."

Like lightning, he assembled the firearm, consulted a large loose-leaf file full of stenciled pages, wrote out a card and put the pistol aside, after having tied a label to the trigger guard.

Martin Beck was not surprised. That was the way Kollberg usually functioned.

"Åsa Torell," mused Kollberg once again. "You would have made a lovely couple."

"Would you want to be married to a policewoman and sit and talk shop on your days off?"

Kollberg appeared to think this over. Then he made a typical gesture, sighing profoundly and shrugging his fat shoulders. "Maybe you're right," he said. "This new one's probably better for you. Rhea, I mean."

"You bet your life she is," said Martin Beck.

"But she talks so damn much," said Kollberg. "And

she's too broad-shouldered and she looks a little narrow in the hips. Doesn't she bleach her hair, too?"

He fell silent, suddenly aware that he might have hurt his old friend's feelings.

But Martin Beck smiled and said, "I could name some other people who talk too much and whose shoulders are maybe a little too broad, not to say chubby."

Kollberg hauled a large automatic out of the box, put it down on his chess problem and said, "Well, Martin, what is it you want? I don't suppose you came here to talk about girls."

"I wondered if you'd do a special little job for me."

"Paid?"

"Yes, for Christ's sake. I've a good budget. Almost unrestricted."

"What for?"

"Protection for this senator from the States who's coming on Thursday. I'm in charge of the security."

"You?"

"I was forced into it."

"And what do you want me to do?"

"Just read through these papers, plus one highly confidential document. Look at it and see if you can spot anything crazy."

"Isn't it crazy enough to invite the guy here?"

Martin Beck did not reply to the question, but said instead, "Will you do it?"

"Kollberg looked appraisingly at the bundle of photostats. "How quickly?" he asked.

"As quickly as possible."

"Okay," said Kollberg. "They say money doesn't smell, and anyway I can't believe the police's money stinks any worse than any other. But it'll probably take all night. What is it that's secret?"

"Here." Martin Beck took a folded document out

of his jacket pocket. "There isn't even a copy of this."

"Okay," said Kollberg. "I'll be here same time tomorrow morning."

"You're as punctual as a bailiff," said Kollberg on Tuesday morning. "I read it all. Twice. Took me all night."

Martin Beck took a long, narrow envelope out of his pocket and handed it over. Kollberg counted the money and whistled to himself.

"Well, it was worth a night's work. This means a night on the town at least, perhaps even this very evening."

"What did you find?"

"Nothing really. It's a good plan. But . . ."

"Well?"

"Well, if there's any point in trying to tell Möller anything, then you might draw his attention to the fact that he has two really difficult moments: when this bastard's standing on Logården with the King, and a less difficult situation when the Senator and the Prime Minister are laying that wreath."

"What else?"

"Nothing, as I said. I think that secret stuff seems a bit crazy. Wouldn't it be better to disguise Gunvald Larsson as a Christmas tree with an angel and the Stars and Stripes on top and put him up in Sveaplan? And let him stay there until Christmas?"

Kollberg placed the papers in a heap in front of Martin Beck, the most important on top, then took a very small revolver out of the box and added, "So that people would have time to get used to such a horrible and dreadful sight, as Malm would say?"

"Anything else?"

"Yes, tell Einar Rönn that he should never again try to express himself in writing, and that if he does, he simply mustn't let anyone else see what he has written. Or else he'll never get promoted."

"Mmm," said Martin Beck.

"Isn't this a pretty little thing," said Kollberg. "A little nickel-plated lady's revolver like American women used to carry in their purses or muffs at the turn of the century."

Martin Beck looked without interest at the nickel-plated firearm as he stuffed his papers into his briefcase.

"Maybe you could hit a cabbage with it at a range of ten inches, presuming that it stayed absolutely still," said Kollberg as he opened the little revolver with one swift movement.

"I've got to run," said Martin Beck. "Thanks for the help."

"Peace," said Kollberg. "Give my regards to Rhea if you like. Otherwise you don't even have to mention my name. That would be acceptable."

"So long, then."

"See you," said Lennart Kollberg, reaching for one of his index cards.

16.

Over the years, more than one person had wondered what it was that made Martin Beck such a good policeman. The question was discussed as eagerly by his superiors as by his subordinates, and was more often dictated by envy than by admiration.

The enviers were apt to point out that he had few cases, and most of them easy to solve. This was true, for the assignments he dealt with were few in comparison with what overwhelmed other departments of Stockholm's police. The Larceny, Narcotics and Violence divisions, for instance, had an enormous work load, and their percentage of solved cases was frighteningly low. A great many reports were simply never followed up and eventually just written off. The Stockholm chief and ultimately National Headquarters always produced the same explanation; shortage of manpower.

In fact, it wasn't easy to be a policeman in Stockholm, where various mobs and syndicates nowadays wreaked havoc quite freely, where drugs were plentiful and the simplest conflict often released insane violence on both sides. The National Commissioner and many others with him had persisted in the reorganization of the old local police system into a centrally directed, paramilitary force with frightening technical resources. The policeman's profession was a dreary one with little or no glamour attached to it, and many of its functions automatically produced hostility and unpopularity. Martin Beck's Homicide Squad, with its established and often exaggerated reputation of excitement and even romance, was an exception.

But Martin Beck had come up through the ranks, and had been a good policeman even when he began patrolling the Jakob precinct over thirty years before. He had always found it easy to talk to people; many problems were easy to solve with the aid of humor and intelligence, and the occasions when he had been compelled to use force could be counted on one hand.

Later on he had developed increasingly as an officer, often having to compromise with stupid superiors, but enduring both that and various inexplicable disciplinary decisions without great injury to his soul. On one point, however, he had always refused to compromise. He liked to work in the field, in direct contact with people and their surroundings.

Shortly after 1950, when he became a detective, he was transferred to the Homicide Squad. He had begun to study criminology and psychology on his own time, and the work in Homicide had interested him. Until the state takeover, he had had the good fortune to have understanding superiors and good colleagues. He had not lost his ability to talk to people and thus had become known as one of the best interrogators on the force.

Although Martin Beck himself had often demonstrated a brilliant and a highly deductive mind, these were not abilities he demanded either of himself or of his colleagues. In fact, if anyone had asked him what was most important to the profession, he would in all probability have replied, "a systematic mind, common sense, and conscientiousness," in that order.

Even if Martin Beck was largely in agreement with Lennart Kollberg about the role of police in society, resignation was unthinkable for him; he was simply too conscientious. His awareness of this caused him to think of himself as an almost painfully dreary figure, and he often got depressed. Things had been considerably better lately, but he was certainly no cheerful Charlie, and had no aspirations to become one.

Among the many characteristics that made Martin Beck an especially good policeman must be mentioned his good memory; his obstinacy, which was occasionally mulelike; and his capacity for logical thought. Another was that he usually found the time for everything that had anything to do with a case, even if this meant following up small details that later turned out to be of no significance. Occasionally these minute considerations led to important clues.

Once he had Lennart Kollberg's positive opinion of their overall plan, he left with a certain feeling of satisfaction, because Kollberg was still the one person he relied on most when it came to questions of policy. It had been a brief meeting and he suddenly decided to pay a call that he had contemplated for a long time but had not had time for until now. Actually, he really didn't have time for it now either, but the rest of the group ought to be quite capable of handling all the other more or less meaningless visits and telephone calls.

With only two days left until the great event, Martin Beck had been supplied with a special official car. It was green, and the policeman at the wheel was a civilian. He asked to be driven to David Bagaresgata, and five minutes later he was standing outside the door to Hedobald Braxén's office.

The bell did not work, so he knocked. A hollow voice called out, "Come in."

Braxén looked absently at Martin Beck, then pushed the blotter to one side of his gigantic desk.

"About six months ago, I testified on your behalf in a case against a girl named Rebecka Lind," said Martin Beck.

"Yes, that girl," said Crasher. "It was good of you to testify. Had a decisive influence."

Crasher was famous for calling curious witnesses. Among others, he had several times tried to get the National Commissioner to testify in cases that involved fighting between police and demonstrators, but naturally that had been unsuccessful.

"You also called a witness who didn't appear. A film director called Walter Petrus."

"Did I?"

"Yes," said Martin Beck, "you did."

"I remember now," he said. "That's quite right, but he was dead, I believe, or was prevented from coming in some other way."

"That's not quite right," said Martin Beck. "He was murdered, the day after."

"Really?" said Crasher.

"Why did you want him to give evidence?"

Crasher did not seem to have heard. After a while Martin Beck opened his mouth to repeat the question, but at that moment the other man raised his hand.

"You're quite right. Now I remember it all. I had intended to use him as a witness to the girl's character and general attitude. But he refused to appear."

"What was his connection with Rebecka Lind?"

"It was like this," said Braxén. "Shortly after Rebecka became pregnant, she saw a newspaper ad offering young girls of attractive appearance well-paid jobs with very good prospects. Her situation was desperate, so she answered the ad. She promptly received a letter instructing her to present herself at a certain address at a certain time. I've forgotten both time and address, but the letter was written on a film company's letterhead and signed by this Petrus. The company was called Petrus Films, I think. She still had the letter and it looked very respectable, printed letterhead and all that."

Braxén fell silent, got up, went over to the cats and poured out some more milk.

"Yes," said Martin Beck. "Then what happened?"

"A pretty typical story," said Crasher. "The address was an apartment that had obviously been used as a studio. When she got there, this Petrus was there with a photographer. Petrus said he was a film producer with international connections. Then he told her to undress. She did not think this all that remarkable, but she wanted to know what sort of film it was."

Braxén returned to his breakfast.

"Go on," said Martin Beck.

Crasher took a gulp from the cup. "According to Roberta, Petrus replied that it was an art film that was to be shown abroad, and that she would immediately receive five kronor if she undressed, so they could see if she would do. She did so, and they inspected her. The photographer said that she would perhaps do despite the difficulty of the part, but that her breasts were too meager and her nipples too small. Then Petrus said that they could stick on plastic nipples. Then the photographer said he would do a trial performance with her on the couch in the room, and he also began to undress. At that point she got scared and began to collect her clothes. They never touched her, but the photographer said that it would be just as well if Petrus told her what it was all about, because if she didn't want to sleep with him, she would never agree to act in the film. So Petrus told her there was nothing to worry about because the film was only going to be shown in sex clubs abroad, and all she had to do was copulate with a dog."

Braxén sat silent for a moment, then said, "There really are extraordinary ways of becoming a millionaire these days. Petrus described a lot of unpleasant things she was supposed to do. She was to be given two hundred and fifty kronor for the first film, but then there would be larger and better parts, he said. The girl . . . what's her name again?"

"Rebecka."

"That's it, Rebecka, yes. She began to get dressed and asked for her five kronor. Petrus said that had only been a joke. She spat in his face and they pushed her out of the apartment half naked, wearing nothing but her socks and sandals. They flung the rest of her clothes down the stairs, and since it was an ordinary apartment house, several people passed her as she was collecting her clothes and putting them on. She told me this while she was under arrest, and asked if it wasn't against the law to treat a person like that. I told her that unfortunately it wasn't. But I went to see this Petrus at his office. He was very haughty and said the whole trade was thick with crazy whores, but that it was in fact true that one of them had spat at him. I tried to get him to testify and he was sent a summons, but he never came. But she was released all the same." He shook his head gloomily.

"And Walter Petrus was killed," said Martin Beck.

"It's not legally justifiable to kill people, is it?" said Crasher. "And yet . . ." He broke off. "Has anything happened to Rebecka? Is that why you're here?"

"No, nothing's happened to her, as far as I know."

Braxén shook his head gloomily again. "I'm a bit worried about her," he said.

"Why?"

"She came here at the end of the summer. She's had difficulties over that American, the one who fathered her child. I tried to explain certain things to her and wrote a letter on her behalf. She finds it a bit difficult to understand this society of ours, and you can hardly blame her."

"What's her address?" asked Martin Beck.

"I don't know. When she was here, she had no permanent address."

"Are you sure?"

"Yes. When I asked her where she lived she said, 'Nowhere at the moment.' "

"She didn't give you any hint at all?"

"No, none at all. It was still summer then, and as far as I can make out, a lot of young people live together, either in the country or else with friends who happen to have an apartment in town."

Braxén pulled out one of his desk drawers and took out a thick notebook with a black cover and an alphabetical register in the margin. He must have had it a long time, because it was frayed with age and a great many thumbings.

He leafed through it and said, "What's her name again?"

"Rebecka Lind."

He found the right page and pulled his old telephone toward him. "We could try her parents."

One of the cats leaped onto Martin Beck's knee and he mechanically stroked the animal's back while trying to follow the telephone call. The cat at once began to purr.

Braxén put down the receiver. "That was her mother," he said. "Neither she nor her husband has heard anything from Rebecka since the trial in June. She also said that it was best that way, since no one in the family understood the girl."

"Nice parents," said Martin Beck.

"Yes, aren't they? Why are you so interested in her, anyhow?"

Martin Beck put the cat down on the floor, got up and went toward the door.

"I don't really know," he said. "But thanks for your help, anyhow. If she turns up, I'd appreciate it if you'd let me know, or at least tell her I'd like to talk to her."

17.

Reinhard Heydt, like Kollberg, thought that everything seemed to be ready. He had moved to a two-room apartment in Solna, acquired by the same front firm that had arranged the apartment in Södermalm.

The Japanese had stayed on in the other apartment. With extreme thoroughness, they had assembled their sophisticated bombs, and their next task was to place them in the selected places, as late as possible.

Long before the information was released to the press, Heydt had purchased all the details of the Senator's schedule, as well as most of the security plans, again from the double agent with the mysterious little firm in Östermalm.

The radio expert arrived slightly late. He was transported by a hired Danish fisherman from Gilleleje to the district of Torekov, passing under the very nose of the National Police Commissioner, who at that moment was pondering his responsibilities in solitude.

The man's name was Levallois and he was considerably more conversational than the two Japanese. He had, however, also brought some rather disturbing news. ULAG's weakness was its communications, which were as yet insufficiently developed; otherwise Heydt would probably have heard earlier. A leak had occurred somewhere, and the police had begun to gather up various bits of information into quite an interesting picture.

Heydt had been seen at the action in India and had also been observed leaving the country after the assassination in Latin America. Ever since, the police had stubbornly tried to establish some kind of identification by circulating through Interpol in Paris what meager information they had to practically every government with a serviceable police or security force.

The leak could not have come from within ULAG, but must have originated in one of the countries in which Heydt had previously been active as a guerrilla mercenary. In any case, they had finally linked his real name with his description. The police in Salisbury were still insisting they had no idea whatsoever who he was, which was probably true, but the authorities in Pretoria, who certainly did not know what he was doing, said that he was a South African citizen, that his name was Reinhard Heydt, that he had not been convicted of any crime in his native country and as far as they knew was not involved in any criminal activity.

Up to that point, the leak did not appear to be especially dangerous, but unfortunately just after that Frelimo in Mozambique, who had him on their blacklist, produced a photograph of him which was sufficiently good to be reproduced and sent out by Interpol. He was not wanted for any crime. Interpol merely stated that the police in the Latin American state were interested in speaking to him and in receiving any information on his present whereabouts.

Heydt silently cursed the occasion when he had been photographed. It had happened two years earlier—a singularly unfortunate accident. During a raid on Lourenço Marques, his group had been split up and he and several others had been taken prisoner by Frelimo guerrillas. They were released a few hours later, but meanwhile someone had photographed them. The photo in question must have been an enlargement of this picture, and if Interpol had sent it out, then the Swedish police would certainly have a copy. This did not, as far as he could make out, complicate the operation itself; but on the other hand, he could hardly leave the country as easily as he had slipped in.

One thing was clear. During the few remaining days, his freedom of movement would be severely limited; in fact he could hardly risk going out. Up to now he had been able to move around Stockholm unhindered, but his outings were over now. And if he absolutely had to go out, he would have to go armed. To be recognized and arrested by a Swedish policeman would have been an ignominious end to a promising career, even though it would not save the famous American's life. The operation was much too carefully doublechecked for that.

Heydt's first response was to get rid of the green Opel. He got Levallois to drive down to Gothenburg, abandon it and legally buy a used Volkswagen.

The apartment on Kapellgatan in Solna was a trifle too small for two people, especially with their two color televisions, three radios and all the Frenchman's technical equipment. They arranged it so that the larger room was used as an operations center, while they slept in the smaller.

Levallois was quite young, no more than twenty-two at the most, and his appearance did not betray his origins. He had a pinkish complexion and fair curly hair. Despite his delicate build, he was, like all those who had been through ULAG's training camps, very experienced in the arts of defending himself and of killing, with his bare hands as well as with a wide variety of weapons.

He had one handicap in Sweden, and that was the language, which was why on Monday the eighteenth Heydt had to get in the car and go into town for the last time before the operation. Levallois was a cautious type, and he had requested the components for a small generator just in case there happened to be a power failure in the middle of the ceremony.

Heydt put on his roomiest jacket, and those who saw him thought he looked unusually pleasant, strikingly tall and broad-shouldered—a Nordic type, blue-eyed and attractively suntanned—never dreaming that under his jacket he was carrying one of the deadliest weapons there is, a Colt revolver of the MK 111 Trooper 357 magnum type, and that he had three hand grenades hooked into his belt. Two of them were American, filled with plastic-covered barbed shafts with wide diffusion. The third grenade had been manufactured in ULAG's own arms workshops. It had a thread coupling with a drag ignition and was intended for his own use in a situation where all hope was gone.

But nothing disquieting happened. He bought four large car batteries and a number of incomprehensible technical items that were on Levallois's list, then returned to the apartment.

The Frenchman appeared satisfied and rapidly constructed the generator. Then he assembled a shortwave receiver and tuned it to the police wave band. They listened to routine messages, most of which Heydt managed to interpret with the aid of police codes he had also bought from the agent in Östermalm. Levallois understood nothing, but seemed satisfied all the same. He busied himself all evening and most of the following day making final adjustments and checking the detonating apparatus until at last he seemed content and announced that nothing could possibly go wrong.

Heydt meanwhile was wondering how they would be able to leave the country. His appearance and build were to some extent a disadvantage, as every form of disguise would be easily seen through.

On the evening of the nineteenth, he lay thinking for a long time in the bath. It would work out somehow; either he could smuggle himself out the same way Levallois had come in, or else he could stay and lie low in the apartment until police activity died down. Some border post could undoubtedly be forced, if he waited long enough. Perhaps there would be some violence, but violence was his specialty and he was firmly convinced that he was far superior to any Swedish policeman he might come up against.

He washed very thoroughly, cleaned his teeth, shaved, sprayed himself in appropriate places and groomed his blond sideburns with great care. Reinhard Heydt was particular about hygiene, so particular that it was almost a neurosis. Finally he massaged skin cream all over his body, spread a clean bathmat on the floor and went into the operations center, where Levallois was deep in an extremely technical book, all the while listening to the police radio, which he did not understand. Then he went to bed.

Heydt slept well and awoke full of confidence. He showered, then cooked a large English breakfast and ate it wearing his elegant bathrobe.

The Frenchman had risen earlier and had neglected to make his bed, which Heydt found slightly slovenly and interpreted as a sign of a none-too-high-class upbringing. Heydt found him in the operations room, the police radio still on and no fewer than three technical books open in front of him.

Levallois did not say good morning. With some reluctance, Heydt placed his hand on the Frenchman's shoulder. For some reason he disliked physical contact, except in certain obvious cases.

Levallois looked up.

"Everything okay?" Heydt asked him.

"Absolutely. Provided that Kaiten and Kamikaze adjust everything properly."

"You can rest easy. They know their job as well as you and I do, and they know the plans inside out. We've decided to do it in the early morning."

"And the risk of someone defusing the bombs? I suppose the police here have a bomb squad?"

"No, strangely enough, they don't. But don't forget that the police in that last place didn't find the reserve charges for several months. And they had bomb squads from both the army and the police, and they also knew where to look."

"Have we any reserve charges?"

"Two. They cover the two other possible routes the motorcade could take into town, if the security boys suddenly have a last-minute flash of intuition."

"The risk seems minimal," said Levallois. "The police never think that far ahead."

"I'm sure you're right. Besides, the other routes are fairly illogical and create a lot of new security problems."

"Well, then, nothing can really happen." The Frenchman yawned. "Everything's hunky-dory, here," he said. "And the Japs won't mess up the final assembling, will they?"

"Out of the question. They can move underground the whole way if they want to. And they've reconnoitered very thoroughly. They placed the mountings ten days ago and no one's found them."

"Sounds okay."

Levallois stretched and glanced around the room.

"The reserve source of power makes me feel much better," he said. "Supposing we were suddenly without current tomorrow. Just dandy."

"There've been no power failures since I've been here."

"That doesn't mean a thing," said the radio expert. "You only need one imbecile with a bulldozer to rip the cable apart somewhere and we've had it."

They listened for a while to the police radio.

"How are we going to get away?" said the Frenchman.

"What do you suggest?"

"Individually, as usual. I'll go direct, the same way I came."

"Mmm," said Heydt. "I'll probably have to wait a while."

Levallois looked relieved. He had no particular wish to die, and knew his chances of getting caught would be vastly increased if the South African suggested accompanying him in the fishing boat.

"How about a game of chess?" said the radioman after awhile.

"Okay."

Heydt played the Marshall variant in Sicilian, a brilliant game invented a long time ago by an American sea captain, who then transformed many a grand master of the time into a loser, gaping with astonishment. Bold moves, ruthless stakes, almost like war.

The only thing wrong with it was that you could catch out a good opponent only once. After that he'd look in an analysis book and learn the right moves, which on the board appeared quite incomprehensible.

They had no chess clock, and the Frenchman pondered longer and longer over his moves, watching his position being torn to shreds despite an early superiority in number of pieces. Finally Levallois sat thinking for an hour and a half over one move, although Heydt knew his opponent's situation was hopeless and had been so for a long time. Heydt went out to the kitchen, made some tea and then washed his arms, hands and face thoroughly. When he went back, the Frenchman was still sitting with his head in his hands, staring at the board.

Two moves later he had to give up.

His expression was offended, as he was a bad loser by nature and also had been taught never to lose. The only loss ULAG approved of was loss of life. In impossible situations, that was to be self-inflicted.

Levallois then sat without saying a word all afternoon, studying his technical books in sulky silence while the police radio continued to pour out messages.

Heydt had by now decided that this country wasn't much of a place to live in. But since he would evidently have to stay for quite a long time to come, he might just as well try to get used to it.

While the Japanese were placing the bombs that night, the one that mattered and the two less important ones, Reinhard Heydt was sleeping soundly and dreamlessly.

Levallois lay awake for some time, thinking about the chess game. When he got back to Copenhagen he would buy a good theory book, he decided.

The two Japanese were back in the apartment in Södermalm by about five in the morning. They were not planning to go out again for quite a while, and they had laid in a store of cans which ought to last them several weeks.

On the bed where Heydt had previously slept lay their machine pistols, loaded and ready to fire, with cleaned barrels and thoroughly inspected mechanisms. Lying next to them was a heap of loaded magazines. And beside the bed was a wooden box filled with adapted hand grenades.

The charges designed for their own final demise they carried on them, even when they slept.

18.

For Martin Beck it was a Wednesday he would remember for a long time. He was not used to this kind of job, with its endless telephone calls and constant arguments with people on different levels of the bureaucracy. He was the first to arrive at Kungsholmsgatan that morning and apparently the last to leave that night. Benny Skacke stuck it out as long as he could, but despite his relative youth, he was so pale and tired that Martin Beck chased him home.

"That's it for the day, Benny," he said.

But Skacke replied, "I'll stay as long as you do, as long as there's something left to be done."

He was as stubborn as a mule, and in the end Martin Beck had to do something he usually avoided, issue an authoritative and incontrovertible order in his capacity as superior officer.

"When I say you're to go home, then I mean that you're to obey a direct order. Do you understand? Go home. Now."

Skacke understood, and with a sulky expression hauled on his overcoat and left.

It had been a god-awful day. The Commissioner had

finished his meditative labors and was back again in top form. Via messengers he dispatched approximately forty-two documents of varying length and content. Most of them dealt with utterly obvious matters that had been arranged and dealt with long ago. In each paper, even if only two lines long, there was an undertone of reproach. He felt he was being insufficiently informed.

More direct comments were left to Stig Malm, who appeared tired and irritable, more or less crippled by his double role of watchdog at work and lapdog at home.

"Beck?"

"Yes."

"The Commissioner wonders why we're going to have only two helicopters in the air when we've got twelve of our own and can borrow more from the navy."

"We think two is enough."

"The Commissioner doesn't. He wants you to reconsider the helicopter question and preferably to consult naval staff on the matter."

"At the start, we'd thought of not using helicopters at all."

"That's absolutely insane. With our own and the navy's machines, we could have complete control of the airspace."

"Why should we have control of the airspace?"

"And if the air force had their way, we could have a squadron of fighter planes and an equal number of assault planes over the area."

"I've told the air force we can't stop them from flying."

"Of course we can't. But instead of establishing a decent relationship with the armed forces, you've deeply offended one of them. Now, will you reconsider the helicopter question?"

"We've already considered it."

"That's not an answer that'll please the Commissioner."

"It's not my assignment to please the Commissioner, at least not the way I see it."

Malm sighed heavily. "It's not easy being coordinator here," he said.

"So go out to your country place and think it all over."

"You . . . you really are the limit. Anyhow, I haven't got a country place."

"But your wife has one, doesn't she?"

Malm had married a fairly large fortune, but those who had met his wife said that she was not only bad-tempered and irritable, but also plain. Plainness was in the eye of the beholder, of course, but Martin Beck had had enough of bad temper and irritability in his eighteen years of married life. Now he felt almost sorry for Malm.

Martin Beck hardly had time to think this thought before the telephone shrilled again. It was the navy this time. Commander someone-or-other.

"I was just wondering whether you want the big Vertol helicopters or our smaller Alouettes. Perhaps a combined group of both? They each have their advantages."

"We don't want any airplanes at all."

"My dear Chief Inspector," the man said stiffly, "a helicopter is not an airplane, it's an aircraft."

"Thank you for the information. I'm sorry if I used the wrong terminology."

"Oh," said the naval man, "there are so many people

who get it wrong. So you don't want any naval helicopters."

"No."

"I got a different impression when I was speaking to the National Police Commissioner."

"There must have been some misunderstanding."

"I see. Goodbye, then, Inspector."

"Goodbye, Commander," said Martin Beck politely.

And it had been like that all day. Decisions had repeatedly been made over his head, then argued over and abandoned, usually by persuasion, sometimes with more brutal wording and tone of voice.

But now the whole plan was complete. Of all those who had been working at Kungsholmsgatan, Melander especially had worked tremendously hard, though quietly, as usual. The others hadn't been exactly idle, either. Rönn, for instance, had been detailed to an assignment that took a great deal of time. Only once during the day had he appeared at headquarters, noticeably red-nosed and with heavy bags under his eyes. Gunvald Larsson had at once said, "How's it going, Einar?"

"Oh, okay, I think. But it's taking longer than I thought it would. And tomorrow I won't have much time. At the most fifteen minutes."

"More like twelve or thirteen," said Gunvald Larsson.

"Oh, dear, oh, dear."

"Take care, Einar."

Martin Beck gazed after Rönn. Gunvald Larsson and Rönn, two totally different types, understood each other's smallest intimation. They were even friends, real friends. Martin Beck had always found it extremely difficult to work with Rönn, and it was out of the question that they should ever meet in their off-duty time or talk to each other about anything but work. He found it easier to work with Gunvald Larsson, despite his abrupt manner and often vulgar remarks. But they were not friends either, even if their relationship had improved over the years, after a very bad start.

The whole plan seemed all right, fairly low-key, much as Martin Beck had wanted it. There were to be a few men stationed on roofs with rifles, but not very many. Certain apartments and attics along the route were to be searched, but they were the exception.

Möller's close-range-security specialists should have an easy task. Of course, certain points were more sensitive than others: the Senator's arrival at the airport and his visit to the Royal Palace. Possibly the homage to the dead King, too, which was now to take place at Riddarholm Church. Gustaf VI Adolf's tomb was not there of course, but the church was centrally located and ideal from a security point of view. Also, most of the other kings of Sweden were buried there, so what the hell.

Naturally this involved certain changes in the timetable, but they were easily accommodated.

All the proposed activities of the distinguished visitor had already been reported in the newspapers, which had managed to dig out the minutest details. There was a certain amount of criticism in the press, but so far no one had actually attacked the police.

At ten past eleven, Martin Beck switched out the lights in all the rooms and locked the doors to the corridor, with an unpleasant sense of having neglected something, though quite what he did not know.

He didn't want to spend the night alone, so he went back to Rhea's. She usually had a kind of open house for her tenants and others on Wednesday evenings, and he felt a great need to talk to people whose thoughts were not forever circling around police cordons, specially trained sharpshooters, helicopters and highly improbable bombs. Since his own driver was off duty that day, he begged a lift in a patrol car and asked the driver to stop in Frejgatan, around the corner from Rhea's block.

Four minutes after Martin Block left headquarters, Gunvald Larsson rode up in the elevator. He unlocked the doors and switched on his desk light, noticing the bulb was still warm.

Beck, he thought. Who else?

He was wet and his hair was mussed. Outside the windows, gangs, thieves, robbers, drunks and junkies reigned over the darkness, the cold and the rain.

Gunvald Larsson was tired. He had not slept the previous night but had lain awake thinking about ULAG, flying presidential heads and such. Then he had missed both lunch and dinner, and for hours, mostly out of doors, had been working with Einar Rönn, who was very much in need of a helping hand. Gunvald Larsson had a formidable constitution, physically and mentally, but it could not stand up to absolutely anything.

They had an electric percolator in the offices and he kept sugar and a few teabags in one of his desk drawers. He poured water into the coffee pot, plugged it in and waited. Since childhood he had known that the use of teabags was about as tasteful as putting condoms in the teapot, but here he had no choice in the matter.

When the tea was more or less as brewed as it could be, he took his private cup out of his desk—the others used plastic cups—then sat down at his desk and at once took several large hot gulps to warm himself up. Then he took all his papers out of his briefcase and began to read. He was in a bad mood, frowning heavily, a wedge of flesh forming above his nose. After a while even his blond eyebrows were furrowed, too.

Something was bound to go wrong, he was sure.

But what?

He fetched Säpo's close-range-security plans from Melander's desk. They were almost illegible because of the myriads of abbreviations in the text, but all the same he worked his way through it page by page, studying the appended tables and sketches thoroughly.

Like the others in the group, he had to admit that the plan seemed unassailable. Eric Möller was a specialist and his assessments correct. Close-range security was an easier game anyhow.

The surveillance of what Möller called "sensitive areas" was to begin at midnight. Gunvald Larsson looked at the clock on the wall. Nine minutes to twelve, so some of the four hundred security police mentioned in the text would now be on their way out to get wet.

He put the papers aside and went on to think about long-range protection. Logården was a suitable spot not only for Möller; the King and this damned American would both be standing there as if on a platform, exposed to expert long-distance snipers from both Blasieholmen and Skeppsholmen, not to mention the boats on Strömmen and along the quays.

But was there really any cause for alarm? The five thinkers—that was to say, himself, Beck, Melander, Rönn and Skacke—had recognized all these dangers long ago. The bridge over to Skeppsholmen had been blocked some hours ago, and the buildings along Blasieholm quay had been rigorously checked, especially the Grand Hotel, which had a great many windows.

Gunvald Larsson sighed and leafed aimlessly through the papers. The sewers and other tunnels under Logården were few and easy to check, provided people either had good rubber coveralls or else did not mind their clothes being ruined.

The clock on the wall clicked. Twelve exactly.

He looked at his own chronograph. The wall clock was wrong as usual, one minute twenty-three seconds slow, to be precise. He got up to put it right.

At that moment, there was a knock on the door.

The members of the group never knocked, so it had to be someone else.

"Come in," said Gunvald Larsson.

A girl came into the room. Well, a woman. She looked to be somewhere between twenty-three and thirty.

After a hesitant look at Gunvald Larsson, she said, "Hi."

"Good evening," said Gunvald Larsson with great reserve. He was standing with his back to his desk, his arms folded. "What can I do for you?"

"I recognize you, of course," she said. "You're Gunvald Larsson from the Violence Division."

He said nothing.

"But you probably don't recognize me."

Gunvald Larsson looked at her. She had ash-blond hair, blue eyes and regular features. Quite tall, five ten or so, quite good-looking, simply and carefully dressed in a gray polo shirt, well-pressed blue slacks and low-heeled shoes. She looked too calm to have anything up her sleeve, but he was almost certain he had never seen her before. He frowned and stared at her with his china-blue eyes.

"My name's Ruth Salmonsson," she informed him. "I work here. In the Investigation Bureau."

"As what?"

"Police assistant," she said. "I'm on duty now. That is, I'm just having a break."

Gunvald Larsson remembered his tea, half turned and swallowed it down in one gulp.

"Do you want to see my card?" she asked.

"Yes."

She took her identity card out of the right-hand back pocket of her slacks and handed it to him. Gunvald Larsson studied it carefully. Twenty-five. That might well be right. He handed it back to her.

"What is it you want?"

"I know you're working on this special job under Chief Inspector Beck, the Stockholm chief and the National Commissioner."

"Beck will do. Where did you hear that?"

"Oh, you know what a lot of talk there is around here. And . . ."

"And what?"

"Well, they say that you're looking for a certain person, whose name I'm not sure about. But I've heard the description."

"Where?"

"In the Identification Department. I've a friend working there."

"If you've got anything to say, then let's have it," said Gunvald Larsson.

"Won't you ask me to sit down?"

"No, I hadn't thought I would. What's it about?"

"Well, a few weeks ago—"

"When?" interrupted Gunvald Larsson. "I'm only interested in facts."

She looked resignedly at him. "It was in actual fact Monday, the fourth of November."

Gunvald Larsson nodded encouragingly. "What happened on Monday the fourth?"

"Well, a friend of mine and I had agreed to go out dancing. We went to the Amarante—"

Gunvald Larsson interrupted her at once. "The Amarante? Can you dance there?"

She did not reply.

"Do they have dancing at the Amarante?" he repeated.

She suddenly seemed timid and shook her head.

"What did you and your friend do then?"

"We . . . we went into the bar."

"Together?"

"No."

"What happened then?"

"I met a Danish businessman, who said his name was Jörgensen."

"Uh-huh. And then?"

"Then we went back to my place."

"Uh-huh. And what happened there?"

"What do you think?"

"I never have preconceived ideas," said Gunvald Larsson. "Especially about other people's private lives."

She bit her lip. "We were together," she said defiantly. "Slept with each other, to put it nicely. Then he left and I've never seen him again."

A vein in Gunvald Larsson's right temple swelled. He walked around the desk and sat down. Then he thumped his right fist on the top of the desk so hard that the electric wall clock stopped, at the wrong time what's more—one minute, thirty-three seconds slow.

"What kind of goddamn joke is this?" he said angrily. "What do you want me to do? Put up notices about the police providing free broads, who can be found in the bar at the Amarante? What are your hours? Mondays from five to eleven, say?"

"I must say I didn't expect such a rigid and old-fashioned attitude," she said. "I'm twenty-five, unmarried and childless, and at the moment wish to remain so."

"Twenty-five?"

"And unmarried and childless," she said. "Are you trying to tell me I have no right to a sex life of my own?"

"No," said Gunvald Larsson. "Of course you do. As long as I'm not mixed up in it."

"I think I can guarantee that you won't be."

Gunvald Larsson caught the sarcasm and again struck the desk with his fist, this time so hard that it hurt all the way to his elbow. He grimaced.

"Female cops who sit in hotel bars and pick up men," he said. "And then come around to bullshit about Danes."

He looked at the stopped clock and then at his watch. "Coffee break must be over now," he said. "Out!"

"I came here to try to be useful," she said. "But that's obviously a waste of time."

"Obviously."

"So I won't tell you the rest."

"I'm not interested in pornography."

"Neither am I," she said.

"What's the rest then?"

"I liked this guy," she said. "He was educated and pleasant, and good in other ways." She looked coldly at Gunvald Larsson. "Remarkably good, even."

Gunvald Larsson said nothing.

"Then ten days later I telephoned the hotel where he said he was staying."

"Oh?" said Gunvald Larsson.

"Yes, and the receptionist said there was no guest by that name staying in the hotel and there never had been."

"Extremely interesting. He probably goes around testing out police girls in different countries for some kind of sexual report. It'll probably be a best-seller. Have you made sure you'll get a cut?"

"You're absolutely impossible," she said.

"You think so?" said Gunvald Larsson politely.

"Anyhow, I met my friend yesterday. She spoke to him for a while, you see, before we went back to my place."

"And where do you live?"

"Twenty-seven Karlavägen."

"Thank you. If I get an address book for Christmas, I'll write it in."

She began to look angry then, and obstinate.

"But I won't get one," said Gunvald Larsson conversationally. "I buy all my Christmas presents myself."

"My friend worked in Denmark for several years and she said that if he was Danish, then he was from a very strange part of the country. She said his Danish was the kind that was spoken at the turn of the century."

"And how old is your friend?"

"Twenty-eight."

"And what does she do?"

"She's studying Scandinavian languages at the university."

Gunvald Larsson mistrusted many things in this world, and one of them was a university education. But now he was beginning to look slightly thoughtful.

"Go on," he said.

"Today I looked into the aliens register and checked. The name isn't there either."

"What did you say his name was?"

"Reinhard Jörgensen."

Gunvald Larsson rose and went over to Melander's desk. "And what did he look like?"

"Much like you, though twenty years younger. And he had sideburns."

"Was he as tall as I am, for instance?"

"Almost, anyhow. But he certainly weighed less."

"Not many people are as tall as I am."

"He may have been a few inches shorter."

"And he said his name was Reinhard?"

"Yes."

"Had he any special identifying marks?"

"No. That is, he was very sunburnt, except . . ."

"Except?"

"Except in places where men aren't usually sunburnt."

"And he spoke Danish?"

"Yes. I thought it sounded pretty authentic. Until my friend brought it up."

Gunvald Larsson had taken a brown envelope out of one of Melander's letter trays. He weighed it in his hand for a moment and then took out a seven-by-ten photograph. He handed it to Ruth Salomonsson.

"Did he look like this?"

"Yes, that's him, but that's about two years old, I'd say. At least."

She peered more closely at the photograph. "Bad quality," she said.

"It's an enlargement extracted from a group photograph on a small negative."

"Anyhow, that's him all right. I'm certain of it. What's his real name?"

"Reinhard Heydt. He seems to be South African. What did he say he was doing here?"

"Business. Buying and selling some complicated machinery of some kind."

"And you met him on the fourth in the evening?"

"Yes."

"Was he alone?"

"Yes."

"When did you last see him?"

"The next morning, at about six o'clock."

"Did he have a car?"
"Not with him, anyhow."
"Where did he say he was staying?"
"The Grand."
"Do you know anything else?"
"No, nothing whatsoever."
"Okay. Thanks for coming," said Larsson, more kindly now.
"Don't mention it."
"I said one or two ill-considered things before."
"All that about free broads and so on?" she said, smiling.
"No," said Gunvald Larsson. "About women police. We need a lot more."
"My coffee break is definitely over now," she said, turning to go.
"Just a moment," said Gunvald Larsson. He tapped the photograph with his knuckles. "This guy's dangerous."
"To whom?"
"Everyone. Anyone. You should let us know if you ever catch sight of him again."
"Has he killed anyone?"
"Many people," said Gunvald Larsson. "Far too many."

In the end, Martin Beck had quite a pleasant evening. There were already seven or eight people around the kitchen table when he arrived, and he had met some of them before.
Among them was a young man named Kent, who a few years ago had said that he was thinking of joining the police. Martin Beck had not seen him since and asked him how he'd made out.

"At the Police College?"

"Yes."

"I got in, but halfway through the term I had to leave. It was an absolute madhouse."

"What are you doing now?"

"Sanitation Department. A garbage man. It's a hell of an improvement."

As was usual around Rhea's kitchen table, the conversation was lively and fluent, moving from one subject to another. Martin Beck sat relaxing in silence, now and again sipping at his wine. He had decided to have no more than one glass. Only once was the notorious Senator mentioned. Some were thinking of demonstrating, others satisfied with grumbling at the government. Then Rhea began talking about Gascony fish soup and lobsters and Brittany, thus putting an end to political arguments.

She was to go away on Sunday, to a sister who was constantly in need of help of one kind or another.

At one o'clock she shooed out all her guests, except Martin Beck, of course, who hardly counted as a guest any longer.

"You'll be absolutely pooped tomorrow if you don't go to bed at once," she said.

She also went to bed at once, but half an hour later she had to get up again and go out to the kitchen. Martin Beck heard her clattering about at the stove, but was too tired to be able to think about *au gratin* ham sandwiches with parmesan, so he stayed where he was.

She came back a little later, thumped about in the bed for a while and then snuggled up close to him. She was warm, her skin soft and covered with almost invisible short fair hairs.

"Martin?" she said softly, testing to see if he was awake.

"Mmm."

"I have to tell you something."

"Mmm."

"When you were here last Thursday, you were very tired and went to bed before me. I read for an hour or two. But you know how damned inquisitive I am, so I opened your briefcase and looked through your papers."

"Mmm."

"There was a file with a photograph in it of someone named Reinhard Heydt."

"Mmm."

"I thought of something that might be important."

"Mmm."

"I saw that guy about three weeks ago. A large, blond man about thirty. We bumped into each other by chance when I was up at your place in Köpmangatan. Then we walked through Bollhus Alley. He was only two steps behind me, so I let him pass. He was a Nordic-European type and I thought he was a tourist, because he had a map of Stockholm in one hand. He had side-burns. Blond ones."

Martin Beck was immediately wide awake. "Did he say anything?"

"No, nothing. He just walked past. But a few minutes later I saw him again. He was getting into a green car with Swedish plates. I'm bad on cars and don't know what make it was. I must have looked rather specially at the letters though, on the plates because I remember they were GOZ, but I forgot the numbers. I'm not sure I even saw them. I've got a bad memory for figures, anyhow."

Martin Beck was at the phone dialing Larsson's number in Bollmora before Rhea even got her legs out of bed.

"New world speed record out of beloved's bed," she said.

Martin Beck waited impatiently while the number rang twelve times. No one answered.

He hung up and called up the central exchange.

"Do you know if Gunvald Larsson's in the building?"

"He was here ten minutes ago."

Martin Beck asked to be connected to the Violence Division. The phone was answered immediately.

"Larsson here."

"Heydt's in town."

"Yes," said Gunvald Larsson, "I just heard. A woman police assistant in the Investigation Bureau had the good taste to sleep with him on the night of the fourth. She seems certain it was him. He made out he was Danish. Nice guy, she said. Spoke a kind of Scandinavian."

"I've got a witness, too," said Martin Beck, "a woman who saw him in Köpmangatan in the Old City about three weeks ago. She saw him getting into a car with Swedish plates in Slottsbacken and she thinks he drove south."

"Your witness," said Gunvald Larsson, "does she seem reliable?"

"The most reliable person I know."

"Oh-ho, yes." Gunvald Larsson was silent for a moment. "The bastard," he said. "He's beaten us and we don't have any time. What do we do?"

"We have to think," said Martin Beck. "If you'll send a patrol car, I'll be with you in twenty minutes."

"Shall I alert Skacke and Melander?"

"No, let them sleep. Someone has to be rested tomorrow. How are you feeling yourself?"

"I was dead beat a moment ago, but I'm ready to go again now."

"Same here."

"Mmm," said Gunvald Larsson. "I don't think we're going to get much sleep tonight."

"It can't be helped. If we can get Heydt, a lot of risks will be eliminated."

Martin Beck hung up and began to get dressed.

"He's that important?" asked Rhea.

"Vitally. Bye, and thanks for this and that. See you tomorrow evening? At my place?"

"Sure," she said cheerfully. She had planned to go there anyhow to watch the news coverage of the event on Martin Beck's color television.

After he'd gone, she lay there thinking for a long time. She had been in a good mood a minute or two before, but now she was feeling depressed.

Rhea was exceptionally intuitive, and she did not like the situation.

19.

Gunvald Larsson and Martin Beck spent the early hours of the morning thinking intensely, but unfortunately they were handicapped by self-reproach, humiliation and deadly fatigue. Both realized that they were no longer young.

Heydt had entered the country despite all their rigorous precautionary measures. It seemed logical that the rest of the sabotage group were also in Stockholm and had been there for quite some time, since it was highly unlikely that Heydt would be alone.

They knew quite a lot about Reinhard Heydt, but

they had no idea where he was and could only guess at what he was going to do. Worst of all, they had no time to find out.

He had at his disposal a green car of unknown make with Swedish plates, possibly with the letters GOZ. Where had he got the car? Stolen it? That seemed an unnecessary risk to have taken, and Heydt was probably not a man to take unnecessary risks. Nevertheless, as soon as possible they checked up on all reports of stolen cars. None matched.

He might also have bought or rented it, but to check all those possibilities would take days, perhaps weeks. They had only a few hours, and during those hours, their quiet offices were to be transformed into a scene of sheer chaos.

Skacke and Melander arrived at seven, listened with gloomy faces to this new development, then set to work on their telephones. But it was all much too late, because in the tracks of messengers came a veritable torrent of people who now suddenly considered their presence highly necessary. The National Commissioner arrived followed closely by Stig Malm, the chief of the Stockholm Police and the chief of the Regular Police. Soon after that Bulldozer Olsson brought his beaming visage into the office, and then came a representative of the Fire Brigade, whom no one had invited; two police superintendents, who as far as could be made out were simply curious; and to crown everything, a government secretary sent by the cabinet, apparently as some kind of observer.

For a brief moment, Eric Möller's unique wreath of hair could be glimpsed in the crowd, but by then everyone had given up hope of being able to do anything properly at all.

Gunvald Larsson realized quite early on that he

would never get back home to Bollmora to shower and change. And if Martin Beck had similar plans, they were soon spiked by the fact that from half-past eight on he was forced to talk on the telephone without a break, mostly to people who had extremely peripheral connections with the Senator's visit.

In the general uproar, a couple of accredited crime reporters also managed to get into headquarters, where they were trying to collect some tidbits of news. These journalists were considered to have favorable attitudes toward the police, and everyone shied away from the very thought of offending them in any way. With one of the reporters no more than a few feet away, the Commissioner turned to Martin Beck and asked, "Where's Einar Rönn?"

"Don't know," lied Martin Beck.

"What's he doing?"

"Don't know that, either," said Martin Beck, if possible even less truthfully.

As he tried to elbow his way away, he heard the Commissioner muttering to himself: "Remarkable. Remarkable way of assuming command."

Shortly after ten, Rönn telephoned, and after a great many ifs and buts managed to get hold of Gunvald Larsson.

"Hi, it's Einar."

"Is everything ready now?"

"Yes, I think so."

"Good, Einar. You must be beat."

"Yes, I must admit I am. And what about you?"

"About as bright as a slaughtered pig," said Gunvald Larsson. "I never got to bed last night."

"I've had about two hours' sleep."

"Better than nothing. Be careful as hell now, won't you?"

"Yes. You too."

Gunvald Larsson said nothing to Rönn about Heydt, partly because far too many outsiders were within earshot, but also because the information would only have served to make Rönn even more nervous than he was already.

Gunvald Larsson pushed his way over to the window, demonstratively turning his back on the others, and stared out. All he could see was the new police superheadquarters under construction and a tiny sliver of a gray and dismal sky. The weather was about what could be expected: temperature about freezing point, a northeasterly wind and repeated showers of sleet. Not especially encouraging for the gigantic number of police on duty out of doors, but hardly encouraging for demonstrators, either.

By half-past ten, Martin Beck had managed to extract his three remaining colleagues from the melée and pilot them into one of the nearby rooms, where Gunvald Larsson at once locked the door and took all the telephone receivers off their hooks.

Martin Beck made a very short statement:

"Only the four of us know that Reinhard Heydt is in town, and that in all likelihood a complete trained terrorist group is also here. Do any of you think that these facts should in any way alter our plans?"

No one replied, until Melander took his pipe out of his mouth and said, "As far as I can see, this is the very situation we always figured on. So I can't see why we should revise our plan at this stage."

"What sort of risk are Rönn and his men running?" asked Skacke.

"A pretty considerable one," said Martin Beck. "That's my personal view."

Only Gunvald Larsson said something off the point.

"If this goddamn Heydt or any of his gang get out of this country alive, I'll take it as a personal defeat. Whether they blow this American to pieces or not."

"Or shoot him," said Skacke.

"It should be impossible to shoot him," said Melander placidly. "All the long-range security is designed to prevent precisely that. On the occasions when he appears outside the bulletproof car, he will have a strong protective guard of policemen with automatics and bulletproof protection. All the areas concerned have been searched continually according to the plan since midnight last night."

"And at the banquet this evening?" said Gunvald Larsson suddenly. "Are they serving the bastard champagne in bulletproof glasses?"

Only Martin Beck laughed, not loudly, but heartily, and was himself surprised that he could laugh in such a situation.

Melander said patiently, "The banquet is Möller's business. If I've got the plan right, then practically every person on duty at Stallmästaregården this evening will be an armed security man."

"And the food?" said Gunvald Larsson. "Is Möller going to cook it himself?"

"The chef and cooks are reliable and will also be searched and carefully supervised."

There was a moment's silence. Melander puffed on his pipe, Gunvald Larsson opened the window, letting in the icy wind plus a little rain and snow and the normal dose of oil specks and industrial fumes.

"I have one more question," said Martin Beck. "Do any of you think we ought to warn the chief of Security that Heydt, and probably also ULAG, are in Stockholm?"

Gunvald Larsson spat contemptuously out the window.

Again it was Melander who provided a logical summary.

"Getting that information at the last moment won't alter Eric Möller's or the close-range security plans for the better, will it? Probably the other way around; there might be confusion and contradictory orders. The close-range-protection people are already organized and quite aware of their task."

"Okay," said Martin Beck. "As you know, there are a few details—more than a few—that only we four and Rönn have the slightest idea about. If things go wrong, we'll be the ones to bear the brunt."

"I've no objection to that," said Skacke.

Gunvald Larsson again spat contemptuously out the window.

Melander nodded to himself. He had been a policeman for thirty-four years and would soon be fifty-five. He had quite a lot to lose by suspension or possible dismissal.

"No," he said finally. "I can't say like Benny that I've no objection. But I'm prepared to take calculated risks. This is one."

Gunvald Larsson looked at his watch. Martin Beck followed his glance and said, "Yes, it'll soon be time."

"Shall we stick strictly to the plan?" Gunvald Larsson asked.

"Yes, as long as the situation doesn't suddenly change in some dramatic way. I'll leave that to your own judgment."

Skacke nodded. Martin Beck said, "Gunvald and I will take one of the really fast police cars, a Porsche, because we'll have to be able to pass along the motorcade quickly, and even swing back if necessary."

There were no more than half a dozen of those black-and-white miracles of speed.

"You two, Benny and Fredrik, go in the radio vans. Place yourselves at the head of the motorcade, between the motorcycle escort and the bulletproof limousine. There you'll have a chance to follow both radio and television, and also to check with our own radio. Apart from the driver, you've also got a radio location expert who's supposed to be tops."

"Good," said Melander.

They returned to their own base, where there was now no one but the chief of the Stockholm Police. He was standing in front of the mirror combing his hair with great care. Then he eyed his tie, which as usual was of plain colored silk. Today it was pale yellow.

The telephone rang. Skacke answered. After a brief, incomprehensible conversation, he put down the receiver and said, "That was Säpo-Möller. He was expressing his surprise."

"Get a move on, Benny," said Martin Beck.

"He was astounded that one of his own men was on the commando section list."

"What the hell's the commando section?" said Gunvald Larsson.

"The man's name is Victor Paulsson. It seems Möller was here this morning and snatched the SC list. He says he needed the group for an important close-range-security assignment. He simply placed his man Paulsson on the list, so from now on it's under his command."

"By all the gods and saints in hell!" cried Gunvald Larsson. "No, it just goddamn can't be true! He's pinched the idiot list! The clod squad. The tic-tac-toe players! The ones who were to be confined to station duty!"

"Well, he's got them now," said Skacke. "And he

didn't say where he was calling from."

"You mean he thought your abbreviation for 'clod squad' stood for 'commando section,'" said Martin Beck.

"No!" said Gunvald Larsson, thumping his forehead with his fist. "It just can't be! Did he say what he wanted to use them for?"

"Just that it was an important assignment."

"Like guarding the King?"

"If it concerns the King, then we've still got time to fix it," said Martin Beck. "Otherwise . . ."

"Otherwise we can't do a damned thing," said Gunvald Larsson, "because now we must go. Hell's blasted bells! Goddammit!"

When they were in the car and driving through town, he added, "It was my own fault. Why didn't I write it out—IDIOT LIST? Why didn't I lock it up in my desk?"

The escort vehicles went separately to the airport. Gunvald Larsson chose to take the route via Kungsgatan and Sveavägen to get an overall view. There were a great many uniformed police about, as well as many in civilian clothes, mostly detectives and police officers from the country. Behind them were already a number of demonstrators with placards and banners, and an even larger number of ordinary curious spectators.

On the edge of the sidewalk in front of the Rialto movie house, opposite the city library, stood a person whom Martin Beck knew well and whose presence astonished him. The man was not large for a policeman, and had a weatherbeaten face and short bowlegs. He was wearing a duffle coat and gray-brown-green-striped tapering trousers, the bottoms tucked into long green rubber boots. On the back of his head perched a safari hat of indefinite color. No one would have guessed he was a policeman.

"Stop a moment, will you?" said Martin Beck. "By that guy in the lion-hunter's hat."

"Who is it?" said Gunvald Larsson, braking. "A secret agent, or chief of the Korpilombolo Security Service?"

"His name is Content," said Martin Beck. "Herrgott Content. He's a police inspector in Anderslöv, a place between Malmö and Ystad in the Trelleborg police district. What the hell is he doing here?"

"Maybe he's planning to hunt moose in Humlegården," said Gunvald Larsson, stopping the car.

Martin Beck opened the door and said, "Herrgott?"

Content looked at him in astonishment. Then he snatched at the brim of his safari hat, so that it came right down over one of his lively eyes.

"What are you doing here, Herrgott?"

"Don't know, really. I was flown up early this morning in a charter plane full of policemen from Malmö, Ystad, Lund and Trelleborg. Then they put me here. I don't even know where I am."

"You're at the corner of Odengatan and Sveavägen," said Martin Beck. "The escort's coming this way, if all goes well."

"A moment ago a drunk came along and asked me to go to the liquor store for him. I suppose he's been shut off. I must look like a real yokel."

"You look in top form," said Martin Beck.

"Lord save us, what weather!" said Content. "And what a grisly place."

"Are you armed?"

"Yes, had orders to be." He loosened his coat and revealed a large revolver clipped to the belt of his trousers, just as Gunvald Larsson liked to wear his, though he preferred an automatic.

"Are you boss of this circus?" said Content.

Martin Beck nodded and said, "And what happens in Anderslöv when you're away."

"Oh, it'll be okay. Evert Johansson's taken over, and everyone knows I'm coming back the day after tomorrow, so no one will dare do anything. Anyhow, nothing happens in Anderslöv since that business a year ago. When you were there."

"You treated me to a fantastic dinner," said Martin Beck. "Would you like to have dinner with me this evening?"

"That time we hunted pheasants?" Content laughed, then answered the questions. "Yes, I would. It's just that I keep getting lots of peculiar orders. I'm supposed to sleep in some empty house, with seventeen others. Quarters, they said. Dear Lord, I don't know."

"It'll be okay," said Martin Beck. "I'll have a word with the chief of the Regular Police. At the moment he's actually my subordinate. You've got my number and address, haven't you?"

"Yep," said Content, patting one of his back pockets. "Who's that guy in there?" He peered inquisitively at Gunvald Larsson, who did not react at all.

"His name's Gunvald Larsson. He usually works in the Violence Division."

"Poor devil," said Content. "I've heard about him. What a job. Very big man for such a small car, by the way. Herrgott Content's my name. It's a silly name, but I've gotten used to it, and at home in Anderslöv no one laughs anymore."

"We have to go now," said Gunvald Larsson.

"Okay," said Martin Beck. "Then we'll see you at

my place tonight. If there's any mix-up, we'll call each other."

"Great," said Content. "But do you think anything special will happen?"

"It's pretty certain that something will happen, but it's hard to say just what."

"Mmm," said Content. "I just hope it doesn't happen to me."

They said their farewells and drove off. Gunvald Larsson drove fast; the car was made for high speeds.

"He seemed okay," Gunvald Larsson commented. "I didn't think there were any cops like him left."

"We've got one or two. But not many."

At Norrtull, Martin Beck said, "Where's Rönn?"

"Well hidden. But I'm a bit worried about him."

"Rönn's okay," said Martin Beck.

The whole route was lined with policemen, and beyond them, spread along the route, were what the police calculated to be ten thousand demonstrators, a figure which was probably a gross underestimate. Thirty thousand was more likely.

As they drove up to the foreign-arrivals building they saw the plane, just about to land.

The operation had begun.

Over the police radio, they heard a metallic voice: "All radio units are to observe signal Q from now on. I repeat: Signal Q to be observed until counterorders given. Only instructions from Chief Inspector Beck will be forwarded. They are not to be answered."

Signal Q was highly unusual. It involved total silence on the police radio.

"Hell, I didn't have time to shower or change," said Gunvald Larsson. "That's that damned Heydt's fault."

Martin Beck glanced over at his colleague and noticed that Gunvald Larsson nevertheless looked considerably better than he did himself.

Gunvald Larsson parked outside the terminal. The plane was not quite down yet. Despite everything that had happened, they had plenty of time. At least several minutes.

20.

The shining aluminum jet landed twelve minutes and thirty-seven seconds early. Then it taxied over to the place that Eric Möller had personally designated as not dangerous.

The mechanical steps were lowered and, still twelve minutes, thirty-seven seconds ahead of schedule, the Senator stepped out of the cabin. He was a tall, sunburnt man with a winning smile and sparkling white teeth.

He looked around the desolate airfield and scrubby forest surrounding it. Then he raised his white ten-gallon hat and waved gaily at the demonstrators and policemen on the spectator's terrace.

Maybe his sight's bad, thought Gunvald Larsson, and he thinks it says "Long Live the Next President" on the placards and banners, instead of "Yankee Go Home" and "Motherfucking Murderer." Maybe he thinks those portraits of Mao and Lenin are pictures of himself, although the likeness isn't especially great.

The Senator descended from the plane and, still smiling, shook hands with the airport chief and a governmental secretary. Behind him on the steps was a large bulky man in a wide checked overcoat. His face seemed hewn from granite, and out of this granite face stuck a huge cigar that looked almost like an extra limb. Despite his overcoat's capacious dimensions, it bulged considerably below the left armpit. This must be the Senator's personal bodyguard.

The Prime Minister of Sweden also had a bodyguard, the first prime minister ever to have one. The political leader of the country had chosen to remain in the VIP room with three other members of the government.

A bunch of Möller's elite agents conducted the Senator and his stonefaced protector to an armored car, borrowed from the army, and they were driven the few hundred yards to the VIP room. (Möller was taking no chances.)

There, the Senator and the Prime Minister shook hands, lengthily and cordially, for the benefit of television and press photographers, but there was no orgy of kissing as when the Russians were around.

The Prime Minister was a slightly edgy, nervous type, with effeminate and slightly sorrowful features. Whatever he radiated, it was not the paternalism for which some of his predecessors had been known and adored. Those who had tried to analyze in depth his appearance and behavior maintained there was clear evidence of a guilty conscience and childish disappointment.

On the other hand, it was immediately noticeable that the Senator was a trained handshaker. With an interpreter from the embassy at his heels, he went up to each person in the room and pressed that person's hand. Martin Beck was the first to benefit, and his immediate reaction was surprise at how firm and trust-inspiring the handshake was.

Only Gunvald Larsson showed a certain annoyance. He had turned his back on the whole gathering and was staring out the window. Outside, Möller's agents were swarming about in the slush while the motorcade vehicles were being backed into place, the bulletproof limousine just outside the door.

A moment or two later he felt a determined tap on his shoulder, turned and found himself staring at Stoneface with the cigar.

"The Senator wants to shake hands," said the bodyguard, the cigar whipping slightly as he spoke.

The Senator smiled even more captivatingly and looked straight into Gunvald Larsson's china-blue eyes. His own were yellow, like those of a Tibetan tiger.

Gunvald Larsson hesitated only a moment, then stretched out his hairy right fist and gripped as hard as he could. It was something he had amused himself with in the navy, and he held on until the politician's smile stiffened into an extremely strained grimace. Stoneface followed the procedure with his eyes, but the cigar did not move as much as a millimeter. The man obviously did not have more than one expression.

Behind the Senator's back, Gunvald Larsson heard the interpreter mumbling something about "commander" and "special police." When he let go of the hand, their foreign guest's features looked set, as if their owner were sitting in a privy.

The photographers were running all over the place, crouching down to get interesting angles. One even lay clicking on his back. The Prime Minister was rushing around too, his bodyguard at his heels. He was anxious to get away, but first the champagne had to be drunk, and they were at least twelve minutes ahead of schedule, a fact the television producer present kept pointing out.

Outside, the motorcycles hummed. Their riders comprised a special corps within the police. They had joined the force because they thought it was fun riding around on motorcycles. They often gave demonstrations on Police Day and similar occasions.

Melander and Skacke did not consider themselves qualified for the VIP room, but were sitting in the radio van. Silence was total on the police wave bands, but the regular radio and television broadcasts all had commentators in action, describing in solemn and important voices the extensive political career of the ex-presidential candidate. They didn't mention his ideological attitudes or reactionary domestic and foreign-policy activities, but they did tell their listeners where he lived, what his dogs were like, how once upon a time he had almost been a baseball star, how his wife had almost become a film star, how his daughters looked like most daughters, how he himself usually did the shopping in the supermarket, how—at least during election campaigns—he wore off-the-rack clothes, how large his private fortune was (very large) and how at one time he would probably have been brought before a Senate committee investigating tax frauds if he had not happened to be chairman of it himself. His wife had opened a charitable home for orphans whose fathers had been killed in the Korean War. As a young man he had advised President Truman to drop the first atom bombs, and when older had been indispensable to a number of different administrations. He started every morning with an hour's ride on his horse, and under normal circumstances swam a thousand yards every day. He had taken an active part in the "solutions" in Thailand, Korea, Laos, Vietnam and Cambodia, said one television reporter—clearly not one of those who leaned to the left—and was also a breath of fresh and youthful air in a world in which political senility was all too commonplace.

The motorcade was now lined up and manned, one minute ahead of the plan.

The Senator, the Prime Minister and an interpreter got into the back seat of the bulletproof limousine. The Prime Minister looked slightly surprised when Stoneface stepped in too, and when the man took the jump-seat opposite him so that the tip of his cigar almost touched the Prime Minister's nose, he was on the point of becoming really annoyed. His own bodyguard had had to ride in another car.

The Prime Minister spoke perfectly good English, so the interpreter seated between them did not have much to do.

"Okay, let's go," said Gunvald Larsson, switching on the engine. The Porsche began to move, and Martin Beck half turned to see if the rest of the motorcade had gotten away as it should. It had.

Inside the car with blue windows, the Senator looked with interest at the countryside, but apart from policemen and an almost unimaginable number of demonstrators, he saw nothing but the somewhat dull bit of countryside between Stockholm and its distant airport. He sat for a long time trying to find something positive to say, then finally gave up, turned to the Prime Minister and smiled his best campaign smile.

The Prime Minister had already used up all his standard phrases and platitudes back in the VIP room. He smiled back.

The Senator kept straightening out the fingers of his right hand. He had never come up against anything like Gunvald Larsson's grip before, despite hundreds of thousands of handshakes.

After a while, Gunvald Larsson drove off into a rest area and stopped, the convoy rolling past them in perfect order and at an adequate speed.

"I wonder what the hell Möller's thinking of using the clod squad for," he said as they sat watching the motorcade pass.

"I expect we'll find out," said Martin Beck tranquilly.

Gunvald Larsson started the engine, stamped on the accelerator and shot past the cavalcade of cars.

The Porsche was in fact doing one hundred and forty miles an hour on the straightaway.

"Good car," said Gunvald Larsson. "How many of these have we got?"

"A dozen," said Martin Beck. "At the most."

"What are they used for?"

"Driving the Commissioner to his country place."

"All of them? Does the bastard ride in twelve cars?"

"Actually they're mainly used for catching speeders and drug peddlers."

They were approaching Stockholm now, though the landscape had grown no less depressing. The Senator peered out through the window again, and then appeared to resign himself.

What had he expected? thought the Prime Minister, smiling unconsciously and maliciously to himself. Lapps in colorful costumes with silver bells on their clothes? Reindeer ridden bareback by natives with hooded falcons on their shoulders?

Then he became aware that Stoneface had moved his eyes slightly and was looking at him, so he hurriedly began to think about important discussions on the balance of payments, the oil crisis and trade agreements.

Shortly afterward, the escort stopped and yet another Porsche with the word POLICE in large letters on each side came up from behind, past the row of vehicles. Apart from Martin Beck and Gunvald Larsson, only very few people knew what was afoot when the black-and-white sports car stopped alongside the limousine and Åsa Torell, who was driving, leaned to one side and opened the door on the left. The Prime Minister changed cars. Without a word, Åsa trod hard on the accelerator and continued toward Stockholm. Immediately the motorcade started up again. The guests followed the procedure with uninterested eyes. It had all taken less than thirty seconds.

An especially large group of demonstrators had gathered at Haga northern gates, and at first it looked as if they had been in a fight with the police. On closer observation, however, it could be seen that the police were standing passively, while the demonstrators fought with a small group of counterdemonstrators waving flags of the USA, the Thieu regime and Taiwan.

"Where's Einar?" asked Martin Beck as they passed Norrtull.

"He's around that corner over there, on Dannemoragatan," said Gunvald Larsson. "We've blocked it in both directions, but you have to leave some things to chance. Suspicious tenants and so on."

"They'll never get further than the emergency center or the police exchange."

In the two-roomed apartment in Kapellgatan, Reinhard Heydt was satisfied that everything was going excellently. He and Levallois were in the operations center, as they called it. Both television sets were on, as were the radios, all broadcasting the same thing: the first visit in a long time of an American statesman of standing. Only one thing irritated Heydt: "Why can't we hear the police radio?"

"They've stopped broadcasting. So have the cars."

"Can there be anything wrong with our equipment?"

"Unthinkable," said Levallois.

Heydt pondered. That Q signal must have meant radio silence. But there was no such signal on his list. It was probably very unusual.

Levallois checked everything again, though he'd already done so countless times. He also tried different wavelengths. Then he shook his head and said, "Absolutely unthinkable. They're simply keeping radio silence."

Heydt laughed to himself, and Levallois looked inquiringly at him.

"Wonderful," said Heydt. "These idiots are trying to fool us by not using their radio."

He glanced over at the television screens. The motorcade was just passing the OBS department store in Rotebro. The radio also gave this information, and added that the crowds of demonstrators were getting heavier. The television commentator didn't say much, except when the cameras panned out over the police and the people along the east side of the route.

A police car was driving about five hundred yards ahead of the escort to clear the way, and another equally far behind to prevent passing.

Gunvald Larsson looked up through the windshield.

"There's one of the helicopters," he said.

"Yes," said Martin Beck.

"Shouldn't it be over Sergel Square?"

"Well, it's got plenty of time. Can you guess who's in it?"

"The Senator," joked Gunvald Larsson. "That would have been brilliant, wouldn't it. Lower a hook for him at Arlanda and drop him down on the Parliament Building roof?"

"Brilliant," Martin Beck agreed. "Well, who do you think's in the helicopter?"

Gunvald Larsson shrugged. "How the hell should I know?"

"Malm. I told him it would be ideal for liaison, and he swallowed it."

"Of course," said Gunvald Larsson. "He's a nut for helicopters."

Reinhard Heydt was beginning to enjoy himself now. He had seen the fight at Haga north and knew the moment would soon be here.

Levallois was still intently watching his instruments and connections.

"The motorcade is now passing Haga southern gates," said the radio announcer. "The streets are absolutely boiling with demonstrators. They're shouting slogans in chorus. It's even worse at Haga Courthouse."

Heydt looked at the television screens to see for himself. The slogans could be heard less well on television and the reporter did not bother to mention them. Instead, he said, "The Senator's bulletproof, custom-built car is now passing Stallmästaregården, where the government is giving a gala banquet tonight."

The moment was very close.

"At this moment, the car with the Senator and the Prime Minister is leaving Solna and crossing the Stockholm city boundary."

Very, very close.

Levallois pointed at the little black box with its white button. He was holding two wires ready to short-circuit some system, presumably in case Heydt dropped dead or got paralysis of the fingers. The Frenchman never took risks.

Heydt let his forefinger rest very lightly on the white button as he watched the television screens.

A few seconds left. He looked at the black-and-white Porsche and thought, What a waste of a damned good car.

Now.

He pressed the button at exactly the right instant.

But nothing happened.

Levallois instantly closed the circuit with his two wires.

Still nothing happened.

The television screens showed the motorcade passing Norrtull and swinging into Sveavägen. Then a stationary camera took over and showed pictures of the crossroads at Odengatan and Sveavägen. Hundreds of demonstrators and curious bystanders behind tight cordons of police.

Heydt noticed a policeman in a safari hat and boots and thought he must be a secret agent.

Then he said calmly, "We screwed up. The bomb didn't explode. It's clearly not our day."

He laughed and said, "Mr. Senator, I give you your life, for as long as it may last."

Levallois shook his head. He had a gigantic pair of headphones on.

"No," he said. "The charge detonated when you pressed that button, just as it should have. I can still hear earth or something falling."

"But that's impossible," said Heydt.

On television, the bulletproof car could be seen passing the city library and shortly after that a large gray building. He knew that was the College of Business Administration.

The demonstrators were as densely packed as they could be now, but the police appeared quite calm and no one tried to break through their lines. There were no raised batons or drawn guns to be seen.

"Bizarre," said Levallois.

"Impossible," said Heydt. "I pressed the button to the right tenth of a second. What happened?"

"Don't know," said Levallois.

Reinhard Heydt detonated the bomb at exactly the right moment for no one to be injured. What he blew up was exactly two thousand ninety-one sandbags and a huge mountain of fireproof fiberglass insulation.

The only casualty with any human connection was Einar Rönn's cap, which was blown to shreds and never seen again.

Rönn had had twenty-five trucks, a repair wagon from the gasworks, three ambulances and two loud-speaker cars, plus a watertender and a firetender with ladders from the Fire Brigade, all standing in Dannemoragatan. He also had thirty handpicked men and women, most of them from the Regular Police, all in helmets, half of them equipped with battery megaphones.

After the motorcade had passed, he'd had a period of twelve to fifteen minutes in which to dam up the section of the street under which the bomb might have been placed. He had also had to block all roads and see to it that people in the area were evacuated to safety. Twelve minutes was not enough time for all that, but fortunately the respite proved to be longer, fourteen minutes and thirteen seconds.

Rönn's helmet fitted him badly, so he hadn't taken his cap off until the very last moment, and then in his distraction he had put it on the heap of sandbags.

One of the trucks had not emptied its load because they couldn't get it started, but it hadn't made any difference. The only thing the bomb achieved was a gigantic plume of sand and a white cloud of fiberglass, plus a sizable gas leak which took several hours to repair even temporarily.

At the moment when the explosion was making several city blocks tremble as if in an earthquake, the Senator was already sitting in the Parliament Building drinking soda water. Stoneface showed his first signs of humanity by taking the unlit cigar out of his mouth, putting it down on the edge of the table and tossing back a huge gulp of whisky from his own flask. Then he clamped the cigar back between his teeth and assumed his normal expression.

The Senator glanced at his bodyguard and explained, "Ray's trying to stop smoking. That's why he never lights it."

The door opened.

"And here we have the Foreign Minister and the Minister of Trade," said the Prime Minister gaily.

The door was opened again. But this time it was Martin Beck and Gunvald Larsson who came in. The Prime Minister looked ungratefully at them and said, "Thank you, but you're not needed here."

"Thanks yourself," said Gunvald Larsson. "We're just looking for Säpo-Möller."

"Eric Möller? He has no business here, either. You can talk to his men. They're all over the place. What was that awful noise I heard just now?"

"An unsuccessful attempt to blow up the Senator's car."

"A bomb?"

"Yes, more or less."

"See to it that those responsible are arrested immediately."

"Quite an order," said Gunvald Larsson, as they walked toward the elevator.

"Reminded me of Malm," said Martin Beck.

"Is it time to go home now?" asked Gunvald Larsson.

"Yes, indeed. And to stay there until Monday morning."

Reinhard Heydt could not figure out what had happened, not even after he read the Friday newspapers.

He was not alone in his bafflement. The National Police Commissioner and Stig Malm immediately summoned Martin Beck and Gunvald Larsson.

21.

Martin Beck and Gunvald Larsson were soon brought before Pontius Pilate. No more than half an hour had passed since the Senator's arrival at the Parliament Building. Radio silence had been broken now and the emergency exchange had been inundated with reports.

Another person who was inundated—though in a more humiliating way—was Stig Malm.

"One hell of a fine liaison officer you are," said the

Commissioner. "I might just as well have been at my place in the country when everything happened. And what did happen, anyhow?"

"I don't really know," said Malm, who was quite noticeably shaking in his shoes. "My dear—"

"I don't wish to be addressed as 'my dear.' I am the senior executive in this country's police force. I demand to be informed of everything that happens within the force. Did you hear? Everything. And at this moment, you happen to be in charge of liaison. What happened?"

"I told you. I don't really know."

"A liaison officer who doesn't know anything," roared the Commissioner. "That's great, isn't it? What *do* you know? Do you even know when you've wiped your ass?"

"Yes, but—"

If Malm had been about to say anything, he was immediately interrupted.

"I don't understand why the head of the Regular Police and Möller and Beck and Larsson and Packe or Macke or whatever his name is can't find time to come and report or even telephone."

"The exchange never lets people through to you unless it's your wife," said Malm, insinuatingly, having collected himself a bit.

"Well, tell me about the attempted assassination."

"I don't actually know anything about it. But Beck and Larsson are supposed to be on their way here."

"Are supposed to be? A liaison officer who doesn't know a damned thing. That's almost sublime. But who winds up being the scrapegoat?"

The same man as always, thought Malm. Then he said, "Our man's name is Benny Skacke, not Macke.

And the expression is *scapegoat.* And 'sublime' is a word that usually means almost supernatural."

Malm was beginning to get almost angry.

The Commissioner lurched and strode rapidly across to one of the heavy curtains by the windows.

"No one corrects me!" he said furiously. "And if I say 'scrapegoat,' then 'scrapegot' it is. If any correcting's going to be done, I'll do it myself."

Climbing the drapes again, thought Malm resignedly. I hope they fall on his head.

There was a knock on the door and Martin Beck and Gunvald Larsson came in.

Martin Beck was no small man, but compared to Gunvald Larsson he looked harmless.

Gunvald Larsson surveyed the scene and said, "Oh, I see the time has come now. Don't let us stop you."

The Commissioner pulled himself together. "Now," he said, "I want to know all about this bomb."

"From the outset, we worked according to Gunvald's theory and recent experiences," said Martin Beck. "There was much to indicate that he was right. ULAG had never before operated in Europe and had only recently begun striking in large cities, despite the increased concentration of police forces. In addition, our honored guest is natural prey for all kinds of terrorist organizations."

"All kinds?"

"Yes. We know that many militant liberation and leftist groups would like to protest against his reactionary attitudes. At the same time, some right-wing elements would like to hit him just to provoke a crisis. Same with pacifist groups, who think he's a threat to world peace. He's the type of politician lots of people are scared of—not scared of him personally, that is, but of what he represents. All of that would tempt ULAG. When he was nominated for president a few years back, a lot of people were ready to vote for almost any other candidate out of fear for what this man's foreign policies might lead to—a direct confrontation between the superpowers and China, for example. He has always been the most active of what they call hawks in Vietnam, and there's no doubt that he worked for the fascist junta in Chile, which was responsible for the murder of President Allende and thousands of other people. The only good thing to be said for him is that he shows a certain amount of moral courage, that he's well-educated and personable."

"I thought you were nonpolitical," said the Commissioner when Martin Beck had finished this long summary.

"I am. I'm just recounting certain facts. I should add that despite the collapse of the Nixon administration, he has maintained his strong political position, in the Senate, in his home state and in the country as a whole."

Martin Beck looked at Gunvald Larsson, who nodded.

"Now we come to the assassination attempt," said Martin Beck. "Quite early on, we realized that ULAG or a similar organization, one of the illegal Palestinian groups for instance, might be about to strike. Since the assassination in June—the one Gunvald witnessed—succeeded despite comprehensive security measures, we became more and more convinced that the same modus operandi—as you always term it, Malm—would be used here. Our inner group consisted of five people with considerable experience, namely Benny Skacke and myself from Västberga, Gunvald Larsson and Einar Rönn from the Violence Division, and an invaluable administrator and appraiser, Fredrik Melander from Larceny. We five each made our own calculation of the most likely place for a bomb attempt on the Senator's car. It turned out that we all hit on exactly the same place."

"Norrtull?"

"Exactly. And if the motorcade was diverted, it would probably have passed other bombs—which, incidentally, we haven't yet been able to find. We decided, therefore, on other measures, of two different kinds."

Martin Beck began to feel his throat going dry. He looked at Gunvald Larsson, who at once took over.

"After the June assassination, I came to two conclusions. One was that the bombs couldn't be located with detectors. More important, I concluded that the person who detonated the bomb was far away from the place, at least out of sight, and that he had no assistants who kept him informed via shortwave radio about just where the victim's car was. How then would he know at what moment the bomb should be detonated? The answer is very simple. He listened to the ordinary radio and television programs, which broadcast live the president's arrival and trip from the airport to the palace. He got further information through the police radio, which had not been silenced. In this way he could see with his own eyes where the motorcade was, and at the same time listen to it on the radio."

Gunvald Larsson cleared his throat, but Martin Beck made no attempt to take over, so he went on.

"With these theories as a starting point, we took a number of steps. First of all, we had a long and involved discussion with the head of broadcasting, who finally agreed not to send anything live. Instead, the general public would see and hear it all on tape just fifteen minutes later. A couple of technicians were sent for and they made a number of objections before they agreed. We then spoke to the news commentators who were to cover the event. They said that as far as they were concerned it didn't make the least bit of difference."

This time Martin Beck was prepared to take up the narrative.

"We stressed the importance of absolute secrecy to all those people. When it came to police radio silence, I spoke to the chief of the Stockholm Police as well as the chiefs in neighboring districts, and although a few raised some objections, they finally went along."

Gunvald Larsson interrupted. "The most difficult assignment we gave to Einar Rönn. Norrtull is heavily trafficked at that hour and we were going to have to evacuate the whole area and simultaneously dampen the effect of the bomb itself as well as a possible and much more dangerous gas explosion."

Gunvald Larsson paused. "It was no easy task, because it had to be completed within fifteen minutes. Rönn had thirty police, half of them women, in Dannemoragatan. He also had two loudspeaker vans, two fire engines, and a large number of trucks loaded with sandbags, mats and fireproof insulation material."

"And no one was injured?"

"No."

"And material damage?"

"A few windowpanes. And the gas pipe, of course. It'll take time to repair that."

"That man Rönn did a fine job," said the Commissioner. "Where's he now?"

"Asleep at home, I imagine," said Gunvald Larsson.

"Why did the Prime Minister change cars without our knowledge?" asked Malm.

"We just wanted him and the Senator to pass the critical spot separately," said Martin Beck.

Malm did not reply.

Gunvald Larsson looked at his watch. "In thirty-three minutes, the ceremony at Riddarholm Church starts. That's Möller's baby, I know, but I'd very much like to be around."

"Speaking of Möller," said the Commissioner, "have any of you seen him?"

"No," said Martin Beck, "but we've been looking for him."

"Why?"

"It's a special matter," said Gunvald Larsson.

"What are the chances of another bomb attempt?" asked the Commissioner.

"Very small," said Martin Beck. "But that's no reason to let up on full security."

"You could say we've managed the first stage," said Gunvald Larsson. "What remains may turn out to be considerably more difficult."

"What do you mean?" said Malm, obviously keen to establish liaison.

"Laying our hands on these terrorists," replied Gunvald Larsson.

22.

The floral tribute designed by the Senator was truly immense. It was the largest wreath Martin Beck and Gunvald Larsson had ever seen and probably also the most vulgar.

The combination of colors created an astonishing impression, even if the Senator's intention had been quite logical. At a distance, the whole arrangement looked like a gigantic life preserver painted by a mentally disturbed seaman.

It was made in four large sections, the first and third made up of red, white, and blue (or rather turquoise-colored) carnations, the second and fourth of cornflowers and yellow daisies. In the borders between the sections representing the star-spangled banner and the Swedish flag, the five kinds of flowers had been mixed, and here and there bunches of green leaves inserted, which were already beginning to wilt. The wreath was surrounded with silvered spruce sprigs, and the whole bordered with elaborately plaited gilded laurel leaves.

On the top rim of the wreath was a large gilded shield with a bald eagle, and behind this emblem protruded the American and Swedish flags arranged in a V. On the lower edge hung a watery blue silk ribbon on which was written in somewhat cramped gilt letters: *To the Memory of a Great Man His Majesty King Gustaf VI Adolf of Sweden from the Hearts of the People of the United States.*

The wreath was lying on the flat bed of a truck parked at the top of Tryckerigatan, and when Martin Beck and Gunvald Larsson arrived, they placed themselves on the steps of Svea Court of Appeals, where the wind whipped their faces. After gaping at the phenomenon on the back of the truck, they went on to study their surroundings.

Riddarholm, which is a small island containing ten or so public buildings, constitutes the most westerly part of the Old City. The railway and the narrow Riddarholm Canal separate it from the rest of the Old

City and there are only three ways to reach it by land. A person could come across the pedestrian walkway on the railway bridge, or from Munkbro harbor up Hebbe steps, or drive to the island across Riddarhus Bridge over the railway and the canal.

These three points were blocked. It had been a simple matter for Eric Möller and his special group to block off the area and prevent unauthorized people from reaching it. Apart from those involved in the official proceedings, only people working in the various offices were allowed through. Demonstrators and bystanders had to remain in Riddarhus Square, on the other side of the bridge.

Ten minutes before the motorcade was to arrive, Möller had sent two men into the church with instructions that no Japanese with cameras round their necks were to be allowed in during the ceremony. These two men chosen from the "commando section" list, were Karl Kristiansson and Detective Assistant Aldor Gustafsson. The former was incredibly lazy by nature, and the latter a lackadaisical young man with a very high opinion of himself.

Gustafsson placed himself inside the entrance and lit a cigar, while Kristiansson wandered around looking at the sacrosanct historical surroundings. He remembered how as a schoolboy he'd been forced to go to museums and such places that bored him almost to death, and then had to write essays on his experiences. It also occurred to him that he hadn't been inside a church since his confirmation.

He returned to his companion, who was still standing by the door, rocking on his heels, enveloped in cigar smoke.

"That Yankee guy'll be coming in five minutes," said Gustafsson. "We'd better get into place."

Kristiansson nodded and loped along behind Gustafsson.

Meanwhile, Martin Beck and Gunvald Larsson were still standing in the freezing wind, looking out over Birger Jarl Square. Security guards were posted around the square, and there was another line of armed men from the truck to the entrance of the church.

Gunvald Larsson suddenly wiped the rain off his face and nudged Martin Beck with his elbow. "Hell's bells!" he said. "I knew it. Look—the clod squad!"

Martin Beck saw Gustafsson sauntering out of the church with Kristiansson in tow and caught sight of Richard Ullholm hurrying along from Wrangel Hill toward the bridge.

Martin Beck looked at the time. Five minutes left. "There's nothing much we can do about it now, except see how things go," he said. "Where is Möller, anyhow?"

Gunvald Larsson pointed at the church and clapped his hand to his forehead. "He's over there," he said, "with the real kingpins of the idiot list."

Eric Möller was striding briskly toward the entrance of the church, followed by Bo Zachrisson and Kenneth Kvastmo. They stopped, and Möller inspected his little troop.

Martin Beck and Gunvald Larsson stayed where they were and watched while Möller spoke to the four men in turn. He did not appear to be his usual calm self, and kept looking at his watch and glancing uneasily over toward Riddarhus Square, where the motorcade would shortly be appearing. He was evidently issuing final orders. Zachrisson and Kristiansson placed themselves on one side of the doors, Gustafsson and Kvastmo on the others.

"I'm not going to budge an inch," said Gunvald Larsson. "Möller will have to deal with this. My God, what a detail! And what a god-awful wreath. Just as well old Gustaf isn't here to see it."

Martin Beck turned up his collar and thrust his hands into his pockets. "Several generations of monarchs will turn in their graves when they lay that thing," he said. "What kind of idiot idea was it to lug it all the way from over there?"

Gunvald Larsson peered through the sleet at the four naval officers, who had now moved over to the truck. "I suppose they thought it would be grander with a procession across the square," he said. "And we've got box seats. I wonder if we're supposed to applaud."

Martin Beck looked over toward the group of press and television men gathered at the end of the bridge beyond the church. Richard Ullholm stood gesticulating in their midst. Eric Möller was on his way toward the bridge to see that the barriers were taken down and to give the people in the television van their instructions.

They were all peering in the direction of Myntgatan, where shouts came from the demonstrators in Riddarhus Square and the motorcade appeared.

Eric Möller was scuttling back and forth, issuing orders left and right, and then gesturing to the naval officers, who stood at attention, ready to lift down the monstrous wreath.

The motorcade crawled over Riddarholm Bridge—first the motorcycle police; then the bulletproof limousine with the Senator, the Prime Minister and the bodyguard, now minus his cigar; then cars of security men, the Prime Minister's bodyguard, the United States ambassador and other prominent diplomats and members of the government.

The young king had been asked to take part in the tribute to his dead grandfather, but he was on a state visit to a neighboring country and could not be present.

The line of vehicles swung to the right and stopped in front of Stenbock Palace, directly opposite the steps where Martin Beck and Gunvald Larsson were standing. The driver hurried out of the front seat of the limousine and put up a large black umbrella before opening the rear door. The Prime Minister's bodyguard came rushing up with another umbrella, and the two potentates got out of the car and began to walk out onto the square, flanked by their umbrella-bearers. Stoneface, who was following close behind, had to manage without protection from the rain, but he didn't seem to notice. There was still absolutely no expression on his face.

Suddenly the Senator stopped and pointed at Birger Jarl, whose huge wet bronze back was turned to them. The entire company behind him also stopped and stared up at the statue.

While the rain poured down on the unprotected and increasingly solemn company, the Prime Minister explained who the statue represented and the Senator nodded with interest, clearly wishing to hear more about the medieval statesman and founder of the city.

The formally clad men who were to take part in the ceremony began to look like drowned cats, and the eyes of the newly coiffed ladies in the company began to shine with something like despair. But the prominent gentlemen remained oblivious under their umbrellas, and the Prime Minister embarked on a long lecture.

Stoneface was just behind the Senator, his eyes fixed on the back of his employer's neck. He followed at a fixed distance, as if drawn by a string, when the two men with their umbrella-bearers slowly strolled around the statue, the lecture continuing, occasionally interrupted by a question from the Senator.

"Christ, either stop talking about Birger Jarl or else

lay the goddamn wreath on him instead," muttered Gunvald Larsson irritably. He looked down at his Italian suede shoes, which were now soaked through and probably ruined forever.

The Senator suddenly seemed to realize that he was not on a sight-seeing tour and that his task was not just to listen to a lecture.

The company began to form up and walk slowly in procession toward the doors of Riddarholm Church. The Prime Minister and the Senator walked in front between the driver and the bodyguard, who were concentrating fiercely and maneuvering the umbrellas so that these would protect the potentates without turning inside out or being torn from their hands by the gusty wind.

"Wouldn't it be great if those two sailed off and floated out over Riddarfjärden," said Gunvald Larsson.

"Like Mary Poppins," said Martin Beck.

Ten feet behind came the wreath-bearers, and after them the rest of the party, pair by pair. The blue ribbon on the wreath flapped in the wind, and the golden emblem with the eagle on it wobbled alarmingly. The two flags, once so artistically folded and draped, now looked more like a couple of well-used dishrags. The four sodden officers were obviously oppressed by their burden.

"Poor devils," said Gunvald Larsson. "I'd never have taken on such a stupid job. I would have felt like an absolute idiot."

"Perhaps they'd have been keelhauled or something," said Martin Beck.

"Speaking of idiots," said Gunvald Larsson, "perhaps we'd better move, so we can keep an eye on the clod squad."

They waited until the end of the procession—four security men—had passed, and then took up positions by the corner of the Appeals Court, from where they had a good view of the entrance to the church. Kristiansson and Zachrisson still stood to the right of the entrance, looking like two stone statues, filled with the solemnity of the occasion. On the left were Kvastmo and Gustafsson, Kvastmo standing stiffly to attention. Victor Paulsson was standing close to the outside wall of the Inland Revenue offices opposite the church. He was probably the most identifiable man in the Security Service, on account of the curious disguises he used to enable himself to melt into the background of his surroundings. Today huge drops fell from the rim of his bowler onto the velvet collar of his coat, and the copy of *Svenska Dagbladet* folded under his arm was in a state of disintegration.

Eric Möller was nowhere to be seen, but Richard Ullholm was still busy keeping the press and television people in their proper places.

The dignified procession slowly approached the church doors. Directly in front of the entrance, the Prime Minister's bodyguard and the Senator's driver stopped, put down the umbrellas and joined Stoneface behind the eminent visitor and his host.

Just as they were about to walk up the steps, someone came out of the church—a young girl, with long fair hair and wide-open brown eyes, lips pressed together in a pale, serious face. She was wearing a suede jacket, a long green velvet skirt and leather boots.

Between her hands she was holding a small shiny revolver. She stopped on the threshold, raised her arms and fired.

The distance between the mouth of the revolver and the point between the Prime Minister's eyebrows where the bullet made a hole in his forehead was no more than eight inches. The Prime Minister tumbled backward against his bodyguard, who was dragged down with him, the umbrella still in his hand.

The girl had jerked back at the recoil, but was now standing quite still as she slowly lowered her arms.

The sound of the shot echoed around the walls, and several seconds seemed to pass before everyone began to react in different ways.

The only person who did not react was the Prime Minister. He had died the moment the bullet penetrated his brain.

"Hell and damnation!" said Martin Beck.

Victor Paulsson dashed across the street, but halfway to the church his pistol fell out of the folded newspaper and disappeared with a splash into a puddle. He rushed up to the group at the church with a soaking wet copy of *Svenska Dagbladét* in his hand.

As the Senator calmly took the nickel-plated weapon from the girl's hand, his bodyguard whipped out a gigantic revolver from inside his wide overcoat. The Senator was still looking at the girl as he handed the murder weapon to Zachrisson, who happened to be standing nearest him.

Stoneface pointed his Peacemaker at the unmarried girl. Even in his gigantic fist it seemed enormous, made for Wyatt Earp's hand, or anyhow John Wayne's. Bo Zachrisson raised the girl's small revolver to shoot the weapon out of Stoneface's hand, but the Senator's bodyguard moved like lightning. Without the slightest change of expression, he hit Zachrisson on the hand with his Colt. Zachrisson yelped and dropped the revolver.

Kenneth Kvastmo, who had hitherto been standing at attention, now threw himself on the girl and twisted her arms behind her back in one swift motion. She offered no resistance, but bent forward with a grimace at Kvastmo's rough treatment.

The Prime Minister's bodyguard had scrambled to his feet and was staring with astonishment at the dead Prime Minister at his feet. He was still holding the umbrella in his hand.

Terrified and astonished cries could be heard from the members of the procession, and reporters and photographers came running up, Richard Ullholm in the lead.

Just as Martin Beck and Gunvald Larsson reached the spot, Eric Möller came hurtling out from somewhere indoors. Barking orders at his bewildered men, he tried to push aside the shocked and distressed people who were beginning to crowd around the dead man.

Martin Beck looked at Rebecka Lind, who was still leaning forward in Kvastmo's grip. "Let her go," he said.

Kvastmo retained his hold on the girl and was just about to protest when Gunvald Larsson walked up and pushed him away. "I'll take her in our car," said Gunvald Larsson, starting to pilot Rebecka through the agitated crowd.

Martin Beck picked up the revolver Stoneface had knocked out of Zachrisson's hand. He had seen a similar weapon quite recently. With Kollberg at the Army Museum.

He remembered what Kollberg had said about the little revolver—you could hit a cabbage with it at a few inches' range, providing that it held absolutely still.

Martin Beck looked down at the dead Prime Minister and at his shattered forehead and thought that was roughly what Rebecka had succeeded in doing.

The confusion was now total. The only people who appeared to be taking the situation quite coolly were the Senator, his bodyguard and the four naval officers, who had now placed their wreath at the feet of the Prime Minister.

Richard Ullholm's face was scarlet as he said to Eric Möller, who was trying to bring some order into the confusion, "I'll report this. It's a gross dereliction of duty and will have to be reported. Scandalous dereliction of duty."

"Shut up," said Möller.

Ullholm's face turned a deeper shade of scarlet, if that was possible, and he turned to Kristiansson who was still standing where he had been placed. "You'll be reported," said Ullholm. "I'll report you all."

"I didn't do anything," said Kristiansson.

"Exactly!" shouted Ullholm. "I'll report just that, just you wait."

Martin Beck turned to Ullholm and said, "Don't stand there gabbing, get on with your job. Get people away. You, too, Kristiansson."

Then he went over to Möller and said, "You'll have to clear this up. I'll take the girl back to the station."

Möller had managed to clear the crowd of people away from the body of the Prime Minister, who was lying on his back on the wet steps of the church, at his feet the grotesque floral wreath, and near the wreath the tall Senator, a troubled expression on his sunburnt face, his cowboy gun still in his hand.

The sound of sirens came from across Riddarhus Square.

Martin Beck put the shiny little revolver into his pocket and began walking over to the car where Gunvald Larsson was waiting with Rebecka Lind.

23.

It was not entirely a new situation for Martin Beck—he himself sitting at a desk, and in the chair in front of him a person who had killed someone. He had been in this situation many times; it was a part of his job.

On the other hand, it was not often that an interrogation could be held less than an hour after the crime had been committed, or that a large number of other police had witnessed the crime, or that the perpetrator was a girl of eighteen, or that the questions *how*, *where* and *when* were already eliminated, leaving only the question *why*.

During all his years as a policeman, he had been confronted with both murderers and victims from all walks of life and of varying status, but never before had the victim in a murder investigation been such an important person as the head of government.

Nor could he remember ever having to deal with a murder weapon of the kind now lying in front of him on his desk. Beside the little nickel-plated revolver lay an old ammunition box made of light-green cardboard with rounded edges and almost illegible printing on the label. The bullet that had bored its way through the Prime Minister's brain had come from that box, and the girl had taken the box out of her shoulder bag and given it to Martin Beck in the car on their way to the police station.

Gunvald Larsson had stayed in the room for only a

short while. He realized that this was a conversation that Martin Beck would deal with best on his own, and after exchanging a look of understanding with him, he had left him alone with Rebecka.

She was now sitting watchfully opposite Martin Beck, her back straight, her hands clasped in her lap and her still childishly round face pale and tense. She had shaken her head when he asked if she would like anything to eat, drink or smoke.

"I tried to get hold of you the other day," said Martin Beck. She looked at him in surprise. Then, after a brief moment, she said, "What for?"

"I asked Mr. Braxén for your address, but he didn't know where you were living. Since the trial last summer, I've occasionally wondered how things were going for you. I thought maybe you were having a rough time of it, that maybe you needed help."

Rebecka shrugged. "Yes," she said. "But it's too late now, anyhow."

Martin Beck immediately regretted his words. She was right—it was too late—and the fact that he had made a halfhearted effort to find her could hardly be much consolation to her in her present situation.

"Where are you living now, Rebecka?" he asked.

"Last week I was staying with a friend. Her husband has been away for a few weeks, so Camilla and I could stay there until he came back."

"Is Camilla there now?"

She nodded, then asked anxiously, "Do you think she'll be allowed to stay there? At least for the time being? My friend will be glad to take care of her for a while."

"I'm sure that'll be all right," said Martin Beck. "Do you want to call her?"

"Not yet. A little later, if that's okay."

"Of course. You also have the right to an attorney. I presume you'd like Mr. Braxén?"

Rebecka nodded again. "He's the only one I know, and he's been tremendously kind to me. But I don't even know his telephone number."

"Would you like him to come here right away?"

"I don't know," she said. "You'll have to tell me what I should do. I don't know what usually happens."

Martin Beck lifted the receiver and asked the switchboard to find Crasher.

"He helped me write a letter," said Rebecka.

"I know," said Martin Beck. "I saw the copy at his office, the day before yesterday. I hope you don't mind."

"Mind what?"

"Me reading your letter."

"No, why should I? Then you know what they answered, too?" She gazed at Martin Beck with a dark look.

"Yes," he said. "Not especially encouraging or helpful. What did you do after you got their reply?"

Rebecka hunched her shoulders and looked down at her hands. She sat in silence for a while before answering. "Nothing. I didn't know what to do. There was no one else to ask. I thought the most important person in the country would be able to do something, but when he didn't bother . . ." She made a small, hopeless gesture with her hands and went on almost in a whisper. "Now it doesn't matter. Nothing matters anymore."

She looked so small and lonely and abandoned as she sat there that Martin Beck felt like going over to her and stroking her smooth shiny hair or taking her in his arms and consoling her. Instead he said, "Where have you been living all fall? Before you went to stay with your friend?"

"Oh, here and there. For a while I lived in a summer

cottage out in Waxholm. A friend let us live there while his parents were abroad. When they came back he didn't dare let us stay, so he moved in with his girl and let us have his place. But a few days later his landlady started making a fuss, so we had to move again. Well, and then we stayed with different friends."

"You never thought of turning to the social services?" asked Martin Beck. "They might have helped you find somewhere to live."

Rebecka shook her head. "I don't believe that," she said. "They would have put the childcare people onto me, and then they would have taken Camilla away from me. I don't think you can trust any of the authorities in this country. They don't care about ordinary people who aren't famous or rich, and what they mean by helping isn't what I call help. They just cheat you."

She sounded bitter, and Martin Beck knew it was no use arguing with her. Nor was there any reason to, as she was largely right. "Mmm," was all he said.

The telephone rang. The switchboard reported that Mr. Braxén was not available either at his office or in court and there was no listing for his home phone.

Martin Beck presumed that Crasher made his home at his office and used only the one phone. Or perhaps he had an unlisted number. He asked the operator to continue to search for Braxén.

"It doesn't really matter if you can't get hold of him," said Rebecka when Martin Beck put down the receiver. "He can't help me this time, anyhow."

"Oh, yes, he can," said Martin Beck. "You mustn't give up, Rebecka. Whatever happens, you must have a defense counsel, and Braxén is a good lawyer. The best you could have. But in the meantime maybe you could talk to me. Do you think you could tell me what happened?"

"But you know what happened."

"Yes, but I mean what happened before. You must have thought about this for some time."

"About killing him, you mean?"

"Yes."

Rebecka was silent for a while, looking down at the floor. Then she raised her eyes, which were so full of despair that Martin Beck expected her to begin crying any minute.

"Jim's dead," she said tonelessly.

"How . . . ?"

Martin Beck stopped when Rebecka bent down for her bag and began rummaging in it. He took his handkerchief, which was clean if somewhat rumpled, out of his jacket pocket and handed it across the desk. She looked up at him with dry eyes and shook her head. He put back the handkerchief and waited until she found what she was looking for in her bag.

"He killed himself," she said, putting an airmail envelope with red-white-and-blue edges in front of him on the desk. "You can read the letter from his mother."

Martin Beck took the letter out of the envelope. It was typed and only one page long. The tone was dry and deliberate, and there was nothing in the writing to indicate that Jim's mother felt either compassion for Rebecka or even grief for her son. In fact, the letter expressed no emotions whatsoever, and thus seemed cruel.

Jim had died in prison on the twenty-second of October, she wrote. He made a rope out of his blanket and hanged himself from the upper bunk of his cell. As far as she knew, he left no explanation, excuse or message for either his parents, Rebecka, or anyone else. She wanted to inform Rebecka, since she knew she was worried about Jim and had a child whose father "might be Jim." Mrs. Cosgrave finished the letter by saying that Jim's way of dying—not his death apparently, but his way of dying—had affected his father deeply and worsened his already weakened health.

Martin Beck folded the paper and put it back in the envelope. It was postmarked the eleventh of November.

"When did you get that?" he asked.

"Yesterday morning," said Rebecka. "The only address she had was my friend's where I lived last summer, and it had been lying there for several days before they found me."

"It's not an especially friendly letter."

"No."

Rebecka sat in silence, looking at the letter in front of her on the desk. "I didn't think Jim's mother was like that," she said at last. "So hard. Jim used to talk about his parents and he seemed to like them an awful lot. Maybe his dad most, of course." She shrugged again and added, "Though parents don't necessarily always like their children."

Martin Beck realized she was alluding to her own parents, but he felt personally affected. He had a son himself, Rolf, who would soon be twenty, and the contact between them had always been poor. Not until after his divorce, or perhaps not until he met Rhea, who had taught him to have the courage to be honest not only with others, but also with himself, had he dared admit that he did not really like Rolf. Now he looked at Rebecka's bitter, stiff face and wondered what his lack of deeper feelings for his son had done to the boy's own emotional life.

He pushed his thoughts about Rolf to one side and said to Rebecka, "Was it then that you decided? When you got the letter?"

She hesitated before answering. Martin Beck suspected that her hesitation was due more to a desire to be honest than to uncertainty. He thought he knew that much about her.

"Yes," she said. "I decided then."

"Where did you get the revolver?"

"I had it all the time. It was given to me a few years ago when my mother's aunt died. She liked me, and I used to be with her a lot when I was little, so when she died I inherited a few of her things; that revolver was one of them. But I never gave it a thought until yesterday and didn't even remember there were bullets for it. I've moved around so much that it's been packed in a case all the time."

"Have you ever fired it before?"

"No, never. I wasn't even sure it worked. It's pretty old, I think.'"

"Yes," said Martin Beck. "It's at least eighty years old."

Martin Beck was not especially interested in guns, and his knowledge of them was limited to what was absolutely necessary. If Kollberg had been there, he would have told them the gun was a Harrington and Richardson 32 single action, Remington model 1885. He would also have been able to identify the ammunition as unjacketed lead bullets in brass cases with short force-loading, manufactured in 1905.

"How did you keep from being discovered? The police blocked the whole of Riddarholm and checked everyone who went there."

"I knew the Prime Minister was going to ride in a . . . a . . . what's it called? I've forgotten."

"Motorcade," said Martin Beck. "A procession, or in this case, a row of cars."

"Yes, with this American. So I read in the newspaper where they were going and what they were going to do, and the church seemed best. Last night, I went there and hid. I was there all night and all day today until they came. It wasn't hard to hide and I had some yoghurt with me so I wouldn't get thirsty or hungry. People came into the church, policemen maybe, but they didn't see me."

The clod squad, thought Martin Beck. Of course they didn't see her.

"Is that all you've had to eat for almost twenty-four hours?" he asked. "Don't you really want anything to eat now?"

"No, thanks. I'm not hungry. I don't need much food. Most people in this country eat way too much. I've got sesame salt and dates in my bag if I need anything."

"Okay, then, but tell me if there's anything else you want."

"Thank you," said Rebecka politely.

"I don't suppose you've slept much, either, over the last twenty-four hours."

"No, not much. I slept for a while in the church last night. Not for long, an hour at the most. It was pretty cold."

"We don't need to talk much today," said Martin Beck. "We can go on tomorrow when you've had a rest. If you like, I'll get you something to make you sleep later."

"I never take pills," said Rebecka.

"The time must have gone slowly during all those hours inside the church. What did you do while you were waiting?"

"I was thinking. About Jim mostly. It's hard to grasp that he's dead. But in some way, I already knew that he would never endure being in prison. He couldn't stand being shut in."

"Jim was sentenced according to the laws of his country—"

"He was condemned here," interrupted Rebecka, leaning forward in her chair. "When they tricked him into going home and assured him he wouldn't be punished, then he was already condemned. Don't say anything else, because I just won't believe you."

Martin Beck didn't say anything. Rebecka sank back into her chair and tucked back a strand of hair that had fallen over her cheek. He waited for her to go on, not wishing to break her train of thought by asking questions or making knowing remarks. After a while, she began again, more slowly.

"I said before I'd decided to shoot the Prime Minister when I heard that Jim was dead. That's true, but I think I'd really thought about it before. I'm not quite sure now."

"But you said you'd never thought about how you owned a revolver until yesterday."

Rebecka frowned. "That's true. I didn't think about that until yesterday."

"If you thought about shooting him before, then you'd probably have remembered the revolver before, too."

She nodded. "Yes, maybe," she said. "I don't know. All I know is now that Jim's dead, nothing matters anymore. I don't care what happens to me. The only thing that matters to me is Camilla. I love her, but I have no means of giving her anything but love. It's terrible to live in a world where people just tell lies to each other. How can someone who's a scoundrel and traitor be allowed to make decisions for a whole country? Because that's what he was. A rotten traitor. Not that I think that whoever takes his place will be any better—I'm not that stupid. But I'd like to show them, all of them who sit there governing and deciding, that they can't go on cheating people forever. I think lots of people know perfectly well they're being cheated and betrayed, but most people are too scared or too comfortable to say anything. It doesn't help to protest or complain, either, because the people in power don't pay any attention. They don't care about anything except their own importance, they don't care about ordinary people. That's why I shot him. So that maybe they'll get scared and understand that people aren't so feeble as they think. They don't care if people need help and they don't care if people complain and make a fuss when they don't get help, but they do care about their own lives. I—"

The telephone rang, interrupting her, and Martin Beck regretted not having given orders that they should not be disturbed. It was probably extremely unusual for Rebecka to be so loquacious; when he had seen her before, she had been shy and quiet.

He picked up the receiver. The operator notified him that they were still looking for Braxén, so far without result.

Martin Beck replaced the receiver, and at that moment there was a knock on the door and Hedobald Braxén came into the room.

"Good day," he said briefly to Martin Beck and went straight over to Rebecka. "There you are then, Roberta. I heard on the radio that the Prime Minister had been shot, and by the description of the so-called perpetrator, I realized who it was and rushed right over."

"Hello," said Rebecka.

"We've been looking for you," said Martin Beck.

"I've been with a client," said Crasher. "A highly interesting man, incidentally. Immensely knowledgeable in a whole range of fascinating subjects. His father was a famous expert on Flemish weaving. That was where I heard the news on the radio."

Braxén was wearing a long greenish-yellowish speckled overcoat stretched tightly across his imposing stomach. He struggled out of it and flung it on a chair. As he put his briefcase on the desk, he caught sight of the revolver. "Mmm," he said. "Not bad. Hitting someone with that isn't easy. I remember once, just before the war, I think, a similar weapon was mixed up in a case against twin brothers. If you've finished here, may I talk to Rebecka for a while?" Crasher rummaged in his briefcase and extracted an old brass cigar case, opened it and took out the chewed stump of a cigar.

Martin Beck got up from the chair behind his desk. "Here you are," he said. "I'll be back in a while."

As he walked to the door, he heard Crasher say, "Well, Rebecka, my dear, this isn't so good, but we'll manage. Chin up. I remember a girl of your age in Kristianstad, it was, in the spring of 1946, the same year as . . ."

Martin Beck shut the door behind him with a sigh.

24.

Martin Beck had judged correctly when he told the Commissioner that the chances of another attempt on the Senator's life were minimal. One of ULAG's principles was that they should strike swiftly, and then disappear without a trace. Repeating an unsuccessful operation immediately in order to achieve better results was considered a dangerous violation of this principle.

In the apartment in Kapellgatan, Levallois had already begun to pack up his equipment, reckoning his chances of getting out of the country to be pretty good as long as he moved quickly. As far as he was concerned, he only needed to get himself to Denmark to feel relatively secure. The Frenchman did not think very much about what had happened. He was not that kind of person.

The situation was quite different for Reinhard Heydt, because the police had his description and would be watching for him.

It was warm in the apartment and he was lying on his back on his bed in an undershirt and white briefs. He had just showered. He had not yet begun to think seriously about how he was going to leave the country. He would probably have to lie low for quite a long time in this room, waiting for the right moment to go.

The two Japanese had similar instructions. They were to stay in the apartment in Södermalm until they could leave it without risk—which meant when the police had given up looking for them and everything was back to normal. Like Heydt, they had laid in a store of canned foods which would keep them alive for over a month. The only difference was that Heydt would not have been able to survive more than a few days on their peculiar food, while his own assortment was to his liking and should last one person a long time, a whole year if necessary.

At the moment he was thinking about something else. How was it possible that they had failed? Way back when he was still in training camp, he had learned that there would inevitably be reverses and casualties; the most important thing was to be sure that neither unsuccessful actions nor dead agents could be traced to ULAG. Still, Levallois was certain the bomb had detonated, and he was almost never wrong. That the two Japanese might have mounted the charge in the wrong place could be considered out of the question.

Heydt was used to making correct calculations and also to solving complex problems. He had not lain on his bed for more than twenty minutes before he realized what must have happened. He got up and went into the operations center. Levallois had already packed his meager belongings and was just putting on his overcoat.

"Now I know what happened," said Heydt.

The Frenchman looked at him inquiringly.

"They fooled us, quite simply. Radio and television were not broadcasting direct; there was a time lag of up to half an hour. When we went into action, the motorcade had already passed."

"Mmm," said Levallois. "Sounds plausible."

"And that explains why the police kept radio silence. The police radio would have revealed the bluff with the radio and television broadcasts."

The Frenchman smiled. "Pretty slick, you must admit."

"I did underestimate the police," said Heydt. "Obviously they're not all fools."

Levallois looked around the room. "Well, these things happen," he said. "I'm off now."

"You can take the car," said Heydt. "I've no use for it now."

The Frenchman thought for a moment. The whole country, especially the area around Stockholm, was probably lousy with police barracks by this time. Although the car was not likely to be traced, it would be a risk.

"No," he said. "I'll go by train. So long."
"So long," said Heydt. "See you sometime."
"Hope so."

Levallois had calculated correctly. He arrived unchallenged at Ängelholm the next morning, and from there took the bus to Torekov. The fishing boat was already waiting in the harbor as agreed. He went aboard at once, but they did not sail until darkness had fallen.

He was in Copenhagen the next morning and thus fairly secure. He went directly to the railway station, and it was while he was waiting there that he saw the morning's headlines.

After Levallois had gone, Reinhard Heydt remained lying on his bed, his hands clasped behind his head. He half listened to the radio as he pondered his first fundamental failure. Someone had tricked him, despite the fact that their preparations had been carried out perfectly. Who was it who'd been cunning enough to blacken his eye with such skill?

When a special news bulletin began, he sat up in bed and listened with astonishment. To crown everything they were now involved in an almost comical coincidence. Heydt found himself laughing.

What was less laughable was the fact that now, more than ever, he could not run the risk of trying to get out. Heydt was glad that he had been sufficiently farsighted to furnish himself with good books, the kind that could be read many times and thought about. It would probably be a long time before he saw Pietermaritzburg again, and being a typical outdoorsman, the waiting might be difficult.

* * *

For Martin Beck, this astonishing day was crowned by a telephone call from Herrgott Content, who said he was free but unfortunately had no idea where he was.

"Isn't there anyone there who knows?" asked Martin Beck.

"No, they're all from Skåne here."

"How did you get there, then?"

"By police bus," said Content. "But it's gone now and isn't coming back to fetch us until early tomorrow morning. All I know is that there's a railway not far from here. The trains are green."

"The subway," said Martin Beck thoughtfully. "Somewhere in the suburbs."

"No, no, these trains aren't underground."

"Tell him to go out and walk to the nearest corner and look at the name," said Rhea, who always eavesdropped on telephone calls.

"That a ghost?" said Content, laughing.

"Not exactly."

"I heard what she said," said Content. "Wait a moment."

He was back in exactly four minutes. "Lysviksgatan. Does that mean anything to you?"

It meant nothing whatsoever to Martin Beck, but Rhea immediately butted in again. "He's in Farsta," she said. "Actually, it'll be murder trying to find his way here—the streets go all over the place. Tell him to wait at the same street corner and I'll pick him up in twenty minutes."

"I heard, I heard," said Content.

Rhea had already gotten her red rubber boots on and was buttoning up her duffle coat as she opened the front door. "Bye," she said, "and may you roast in hell if you as much as touch the switches on the stove."

"That's a polite lady you've got there," laughed Content. "What's her name?"

"Ask her yourself," said Martin Beck. "See you later."

Exactly forty-four minutes later, she returned with Content. Their first meeting had clearly been successful, as Martin Beck heard them laughing and both talking at once as they got into the elevator. As soon as she came in, she flung off her outdoor clothes, glanced at the clock and hurtled out into the kitchen.

Content inspected the apartment and finally said, "Not so bad living in Stockholm." And then, "What really happened today? A policeman in this town just doesn't know a goddamn thing. You just stand there where they tell you to."

He was right. In situations like this, the policemen in the streets knew just about as much as the soldier in the field—in other words, nothing whatsoever.

"A girl shot the Prime Minister. She'd hidden inside Riddarholm Church and the security men who were supposed to be covering the area slipped up."

"I can't say I was one of his admirers," said Content. "But it does seem a bit pointless. They'll find another one just like him inside half an hour."

Martin Beck nodded, then asked, "Has anything been happening in Anderslöv?"

"Lots," said Content. "But only nice things. Kalle and I saved the liquor store, for instance. Someone wanted to close it, but against such powerful foes as the priest and the chief of police, most people fight in vain."

"And how's Folke Bengtsson?"

"Well, I think. He seems the same as ever. But some crazy Stockholmer bought Sigbrit Mård's home as a summer place." He laughed loudly. "And something peculiar happened to Bertil Mård."

"What?"

"I was going to ask him a few questions about the estate and all that. But it turned out he'd sold the house and the café and every single thing he possessed and gone to sea again. I wonder what prompted him to do that."

Martin Beck did not reply. He himself had done the prompting.

"Well, we sent out all sorts of inquiries, and in the end we got a fantastically grand letter from a shipping company in Taipei in Taiwan. They said that Captain Mård had been hired by them four months earlier in Liberia and was now captain of the M.S. *Taiwan Sun,* which was on its way from Sfax to Botafogo with a cargo of esparto grass. Then I gave up. But I did wonder just one thing. Mård had almost drunk himself to death and couldn't have gotten a clean bill of health. How the hell could he become captain of a goddamn huge boat like that?"

"If you stick five hundred dollars under the nose of the right doctor in Monrovia, you can probably get a certificate saying you've got a wooden leg and a glass eye," said Martin Beck. "The only thing that surprises me is that Mård never thought of it himself."

"Himself," said Content. "So it was you who . . ."

Martin Beck nodded.

"Then there were a number of points in the investigation of Sigbrit's murder that surprised me," Content went on. "For example, they said that the murderer, whatever his name was, had a coronary and died when the police came for him."

"So?"

"So you don't get coronaries to order like that. When

I saw the man's doctor by chance later on in Trelleborg, he mentioned that the guy had severe heart trouble. He wasn't supposed to smoke or drink or walk up stairs or get excited. He wasn't even supposed to scr—"

Rhea came into the room and Content stopped.

"What wasn't he supposed to do?" she asked.

"Screw," said Content.

"Poor man," said Rhea, going back into the kitchen.

"Another thing," said Content. "When his car was stolen, it wasn't even locked, and the garage doors were wide open. Why? Well, naturally because he hoped someone would steal the car, since he knew it was evidence in the Sigbrit Mård case. The car had been standing out like that ever since the murder, but not before. If it hadn't been for his damned old lady, he'd probably never even have reported the theft of the car."

"You should be in the Homicide Squad," said Martin Beck.

"What? Me? Are you crazy? I'll never think about such things again, that I promise you."

"Who said 'damned old lady'?" shouted Rhea from the kitchen.

"She's not a woman's libber, is she?" asked Content, lowering his voice.

"I don't think so," said Martin Beck.

"It was me!" shouted Content.

"Good," said Rhea. "As long as you didn't mean me. Food's ready. Out in the kitchen, quick, before it gets cold."

As much as Rhea liked cooking, she disliked guests who just shoveled everything inside them indiscriminately and without comment.

The police inspector from Anderslöv was a model guest. He was a pearl in the kitchen himself and tasted everything very carefully before saying anything; and when he had anything to say, it was always very positive.

When they put him into a cab on Skeppsbron some hours later, he was looking more contented than ever.

On Friday the twenty-second of November, Herrgott Content was once again at his post opposite the library on Sveavägen. As the motorcade passed Martin Beck raised his hand in salute.

"Were you waving to that moose hunter?" asked Gunvald Larsson acidly.

Martin Beck nodded. He and Gunvald Larsson had tossed for who'd have to go to last night's banquet, and for once luck was with Martin Beck. He and Content had feasted on Rhea's cooking while Gunvald Larsson suffered.

The banquet at Stallmästaregården had been a melancholy business, but both the Senator and the hastily arranged provisional Prime Minister had kept the flag flying. In their official speeches, both referred to the "tragic episode," but neither had gone further than that. Otherwise, the speeches contained the usual guff about friendship, peace, equal opportunities and mutual respect. Gunvald Larsson thought it sounded as if both statesmen were using the same speechwriter.

Möller's security arrangements functioned without a hitch this time, and there was no sign of his "commando section."

Gunvald Larsson had found the evening paralyzingly boring and had opened his mouth only once. Looking at the colossal bump under Stoneface's jacket, he had said to Eric Möller, who at that moment just happened to be in the cloakroom, "How is it that guy is allowed to carry arms abroad?"

"Special permission."

"Special permission? Given by whom?"

"The person in question is no longer alive," said Möller unmoved.

The Säpo chief left, and Gunvald Larsson sank into his own thoughts. His legal knowledge was not overwhelming, and he was wondering to what extent permission from dead people to commit illegal acts could be regarded as valid, and for how long. Unable to find an answer to this question, he took to studying Stoneface and soon found himself feeling sorry for the man. What a goddamn awful job, he thought. Especially if you had to go around with an unlit cigar stuck in your face.

The Senator's smile was subdued, as was the event as a whole, and the party did not continue into the wee hours.

The next morning there was a great deal of speculation over whether the King would cancel the luncheon or not. In view of the previous day's events and the fact that he had just returned from a state visit to Finland, he would have been quite justified in doing so. But nothing was heard from the Court, so Martin Beck's group went ahead with the complicated plan that had been laid down for this particular event.

As the Adjutant had said, the King was not afraid. He walked out onto Logården and personally greeted the Senator, bidding him welcome to the palace. The only indication that there had been some contact between the Court and the U.S. embassy was that Stoneface had to remain in the bulletproof car. After the Senator had ascended what the security forces referred to as the "sensitive steps" unscathed, the car finally parked in the palace yard itself. When Martin Beck glanced through the bluish glass as he walked past, he saw the bodyguard put aside his cigar and take out a can of Budweiser and something that was undeniably a lunchbox.

Apart from this little detail, nothing unforeseen occurred. The luncheon had been the King's private arrangement, and what was said or done on this occasion concerned no one but the participants. The demonstrators outside the palace had been insignificant in comparison with what had been expected, and at the meeting in Logården there had been roughly as many shouting "We want our king" or "Yankee go home."

The time factor was an important consideration for the police, especially for Gunvald Larsson, who with the chief of the Regular Police was in command of the whole long-range-security force. Gunvald Larsson frequently looked at his chronograph, and each time saw with some surprise that they were exactly on schedule. People in high political and official positions generally stuck to agreed times, and neither the monarch nor the Senator broke the timetable. The Senator walked up the north steps to Logården at exactly the right moment, and the King was there to greet him. They shook hands and walked in through the east entrance of the palace precisely as calculated.

With their entrance into the palace, the most critical moment was past, and Martin Beck and various other people all heaved a sigh of relief.

The meal came to an end on the dot. The Senator stepped into the bulletproof car fifteen seconds behind schedule. There was no sign of Möller, as usual, but he was undoubtedly around somewhere. The motorcade formed up, and the long trek to Arlanda began. Möller had barricaded the palace yard with his best men—he had a number of good men at his disposal—and this time the whole area was searched in good time and with great thoroughness.

The motorcade made a small diversion to avoid the explosion area, where gasworks personnel were far from having completed the repair work, then traveled at greater speed than on the previous day.

As before, Gunvald Larsson drove the fast Porsche fairly unconventionally, passing up and down the column. He was very quiet, thinking mostly about Heydt and his companions, who had almost certainly gone underground for some time.

"There are a few good clues," he said to Martin Beck. "The car and the description of Heydt."

Martin Beck nodded.

Much later, Gunvald Larsson said, almost to himself, "And this time you won't get away. There are two things that have to be done. Find the firm that sold or rented out that green car. And then wait them out. We must put a couple of men on that at once. But who?"

Martin Beck pondered for a long time and finally said, "Rönn and Skacke. It won't be easy, but Skacke's as stubborn as a mule, and Rönn's good on routine."

"You didn't think that before."

"People change over the years. Myself included."

There were many demonstrations along the route, but far fewer than on the previous day. Most people had had a hard night in tents in bad weather, and it seemed that the unexpected development had caused the majority to lose heart. There were no incidents, just a great many placards which were soon ruined by the foul weather.

Glasses of champagne were once again being served in the VIP room at the airport. Gunvald Larsson again calmly poured his into the nearest flowerpot as the Senator, his smile now more relieved than subdued, went from person to person shaking hands. When he came to Gunvald Larsson, he put his hand into his trouser pocket and contented himself with a nod and his best and most charming campaign smile. Over his shoulder, Stoneface gazed at Gunvald Larsson with a kind of sorrowful understanding, one of the few occasions on which he had seemed to convey something close to ordinary humanity.

The Senator made a neutral and routine speech of thanks—concise, short and simple, once again mentioning the "tragic episode"—then he went to the Säpo jeep which was to take him to the plane. It had been standing far out on the field and was very well protected. With him in the vehicle were Martin Beck, Möller, and the same governmental secretary involved in the reception ceremony the day before, now hastily promoted to minister without portfolio; and lastly the man with the stone face and cigar.

"Dirty motherfucking pig," yelled a black deserter from the spectator's gallery as the Senator went up the steps to the cabin.

The Senator glanced up at the man and smiled and waved delightedly.

Ten minutes later the plane was in the air.

It climbed steeply, swung around in a long shining aluminum curve to get on its proper course, and within a minute was out of sight.

In the car on the way back to Stockholm, Gunvald Larsson said, "Hope the plane with that bastard in it crashes, but I suppose that's asking too much."

Martin Beck glanced sideways at Gunvald Larsson. He had never before seen him look so serious. Gunvald Larsson stamped on the accelerator and the speedometer rose to about one hundred and thirty miles an hour. The traffic appeared to be standing still.

Neither of them said anything until the Porsche was parked in the police station yard.

"Now the real job starts," said Gunvald Larsson.

"Finding Heydt and the green car?"

"And his companions. People like Heydt never work alone."

"You're probably right," said Martin Beck.

"A green crate with GOZ on the license plate," said Gunvald Larsson. "Do you think we can rely on her remembering those letters correctly after such a long time?"

"She doesn't usually say things she's not sure of," said Martin Beck, "but anyone can get that sort of thing wrong."

"And she isn't colorblind or anything like that?"

"No."

"If the car wasn't stolen, then it was either purchased or rented. Under any circumstances, it must be traceable."

"Exactly," said Martin Beck. "It'll be a pleasant job for Skacke and Rönn. If they do the footslogging, then Melander can see to the telephone."

"What shall *we* do then?"

"Wait," said Martin Beck. "Wait and see what happens. Just like those ULAG boys. They know now that something's gone wrong and they'll probably be ultracautious, lying low somewhere."

"Yes, that seems likely."

They were correct, but only seventy-five percent correct.

This was the situation on the afternoon of Friday the twenty-second of November:

Reinhard Heydt was in his apartment in Solna and the two Japanese were considering the situation from their apartment in Södermalm.

The Senator was sleeping soundly in a reclining chair as his private plane thundered on westward over the sea.

Stoneface could stand it no longer. He took out the bookmatches advertising Stallmästaregården and lit his cigar.

Martin Beck and Gunvald Larsson were issuing instructions to their colleagues. Rönn yawned; Melander knocked the ashes out of his pipe and looked ostentatiously at his watch; and Skacke, constantly in search of brownie points, listened attentively.

A few hundred yards away, Rebecka Lind was once again in court for formal arraignment proceedings. These had been delayed because the case had been allotted to Bulldozer Olsson, who considered it far too simple. As he was also terrified at the thought of having to listen to Crasher's tirades, he suddenly declared himself ill, although he was in his office. His replacement was a woman, who immediately demanded confinement and what was called a "thorough investigation into the mental state of the accused," a procedure that often took several months.

Rebecka said nothing. She looked utterly alone in the world, although she had a kindly looking policewoman on her left and Hedobald Braxén on her right.

When the prosecutor had finished, they all waited impatiently for what Braxén had to say, because the court officials wanted to go home and the reporters were anxious to rush off to the nearest phone.

But they had to wait a long time before Crasher spoke. First he regarded his client with sorrow, belched twice, and let his belt out another notch.

Finally he said, "The prosecutor's version is completely inaccurate. The only thing that is undoubtedly true is that Rebecka Lind shot the Prime Minister dead. By this time, practically the entire population of the country must have witnessed the event on television, which as recently as an hour ago broadcast the entire episode for the sixteenth time. As Rebecka's defense counsel and legal adviser, I have come to know her quite well and I am convinced that her mental state is far healthier and less perverted than that of anyone else present, not excluding myself. I hope to be able to prove that at the trial, which I hope will take place sometime in the future.

"The fact is, Rebecka Lind has on repeated occasions during her short life been confronted with a system whose arbitrariness we all have to submit to. On not one single occasion has society, or the philosophy that created it, given her any help or offered her its understanding. When the prosecutor urges an investigation into her mental state on the grounds that the crime lacked motive, this is at best an outburst of sheer unadulterated foolishness. In fact, Rebecka's action had political foundations, although she herself does not belong to any political group and certainly lives in happy ignorance of the political system that dictates practically everything that happens to us in this country. Let us not forget that the preposterous doctrine that war is the logical conclusion of politics is still valid today, and that this maxim has been created by well-paid theorists in the service of this capitalist society. What this young woman did yesterday was a political act, even if unconscious. I maintain that Rebecka Lind sees the corrupt rottenness of society more clearly than thousands of other young people. As she lacks political contacts and has little idea of what is involved in a mixed-economy government, her clarity of vision is even greater.

"Recently—no; for as long as I can remember, large and powerful nations within the capitalist bloc have been ruled by people who according to accepted legal norms are simply criminals, who from a lust for power and financial gain have led their peoples into an abyss of egoism, self-indulgence and a view of life based entirely on materialism and ruthlessness toward their fellow human beings. Only in very few cases are such politicians punished, but the punishments are token and the guilty persons' successors are guided by the same motives. I am perhaps the only person in this courtroom old enough to remember politicians like Harding, Coolidge and Hoover. Their actions have been condemned, but has there been any significant improvement since those days? We have lived through Hitler and Mussolini, Stroessner, Franco, Salazar, Chiang Kai-shek, Ian Smith, Vorster and Verwoerd, and the generals in Chile, men who, when they have not led their people to the edge of disaster, have in their own self-interest treated their own citizens in the manner of a military power oppressing an occupied country."

The magistrate looked irritably at the clock, but Crasher continued unmoved.

"Someone once said that our country is a small but hungry capitalist state. This judgment is correct. For a purehearted thinking person—this young woman, for instance, who will shortly be taken into custody and whose life has already been ruined—a system such as ours must seem incomprehensible and hostile. She realized however, that someone must bear the responsibility, and when this person cannot be reached or contacted by ordinary human methods, she is overwhelmed with despair and mindless hatred.

"That I have spoken at such length is due to the fact that my experience of the law tells me that Rebecka

Lind will never be tried and that what I have now said is the only thing that will ever be said in her defense. Her situation was in fact hopeless, and her decision for once in her life to strike back at those who had destroyed her life is understandable."

Crasher rested a moment, then said in conclusion: "Rebecka Lind has committed a murder and naturally I cannot oppose her arrest. I, too, plead for an investigation into her mental state, but on quite different grounds from the prosecutor's. I have a faint hope that the doctors in whose hands she will find herself will come to the same conclusions and convictions as my own: that she is wiser and more right-thinking than most of us. In that case she can be brought to trial in a manner worthy of a just state. But unfortunately, my hopes are not great."

He sat down again, belched and gazed sorrowfully at his unkempt fingernails.

It took the magistrate less than thirty seconds to declare Rebecka Lind under arrest and order her to be taken to the State Psychiatric Institute for long-term evaluation.

Hedobald Braxén had been right. The valuation took almost nine months and the result was that she was transferred to a mental hospital for psychiatric care.

Three months later she took her own life by throwing herself against a wall with such force that her skull was shattered.

Her death was listed as accidental.

25.

It took Einar Rönn and Benny Skacke slightly more than a week to locate the right car-rental firm. Heydt had not patronized any of the larger established companies like Hertz or Avis but had sought out a small private company.

The car he had rented was an ordinary make, in fact an Opel Rekord. It was green and the registration number was FAK 311. It could be presumed with some certainty that he had changed the license plates almost at once. He had used the name Andrew Black and had also of course given a phony address. Unluckily for him, however, because of his lack of knowledge of the network of streets in Stockholm, the address he chose happened to be in the same general area he and the Japanese were actually living in. Thus when Skacke and Rönn made a routine house-to-house check of the area, they were surprised when they soon got a bite.

"Excuse me, but have you ever by any chance seen this man," said Benny Skacke for about the eight hundred and fiftieth time, after first showing his identity card.

"Oh, yes," said the woman who had opened the door. "He had a green car and lived in this house, on the eleventh floor, with two Japanese gentlemen. They're still there, as a matter of fact. A small one and another one who is terribly big. But the man in the photograph left about three weeks ago. They were all very polite and nice when you happened to meet them in the elevator. Businessmen. It's a company apartment."

"So the Japanese are still there, are they?" said Rönn.

"Yes, but they haven't been out for an awfully long time. And before that they brought back big boxes of food from the supermarket by the bus stop."

This woman was clearly one of the observant types, or more precisely damned nosy. Skacke did not miss the chance of asking, "Could you tell me how long it is since either of the Japanese gentlemen has been seen outdoors or in the elevator?"

"Not since that dreadful murder on Riddarholm." She struck her forehead and said with undisguised interest. "You don't think—"

"No, no, not at all," Rönn said immediately.

"Anyhow, the person who committed the murder was caught right away," Skacke reminded her.

"Of course," said the woman. "That girl couldn't have dressed up as two Japanese, could she?" She laughed, then said, "I've nothing against those two yellow men, really. Nor the man in the photo. He was a good-looking man, actually."

Seventeen days had passed since the bombing and the astounding murder, and headquarters now had two difficult problems. First, was Heydt still in the country or had he managed to get out? And second, how would they tackle the problem of the two Japanese, who were surely armed to the teeth and probably had orders to resist to the last. They might even blow themselves and any possible assailants to pieces rather than give themselves up.

"I want to get those devils alive," said Gunvald Larsson, gazing gloomily out the window.

"Do you think that's the whole terrorist group?" Skacke asked. "These two and Heydt?"

"They were probably four," said Martin Beck. "And the fourth has no doubt gotten away."

"What makes you think that?" asked Skacke.

"I don't know."

Martin Beck often guessed correctly, and many people called it intuition. But according to his own view, intuition did not play an important part in practical police work; he even doubted that such a quality existed.

Einar Rönn was in the Tanto area, in an apartment the police had almost had to expropriate by force. They finally succeeded with bribery, which included paying the tenant's full board at one of the most luxurious hotels in town.

Rönn was protected from observation by a net curtain which could not be seen through as long as he didn't switch on a light or strike a match. He did neither. Rönn was no smoker, and the half-pack of Danish cigarettes he carried around in his jacket were only a service for especially nicotine-hungry suspects.

In six hours he had seen the Japanese twice through his excellent field glasses as they moved about in the apartment across the way. On both occasions they had been armed with machine pistols. The distance between the buildings was about four hundred yards and if Rönn had been a good shot, which he certainly was not, and if he had had a good rifle with a telescopic sight, he would have been able to put at least one man out of action, the large one perhaps, who had first moved the curtain.

Rönn was relieved by Skacke ten hours later, and by then he was fairly tired of the whole affair. Skacke was not entirely satisfied with his instructions.

"Gunvald Larsson says we've got to take them alive," he said acidly. "But how are we going to do that?"

"Well, Gunvald doesn't like killing people," said

Rönn, yawning. "You weren't in on that roof job in Dalagatan four years ago, were you?"

"No, I was working in Malmö then."

"Malmö," said Rönn. "The city where even the police superintendents are corrupt. Nice place." He added hastily, "I didn't mean that you had anything to do with that, of course. Of course not."

He put on his overcoat and walked to the door, then turned. "Remember, don't touch the curtain," he warned.

"No, of course not."

"And if anything important happens, dial the number on that paper there at once. You'll be put through directly to Beck or Larsson."

"Sleep well," said Skacke, seeing before him ten hours of apparently pointless vigil.

As the night wore on, the lights dimmed in the windows across the way. At first Skacke thought the two men had gone to sleep, but one light was still on and he gradually realized this probably meant they were sleeping in shifts. This was confirmed shortly after midnight, when for the first time he caught sight of one of the men. It was the smaller of the two, drawing back the curtain and looking out. He apparently saw nothing much of interest, but Skacke had a good pair of night binoculars and clearly saw the machine pistol resting in the angle of the man's right elbow. Skacke thought about the fact that the men had to keep watch in two directions, while the police could limit themselves to covering one side of the building, where the front and basement entrances were.

After a while, Skacke saw one of the increasingly common gangs of delinquents coming along the street, smashing the globes on the streetlights until the whole area lay in darkness. There were boys as well as girls in the mob, but at this distance it was not easy to tell which was which. One of the Japanese, again the smaller one, peered out to see what was happening.

When Rönn came at seven in the morning, Skacke told him, "I've seen one of them twice. He was armed, but he seemed pretty peaceful in comparison with our own hooligans."

Rönn pondered the word "hooligan"; he had probably not heard it since Field Marshal Mannerheim had spoken on the radio, and that must have been a very long time ago.

Benny Skacke left and Einar Rönn took his place by the net curtain.

They were not exactly having an amusing time at the police station in Kungsholmsgatan, either. Fredrik Melander had gone home shortly after midnight, but he lived close-by and could easily—well, with some difficulty—he recalled.

Martin Beck and Gunvald Larsson stayed long after the dismal, dirty, gray and depressing dawn began to creep up over the roofs, leaning over photostats, plans of buildings, drawings and maps of the Tanto district, sunk in their thoughts.

Just before Melander left, he had made a remark: "And that's a standard apartment building is it, with emergency stairs?"

"Yes, it is," said Gunvald Larsson. "So what?"

"And the emergency stairs back onto the apartment, don't they?"

Now it was Martin Beck's turn to ask, "So what?"

"I happen to have a brother-in-law who lives in one

of those buildings," said Melander, "and I know how they're built. When I was going to help him put up a mirror, quite a big one I must admit, half of it fell straight through the wall out into the emergency stairway, and the rest of the wall collapsed into their neighbor's living room."

"What did the neighbor say to that?" said Gunvald Larsson.

"He was a bit surprised. He was watching TV. Soccer."

"What's your point?"

"My point is that perhaps that's something to think about, especially if we're going to take them from three or four directions."

Then Melander had gone home, obviously anxious about his indispensable night's sleep.

While things were comparatively calm at Kungsholmsgatan, Martin Beck and Gunvald Larsson began transforming Melander's idea into what with a certain goodwill might be called the embryo of a plan.

"Their attention will be concentrated on the door, especially as there's only one," said Martin Beck. "They'll be expecting someone, you for instance, to kick down the door and come hurtling in with a posse of policemen at your heels. If I've got those guys' methods right, they'll kill as many as possible. Then, when all hope is gone, they'll blow themselves to pieces, hoping to take some of us with them free of charge."

"I still want to take them alive," said Gunvald Larsson darkly.

"But how? Shall we starve them out?"

"Good idea," said Gunvald Larsson. "And then on Christmas Eve we'll send the Commissioner in dressed as Santa Claus with a big dish of rice pudding. They'll be so surprised, they'll give themselves up at once. Especially if Malm joins in with twelve helicopters and three hundred and fifty men with dogs and armor plate and bulletproof vests."

Martin Beck was standing by the wall in his usual stance, elbow propped on the old metal filing cabinet. Gunvald Larsson was sitting at his desk picking his teeth with a letter opener.

Neither of them said more than one word at the most for the next hour.

Benny Skacke was a good shot. He'd had the chance to demonstrate this not only at the shooting range, but also on the job. If he had been a headhunter, his collection would have been enhanced by the somewhat ugly head of a Lebanese who had at the time been considered one of the ten most dangerous men in the world.

Skacke also had excellent night vision. Although it was black as soot outside and the Japanese were very economical with the light, he could see they were going to have a meal. Dinner was clearly a ritual affair. They put on white clothes, rather like judo costumes, and knelt on each side of a square cloth apparently covered with plates and small bowls.

It looked peaceful and leisurely. Until he discovered that they each had a machine pistol with spare magazine within easy reach.

His own rifle was standing out in the hall, a Browning High Power Rifle Medallion Grade 458 Magnum. Skacke was convinced he had a chance of hitting both men before they had time to take shelter or shoot back.

But what would happen then? And what about his instructions?

Skacke reluctantly gave up any sharpshooting ideas and stared gloomily out into the darkness.

Martin Beck and Gunvald Larsson had a very hard nut to crack. But first they had to get a few hours' sleep. They went and lay down in two of the empty cells, having issued orders that they were not to be disturbed by anyone except mass murderers and other perpetrators of especially serious crimes.

Shortly before six they were on their feet again. Gunvald Larsson telephoned Rönn, who had also just awakened and sounded slightly punchy.

"Einar, you needn't go to Tanto today."

"Um? Really? Why not?"

"We need to have a talk with you down here."

"Who'll relieve Skacke?"

"Strömgren or Ek'll have to do that. It's not exactly an overwhelmingly difficult assignment."

"When do you want me to come?"

"As soon as you've read the newspaper and had your coffee, or whatever you usually do in the mornings."

"All right. Fine."

Gunvald Larsson hung up and stared at Martin Beck. "Three men should be enough," he said finally. "One from the balcony, one through the door and one from that emergency stairway."

"Through the wall."

"Exactly."

"You're good at crashing through locked doors," said Martin Beck. "But what about walls?"

"Whoever goes through the wall is going to have to have a pneumatic drill with a silencer. Artificial sound effects probably won't wholly cover the noise even then, and all the time they'll be keeping an eye on the door, too, so in my view the man coming from the balcony has the best chance. Doesn't that sound right to you?"

"Yes, but which three men do we use?"

"Two seem obvious," said Gunvald Larsson.

"You and me."

"It was our idea, and it's going to be difficult to carry out. Can we put that responsibility onto anyone else?"

"Hardly. But who . . . ?"

"Skacke?" Larsson suggested with considerable hesitation.

"He's too young," said Martin Beck, "and he's got small children. He's learning, but he's still pretty inexperienced, especially in practical matters. I couldn't stand to see him lying dead in that apartment the way I saw Stenström lying dead in that bus."

"Then who *could* you stand to see lying dead up there?" said Gunvald Larsson with unusual sharpness.

Martin Beck did not reply.

"Melander's too old," said Gunvald Larsson. "He would volunteer, of course, but he'll soon be fifty-five, and he's done more than his share of that kind of work. He's a bit slow, too. Of course, we're not so young either, for that matter, even if we aren't slow."

"So that leaves—"

"Einar," said Gunvald Larsson. He sighed deeply. "I've thought about it for hours," he said. "Einar has certain disadvantages which we both know perfectly well, but he has one great advantage. He's worked with us for a long time and knows how we think."

Martin Beck longed for Kollberg. It was no doubt true that Rönn knew how Gunvald Larsson thought, but it was just as certain that he didn't know how Martin Beck thought—or if he did, he never showed it.

"We'll have to talk to him," said Martin Beck. "This isn't the sort of assignment you just give to people and say, 'Now just do this and that.' "

"He'll be here soon," said Gunvald Larsson.

While they were waiting, Strömgren was sent to the apartment in Tanto. Skacke was too tired to show any surprise. He put his fine rifle into a case that looked as if it held some kind of musical instrument. Then he left the building, got into his fairly new car and went home to bed.

Rönn's red nose did not appear in the doorway until just before nine. He had taken his time, among other things because of Gunvald Larsson's tone of voice, which had not promised any happy surprises, and also because it had been a long time since he'd had a chance to relax. Then he had taken the subway into town, since he basically disliked driving a car.

After greeting the other two men he sat down, guardedly, watching his colleagues. Martin Beck decided that as Gunvald Larsson had been a buddy of Rönn's for years, he could do the talking. Gunvald Larsson thought so too.

"Beck and I have been thinking for several hours about how we're going to get at those guys in Tanto, and we think we've come to a possible solution."

"Possible" is the word, thought Martin Beck, as Gunvald Larsson began to outline the plan.

Rönn sat silently for a long time, and then looked at them, a swift glance at Martin Beck, as if he had already seen him too many times and knew what he was about, and a far longer examination of Gunvald Larsson. The silence was almost unbearable. As they had told Melander from the start to take all calls, there was not even the hope that a telephone ring would break the tension.

Finally, after what must have been several minutes, Rönn said, "Where I come from, they call that suicide."

Then he said, "Have you shown this so-called plan to Melander?"

"Yes," said Martin Beck. "The basic idea was his, as a matter of fact."

"What basic idea? That he wouldn't have to get involved himself?"

Gunvald Larsson and Martin Beck had a hard time hiding their disappointment at Rönn's opinion of their plan. But Rönn suddenly walked across to the window, peered out into the sleet and said sorrowfully, "Well, I suppose I'll do it. Bring the wretched thing here so I can read it through again."

And about half an hour later: "I presume the idea is that you rush through the door, while Martin climbs down from the balcony above theirs."

"Yes," said Gunvald Larsson.

"And I come crashing through the wall with a roar. What time will all this happen?"

"What time do they usually eat?" asked Martin Beck.

"Nine," said Rönn. "First meal on the dot at nine, and it's usually a pretty long one with lots of courses."

"Then we'll get them at five past nine."

26.

It was Friday the thirteenth of December, but no one made any jokes about that.

If any one of the three of them had ever doubted

that ten pneumatic drills in an enclosed space would make an almost incomprehensible racket, especially with two crazily clattering trench-diggers and four hysterical paving machines as background, he was quickly disabused of that notion at two minutes to nine A.M. that morning.

Rönn was operating in the stairway with three men. Together they were doing a pretty smart job of boring holes just deep enough so that the wall would collapse at the slightest pressure. Rönn, incidentally was one of the few people present who had ever used a pneumatic drill before. The heavy machinery outside was manned by policemen wearing coveralls borrowed from the Highway Department.

Gunvald Larsson, who was outside by the elevators, had quickly decided that drilling wasn't his forte. Although he'd turned purple in the face with the effort, the drill had kept slipping away and he'd only succeeded in kicking up a horrible din.

Martin Beck, meanwhile, was lying stretched out on the balcony one floor up, a light aluminum ladder beside him. The family that lived there hadn't raised any serious objections when the police appeared and evacuated them to another floor. The other apartment on the floor where the Japanese lived was empty. The buildings were so poorly built and the rents so high that many people who could afford to live in them preferred to move elsewhere. In fact, the multinational company that owned this building had recently sued the multinational giant that built it. The suit claimed breach of contract in respect to negligence, faulty materials, fraud and all the usual abuses involved in large-scale housing developments.

Through a crack in a drainpipe, Martin Beck could see straight down onto the balcony below. The two

Japanese had been out twice to look down at the earth-movers and the paving machines.

Martin Beck's group had estimated preparatory work inside would take eight minutes, and that was what it took. At five minutes past nine on the dot, Gunvald Larsson kicked in the door and hurtled into the apartment. The door, which was made of imitation wood, was immediately transformed into a buckled scrap of unidentifiable trash.

The larger Japanese leaped up from his breakfast, his machine pistol in his hands, and turned to face Gunvald Larsson. But at the same moment the whole wall to the right of him appeared to give way. Large sections of it came crashing into the room, together with Einar Rönn, looking truly ferocious with his Walther pistol drawn. And exactly at that same instant, Martin Beck kicked in the balcony door, discovering what great fun it was to kick in a door, even if this one was only glass and Masonite.

There was nothing wrong with the training and courage of the two Japanese, nor with their knowledge of the rules of strategy. They had been taken by surprise despite all their precautions and were under attack from three different directions. If they tried to resist, the three men in orange coveralls, presumably police, would simply shoot them dead. They said nothing, but the larger one half-turned toward Rönn and the shattered wall. Gunvald Larsson seized the opportunity and struck him from behind with the butt of his 38 Master, a fine weapon which Gunvald Larsson had purchased with his own money, but had never fired at a human being.

Almost simultaneously, two small wooden boxes of about the same size and appearance as ordinary cigar boxes fell to the floor from the white sheet that served as a breakfast cloth. From each box ran a thread fastened to the bearer's wrist.

It was not difficult to figure out what they were—two compact bombs, the threads leading from each man's wrist to a detonator. If one of them had time to jerk the thread . . .

And why wouldn't they have time? A swift jerk, the bomb would go off and that would be that.

Gunvald Larsson was perplexed. Then he noticed that across the room the giant he'd struck was beginning to come to and was already jerking at the thread. Five, ten seconds appeared to be left of life.

Gunvald Larsson called out, almost in desperation, "Einar! The thread!"

Then Rönn did something neither he nor anyone else would ever understand at all. Although he was one of the force's most hopeless shots, he raised his Walther an inch or two and shot off the thread to the detonator with almost inhuman precision.

When the thread lay in a meaningless little heap on the floor, Gunvald Larsson threw himself with a bellow onto the man, who was in fact as large as Larsson himself.

While the two battled, Rönn turned to Martin Beck and the other Japanese and said calmly, "Martin, the detonating thread."

Faced with two opponents and virtually disarmed since Martin Beck had struck his machine pistol out of his hands, the smaller man did something for which he could not afford the time. He looked at Rönn with a kind of strange understanding as he gathered up the slack in the detonating thread in his right hand in order to pull it. As he looked at Rönn and at the pistol, he seemed to be thinking: Why doesn't he kill me?

With the man's gaze thus fixed on Rönn, Martin Beck

took a pair of office scissors out of his inside pocket and quite undramatically snipped off the thread. And when the man turned in surprise to Martin Beck, Rönn coldly clubbed him from behind with the butt of his revolver. The Japanese collapsed without so much as a sigh and Rönn knelt down and clicked handcuffs onto him. Martin Beck pushed the cigar box to one side with his foot. It should have been harmless by then, but they couldn't be certain.

The larger Japanese was at least twenty years younger than Gunvald Larsson and enormously strong, nimble and skilled in the techniques of judo, jiu-jitsu and super-karate.

But what use was that against a Gunvald Larsson in a mindless rage? He felt the hatred welling up inside him, a wild, uncontrollable hatred against these people who killed for money without caring who they killed or why. After a few minutes' bitter struggle, Gunvald Larsson got the upper hand and proceeded to smash his opponent's face and chest repeatedly against the wall. On the last two occasions, the Japanese was already unconscious, his clothes soaked with blood, but Gunvald Larsson kept his grip and raised the large limp body, ready to strike again.

"That's enough now, Gunvald," said Martin Beck quietly. "Put the handcuffs on him."

"Yes," said Gunvald Larsson. His china-blue eyes cleared.

"That doesn't happen to me often," he apologized.

"I know," said Martin Beck.

He looked down at the two unconscious men. "Alive," he said almost to himself. "It worked after all."

"Yes," said Gunvald Larsson, "it worked." He rubbed his tortured shoulders against the nearest doorjamb and said, also more or less to himself, "He was goddamn strong, that one."

What happened next could only be regarded as an absurd anticlimax.

Martin Beck went out onto the balcony and signaled for the noise to stop. When he came back, Rönn and Gunvald Larsson were struggling out of their orange coveralls.

A policeman unknown to them peered in through the ruined door and gave a kind of all-clear signal to someone behind him. One of the elevator doors opened and Bulldozer Olsson rushed with small tripping steps into the apartment, his head lowered.

He first looked at the unconscious Japanese, then at the ruined apartment, and finally let his jolly eyes sweep over Martin Beck, Gunvald Larsson and Einer Rönn. "Great job, boys," he said. "I never thought you'd make it."

"Didn't you?" said Gunvald Larsson acidly. "What the hell are you doing here, anyhow?"

Bulldozer Olsson ran his fingers once or twice down the giant cravat of the day, an American political party tie featuring white elephants on a green background. Then he cleared his throat and said,

"Hitadichi and Matsuma Leitzu, I herewith declare you under arrest for attempted murder, terrorism and armed resistance to officers of the law."

The smaller of the two men had come around and said politely, "Excuse me, sir, but that's not our names." He paused briefly and then added, "If what you said was supposed to be our names."

"Oh, the name business will probably sort itself out," said Bulldozer happily. He gestured toward the policeman behind him.

"Okay, take them to Kungsholm. Have someone explain their rights to them, and tell them they'll be formally arraigned tomorrow. If they haven't got a lawyer of their own, we'll appoint one." He paused, then added, "Though preferably not Crasher."

Some of Bulldozer's men came into the apartment, and the two men were taken away, one of them on his own two feet, the other on a stretcher.

"Yes," said Bulldozer, "first-class job, boys. As I said. An excellent piece of work. But I still don't understand why you do this kind of thing yourselves."

"No," said Gunvald Larsson, "you wouldn't understand that."

"Larsson, you're a peculiar man," said Bulldozer.

Then the crumpled blue suit floated away with the public prosecutor inside it.

"How the hell . . . ?" said Gunvald Larsson when Bulldozer had vanished.

Martin Beck was wondering the same thing but said nothing.

It was all too simple. Bulldozer had tabs everywhere. He stuck his nose into everything and then tried to take the credit. Martin Beck had been almost certain that Bulldozer hadn't succeeded in placing an informer within the Homicide Squad, but now it appeared that he did have a man in the Violence Division.

Who?

Ek? Strömgren?

Strömgren seemed possible, but he'd never admit it.

"Well," said Rönn, "the fun's over now, is it?"

"Fun?" Gunvald Larsson gazed at Rönn for a long time, but abstained from further comment.

Martin Beck was studying the boxbombs. The crime lab would shortly take care of them.

Four hundred yards away, Strömgren sat smoking behind the net curtain. Since his conversation with

Bulldozer an hour earlier, he had done more or less nothing except chain smoke. He was thinking that perhaps now at last he would be transferred to Bulldozer's special group and get his much-sought-after promotion.

Benny Skacke was home in bed. His occupation at that moment was of a private nature.

"And where the hell is Heydt?" said Gunvald Larsson dejectedly.

"Can't you think about anything else?" said Rönn. "At least for the moment?"

"What, for instance?"

"Well, for instance, that I shot through that string. That was as good as impossible."

"How many points did you get at the last training competition?"

"Nil," said Einar Rönn, his neck reddening.

"Goddamn strong, that one," said Gunvald Larsson again, grasping the small of his back.

Fifteen seconds later he repeated it to himself: "Where the hell is Heydt?"

27.

The formal proceeding against the two Japanese took place on the morning of the sixteenth and was one of the most farcical that had ever been enacted in any Stockholm courthouse.

In Sweden, the prosecutor in a case is supposedly appointed by drawing lots, presumably to create an illusion of justice. But if there had been any lot drawing, which was highly unlikely, then Bulldozer had certainly seen to it that his name appeared on all the lottery slips, because he behaved with a confident pomposity and an easy grandeur that made the very idea of anyone else in the role seem ridiculous. His suit was newly pressed, or rather had been earlier that day, his shoes polished, his tie a bright green with red oil rigs, maybe a personal gift from the Shah of Iran—which was what he himself maintained.

He had especially requested Martin Beck, Gunvald Larsson and Einar Rönn to be present, and the court was also packed with people who had come either out of sheer curiosity or else out of a sense of their duty to keep themselves informed. In the latter category were the National Police Commissioner and Stig Malm, who were enthroned on the front spectator bench. Slightly less prominent was the foxy-red halo around the Säpo chief's bald head. As far as was known, this was the first time Möller had shown himself in public since the twenty-first of November.

The two Japanese had been assigned a defense counsel compared to whom Hedobald Braxén was Clarence Darrow and Abraham Lincoln rolled into one. After Gunvald Larsson's treatment, the larger of the two terrorists looked like a mummy in some old Boris Karloff movie, but the smaller smiled politely and bowed whenever anyone happened to look at him.

Everything was complicated by the fact that the two Japanese were now playing dumb, so interpreters were needed.

The weakest point in Bulldozer's case was that he did not in fact know the names of either of the accused. As an introduction, he read out fourteen different names from an Interpol list of wanted men. As each name was read out, the mummy and his more obliging friend shook their heads.

Finally the judge lost patience and allowed the interpreter to ask the Japanese for their names and dates of birth.

To this, the obliging one replied that their names were Kaiten and Kamikaze, and he also gave their birthdates. The mummy would not even speak.

Martin Beck and Gunvald Larsson looked at each other in astonishment, but no one else reacted. Clearly they were alone in knowing that Kaiten meant human torpedo, and Kamikaze suicide pilot. Actually, the men had also given the birthdates of Admiral Togo and Admiral Yamamoto, which would make them about a hundred and seventy and a hundred years old respectively, although anyone could see that neither of them was a day over thirty.

However, the Court swallowed all this information and the clerk industriously wrote it all down.

Bulldozer then declared them under reasonable suspicion of having committed a huge number of crimes, such as treason, attempted murder of the Prime Minister, the King, the American Senator, and eighteen other persons specified by name, including Gunvald Larsson, Martin Beck and Einar Rönn. He went on to armed subversion, damage to the city gas mains, illegal possession of arms, illegal entry into the country, gross damage to the apartment house in Tanto, larceny, smuggling of arms, violent resistance to the police, preparation for narcotics offenses (they had found a bottle of cough medicine containing tincture of opium in the apartment), offenses against the food laws (there had been a dismembered dachshund in the icebox), and illegal possession of a dog, forgery of documents, and violation of the laws on games of chance. On the last charge, he had judged the strange wooden tiles as a game of chance.

When he reached that point, Bulldozer suddenly rushed out of the courtroom without a word of explanation. Everyone watched in astonishment. He came back a few minutes later, contentedly tripping ahead of six or seven laborers who came puffing in carrying a coffin-shaped wooden crate and a large folding table.

He proceeded to take quantities of material evidence out of the crate—parts of bombs, hand grenades, ammunition and so on. Each object was shown to the spectators and the judge, after which it was placed on the table.

The crate was still half full when Bulldozer took out the dachshund's head wrapped in cellophane, which he first showed to the National Police Commissioner and then to Stig Malm, who at once threw up on the floor. Encouraged by this success, Bulldozer took off the wrapping and thrust the head under the judge's nose, whereupon the judge took his handkerchief out of his top pocket, held it in front of his mouth and said in a choked voice, "That will be sufficient, Mr. Public Prosecutor, that's sufficient."

Bulldozer then began to take out the remains of the decapitated dachshund, but the judge said emphatically, "I said that would be sufficient."

Bulldozer brushed a slight disappointment from his face with his tie, did a lap around the courtroom, stopped in front of the mummy, and said, "I herewith request formal arraignment of Messieurs Kaiten and Kamikaze. May I add that I am expecting further evidence from abroad."

The interpreter translated. The mummy nodded. The other Japanese smiled courteously and bowed.

The defense counsel now had the floor. He was a

dry man, in appearance rather like a stubbed-out cigar, long since extinguished and abandoned.

Bulldozer looked absently down into the crate. He picked out the hindquarters of the dachshund with its attached tail and demonstrated the evidence to the chief of State Police until the latter turned purple in the face.

"I oppose the arraignment," said the defense counsel.

"Why?" asked the judge, a flash of genuine surprise in his voice.

The defense counsel sat in silence for a moment, then said, "I don't really know."

With this brilliant remark, the proceedings collapsed, the two Japanese were declared under formal arrest, and the spectators poured out.

In the apartment in Kapellgatan in Solna, Reinhard Heydt was lying on his bed, thinking.

He had just taken a bath and the route from the bathroom to the bed was covered with outspread white towels. He himself, on the other hand, was undressed. In the bathroom, he had looked at himself in the mirror for a long time and had made two discoveries: one, that his suntan had begun to fade; and two, that there was nothing he could do about it.

For the first time, a ULAG operation had been a total fiasco. Not only had they flopped, but two activists, including one of their best, had fallen into the enemy's hands alive.

Levallois had indeed gotten away, but that was not much consolation.

Their enemies were countless; in this case they appeared to be primarily represented by the Swedish police. He had seen on television the person who was said to be the "brain behind the capture of the two

Japanese terrorists," Chief Public Prosecutor Sten Robert Olsson. He appeared to be a chubby-cheeked man with a startling tie and satisfied expression.

There was something fishy about it all. Had this Olsson, "Bulldozer" as he was called, really been responsible for their defeat? Heydt found this difficult to believe—or rather, he was almost certain that it was an outright lie.

No, somewhere else there was another man lying on his bed, trying to figure out where Heydt was and what he might be planning to do next. And that man, whoever he was, constituted the greatest risk.

Perhaps it was that chief inspector who had appeared on television in connection with the strange events of the twenty-first of November. Heydt had noted the man's appearance and his name. Chief Inspector Beck.

Would it be worth trying to lure Beck into meeting with him? Heydt knew from experience that dead men made the least dangerous opponents.

But on the other hand, was this Beck really the person most dangerous to him?

The more Heydt thought about what had happened, the more certain he became that his main opponent was someone else. Perhaps it had been this man Bulldozer who had tricked him and Levallois on the twenty-first of November.

But no. After looking at them both, he had been convinced that it was neither of these two—anyhow certainly not Olsson—who had magically managed to capture "Kaiten" alive without anyone being killed or even seriously injured. The big Japanese had been one of the physical aces in the same training group as Heydt. Just overpowering him should have been a virtual impossibility. Heydt himself wouldn't have liked to try it and would have judged his chances minimal.

Reinhard Heydt was a dangerous man, which he was proudly aware of. He had indeed come out at top of the course, but even so had had considerably lower grades than Kaiten in the physical disciplines.

Also, it was said that Kaiten and the other man had been overpowered and captured inside the apartment. That should have been impossible. And yet someone had done it, and it did not appear to have been any kind of mass conscription of police. Only three or so men, with Beck as leader, and one of them had put Kaiten out of action without killing him or being injured himself.

That man was dangerous, but who was he? Beck? Or perhaps one of the best CIA agents? That was always also a possibility.

Or could it really have been a Swedish policeman?

From what Heydt had seen of the Swedish police, that seemed out of the question. On three occasions he had seen this country's National Police Commissioner on television, and once some kind of departmental administrator. Both had seemed to him, if not exactly idiots, then at least blown-up bureaucratic ciphers, with very vague ideas about their work, and a certain propensity for making meaningless, bombastic speeches.

The country's security forces did not appear in public, understandably enough, but they seemed to be generally derided, though they could hardly be as incompetent as people said. They seemed to have had a hand in only a part of the arrangements for the Senator's visit—primarily the part that had been most disastrous from the police point of view. But the rest of the planning had been clever; Heydt was the first to admit it. Someone had tricked him.

Who?

Could it be the same someone who had beaten Kaiten and put him under lock and key? Someone who was sufficiently interested in Reinhard Heydt to be truly dangerous to him?

It seemed so.

Heydt turned over onto his stomach and spread the map of Scandinavia out in front of him. He would soon be leaving the country and he had tentatively decided where he would go first. To Copenhagen. Levallois and several other sympathizers were there.

But how was he to get there?

There were several possibilities. Some he had long since abandoned—scheduled airline flights, for instance, as they were too easy to control. Levallois's method, too, which had probably been fine for him; he had spent five years building up the necessary contacts. Heydt had no such contacts. The risk of being betrayed was far too great.

To go to Finland also looked dangerous, partly because communications were well controlled, and partly because the Finnish police were said to be more dangerous than their colleagues in the other Scandinavian countries.

The exits remaining were few, but promising. Personally, he was most tempted to go by train or car to Oslo, and from there by passenger boat to Copenhagen. The boat itself would be a satisfactory retreat, maybe involving a pleasant cabin and elegant saloons.

But was that way the safest? Sometimes Heydt thought so, and sometimes he found the ferry from Helsingborg to Helsingör more tempting from a security point of view. Just before Christmas, that route would be extremely overcrowded. That was even truer of the hydrofoils between Malmö and Copenhagen, where things were chaotic at every season of the year.

There were other ways, the ferries and small boats from Landskrona to Tuborg and Copenhagen, for instance. And also the car ferries from Helsingborg, Malmö and Trelleborg to the German Federal Republic and from Ystad to Swinemünde, which was in Poland now and called something peculiar, Swinouscie or something like that.

But the passport police were thorough in Poland and East Germany. No, it would have to be the large passenger boat from Oslo to Denmark, the Helsingör ferry or the commuter hydrofoils between Malmö and Copenhagen. When the Christmas rush was at its worst.

Though he hadn't yet really decided, to be on the safe side he had already booked a luxury cabin on the *King Olav V* from Oslo.

He studied the map, stretching so that his joints cracked.

He thought for a moment about Kaiten and Kamikaze, but without anxiety. No police brutality or torture would make them reveal anything.

On the other hand, perhaps it would be a good idea after all to get rid of this fellow Martin Beck. A police force could seldom afford to lose the few good brains it had. Heydt had a rifle with a night telescopic sight. He had assembled it a few days earlier, and it was now standing in the wardrobe, ready for use.

But was it really Martin Beck who had taken Kaiten and Kamikaze and was now undoubtedly trying to lure him into the trap? He doubted it. But still, one couldn't be sure.

Naked, Heydt went to the wardrobe and took out his rifle, dismantled it and thoroughly inspected the parts. Everything was in order. He began to assemble the rifle again, and finally took a handful of cartridges out of his false-bottomed suitcase, loaded the gun and put it under his bed.

Reinhard Heydt was right, even if his invisible opponent was farther away than he imagined.

Even by city standards, it was a long way from Solna in the northwest to the dreary suburb of Bollmora where Gunvald Larsson lived, south and also quite a bit to the east of the city.

Gunvald Larsson had just returned from the supermarket, where everyone had seemed more or less neurotic because of Christmas. Driven almost to distraction by the fifth consecutive repetition of "Rudolph the Red-nosed Reindeer" on the piped-in music system, Gunvald Larsson bought the wrong kind of cheese—Swedish Camembert instead of Danish Brie—and on top of everything else, the wrong kind of tea—Earl Grey instead of Twining's Lapsang Souchong. He had finally struggled his way through the check-out line and left the store, tired, battered and irritable.

After his meal he lay in the bath for a long time, thinking about the various possibilities. Then he toweled himself down, put on clean silk pajamas, his slippers and bathrobe, unfolded his large map of Scandinavia and placed it on the floor. He lay facedown on his bed after fiddling for a while with the pillows, for the struggle with Kaiten had left various bruises from blows on his chest and thighs. Then he devoted all his attention to the map.

There had been a time, lasting in fact for several years, when Gunvald Larsson had never taken his work home with him, and he had often managed to forget he even was a policeman the moment he entered his own home. But that time had passed.

Right now he was thinking exclusively about Reinhard Heydt. At this point he felt he almost knew the man and he was convinced that Heydt was still in the country. He was also almost certain that he'd make use of the crazy confusion of Christmas to try to slip out.

Gunvald Larsson had drawn some blue and red arrows on to his map. The red arrows predominated; they were the escape routes he reckoned most likely, and also the most difficult to control. The blue arrows were the most sophisticated possibilities. A number of blue arrows led eastward, mostly to Finland, a few to the Soviet Union, and some to the south, to Poland, East Germany and the German Federal Republic. To the west, blue arrows pointed from Gothenburg toward Tilbury Docks at the mouth of the Thames, to Immingham and to Fredrikshavn in Jutland, and from Varberg to Grenå.

There were blue circles around the fortunately not too numerous international airports. They would be easy to watch, especially since the recent wave of hijackings had prompted the establishment of relatively good control points that only needed stirring up a bit.

The really hot lines were in other directions. Red arrows ran down the main highway to South Norway, the European highways numbers six and eighteen and the railway to the capital of Norway. From Oslo, Gunvald Larsson had also drawn in the sea route to Copenhagen with a broad red line, which he looked at thoughtfully for a long time.

Then he lowered his eyes to South Sweden. The broad red line from Helsingborg to Helsingör indicated the Danish train ferries, the Swedish car ferries and the smaller passenger boats on that route. The sailing frequency between Sweden and Denmark was highest at just this point, usually only fifteen minutes between sailings, often less.

Landskrona had two separate lines to the Danish capital—the car ferry to Tuborg harbor and the smaller passenger boats to the inner harbor—but the boats sailed at longer intervals, and not even at the height of the Christmas rush were there more travelers than could be reasonably checked. He was content with blue arrows there.

In Malmö the situation was quite different. The route to Copenhagen included a train ferry to the free port; two shipping companies with medium-sized passenger boats which sailed right into the inner harbor of the Danish capital; and the famous hydrofoils, which in critical situations—for instance on national holidays—commuted back and forth with double trips and no special timetable. On top of all this, there were the car ferries from Limhamn to Dragør in Amagar, a line that on the days before Christmas often ran no fewer than five ships.

Gunvald Larsson stretched and thought for a while longer. If he were in Heydt's position, he wouldn't hesitate very long. He would get himself to Oslo by car, or preferably by train, and then continue by boat to Copenhagen. Stopping him there would be the business of the Danish police and thus almost impossible. Once he got to Copenhagen, the whole world would lie more or less open to him.

But Heydt might be thinking differently, and perhaps had never been a seaman. In which case he would probably make use of the most crowded route, and that was in Helsingborg or Malmö.

Gunvald Larsson rose and folded up the map.

Control would have to be concentrated on three

points; the roads to Oslo and the ports in Malmö and Helsingborg.

The next morning, Gunvald Larsson spoke to Martin Beck.

"I lay awake all night studying the map," he said.

"So did I."

"And what conclusion did you come to?"

"That we should ask Melander," said Martin Beck.

They went into the next room, where Melander was trying to get his pipe to draw.

"Were you up all night looking at the map?" Gunvald Larsson asked him.

It was a stupid question, as everyone knew that Melander never lay awake at night; he had more important things to do, namely sleeping.

"No," said Melander. "I certainly wasn't. But I looked at it this morning while Saga was getting breakfast, and for a while afterward."

"And what conclusion did you come to?"

"Oslo, Helsingborg or Malmö," said Melander.

"Mmm," said Gunvald Larsson.

They left Melander fiddling with his pipe and went back to Martin Beck's still temporary office.

"Did that agree with your own conclusions?" said Martin Beck.

"Exactly," said Gunvald Larsson. "And yours?"

"Yes."

They were silent for a moment, Martin Beck standing in his usual old place by the file, pinching the bridge of his nose between the thumb and forefinger of his right hand, Gunvald Larsson over by the window.

Martin Beck sneezed.

"Bless you," said Gunvald Larsson.

"Thank you. You think Heydt's still here?"

"Certain of it."

"Certain," said Martin Beck. "That's a strong word."

"Maybe," said Gunvald Larsson. "But I feel certain. He's somewhere and we can't find him. Not even his damned car. What do you think?"

Martin Beck didn't reply for a long time. "Okay," he said finally. "I think he's still here, too. But I'm not certain." He shook his head.

Gunvald Larsson said nothing, staring gloomily out at the almost completed colossus outside.

"You'd like to meet Reinhard Heydt, wouldn't you?" Martin Beck said.

"How do you know that?"

"How long have we known each other?" asked Martin Beck in return.

"Ten or twelve years. Maybe a little longer."

"Exactly. And that answers your question."

Another silence, a long one.

"You think a lot about Heydt," said Martin Beck.

"All the time. Except when I'm asleep."

"But you can't be in three places at once."

"Hardly," said Gunvald Larsson.

"Then you'll have to choose. Which one do you think's the most likely?"

"Oslo," said Gunvald Larsson. "They've got a mysterious booking on the Copenhagen boat for the evening of the twenty-second."

"What sort of boat?"

"*King Olav V*. Luxury boat."

"Sounds all right," said Martin Beck. "What sort of booking?"

"An Englishman. Roger Blackman."

"Norway's lousy with English tourists all year round."

"True, but they seldom travel that way. And this

Blackman can't be traced. At least the Norwegian police can't find him."

Martin Beck thought, then said, "I'll take Benny with me and go to Malmö."

"Skacke?" said Gunvald Larsson. "Why don't you take Einar instead?"

"Benny's better than you think. And he also knows Malmö. There are a number of other good men there, too."

"Really?"

"Per Månsson's good, for instance."

Gunvald Larsson grunted, as he often did when he didn't want to say yes or no. Instead he said, "Which means that Einar and Melander will have to go to Helsingborg. Helsingborg's damned difficult."

"Right," said Martin Beck. "So they'll need proper backing. We'll have to arrange for that. Do you want Strömgren to go with you to Norway?"

Gunvald Larsson stared stubbornly out the window and said, "I wouldn't want to go piss with Strömgren. Not even if we were alone together on a desert island. And I've told him so."

"Your popularity is easily explained."

"Yes, isn't it?"

Martin Beck looked at Gunvald Larsson. It had taken him five years to learn to put up with him, and equally long to begin to understand him. In another five years, maybe they would like each other.

"Which are the critical days?"

"The twentieth to the twenty-third inclusively," said Gunvald Larsson.

"That means Friday, Saturday, Sunday and Monday?"

"Probably."

"Why not Christmas Eve itself?"

"All right. Christmas Eve too."

"We'll have to figure on full alert," said Martin Beck.

"We're already on full alert."

"— full alert, plus the five of us from tomorrow evening on," said Martin Beck. "Right on through the Christmas holiday if nothing happens before that."

"He'll go on Sunday," said Gunvald Larsson.

"According to you, yes. But what's Heydt thinking?"

Gunvald Larsson raised his arms, placed his large hairy hands on the window frame and went on staring out into the gray misery outside.

"In some funny damned way, it's like I knew Heydt," he said. "I think I know how he thinks."

"Do you really?" said Martin Beck, moderately impressed. Then he thought of something else. "Think how pleased Melander will be," he said. "Freezing at the ferry station in Helsingborg. On Christmas Eve."

Fredrik Melander had at his own request been transferred first from the National Homicide Squad and then from the Violence Division in order to avoid having to be away from home, despite the fact that he was miserly and the transfers had cost him a raise in salary as well as a promotion.

"He'll have to put up with it," said Gunvald Larsson.

Martin Beck said nothing.

"You know, Beck," said Gunvald Larsson, without turning his head.

"Yes, what?"

"If I were you, I'd be careful. Especially today and tomorrow." Martin Beck looked surprised. "What the hell do you mean? Should I be scared? Of Heydt?"

"Yes."

"Why?"

"You've been in the newspapers a lot, and on radio

and television lately. Heydt's not used to being tricked. And it might be in his interest to pin our attention down. Here. To Stockholm."

"Oh, shit," said Martin Beck, and left the room.

Gunvald Larsson sighed deeply and went on staring out the window with his unseeing china-blue eyes.

28.

Reinhard Heydt was standing in front of the bathroom mirror. He had just shaved, and now he was combing his sideburns. For a moment it occurred to him that perhaps he ought to shave them off, but he immediately abandoned the thought. The idea had come up before, in different circumstances. His superior officer had suggested it, almost ordered it. He studied his face in the mirror. His suntan was fading a little more every day. But there was nothing wrong with his appearance. He had always approved of it himself, and no one else had ever commented adversely on it. Let them try.

From the bathroom he went into the kitchen, where he had just breakfasted, then on into the bedroom and out into the large room where he and Levallois had had their operations center about a month earlier, now rather bare and empty.

As he never went out, he knew nothing about what was in the newspapers, but television and radio were devoting a great deal of attention to the capture and the court proceedings, returning again and again to the subject. Now it seemed clear that the man Olsson was at most an administrator. The really dangerous person seemed to be the policeman who was mentioned so often—Martin Beck. Beck must also have been the one who thwarted the assassination attempt the month before. It seemed incomprehensible that such a person should exist in a country like Sweden.

Heydt strode with long silent steps from room to room in the none too spacious apartment. He was barefooted and wore only a white undershirt and white briefs. He hadn't brought much in the way of clothes, and since he never went out now anyhow, there wasn't much reason to dress. He washed his underclothes in the bathroom every evening.

Heydt had two problems that had to be solved immediately. The first was the question of his escape from the country. He knew exactly when he was going to leave, but was still hesitating over which route to take. He'd made up his mind that today, the nineteenth of December, he would decide. It would probably be via Oslo and Copenhagen, as he had thought from the first, but the other possibilities were still open.

Question number two was even more delicate; he had not even begun to contemplate it until Kaiten and Kamikaze were captured.

Should he liquidate Beck?

What would be the advantages?

Heydt never thought in terms such as revenge. For one thing, he completely lacked such emotions as disappointment, jealousy, humiliation and fear. For another, he was a pure realist; all his actions were dictated by practical considerations. In training camp he had learned to make his own decisions, weigh them carefully and put them into action without hesitation.

He had also learned that careful planning was at least half the battle.

Still without having decided, he fetched the first volume of the telephone book from the shelf, sat down on the bed and leafed through it until he came to the right page. It was no more difficult than that. He read: *Beck Martin, Chief Inspector, Köpmangatan 8, 22 80 43.*

He took the blueprint of the city plan from the shelf in the wardrobe. He had a good memory, and he recalled walking along that particular street six weeks or so ago. It was quite near the Royal Palace. The city plan was very detailed and he at once found the right building. It was in a kind of alley, not facing the street, and the surrounding buildings looked promising.

He spread out the blueprint on the floor, then took his rifle from under the bed. Like all ULAG equipment, the gun was perfect, of English manufacture and equipped with a night telescopic sight. He dismantled the weapon and packed it in his briefcase. Then he sat down again on his bed and thought.

The point of taking Martin Beck out of circulation was twofold: one, the police would be robbed of one of their best and most dangerous men; and two, their attention would focus on Stockholm.

But there were some disadvantages, too. First of all, police activity would be sure to be enormous. And secondly, every possible exit would be even more effectively checked. On the other hand, these measures would only be taken in time if the elimination of Martin Beck was discovered almost at once.

One thing was certain: If Chief Inspector Beck was to be eliminated, it should happen at his home. Early on in his researches, Heydt had discovered that Beck was divorced from his wife and lived alone.

It was a difficult decision. Heydt looked at his wristwatch. He still had a few hours left before definitely having to decide either question.

Then he wondered whether the police had found the car. There'd been no mention of it in the news reports, so perhaps it was still standing where Levallois had abandoned it. The beige Volkswagen purchased in its stead was parked not far from the apartment.

He thought about it for a few seconds, then again began his wandering through the rooms.

On the morning of the same day, Martin Beck sent Benny Skacke on ahead to Malmö. Skacke went by car because he wanted a chance to pad his mileage expenses, but Martin Beck usually felt ill on long car journeys and decided to take the night train. Another, perhaps more telling factor in this decision was that even if Christmas was spoiled, he would at least have half an evening with Rhea. If she put in an appearance. He never knew for sure whether she would.

Rönn and Melander had gone to Helsingborg by train, with the gloomiest expressions he had ever seen on their faces, and Gunvald Larsson, who liked driving, had left very early in the morning in his peculiar East German luxury car from Eisenacher Motorwerke. The make was in fact EMW, but nearly everyone thought it was a BMW misspelled.

If Rönn and Melander had been as sour as vinegar, Gunvald Larsson had seemed expectant, and Skacke simply happy. Benny Skacke was a merit-point hunter, and here perhaps was another within reach.

Martin Beck had not been able to get hold of Rhea, but had left a message at the Social Service headquarters' exchange. He thought he'd go home, but before he got his overcoat on, the telephone rang. Torn between duty and more human instincts, he went back to his desk and lifted the receiver.

"Beck."

"Hammargren," said someone with a Gothenburg accent.

The name meant nothing to Martin Beck, but he presumed the man must be a policeman. "Yes, what is it?"

"We've found the car you're looking for. A green Opel Rekord, with false plates."

"Where?"

"Skandia harbor, here in Gothenburg. Where the *Saga* ties up. Lloyd's boat. It could have been standing there for a couple of weeks before anyone noticed."

"And?"

"Well, there aren't any fingerprints. Wiped off, I guess. All the papers were in the glove compartment."

Martin Beck was depressed, but his voice was normal when he said, "Is that all?"

"Not really. We questioned the crew of the *Saga*. Started at the top with Einar Norrman, Lloyd's chief skipper, and then talked to all the officers. Then we took the intendant, Harkild, and went right through the staff, especially stewards and cabin staff. But not one of them recognized that guy in the picture, Heydt."

"Intendant?" said Martin Beck. "Don't they call them pursers anymore?"

"Well, the *Saga*'s not the *Suecia* or the *Britannia* exactly, is it? They call the purser the intendant nowadays, and the steward in the dining saloon is called the headwaiter. They'll start saying wall instead of bulkhead and left instead of starboard soon. Then . . ."

"Yes?"

"I was going to say that then boats can go to hell, and you might as well fly instead. Einar Norrman said, incidentally, that he hasn't even worn his cap for six months now. The skippers'll soon be passing out for lack of fresh air."

Martin Beck felt sympathy for this Gothenburg policeman, but now it was a matter of steering the conversation back onto the right track. "About Heydt . . ." he said.

"Nothing," said Hammargren. "I don't think he ever went on board. With his looks, someone would have remembered him. But the car was standing there out at Hisingen."

"And the lab examination?"

"Nothing there either. Absolutely nothing."

"Okay. Thanks for the call."

Martin Beck energetically massaged his scalp. The car could be a red herring; it was more likely that Heydt had left the country on a less noticeable boat than the *Saga*. Gothenburg had a large harbor and a great many ships left it every day. Some of them took passengers and were licensed to do so. Just as many, especially small-tonnage ones, carried travelers who wished to remain anonymous and could afford to pay for the privilege.

In sum, it was possible that Heydt had left the country several weeks ago and was already far out of reach.

He looked at the time. It was too early to recall any of his colleagues. Maybe it would be a mistake to bring them back, anyhow. What if the car was a one-hundred-percent red herring and Heydt hadn't left the country at all? It was a great loss that the man in Gothenburg didn't know whether the car had been there even before the bombing. That would have made it certain. Now everything was one large question mark.

Martin Beck slammed the door of his temporary office and went home. Car or no car, it was probably best to stick to the plan. The train did not leave the central station in Stockholm until just before midnight. He still had plenty of time.

There was a film of ice on the roof, but it was not especially cold. Reinhard Heydt lay absolutely still, the warmth of his body sufficient to melt the veil of ice underneath and around him.

He was wearing a black jersey with a polo neck, a black woolen cap pulled down over his ears and forehead, black corduroy trousers, black socks and black shoes with crepe soles that he had smeared with black shoe polish. He was also wearing long thin black gloves.

The rifle had a black barrel and a dark-brown butt, and the only thing that could possibly give him away was a reflection in the night sight, but the lens was smoked and especially coated to prevent reflections.

Of course the idea was that he should not be visible, and although he could not have known it himself, a person with normal sight would not have been able to see him from a distance of six feet, assuming that such a person, for some extraordinary reason, were suddenly to appear on the roof.

He had reached the roof easily through a hatch a few feet away. His Volkswagen was parked in Slottsbacken, and on the street he had worn a light-colored raincoat. This was now lying with his briefcase, tucked into a niche in the grubby attic below.

The situation was perfect. In fact he could see all of Martin Beck's windows, since they all faced east. So far, however, the apartment had been silent and dark.

The rifle was especially constructed for sniping in the dark, and he found he could even make out details in the rooms, although all the lights were out. Behind him the devilish racket of the traffic on Skeppsbron formed a perfect background. The English rifle was comparatively quiet and the sound of a single shot would undoubtedly be drowned in the cacophony of car engines, squealing brakes and backfiring exhaust pipes.

The distance to the four windows was no more than fifty or sixty yards; if it had been ten times as far, he would still have been certain to hit his target.

Heydt was no longer lying still. He was moving his fingers and legs a little so as not to stiffen up. He had learned all that a long time ago—lying almost still, but giving his small muscles a little exercise so that none of them would let him down at the decisive moment. Now and again he checked the sight, which was truly a technical masterpiece.

He must have been on the roof for about forty minutes when a light was suddenly switched on in the elevator shaft and shortly afterward in the farthest of the four windows. Heydt pressed the butt against his shoulder and placed his finger inside the trigger guard, letting it stroke the trigger. He was familiar with his weapon and knew exactly where the pressure point lay.

His plan was simple. It entailed acting immediately, shooting this man Beck as soon as he showed himself and then swiftly but calmly removing himself from the area.

Someone passed the first window, then the second and stopped in front of the third. Like all good snipers, Heydt relaxed, his body filling with a pleasant, satisfying warmth as the rifle, in some mysterious way, became a part of himself. His right forefinger rested on the trigger without a tremble. His physical and mental self-control was complete.

Someone was standing with his back to the third window.

But it was the wrong person.

It was a woman.

She was small and quite broad-shouldered. Straight blond hair and a short neck. She was wearing a brightly colored blouse, a tweed skirt down to her knees and, presumably, tights.

Suddenly she turned around and looked up toward the sky.

Heydt had already recognized her before he saw her straight blond bangs and searching blue eyes. Six weeks had passed since he had seen her. Then she had been wearing a black duffle coat, faded blue jeans and red rubber boots. He also remembered exactly where he had seen her, first here in Köpmangatan, then in an alley, the name of which he had forgotten, and shortly afterward in Slottsbacken.

He had no idea who she was, but he recognized her at once, and if he had been equipped with such a capacity, he would have been surprised to see her. Instead, he observed her hair through the telescope sight and thought that perhaps she did not bleach it, as he had thought the first time.

A man came into his field of vision, quite a tall man with a broad forehead, straight nose, thin but wide mouth and strong jaw. Heydt at once recognized him from television. This was his enemy, Martin Beck, the man who had transformed the assassination into a miserable fiasco, then put Kaiten—the most physically dangerous of all ULAG's agents—out of action and the man who would now have to be eliminated to facilitate Heydt's own retreat from the country.

The man put his arms around the woman, turned her around and pulled her toward him.

He did not look particularly dangerous, thought Heydt, raising the barrel a trifle so that the cross hairs of the night sight lay exactly between the policeman's eyes. It would have been easy to kill him then, but after that he would also have had to kill the woman, and it all would have had to happen very quickly. Everything depended on how she would react. He had not seen much of her, but something told him she was probably very quick-thinking. If she were swift enough, she might have time to take shelter after the first shot and raise the alarm, and in that case his situation up there on the roof would not be particularly enviable. If there were enough police nearby, he would no longer be protected by the darkness and his isolated position. Instead he would find himself in a deathtrap, with no means of flight and no path to safety.

Heydt analyzed the situation, clearly and swiftly, and decided that there was still plenty of time. He could wait and see what happened.

Rhea Nielsen stood on tiptoe and bit Martin Beck playfully on the cheek.

"I have regular working hours nowadays," she said. "And superiors. It looks a bit peculiar when a policeman comes and fetches me three quarters of an hour early."

"The circumstances are a little special," said Martin Beck. "And anyway I didn't want to go home alone."

"What circumstances?"

"I've got to go away this evening."

"Where to?"

"To Malmö. I should really have gone already."

"Why haven't you then?"

"There was something I thought I'd better take care of first."

"What? Where? In bed?"

"For instance."

They moved away from the window. She ran her fingers roughly over one of his model boats, peered suspiciously at him and said, "How long will you be gone?"

"Don't know for sure. Might take three or four days."

"Over Christmas Eve then? Damn. I haven't even had time to buy you a present."

"I haven't got yours yet either. But I'll probably be back on Christmas Eve."

"Probably? Don't I look nice today, by the way? Skirt, blouse, tights, real shoes, tartan bra and matching panties."

Martin Beck laughed.

"What are you laughing at? My femininity?"

"That's not in your clothes."

"You're sweet," she said suddenly.

"Do you think so?"

"Yes, I do. If I read your thoughts correctly, then we should immediately rush off to bed."

"You read my thoughts absolutely correctly."

She kicked off her shoes, which flew in different directions, then said, "In that case I'd better check up on the fridge and pantry first, so there won't be hunger riots afterward." She went out to the kitchen.

Martin Beck went over to the window and looked out. The sky was actually clear and the stars were out —a meteorological miracle at this time of year.

"Where did this lobster come from?" she called out.

"Hötorg market."

"I can do lots of good things with it. How long have we got?"

"That depends on how long you spend messing

around in the kitchen," he said. "No, we've got plenty of time. Hours."

"Okay, I'm coming. Have you got any wine?"

"Yes."

"Good."

Rhea undressed on her way to the bedroom, beginning by flinging her blouse on the kitchen floor. "It scratches," she explained.

By the time she reached the bed, she had nothing on but the tartan bra. "You take it off," she said with burlesque coquettishness. "It's a rare occasion, since I almost never wear one."

They did not pull down the blinds, since normally there was no way anyone could see into the apartment.

From his place on the roof, Heydt could not see the bed, but he observed that the light dimmed in the bedroom, and he was quite able to figure out what was going on.

After a while, the lights went up again and the woman came to the window. She was naked.

Through the telescope sight, he gazed dispassionately at her left breast. The cross hairs lay just over the large brown nipple, the enlargement in the night sight was so great that it filled his whole field of vision. He could even see that there was a blond hair about half an inch long growing just above the nipple. It occurred to him that she ought to have it removed.

Then he lowered the barrel a trifle. The cross hairs lay over a point immediately below her left breast. Her heart. He pulled the trigger toward him half a millimeter and felt it against the point of pressure. If he pulled the trigger yet another half-millimeter, the gun would go off and the bullet would strike her in the heart. With the super high speed ammunition he used, she would be thrown backward across the room and be dead before her back even struck the far wall.

Rhea was still standing by the window.

"What stars!" she said. "Why do you have to go to Malmö? Is it still that character with the sideburns? Heydt?"

"Yes."

"Do you know what I think he's doing at this moment. Sitting in Bali fishing for goldfish with a hula-hula girl on his lap. Come on, let's fix that lobster."

Fifty yards away, Reinhard Heydt was deciding that this whole project was uninteresting and pointless. He wriggled down through the hatch, dismantled his rifle and put the parts into the briefcase. Then he put on his light-colored raincoat and left.

As he walked calmly down Bollhus Alley, he decided when, how and where he would leave the country.

29.

Since Martin Beck and his generation had been children, Christmas had changed from a fine traditional family festival into something that might be called economic cheapjackery or commercial insanity. For over a month before Christmas Eve, almost desperate advertisements for practically everything hammered at people's nerves, intent on squeezing their money from them right down to the last possible coin. Christmas was supposed to be in many respects a festival for children, but many children suffered from nerves and exhaustion several weeks before the great day finally arrived.

It had also become a festival of travel. The whole population seemed gripped by a manic need to be on the move. The lines of cars were endless, and charter flights to Gambia, Malta, Morocco, Tunis, Malaga, Israel, Canada, the Canary Islands, Algarve, the Faroes, Capri, Rhodes, and various other places less inviting at that time of year, were all fully booked. The state railways had to put on extra trains, and singularly uncomfortable buses rumbled off to the strangest places, like Säffle, Bogholm and Hjo. Even the Djurgård ferry and the boats to Visby were full.

Martin Beck could not sleep on the night train to Malmö, although in his capacity as a senior official he was able to travel first class. His sleeplessness was partly due to the fact that his companion in the bunk above not only snored, talked in his sleep and ground his teeth, but also frequently climbed down to pass water, as it was called in tasteful language. As the train was rattled through the shunting yard in Malmö, Martin Beck's fellow traveler was peeing for the fourteenth time, apparently suffering from some malfunction of the bladder.

Martin Beck's thoughts, however, were elsewhere—mostly with Reinhard Heydt.

A few hours earlier, when Rhea had been standing naked by the window on Köpmangatan and he had been lying in bed admiring her back and muscular calves, he had suddenly recalled Gunvald Larsson's warning, and had virtually jumped up and jerked her from the window. Gunvald Larsson almost never said such things, anyhow not without grave reason. A moment later, while Rhea, with a hideous clatter and talking continuously, was transforming the lobster into a delicious dish of her own devising—half Lobster Vanderbilt, half Lobster Rhea Nielsen—he had walked through the apartment and pulled down all the blinds.

Naturally Heydt was dangerous, but was he actually in Sweden?

And was this question mark sufficient reason for Martin Beck to ruin Christmas for four loyal colleagues, three of whom also had children?

Well, the future would tell. Or perhaps the future would tell nothing, anyhow not about Reinhard Heydt.

Deep down, Martin Beck hoped that Heydt would take the Oslo route so that Gunvald Larsson would have the chance to slug him on the jaw. Gunvald Larsson could not receive a better Christmas present.

Then he thought for a while about the calm that Melander and Rönn were probably spreading all through the Helsingborg police force. But they were good men—Melander always had been, and Rönn had become so against many people's expectations—and if Heydt tried to get out that way, he would probably have little chance of success.

But Malmö . . . well, Malmö was pure hell when it came to border control. Practically all the drugs in the country were funneled in by that route, as well as most other contraband.

The man with bladder trouble was first down to the floor, and as Martin Beck could not be bothered to turn over, he had the pleasure of a worm's-eye view of his fellow traveler dressing. Socks and underpants and a string undershirt swirled past, followed by a great tussle with trousers and suspenders, before Martin Beck had a chance to get his own clothes on.

He jogged across to the Savoy, where he always used to stay, even if at long intervals, and was given an exuberant welcome by the porter in his long greatcoat.

He went up to his room, shaved and showered, then took a cab to the police station, where he was soon shown into Per Månsson's office. The Malmö police had had a difficult, even oppressive year, but this was not evident from Månsson, who was chewing more tranquilly than ever on one of his eternal toothpicks.

"Benny isn't here," said Månsson. "He practically lives down at the flying-boat terminal." In Malmö for some reason they called hydrofoils "flying boats."

"And otherwise?"

"Otherwise we've checked damned well everywhere," said Månsson. "The problem, of course, is that so many people are traveling at this time of year. In both directions. Pure chaos. But . . ."

"Yes?"

"His looks are on our side. As big as hell, this guy Heydt. Maybe he could crawl on all fours and get by as a dog, if it weren't for the fact that you can't take dogs into Denmark anymore. The foxes over there have rabies."

"Well," said Martin Beck, "there are a lot of tall people. Heydt isn't as tall as Gunvald Larsson, for instance."

"But you could frighten the life out of little kids with Larsson," said Månsson, taking another toothpick from his pen tray.

"What do you think? You know this sort of traffic."

"Mmm," said Månsson. "Sometimes I wonder whether I know anything at all. The train ferry *Malmöhus* is the easiest to check. He hasn't got a chance there. Then come the so-called big boats, *Ørnen, Gripen* and *Öresund.* Not so good with the car ferries in Limhamn, *Hamlet* and *Ophelia,* or whatever their names are. But the worst of all, that's the flying-boat terminal—sheer hell."

"Hydrofoil," said Martin Beck.

"Okay, they're hell, anyhow. They come and go all the time, and the terminal building is so packed with people, you can hardly get your nose in."

"I understand."

"You won't understand a thing until you've actually seen it with your own eyes. The seaman who's supposed to check the tickets gets trampled underfoot, and the passport police have a room to hide themselves away in, otherwise they'd be as flat as pancakes in ten minutes. You could push them under the doors to their wives when they got home." Månsson fell silent, a toothpick stuck in his teeth. Then he added, "To use a corny old joke."

"Then what's Skacke doing?"

"Benny? He's standing out on the quay, freezing in the wind, blue in the face. And he's been standing there since he got here yesterday evening."

Gunvald Larsson was also freezing, though he had some important and some less important reasons for doing so. It was certainly several degrees colder on the Norwegian-Swedish border than in Malmö, but on the other hand he was purposefully clad in long johns (which he loathed), thick corduroy trousers, ski pants, thick socks, sheepskin jacket and cap.

He was standing almost on the actual border, his back against a pine tree, attentively observing the endless stream of cars, the customs shed, the border barrier and the provisional roadblock, absently listening to the veritable storm of abuse motorists were raining down onto the inquisitive police. Wasn't there supposed to be free travel here? Had Norway suddenly become as difficult to get into as Saudi Arabia? What had happened to Scandinavian cooperation? Was it because of the North Sea oil? Or because all Swedish policemen were idiots? Why the hell should my name be Heydt? And what business is it of the police what my name is anyhow? As long as I'm a Swedish citizen, it's none of your business whether my name's Päronqvist or Laurel and Hardy. Look at the damned tie-up you've caused anyhow.

Gunvald Larsson sighed and looked at the line of cars. It had in fact begun to get remarkably long, while the vehicles coming from the opposite direction swept unhindered into Sweden from dear old Norway. Some of the policemen at the barrier were also behaving unusually stupidly. Every man was equipped with Heydt's photograph and a description. They knew he spoke bad Swedish, but passable Danish, and also that he was about thirty years old and six feet tall. Yet some were harassing bald sixty-year-olds with marked Värmland accents for as long as ten minutes. Larsson sighed. Doing penance for the inbuilt stupidity of the police force had cost him years of his life. Now it was time for Don Quixote to take over.

Nearly all the cars had their roof racks loaded with skis, snow shovels and reindeer antlers, the latter having been sold to them by some smart operator at grossly inflated prices on the Swedish side of the border. Gunvald Larsson watched it all with profound distaste.

He liked Lapland very much indeed—but only in the summer.

Rönn and Melander were not out freezing in the cold. They were sitting in relatively comfortable chairs in a glass-walled cabin the police in Helsingborg had provided especially for them. Two excellent electric heaters maintained a pleasant warmth inside, and at regular intervals young policemen came in with Thermoses of coffee, plastic cups, and plates of cakes and Danish pastries. The stream of traffic had been directed past the cabin's glass walls, and if a traveler required special examination, two excellent pairs of prism binoculars were at their disposal. They were also in radio communication with the police who were checking car and train passengers.

Nevertheless, Rönn and Melander were looking equally bad-tempered, since despite their relative comfort their Christmas was going to hell. They didn't say much, except when they got hold of a private telephone and could call up their wives and complain.

This was the situation on Friday the twentieth of December, four days before Christmas Eve. Saturday was worse, as even more people were free from work, and the crowds crossing Öresund were enormous.

Martin Beck went down to the quay outside the hydrofoil terminal, fighting his way through the hysterical crowd of people who had no reservations but nevertheless hoped to get on the next boat. It turned out that the man clipping the tickets for the *Løberen* was Danish and extremely distrustful of people who claimed to be chief inspectors of police but were unable to produce their identity cards. Martin Beck had changed jackets and, naturally, had left his card back in the hotel room. He was finally saved by Benny Skacke, who by this time was well known to the ticket-clipping seaman.

Martin Beck stepped out into the sharp, mean, wet wind so typical of winter in South Sweden, especially in Malmö. He looked at his myrmidon, behind whom a row of Santa Clauses were handing out handbills advertising some of what the capital of Denmark had to offer despite the economic crisis and threatened devaluation.

Skacke looked terrible; his cheeks were a pale violet color, his forehead and nose dead white, and above his woolen scarf his skin was almost transparent.

"How long have you been standing here?" said Martin Beck.

"Since a quarter past five," said Skacke shakily. "The first sailing, in fact."

"Go and get something hot to eat at once," said Martin Beck sternly. "Now. Right away."

Skacke vanished, but fifteen minutes later he was back again, his color now slightly more normal.

Nothing much happened on Saturday, apart from a number of people who got very drunk and started fights. Martin Beck thought about an article he'd read recently that said Swedes, Americans and perhaps Finns did more fighting than any other people. It was probably one of those generalizations, but sometimes it appeared to be true.

At about ten in the evening, Martin Beck went back to his hotel. The overindustrious Skacke remained, determined to stay at his post until the last boat sailed. He clearly had no faith in his erstwhile colleagues on the Malmö force.

Martin Beck fetched his room key and headed for the elevator but then changed his mind and went into the bar. There were plenty of guests there, as always just before Christmas, but one of the barstools was empty, so he sat himself down.

"Well, well, good evening," said the bartender. "Whisky with ice water as usual?" The man had an infallible memory.

Martin Beck hesitated. Ice water did not sound particularly tempting after all those hours on the windy quay. He glanced at the guest beside him who was drinking something golden-looking out of a large glass. It looked pretty good. Then he looked at the guest himself, a youthful man in his fifties with a beard and glossy hair.

"Try it," said the man. "A Gyllenkrok, or Golden Hook, as the Americans call it. It's the bar's own invention."

Martin Beck took his advice. The drink was good, and he tried in vain to figure out what was in it. He glanced again at the man who had recommended it, and said suddenly, "I recognize you. You're the botanist and reporter who found Sigbrit Mård at Lake Börringe last autumn."

"Ugh," said the man. "Don't talk about things like that. Not here, anyhow."

A moment later he glanced at Martin Beck and said, "Of course. And you're the police inspector from Stockholm who questioned me afterward. What's up now?"

"Just routine," said Martin Beck, shrugging his shoulders.

"Oh, well," said the finder of the corpse, "it's none of my business."

Three minutes later, Martin Beck said goodnight and went to bed. He was so tired that he couldn't even summon up the energy to call Rhea.

Sunday the twenty-second of December, and even worse chaos at the hydrofoil terminal. The stores were apparently still open, because the Santas with their handbills were more numerous than ever. There were also large numbers of children among the crowds of passengers. It was midday, rush hour, high season for everything except for passable weather. The wind was from the north, wet and bitterly cold, blowing straight in through the harbor entrance and sweeping mercilessly onto the unprotected quay.

Two boats were just about to sail, a Danish one called *Flyvefisken* and a Swedish one called *Tärnan.* They were simply being packed and sent off as quickly as possible.

The Danish boat cast off, and Benny Skacke, who had been standing by the gangway, began to walk toward the Swedish boat. Martin Beck was standing by the exit, just behind the Swedish seaman clipping tickets like lightning while he simultaneously clicked a mechanical counter with his other hand to check the number of passengers.

The wind was hideous and as Martin Beck turned his head down and away to protect his face a little, he heard someone say something in Danish to the ticket man. He turned.

There was no doubt about it.

Reinhard Heydt had gotten past the ticket taker as well as all the policemen outside and was already only a yard away from him, on his way toward the gangway. His only luggage was a brown paper bag with a Santa Claus printed on its side. Skacke was twenty-five yards away, still halfway between the boat that had just sailed and the one just about to cast off, when he looked up, at once recognized the South African, stopped and felt for his service pistol.

But Heydt had seen Skacke first and immediately identified him as a policeman in civilian clothes. When Skacke looked up at him and thrust his right hand under his coat, the situation was quite clear to Heydt.

Someone was going to die within the next few seconds, and Heydt was certain it would not be him. He would shoot this policeman, then jump over the fence into the street and escape through the traffic. He dropped the bag and his hand flew to the gun inside his jacket.

Benny Skacke was quick and well trained, but Reinhard Heydt was ten times quicker. Martin Beck had never seen anything like it, not even in the movies.

But Martin was quick on the uptake, too. He took a step forward and said, "Just a moment, Mr. Heydt . . ." simultaneously grasping Heydt's right arm. The South African already had the Colt in his hand and, with all his strength, slowly raised his arm while Martin Beck struggled to hold it down.

With his life at stake and Martin Beck offering him a chance to stay alive, Skacke aimed his Walther and shot to kill.

The bullet struck Heydt in the mouth and lodged in the top of his spine. He died instantly—and at the moment of death pulled the trigger. The bullet struck Benny Skacke high in the right hip and spun him around like a top, straight into the row of Santa Clauses.

Skacke was lying face-down, bleeding profusely, but he was not unconscious. When Martin Beck knelt down beside him, Skacke said at once, "What happened? Where's Heydt?"

"You shot him. Killed him instantly."

"What else could I do?" said Skacke.

"You did right. It was your only chance."

Per Månsson came rushing up from somewhere, surrounded by an aura of freshly made coffee.

"The ambulance will be here in a jiffy," he said. "Lie still, Benny."

Lie still, thought Martin Beck. If Heydt had had

another tenth of a second of life, Benny Skacke would have lain still forever. Even another hundredth of a second could have made Skacke an invalid for life. Now he would be all right. Martin Beck had seen where the bullet had struck and it was well out in the hip.

A crowd of policemen had appeared and began to clear the gawkers away from the dead man. When the wail of the ambulance sounded, Martin Beck went over and looked at Heydt. His face was slightly distorted, but on the whole he looked pleasant even dead.

The man who answered at the border station at Europe Route Eighteen sounded somewhat irritable. The telephone had rung far too damned often and the line of cars was also growing longer and longer and more and more impossible to survey.

"Yes," said the border policeman, "he's here all right. Wait a moment." He put his hand over the mouthpiece. "Gunvald Larsson?" he said. "Isn't that the big slob in the millionaire clothes hanging around over by that tree there?"

"Yes," said colleague. "I think so."

"He's wanted on the telephone. This goddamn guy Heydt."

Gunvald Larsson came in and took the receiver. His remarks were so monosyllabic that it was hard to make anything of what he said.

"Oh, yes . . . Uh-huh . . . Dead? . . . Injured? . . . Who? . . . Skacke? . . . And he's okay? . . . Right. So long."

He put down the receiver, looked at the men at the border station and said, "You can let the traffic through now, and take down the barriers. We don't need them anymore."

Gunvald Larsson suddenly felt that he had not slept for a long long time. He drove only as far as Karlstad, then gave up and stopped at the city hotel.

In Helsingborg, Fredrik Melander replaced the receiver and smiled with satisfaction. Then he looked at the time. Rönn, who had been eavesdropping, also had an extremely satisfied expression.

They would be able to celebrate Christmas at home.

Friday the tenth of January 1975 was just the kind of evening everyone hopes for more of. When everyone is relaxed and in tune with themselves and the world around them. When everyone has eaten and drunk well and knows they are free the next day, as long as nothing too special or horrible or unexpected happens.

If by "everyone" we mean a very small group of humankind.

Four people, to be exact.

Martin Beck and Rhea were spending that evening with Lennart Kollberg and his wife, and together they had created the conditions for as good a time as anyone could wish for.

No one said very much, but that was mostly because they were playing a game called "crosswords," a game that seemed very simple. Each had a pen and piece of paper on which were drawn twenty-five squares, and each person in turn said a letter of the alphabet. The players had to fill in the given letters, and none other, and try to make words that read either across or down.

They were not allowed to look at each other's papers.

"X," said Kollberg, for the third time in the same game, and they all sighed heavily.

There was possibly one fault with this game, thought Martin Beck, and that was that Kollberg won four times out of five—and the fifth time, Rhea won. But when it came to games, both he and Gun Kollberg were used to being losers, so it didn't matter.

"X, as in ex-policeman," said Kollberg, breezily, as if they all didn't know how impossible it was to squeeze in one more example out of that hopeless letter.

Martin Beck stared for a moment at his paper, then shrugged his shoulders and gave up.

"Lennart?"

"Mmm," said Kollberg.

"Do you remember ten years ago?"

"When we were hunting for Folke Bengtsson and the police had just been nationalized? Yes, I do, and I guess that is a time to remember. But everything that happened afterward? No, goddammit."

"Do you remember that was when it all began?"

Kollberg shook his head. "No, I don't. And what's worse, I don't think this is where it's going to end."

"Y," said Rhea.

Which shut everyone up for a moment.

A little later, the time had come to count the scores. Two points for a two-letter word, three for a three-letter word, and so on. Martin Beck scribbled the numbers on his paper. He was last as usual.

"Although one thing's certain," said Kollberg, "and that is that they made a terrible mistake back then. Putting the police in the vanguard of violence is like putting the cart before the horse."

"Ha! I won!" said Rhea.

"You sure did," said Kollberg.

Then he said magnanimously to Martin Beck, "Don't sit there thinking about all that now. Violence has rushed like an avalanche throughout the whole of the Western world over the last ten years. You can't stop or steer that avalanche on your own. It just increases. That's not your fault."

"Isn't it?"

They all turned their papers over and drew more squares. When Kollberg was ready, he looked at Martin Beck and said, "The trouble with you, Martin, is just that you've got the wrong job. At the wrong time. In the wrong part of the world. In the wrong system."

"Is that all?"

"Roughly," said Kollberg. "My turn to start? Then I say X—X as in Marx."

About the Authors

Maj Sjöwall and Per Wahlöö met as journalists working on different magazines. Over lunch one day they shared what turned out to be a common interest and the beginning of a literary collaboration and a marriage—the concept of the crime novel as a mirror to society. Together they planned a series of ten books, which they said would trace "a man's [Martin Beck's] personality changing over the years, as the milieu and the atmosphere, the political climate, the economic climate, and the crime rate change."

Begun in 1965 with *Roseanna* and ending in 1975 with Per Wahlöö's death and the completion of the tenth book, *The Terrorists,* the Martin Beck series has come to represent a unique achievement in the field of mystery fiction. The books, originally written in Swedish, have been published in every major country and have won many awards, including the Mystery Writers of America's Edgar for the best mystery novel of 1970 (*The Laughing Policeman*). The Wahlöös have been hailed as "the reigning king and queen of mystery fiction."